ADEQUATE

YEARLY

PROGRESS

Cover design by The Book Designers
Interior design by Pauline Neuwirth, Neuwirth & Associates

Library of Congress Cataloging-in-Publication data is on file
with the publisher.

Printed and bound in the United States of America

ADEQUATE YEARLY PROGRESS

A NOVEL

ROXANNA ELDEN

RIVET STREET BOOKS

For Erica, my toughest grader, my favorite teacher

LANGUAGE ARTS

BRAE HILL VALLEY High School did not sit atop a hill. Nor was it nestled in a valley. Nor was it on a brae. When Lena Wright had moved to Texas, hoping it might one day feel like home, she'd noted how many of the streets were named Brae Something, or Something Brae, and looked up the word. *Brae* was a Scottish term for *hill*. Lena appreciated the irony of this: Like everything else in this sprawling, landlocked city, her workplace rested on level ground, within a few miles of a sunbaked six-lane freeway.

The school, too, might have been interchangeable with any other school. A marquee in front of the entrance revealed only that school started on Monday. Last year's graffiti was hidden by a fresh coat of Band-Aid-colored paint. Even the fences and the steel grates over the windows might not, by some other freeway exit, have been that bad.

But Brae Hill Valley was not by some other freeway exit. That was why Lena had chosen it. The streets that led her to work were ones on which she imagined nervous drivers might subtly lock their doors. Not Lena, though. She'd moved into an apartment just a mile from the school, and her car doors were still unlocked when she pulled into the parking lot, grabbed her ankara-print messenger bag, and hoisted a box from the back seat onto one hip—though her hips weren't wide enough to be much help. She had a nearly curveless body, punctuated by a head of curls that refused to form respectable dreadlocks, and light skin that sometimes made people ask if she was "all black." Which she *was*.

She steadied the box with both hands as she headed past the practice field toward the school. Coach Ray—winner of football championships, manager of scandals—flashed her a red-faced grin. A nylon flap on his fisherman's hat protected his neck from the sun as his players zigged and zagged through a maze of orange cones. On the far end of the field, the marching band repeated the first few bars of a song. Lena couldn't believe they'd been practicing in this heat all summer.

She waited until a line of JROTC students marched past, then yanked open the door to a welcome blast of air conditioning. A familiar sign above the office door proclaimed, AT BRAE HILL VALLEY HIGH SCHOOL, FAILURE IS NOT AN OPTION!—though this was not an entirely accurate statement. In fact, near the end of the previous year, Lena had often joked that failure was one of the most popular options at Brae Hill Valley. Today, however, she entered the office with no urge to be sarcastic. It was August. Her spark of late-summer hopefulness burned even brighter than usual, and the year ahead shined like the school's freshly waxed floors.

Around her, other teachers shared their favorite seasonal greeting.

How was your summer?

Too short!

Ha-ha. Mine, too.

Lena smiled but hoped she'd be able to avoid the small talk. As a spoken-word poet, she hated the feeling of wasting words. Plus, there was only one more day to prepare before tomorrow's marathon of meetings. She put down the box and checked her mail, flinging a summer's worth of catalogues into the recycling bin. They landed with a loud *thunk*. Maybelline Galang, who stood sorting her own mail according to some meticulous math-teacher logic, looked up in disapproval.

"My new filing system," Lena explained. She grabbed the remaining envelopes and stuffed them into her bag, crumpling them in the process. Something about Maybelline's aggressively appropriate presence compelled Lena to flaunt acts of noncompliance.

She turned away before Maybelline could react and spotted Kaytee Mahoney, whose blond ponytail was, as always, a little loose and slightly off center.

"Hey, you made it back for a second year, huh?"

A flicker of guilt crept into Kaytee's smile. She tugged at the bottom of her sweater as if worried it was too small.

"Girl, I'm just playing." Lena laughed, trying to backtrack. The truth was she liked Kaytee, an eager second-year teacher from the TeachCorps program perpetually weighed down by an assortment of bags. Kaytee activated a primal feminine instinct in Lena that, put into words, would have sounded something like *I could give you a makeover.* "But this year, we have to get you to relax a little."

Kaytee's smile returned to its previous wattage. "No way! This year I have to work even harder. I've got OTWP classes for the first time."

"Ooh. Ouch." OTWP stood for Open to Wonderful Possibilities, the newest name for the remedial classes whose title changed every few years. Each upbeat term was a new attempt to outrun the previous name's stigma. "I feel you, though. I've got OTWP reading."

"No. No, no, no!" clarified Kaytee. "I'm actually looking forward to it. I just have to let them know I don't expect *any* less from them because of that OTWP label."

"Well, sounds like you're on the right track!" Lena tried to keep the doubt out of her voice as she bent to pick up her box. Nobody liked teaching OTWP classes.

"Good morning, Ms. Wright!"

"Yes, good *morning*, Ms. *Wright!*"

Even before she stood up, Lena recognized the voices of Mrs. Reynolds-Washington and Mrs. Friedman-Katz. The two middle-aged women shared a love of tremendous jewelry, brightly colored pantsuits, and other people's business that transcended all barriers of race and religion. Their bond was so strong that Mrs. Reynolds-Washington overlooked the fact that Mrs. Friedman-Katz was Jewish and would never be right with Jesus ("At least she believes in God!"), and Mrs. Friedman-Katz barely seemed to notice that Mrs. Reynolds-Washington was black ("Did you know her son is studying to be an orthodontist?").

"Good morning, Mrs. Reynolds-Washington. Mrs. Friedman-Katz." Lena nodded to each of the women, trying not to invite conversation. The two were like bees spreading pollen, gathering material for tomorrow's gossip as they shared today's. Lena had little interest in hearing gossip. She had even less interest in being its subject.

"I see your hair is growing in, hon," said Mrs. Friedman-Katz, reaching out to pat Lena's curls. "It looks very pretty now."

"Thanks." Lena ducked instinctively. Ever since she'd gone natural, white people had wanted to touch her hair. It was a topic she often raised when she met other black people with natural hair, though this was regrettably rare. Texas was the kingdom of relaxer and hair weave.

"We were worried about you for a while there, dear, with that bald-headed look," added Mrs. Reynolds-Washington.

"Okay, well." *That was two years ago,* Lena wanted to say, but she settled for "Glad you like this better." Shifting the box to show she really had better be going, she headed for the exit.

"I guess you've already heard the latest about our friend Nick Wallabee," said Mrs. Friedman-Katz.

Lena turned around to push the door open with her back, realizing too late that this made her look interested.

"Oh, yes." Mrs. Reynolds-Washington joined in, believing they'd re-engaged their target. "It was in the paper this morning. Or don't you read the news, *Miss Phil-a-delphia?*" Her tone suggested she knew all she needed to about Lena's hometown, some big city Up North where everyone was in a hurry and no one went to church.

"Thanks," said Lena, escaping into the hallway. "I'll definitely check it out."

Mrs. Reynolds-Washington's voice trailed behind her. "I swear, these young people do *not* pay attention to the news anymore. They're almost as bad as the kids!"

Luckily, the office door closed, cutting off the sound. Let someone else get roped into that one. The last thing Lena wanted to talk about right before school started was Nick Wallabee, a political celebrity who had never worked at a school himself but whose best-selling book was apparently full of "easy fixes" for education. Any conversation about him quickly turned into a morale-draining gripe session.

Her footfalls echoed off the empty lockers as she hurried down the hallway. Behind her, more teachers streamed into the school and headed to the office. They toted tote bags, rolled rolling crates, and reached the consensus that summer had been too short.

She'd almost reached her classroom door when she heard a voice call, "Leeeena Wright!"

Lena turned to see the tan, friendly face and buzzed hair of Hernan D. Hernandez. "Let me guess," she said. "Your summer was too short?"

"Nope—just about the length I expected."

Lena laughed, relieved. Hernan was one of the few people in the school with whom conversations didn't feel like small talk. There was something effortless about being around him that made Lena seek him out at faculty meetings and happy hours. He was even kind of cute, though not exactly her type. She balanced the box on her knee as she dug for her keys.

"Here, let me get that for you."

"Thanks!" Her classroom lights blinked on, illuminating the still-empty bulletin boards. "See you at the meeting tomorrow?"

"Yeah, see you there." Hernan put the box on a desk and paused before heading out the door. "Should be an interesting one this year."

"Aren't they always?" Lena rummaged through her desk drawer to find her stapler as the sound of Hernan's steps faded down the hallway. Under other circumstances, she would have liked to catch up with him, but right now she had decorating to do.

She spread out the photos she'd collected for her bulletin boards. There were printouts of Mexican festivals and crowded outdoor markets in Kenya, plus her own snapshots of Philly's crowded streets and brick row houses. Most of the photos, however, were pictures she'd taken near the school: Strip malls populated with Laundromats and liquor stores. Restaurants advertising tacos and Salvadoran pupusas. A man selling rugs from the back of a pickup truck. A bare storefront whose hand-lettered sign read, SHRIMPS YOU BUY WE FRY.

Her first literature lesson would focus on setting. She'd begin with these photos and add pictures for each story they read, then encourage students to bring in photos of their own. She wanted them to understand that stories didn't just happen; they happened in a time and place inseparable from the way the action unfolded.

It was a revelation that had hit her with a jolt over the summer, as she listened to poetry at a rally against police violence: Now more than ever, her students needed to read things that made them question the world around them. They needed to write more clearly, think more deeply, and have more discussions in which they could give voice to their reality. And this year she could make it happen. Her first two years at the school had taught her that if she stayed under the administrative radar and seemed cooperative, she wouldn't have to spend so much time doing test prep. She could finally stop making her students work for the curriculum and start making the curriculum work for them.

And yet, as she stapled the photos to the boards, something nagged at her. Bits of the morning's conversations were floating back into her memory, sticking like dust on a fresh coat of paint. Hernan had said the faculty meeting would be an interesting one. And there had been a little too much excitement in Mrs. Reynolds-Washington's voice when she'd mentioned the newspaper, which, in truth, Lena had not read.

She turned on her sluggish classroom computer and waited for the day's headlines to load. And then there it was: "Best-Selling Author Named Superintendent of Schools." Underneath that: the instantly recognizable headshot of Nick Wallabee.

Suddenly, the stapler hung heavy in Lena's hand. She couldn't concentrate, couldn't reignite the sense of possibility she'd felt minutes earlier. It was as if she'd spent the summer guarding a freshly lit candle, eager to pass its flame on to her students. And now it had just started to rain.

"Heeeey, guuurl!"

Lena turned to see Breyonna Watson, who was patting her shiny, shoulder-length weave with a manicured hand. When Lena lamented Texas's deficit of natural hair, Breyonna was the first example that sprung to mind.

"Hey, Breyonna. What's up?" It was a reluctant greeting; Breyonna only stopped to talk if she had something to brag about. She carried a monstrosity of a purse covered with some designer's initials. The sorority keychain around her neck hung over a sweatshirt from a lower-end college that Lena's parents would have referred to as an *at-least-I-went-to-college* college. This last thought, however, was so snobbish Lena shoved it immediately from her mind. She concentrated instead on hating Breyonna's purse.

"What's up? Nothing . . . unless you count this!" Breyonna extended her weave-patting hand to display a large diamond, sparkling under the fluorescent lights.

"Congratulations," said Lena, though she had trouble getting excited about diamonds, considering the atrocities they caused in Africa.

"Thank you!" Breyonna let out a happy, *check-out-my-fat-rock* screech that died down when Lena didn't join in. "But enough about me. How was *your* summer, guuurl?"

Lena sighed. "Too short."

SCIENCE

HERNAN D. HERNANDEZ slipped in at the back of the auditorium. The back-to-school faculty meeting hadn't officially started yet, but it felt too late to walk to the front of the room to join the rest of the science department. He slid into a nearby seat, its springs sighing at the year's first interruption.

A presenter from the district stood on the stage, grinning at no one in particular. She was one of those heavily accessorized, well-connected former teachers who had long ago retreated to offices within the district headquarters, emerging at the beginning of each school year to give PowerPoint presentations. Behind her, a screen glowed with a picture of a beach at sunrise, hundreds of sea stars dotting the sand.

All of which suggested they were going to start with the starfish story.

Hernan pulled a pen from his computer bag. The bag had spent the summer in his closet, and its reemergence was one of many reminders that summer was over—no more soccer games with his nephew, no more helping his father in the backyard or experimenting in the greenhouses of the Hernandez Plant Nursery. For the next ten months, he'd spend most of his time indoors.

"Good morning, y'all!" said the presenter.

Conversation sounds dwindled as a few teachers returned the greeting.

"I know everyone is sleepy, but we can do better than *that*! I said good *morning*!"

"*Gmrning.*" It came out as a grumble. This crowd spent too much time around teenagers to respond to demands for cheerfulness. Plus, everyone now sensed that the presentation would start with the starfish story, which rarely preceded good news.

The door behind Hernan opened to let in a few more stragglers. He turned in time to see Lena Wright appear in its frame, the light of the hallway behind her. Her silhouette was slim and graceful, topped by an unruly crown of curls extending in all directions. She paused as if assessing whether it was too late to sit with the English department. Then she turned her attention to the back rows, brightening when she spotted Hernan. His faculty-meeting experience improved considerably as she slid into the seat next to him.

"Did I miss anything?" she whispered.

"Not much." Hernan gestured toward the screen.

"I'd like to start with a little inspiration this morning!" said the presenter.

Lena squinted at the beach scene, massaging her temples with one hand as if she had a headache. She had short nails and thin fingers, her bone structure as delicate as the wing of a bat. "Uh-oh. Is she going to tell us the starfish story?"

"Once, a man was walking along a beach," the presenter began. "On the beach lay *hundreds* of starfish."

"Looks like it." Immediately, Hernan lamented the answer's lack of cleverness. Growing up with two sisters should have given him an edge in talking to women. Instead, it had trained him to make women see him as a brother. Though they didn't *always* see him this way, he reminded himself. His younger sister, Lety, sometimes mentioned college friends who'd asked about him, and he knew he wasn't bad-looking, though he would've liked to be taller. He'd inherited the same tan skin and sharp features as his sisters, and a tendency toward outdoor activity kept him in shape. In his classroom, talking to students about biology, he felt confident, interesting—maybe even charming. And yet, around the women who interested him most, he seemed always to miss some crucial opening, some moment of possibility that floated past without his reaching out to grab it. His dealings with Lena were no exception. Even at this moment, her presence alternated between lifting his spirits and intimidating the hell out of him.

"The starfish had been stranded by the tide!" The presenter's eyes widened as she read the creatures' dramatic fate from the next slide. "Soon, the sun would rise and *bake* them to *death!*"

"She seems pretty surprised by this story line," whispered Lena.

"Maybe she's never heard it before."

Lena let out a whoosh of breath that might have been a laugh.

"In the distance, the man could see a young boy going *back* and *forth* between the *surf's* edge and the *sand*." The presenter's habit of speaking slowly and emphasizing words suggested her past teaching experience had been in elementary school. "He was picking up the starfish, *one by one*, and *throwing* them back into the sea."

Click. A dancing cartoon starfish appeared on the screen. The pointy-headed figure shimmied on the starfish appendages that served as legs and waved the starfish appendages that served as arms.

"Nice touch with the graphics," said Lena. "Really adds to the story."

"Well, they definitely got the science part right. That's exactly how a starfish would dance if it could stand on its side."

Lena laughed aloud. The treads of Hernan's confidence regained their grip.

Click. Smile. "The man couldn't *believe* this young boy thought he could make a difference by throwing just *one* starfish at a *time* back into the water. There were *far* too many starfish stranded on that beach to save them *all!*"

Hernan tried to think of something noteworthy enough to spark conversation. Lena wasn't really his friend so much as a colleague who often ended up at the same happy hour. He'd first noticed her when she'd started working at the school two years earlier, strutting the hallway with braids held back by a colorful cloth headband. His real interest in her, however, had started the morning she showed up completely bald. There had been competing explanations from Mrs. Friedman-Katz, who believed Lena was a cancer patient ("poor thing"), and from Mrs. Reynolds-Washington, who believed she was a lesbian ("I always knew that girl was a little strange"). Hernan had hoped neither rumor was true and had been relieved as Lena's hair grew into a halo of wild curls.

Click. "The man approached the little boy who was picking up the starfish. 'You must be *crazy*,' said the man. 'There are *so* many miles of beach covered with starfish. You can't *possibly* make a difference by saving just *one starfish at a time!*'"

Hernan surveyed the landscape of seated teachers. The science and math departments were in their usual seats up front, within the sight lines of the presenter. The coaches lined the back of the room, where they could slip out to check the action on the field. Any teachers who could get away with it were working discreetly on other things. Occasionally they looked up with exaggerated intensity, as if absorbed by the suspense of the starfish story.

"Let's have one of you read the next line from your packet!" The presenter's mouth was still smiling, but her eyes had noted the audience's drifting attention.

From the back of the room, a voice called, "What packet? I never got a packet."

Another voice chimed in. "I don't have a packet, either!"

"Oh . . . well . . . they should be circulating from the front to the back. Has anyone seen the packets?" A few teachers near the front raised their hands. Among them was Maybelline Galang, who strained toward administrative praise like a flower toward the sun. She was taking notes as if she'd never heard the starfish story in her life.

"I got the last one," said a voice a few rows behind Maybelline.

"Okay." The presenter's voice was losing its zest. "It looks like we don't have quite enough copies, so if you don't have a packet, please share with someone next to you, and maybe some of y'all in the back can move up to share with someone in the front?"

A few latecomers took the opportunity to hurry up the aisles and sit with their departments. Hernan was glad to see Lena wasn't one of them.

"My packet is missing pages one and two," said another voice.

"Oh . . . right," said the presenter. "I meant to tell y'all—the page numbers are a little off. So, the packet starts on page three, and it's stapled on the right instead of the left, but if you just flip over page three, you'll see page two . . . You see it? Page one is behind that. Okay, great! We're on page four."

Click. The reddish glow of another ocean sunrise cascaded over the teachers, some of whom were now fumbling with the misstapled packets. Others bent over their laps, still trying to complete paperwork by the low light of the new slide.

"So, just to review: The man didn't think the boy could ever make a difference, right? Since there were so many starfish washed up on the beach? And the boy can only save one at a time, right? Right, everyone?" She waited until a few teachers nodded before advancing the slide.

"The little boy picked up one more starfish and threw it back into the ocean. Then he turned to the man and said, 'It sure made a difference to *that* one!'"

She paused, gazing at the teachers in front of her as if watching butter sink into a warm muffin. Then she continued. "I think that story really speaks to the difference a great teacher can make, which leads me to what I'm so excited to discuss with you all today! I'll give you a hint."

Click. The beach scene disappeared, replaced by a bright blue sky. Across the sky, written in cloud letters, stretched a single word: *believe*. "I want you all to help me finish this sentence: If you believe, your students will . . ."

The teachers sat silently, bracing for the unpleasant news that always dropped at the end of the starfish story.

"It rhymes with *believe*."

"Deceive?" called a voice from the back of the room.

Hernan knew Mr. Weber, the school's union representative, was just stalling. "Believers make achievers" was the most often quoted line from Nick Wallabee's book, the cover of which featured a photo of Nick Wallabee standing in a sparse classroom, foot planted on an empty student desk, gazing defiantly into the camera on behalf of children. The news that he was now their superintendent had elevated Mr. Weber's predictable drizzle of sarcasm and conspiracy theories to a raging thunderstorm.

"You're close!" said the presenter. "But maybe something a little more positive?"

"New Year's Eve?" offered another voice.

"Good guess . . . getting closer!"

"Sleeve!"

"Um . . ." She was running out of ways to gently correct wrong answers.

"*Achieve.*" It was Maybelline Galang.

"She *would* be the one to mess that up," whispered Lena.

"Very good!" said the presenter. "And that's what we want all our students to do: *Achieve!* Accomplish great things!" It seemed she'd added this last part for those who might not know what the word *achieve* meant and thus might not catch the cleverness of the rhyme. "And we know they can do that as long as their teachers *believe* in them. There's real research and statistics about this. That's why when I was a teacher I used to tell my students: Reach for the moon! Even if you miss, you'll land among the stars!"

Hernan noted some scientific discrepancies in the moon-and-stars metaphor. For one thing, the moon was much closer to Earth than the stars were. Also, stars were huge, burning balls of gas millions of light-years away from one another, so you could in no way "land among" them, nor would you want to. These were just the most glaring errors he could have pointed out, possibly drawing another laugh from Lena. But then he worried the whole thing might sound too science geek—ish, like his earlier urge to point out that "starfish" were not actually fish. The correct term for them was *sea stars*. In the end, the comment-making window closed before he said anything at all. He sat, trapped in silence, gazing into the blue PowerPoint sky.

The presenter's jargon cut mercifully into his awkwardness. "So this year, with the help of our new superintendent, our district is going to help teachers really take ownership of student achievement!" She stared into the corner farthest from Mr. Weber, who was waving his hand to get her attention. "It's going to be such an exciting year!"

Mr. Weber dropped his hand and bellowed, too loud to be ignored, "This is another way of saying our jobs will depend on students' TCUP scores, right?"

"Actually, test scores are just one part of the evaluation formula, which we are developing *right now* with our new superintendent." Her speed increased, as if she'd just remembered this part of the presentation was to be delivered quickly, using big words and long sentences.

"It's going to be a really collaborative effort to get our students where they need to be. So exciting!"

"Now, wait," Mr. Weber interjected. "Just so I'm clear: This means our jobs will depend on test scores *and* some formula that hasn't even been developed yet?"

"I'm so glad y'all are asking so many great questions, and I'm actually really excited to announce that this year's evaluation will include a category called the Believer Score. That's going to let you all *gain* points by proving you believe all students can learn. It's going to be a total paradigm shift!"

The auditorium buzzed. This, it seemed, was the bad news presaged by the starfish story.

"And how will they be calculating this 'Believer Score,' exactly?" Mr. Weber was standing now.

"I'm so glad you're asking!" The presenter's smile hung on like a bull rider at a rodeo. "For now, just be ready to show that you fully embrace any new initiatives."

The collective grumbling intensified.

"In other words," translated Lena, just barely lowering her voice now, "we have to act excited about anything they tell us to do?"

The presenter strained to maintain her cheerful tone as she increased her volume. "I know change is hard, everyone, but remember: We've been changing since we were born! And let's not forget that this is really about the students!"

Hernan willed himself to think of something clever to say about the Believer Score, but nothing came to mind. His awkwardness returned and coagulated around him as the noise in the room grew.

It was Lena who finally spoke again. "Have you heard anything about this Believer Score stuff?"

"A little," said Hernan. "But I wouldn't worry about it. Doctor Barrios is good at keeping the heat off the school."

"You sure? Weber doesn't seem to be the only one worried this time around."

She was looking to him for reassurance, he realized. And why not? This was only Lena's third year at a school where he'd worked for seven.

His awkwardness lifted. He didn't need some clever line—he had experience. "Yeah, Doctor Barrios is like the superintendent whisperer."

Lena laughed. Again.

"In fact, that's probably why he's not here right now. He's probably becoming Nick Wallabee's new best friend as we speak."

Even as Hernan said it, he realized he had no idea if this was actually the case. But it was possible. For as long as he could remember, the principal had never missed a back-to-school meeting.

On a related note, the teachers in the auditorium had never been so noisy.

"The superintendent whisperer, huh?" said Lena. "Yeah, I guess I could see that."

She looked relaxed again, and Hernan had a burst of inspiration. "How about this? If they're still bothering us about any type of initiative by this year's first happy hour, I'll buy you a drink." Now, he thought, they'd have a reason to go to the same happy hour.

"Sure. Wait—do we have each other's numbers?" She spoke loudly this time. Everyone in the auditorium was talking by now.

The presenter had already counted to three and was now saying, "Clap twice if you can hear me!" But only Maybelline Galang and a few other teachers were clapping.

As he offered Lena his number, Hernan felt a great swell of hope for the year ahead. His optimism rose like the sun in the presentation slides, melting away any worries he might have had about the Believer Score or anything else the new superintendent might dream up.

Lena tapped the contact information into her phone. Her other hand traveled absentmindedly to the back of her neck, twisting a tiny curl that started just below her ear.

Hernan wondered what it might be like to touch that spot.

ADMINISTRATION

DR. MIGUEL BARRIOS, EdD, often joked that he wasn't fat—he was Texas-sized, and everything was bigger in Texas. Except, apparently, the press-conference area in the lobby of district headquarters.

There, behind a lectern, facing a congregation of his supporters, stood Nick Wallabee: The man with *the answers*. The man who *needed no introduction*.

"I want to start by thanking our teachers for all they do. Please, everyone, give our teachers a hand." It was a strange choice for an opening line, given Wallabee's reputation, but maybe thanking teachers for all they did was so mandatory even someone like Nick Wallabee had to do it.

Dr. Barrios joined in the polite applause as he wedged his bulk farther into the group. He'd expected a bigger crowd, one in which he could have concealed himself while he waited for the right moment, but this would have to do. He inched toward a spot where he hoped the superintendent could see him and the cameras couldn't. For a principal, unexpected media attention never brought anything good.

Wallabee pounded the lectern. "We are lucky to have some outstanding teachers in this city who believe that *all* of our children can learn!"

The cameras panned the area to capture the growing applause. Dr. Barrios turned away from them, examining the faces behind him. There were no actual teachers at the event. They were at work today, setting up for the year ahead. He, too, would have liked to be at work. He'd missed his own back-to-school meeting for this, leaving a district presenter in charge. This might have seemed negligent to some, but Dr. Barrios knew that repairs, supplies, and other favors came more easily when a principal could get the right person on the phone. Beginning today, that person was Nick Wallabee.

And so Dr. Barrios was here, wearing one of his newer shirts, crammed in among the cluster of admirers who'd come to see the new superintendent announce the Believers Make Achievers Zone. This was to be a group of schools with poor students and poor test scores that the superintendent would handpick for special attention. It was unclear, at this point, what *believing* meant, but Wallabee had famously promised to assign a numeric value to it and show its link to *achieving*, which meant test scores. Mr. Weber and the union contingent had grumbled mightily about this. Apparently Global Schoolhouse Press, which had published Nick Wallabee's book, also produced Texas's standardized tests.

But Dr. Barrios was not here to dig up snakes. He was here to make sure his new boss understood what his previous bosses had understood: The principal of Brae Hill Valley High School was the kind of likeable guy whose school didn't need special attention. All he needed were some basics, like flexibility in the budget to renew the copy-machine warrantee and hire a couple of extra security guards, plus some breathing room so he and his teachers could work in peace. In return, he was happy to make his boss look good. He hoped his smile from the middle of the throng conveyed all of this to Nick Wallabee.

It was unclear what Wallabee noticed, however. The superintendent's voice was building to a righteous rumble as he courted the cameras and crowd. "I've always said we should pay our top educators the way we pay our top professional athletes!"

The crowd bubbled with approval. Dr. Barrios nodded along, though he sensed Wallabee was pulling back the slingshot.

"We should hold parades for our best teachers! We should fill stadiums with fans of our best teachers!"

Dr. Barrios had to admit it: The guy was a master of the applause line.

"Unfortunately"—Wallabee's voice dropped, his face suddenly serious—"we also have schools in which teachers do *not* believe in children the way they should, and the test scores at these schools reflect that."

Dr. Barrios rearranged his face to express the appropriate level of concern. Part of him hated this willingness he'd developed to express outrage on demand, to shake hands and smile and laugh at unfunny jokes. Yet a larger part was proud. Miguel Barrios, son of a father who'd worked too hard for too little and a mother who'd spent most of his teenage years dying, hadn't just gotten his degrees, though he'd done that, too. He'd decoded the unwritten instructions not covered in any doctor-of-education courses and—mostly—used this knowledge to benefit his school. Certainly, no one would call him a visionary or publish a book with his face on the cover. But he took pride in being a principal who remembered the view from the front of the classroom. He'd worked hard to make Brae Hill Valley a place where teachers could focus on their jobs and block out the clanking machinery that kept the whole system chugging forward.

The occasional photo op was a small sacrifice toward this end.

"I know there are some adults"—Wallabee's tone had changed so completely that he nearly spat the word *adults*—"who take issue with being held accountable for our kids. But my priority here is children! I remember something my mama used to tell me. She would say, 'Son, sometimes you got to break a few eggs to make an omelet.' And you know I didn't argue with my mama." He paused for a few audience laughs before continuing. "And when that omelet is our children, and when those eggs are cheating our children of the education they deserve, then I declare those eggs *public enemy number one!*" With that, the superintendent abruptly stepped from behind the lectern, exchanging handshakes and shoulder clasps with supporters as he glided toward the exit.

The moment had come. Positioning himself near the door, Dr. Barrios reached out for a camera-friendly handshake. "Great speech. I'm Doctor Miguel Barrios, principal over at—"

"Nice to meet you, Doctor Barrios." Wallabee did not extend his hand.

Someone pushed open the door, and Wallabee stepped into the

sunlight. The camera crews followed, brushing past Dr. Barrios as if to underscore how quickly his chance had come and gone.

Except it couldn't end like this. Whatever his ambitions for the future, Wallabee was new in town. He'd soon learn it helped to have a friendly principal around. When he figured it out, the first name that sprung to mind had to be Miguel Barrios, EdD.

Dr. Barrios pushed through the doors, scrambling through Texas's late-summer humidity to catch up with the superintendent. "I just want to be one of the first folks to welcome you to our district and say we'd love to have you visit Brae Hill Valley High School." This was a lie. Principals didn't want a visit from the superintendent any more than teachers wanted a visit from the principal. But it was a friendly lie.

Wallabee edged toward the nearest camera before answering. He wore a layer of chalky makeup that was disconcerting up close. "I'll be paying close attention to your school, Doctor Barrios. I assure you of that."

"That's great to hear." This was an even bigger lie. "And don't forget to come on down and watch the Killer Armadillos play some football." Dr. Barrios followed this with the type of smile that football-lovin' Texan men gave one another when talking about football-lovin' Texan subjects.

"Well, I do love a good football game as much as the next person, Doctor Barrios." Then, having reassured Texas of his love for football, Wallabee turned fully toward the cameras. "But I'm expecting school leaders to stand up for student achievement, not just sit in the stands defending the status quo."

Defending the status quo. The line dropped onto Dr. Barrios with an almost physical force. Accusing someone of defending the status quo in education was like accusing them of defending Goliath in the story of David and Goliath. It was a charge that had to be answered. But this was the new boss, and Dr. Barrios had come here for a reason . . . The fishbowl of heat closed in on him, beading sweat along his hairline.

Wallabee, with his thick coating of makeup, should have been sweating, too. Yet the superintendent seemed impervious to the weather. His skin was unreflective, his hair unmoving. "We've got too many students who can win on the football field but not in college and the workforce."

"Oh, yes. Of course. I just thought you'd enjoy our tradition of . . ." Dr. Barrios's voice trailed off as a microphone nudged closer. Buzzwords failed him.

Nick Wallabee gazed deep into the lens of a camera. "Our children deserve teachers and school leaders who will make sure they win in *life*." Then he turned and pointed a forefinger at Dr. Barrios's chest. "So I ask you, Doctor Barrios: Are *you* a leader who will do whatever it takes to win for children?"

The correct answer was clearly an enthusiastic yes, but Wallabee did not wait for an answer. A woman with a headset whisked him away to pose for another picture.

Another picture. A damp realization settled upon Dr. Barrios: Nick Wallabee didn't need a picture of himself shaking hands with a principal. He needed a picture of himself putting a principal on notice. He needed someone to represent the status quo. He needed a Goliath.

Suddenly, Dr. Barrios felt very much like Goliath—heavy, out of breath, and dizzy from an unexpected impact. He imagined the teachers at his school, putting the finishing touches on their classrooms and first-day lesson plans. Tomorrow, they'd see his picture in the paper and learn he'd cemented their spot in the Believers Make Achievers Zone, with all that this designation entailed.

How he longed to be in his truck, with its air conditioning and privacy and large, soft seats. But the parking lot in front of him seemed endless. It radiated heat, blurring the air, sticking him to the ground where he stood. He wiped his face with his shirtsleeve, feeling wet spots under his arms where sweat had soaked through the fabric.

It wasn't until he dropped his arm that he saw it: one lingering camera, still pointed in his direction, filming his response.

MATH

MAYBELLINE GALANG HAD spent her final days of back-to-school preparation listening to the murmur of a Pakistani news channel from Apartment 206. This had mingled with a Spanish-language soccer broadcast thumping through the wall from 204, which suggested there were now *eight satellite dishes on the street side of Building 2*. Satellite dishes were *fixtures not removable without damage to the premises*, she wrote in an e-mail to building management, which made the dishes *a clear violation of Article 16 of the Brae Estates lease*.

She'd sent many such e-mails, printing and filing each for her records. Still, the dishes remained, spreading like gray mushrooms along the side of the building.

Today, however, a sense of promise rumbled within her. It had begun the moment she'd seen Dr. Barrios's picture in the paper with his sweaty armpit exposed. Brae Hill Valley was in the "Believers Make Achievers Zone," the article had said. The new superintendent would be watching. Judgment day was upon them, and soon the world would know: Maybelline Galang was *in compliance*.

Not like her colleagues. Not like her neighbors.

Definitely not like her sister, Rosemary.

Thirty-four years earlier, their mother had arrived from the Philippines alone and pregnant with twins. She'd raised the girls on a home-care nurse's thin paycheck and thinner patience, and she'd had two main rules:

1. Don't depend on a man.
2. Don't ever, ever become a nurse.

Maybelline had followed these rules and all the others, too. She'd kept her side of the bedroom spotless, while Rosemary's stayed a mess. She'd brought home As, while Rosemary offered Cs and excuses. It should have been no surprise, then, that as soon as the girls graduated high school, Rosemary decided nursing was exactly what she wanted to do. Or that after taking four years to complete what should have been a two-year degree, she started her first nursing job and immediately hated it. Rosemary was like that.

Maybelline, meanwhile, had majored in math. She'd even found a program that would offset some of her student loans if she worked in a low-income school. These were accomplishments as undeniable as a report card full of As on a refrigerator. But as with so many of Maybelline's accomplishments, the noisy clamor of Rosemary's existence drowned them out. The week Maybelline signed her contract with Brae Hill Valley was the same week Rosemary announced she was breaking their mother's other main rule: She was quitting her job to marry an ear, nose, and throat doctor she'd met at the hospital.

At the time, this had seemed like just another of Rosemary's attention-stealing moves. Eleven years later, however, Rosemary and the ear, nose, and throat doctor were still married. They lived with their daughter, Gabriella, in an orderly, satellite dish–free suburb zoned to Grumbly Elementary, a school with such a good reputation it didn't even need a nice-sounding name.

Maybelline, who shared the apartment and its attendant expenses with her mother, did not depend on a man. She had not become a nurse. And for her daughter, Allyson, she had rules of her own:

1. Don't depend on a man.
2. Don't ever, ever become a teacher.

Also, added at this very moment:

3. "There is no way you are wearing those pants to school."

"Why not?" Allyson was wearing a pair of too-tight stretch pants, the phrase *You Wish!* scrawled across the butt in sparkly letters. She accessorized these with the fiercest look her childish features could manifest.

"Because you are ten years old."

"Ten *and a half*."

"Exactly."

"Gabriella wore these before she gave them to me, and she was only ten then."

Technically, Gabriella had been ten *and a half*, but that wasn't the point. Maybelline and Rosemary had different standards for how girls should dress. There was also the issue that Gabriella, the product of two slim parents, was smaller than her younger cousin. Allyson took after her father. Only the largest of Gabriella's hand-me-downs fit her, and these pants were not among them.

"Allyson, we don't have time for this. Go put on the clothes we picked last night."

"You mean the clothes *you* picked."

"Go put them on. We can't be late to your aunt's house."

Years earlier, when Maybelline had first considered using Rosemary's address to register Allyson for school, Coach Ray had reassured her it was no big deal. Football coaches helped players do this all the time, he said.

Also, to be fair, the rules did not explicitly say the child had to live at the address. They only said one of the utilities had to be under the name of the child's primary guardian. The bills in the apartment were registered to her mother, and it had been easy enough for Maybelline to put her name on Rosemary's energy bill. She'd done it for a few other bills as well. In fact, on paper, Rosemary's house might as well have been Maybelline's. Moreover, it was simply out of the question to send Allyson to the local elementary school, Sunshine Gardens, where there would be no more respect for rules than there was at the apartment complex.

By the time Maybelline and her sulking daughter pulled up to Rosemary's house, the garage was already open. Rosemary stood next to her new SUV wearing bulging designer sunglasses she'd probably seen on one of her reality shows. Even on the first day of school, she was wearing workout clothes. No wonder she had no standards for whether her daughter dressed appropriately.

"What?" said Rosemary from behind the sunglasses.

"Nothing." Maybelline looked away. There was no use starting an argument unless she wanted Rosemary to get into her whole thing about how just because she didn't *work outside the home* didn't mean she had nothing better to do than take care of someone else's kid. "Have a good first day, everyone."

"Whatever," said Allyson. "I look stupid."

"What's wrong?" Rosemary asked her.

"I'm wearing this baby outfit on my first day of school."

"You look fine," said Rosemary. "Just hurry up. I have a class at Fantastic Fitness after I drop y'all off. If I'm late, I'll lose my spot."

Maybelline took a deep breath and looked at her dashboard clock. "I'll pick you up around five, okay, Allyson?"

"Yeah. Right. Sure you will."

"Maybe a little after, but try to get your homework done here. Okay?"

"It's the first day. I'm not going to *get* homework." With that, Allyson grabbed her purple shoulder bag, slid off her seat, and stomped into the garage.

Gabriella emerged from the house. She was carrying a backpack, and Allyson gave Maybelline a look that said they'd be having yet another argument about why Allyson had to wear a shoulder bag when *eeeeveryone* else had a backpack. But Maybelline couldn't discuss that today. Not any time this week, either. There was just too much work at the beginning of the school year.

"I have to go to the bathroom," Allyson said to Rosemary. "Really bad."

"Hurry!"

Maybelline pulled away from the curb, waving to her sister and niece and to Allyson's back. Then she glanced at the clock: There was still time. Even with first-day-of-school traffic, she'd be able to drive to the far edge of Rosemary's gated community before doubling back toward the expressway. This was a ritual Maybelline had developed, though she never spoke of it. She would never admit how calming it was, passing all these houses painted the same six colors, lawns that never dared to grow past regulation height, row after symmetrical row, until a series of crisp ninety-degree turns left her at the far end of the street she'd started on.

Finally, she headed toward the exit gate, so lost in the order of it all that she was almost on Rosemary's block before she noticed the SUV, still idling at the curb.

The sight of it made Maybelline pause midbreath. She pulled behind a parked car and lowered her head, watching the SUV through the windows of the car in front of her. Rosemary waited in the driver's seat, tapping her garage-door clicker on the steering wheel as she looked toward the house. A few seconds later, Allyson emerged, walking fast and looking so happy that Maybelline wondered if her daughter always became pleasant once she was out of sight.

But no. Something else was different. Maybelline couldn't place what it was until Allyson climbed into the SUV's rear seat, revealing the sparkly letters scrawled across the back of her pants.

Maybelline's heart thumped. She wanted to lean on her horn, then drive up beside the SUV and demand that Allyson change back into her school clothes. *Right. Now.* But that would make them all late. Plus, how could she explain why she was still there? Her only hope was that Rosemary would notice the pants, and she stared hard at the SUV, willing this to happen.

But Rosemary's eyes were fixed on the garage door as it rolled closed, protecting the orderly life that lay inside. Until the girls arrived at school, the message on the back of Allyson's pants was for Maybelline's eyes alone:

You Wish!

THE MYSTERY HISTORY TEACHER

www.teachcorps.blogs.com/mystery-history-teacher
MAKING EDUCATIONAL INEQUITY "HISTORY"

Happy new school year, everyone! For any new readers, here's what you need to know about me: This is my second year teaching high school American history—which explains the title of the blog. ;-) I'm also a proud member of the TeachCorps program, which addresses the civil rights issue of our day: educational inequity for low-income, minority students, often caused by the low expectations of their teachers. That's why I'm starting the year by letting my students know I've set gigantic goals for them. I am determined to prove to them that no matter what their past experiences have been, they can and *will* succeed in my class.

I've set some gigantic goals for myself also. Rereading my notes from TeachCorps boot camp made me realize I need to do a better job of reaching across the communication divide to build on my students' unique cultural paradigms. Also, I want to lose the ten pounds I put on last year.

Today is the first day of school. I've got a yogurt and an apple packed for lunch and a PowerPoint presentation ready so I can start investing my students in high achievement on day one. Wish me luck!

"Good morning." Kaytee reached out to shake hands with her first student. "I'm Ms. Mahoney. Please find a seat and begin the bell-ringer activity."

She gestured to the directions on the Smart Board:

Take out a blank piece of paper and complete the following sentence: "Democracy is . . ." Keep this paper at your desk. It will be your exit ticket.

The student took out a notebook and began working. So far, so good.

Kaytee continued her introductions as students arrived, trying to block out the voice of Ms. Grady, who was loudly addressing her own students next door: "Son, fix that shirt collar. And you, young man—I hope you do not think you're coming into this classroom with your pants leg rolled up."

In the hallway, two boys stopped in front of Ms. Grady's door and pulled out their schedules for a final look.

"Damn," one of them muttered, hitching up his beltless pants and holding them in place through his shirt. "We got Scarface."

Ms. Grady's nickname reminded Kaytee of a line she'd read during the blur of her high school Advanced Placement classes: *If a woman is beautiful enough, a small scar only enhances her beauty.* But Ms. Grady was not that beautiful, and her scar was not that small. It curved down one cheek like a zipper, turning an already intimidating presence into a teacher look that was impossible to talk back to. Sometimes Kaytee even wondered if Ms. Grady was proud of the scar.

The jagged-edged voice cut into Kaytee's thoughts again. "What do you mean you don't have paper? Where did you think you were going this morning, the circus?"

In her pity for Ms. Grady's class, Kaytee worked even harder to shake hands with each of her own incoming students. She greeted a boy named Brian Bingle, followed by a girl named Milagros, which Kaytee knew was Spanish for miracle. Such hopeful historic and religious names were common among Latino students, Kaytee remembered from the previous year. African American students, on the other hand, often had names with punctuation in them or that combined their parents' first names.

This was just in some cases, though, of course. She wasn't saying *all* of them had names like that. And anyway, there was nothing abnormal, nothing *other*, as they'd discussed in TeachCorps diversity training, about a name like Moses, or Ulysses, or Kar'Natium.

The voice of the assistant principal, Mrs. Rawlins, crackled through the PA system, reminding students to hurry. They were coming in bigger groups now. Some students still stopped to shake Kaytee's hand or return her greeting. Others walked past without any sign that they saw her, searching for desks next to their friends and beginning loud conversations.

"Please begin the bell ringer," Kaytee said. "On the board. Quietly, please!"

Finally, the PA clicked off, the crowd in the hallway dwindled to a few confused freshmen, and Kaytee shut her door. "Good morning, everybody! Let's just start with a show of hands—who's done with their bell-ringer activity?"

The students who had arrived early raised their hands. A few others were still working. But several students hadn't written anything at all. Some didn't even have paper on their desks.

"Okay. Um, please take five minutes to finish your bell-ringer activity. The directions are on the board."

A few more students began writing.

For the remaining motionless kids, Kaytee paraphrased the directions. "What do you think of when you hear the word *democracy*? Answer that question on your paper." She paused, then added, "This will be your exit ticket."

A short boy in the back turned to the girl next to him. "Hey, you got paper?"

"Please raise your hand if you have any questions," said Kaytee.

The boy's hand shot up. "What's an exit ticket?"

"Raise your hand, please, and wait for me to call on you."

The hand remained in the air.

"Yes," said Kaytee. "Please tell me your name so I can start to learn people's names. Then ask your question."

"What's an exit ticket?"

"Okay, and your name is . . . ?"

"Jonathan."

"She told you say your name and *then* ask the question, stupid," said the girl next to Jonathan. Letters across her large hoop earrings spelled *Yesenia*.

"An exit ticket is the assignment you'll turn in as you leave this classroom each day," Kaytee said. "It's your ticket to leave the room."

"Okay. Thanks." Jonathan turned back to Yesenia. "You got paper?"

Yesenia ripped a page from her spiral notebook and handed it to him.

The attention in the room was developing small cracks. A student near Kaytee put his head down on top of his finished assignment. Others peeked at cell phones.

"It looks like most of you are finished," said Kaytee. "Who wants to share what they wrote about democracy?"

For the first time, the class was completely silent.

"Anyone?"

No one.

"Jonathan! Why don't you start? What does democracy mean to you?"

"It's like when you vote," said Jonathan, whose paper was still blank.

"Good. Let's start there. Who wrote something about voting to elect a leader?"

A few hands went up.

"What else?"

Silence.

"Come on, guys. This is tenth-grade American history. You've got to know *something* about democracy."

To her relief, Yesenia's hand shot into the air.

"Yes. Yesenia, right?"

"I'm in eleventh grade. Why am I in a tenth-grade class?"

"Did you take American history last year?"

"Yeah. But I failed." A few kids in the class laughed.

"Now who's stupid?" said Jonathan.

"Hey!" Kaytee must have sounded angry, because students looked at her in surprise. She raised her voice. "*No one* in this class is stupid. Do you hear me? *No one.*"

Thirty-four pairs of brown eyes were now focused on her.

She stared back, a new feeling of determination smoldering behind her gaze. "I don't know what your school experiences have been like in the past, but if you've failed, it's because the adults in charge of your education have *let* you fail. Not in my class, though. In here, you are going to succeed." She softened her tone. "*We* are going to succeed. But to do that, we are going to have to work together."

There was an empty bulletin board near the door, and now she marched over and pointed to it. "You see this bulletin board? It's supposed to have a list of rules on it, but for now, it's empty. That's because I'm not going to make rules for you. We're going to work together to create norms and expectations we all agree on. Because I *know* you are capable. In fact, I made a presentation about exactly what I expect of you this year."

Kaytee turned to a tall African American student sitting next to the light switch. He'd been quiet the whole class, but an ominous knot of muscle in his jaw made Kaytee wonder if he was a potential behavior problem.

Not problem. Challenge. Behavior *challenge.*

And not because he was African American. That would have been totally *pathologizing* him as *other.* Just because he looked so . . . potentially angry.

"Brian, right? Brian Bingle?" She made sure her tone modeled the same type of respect she would request from her students. Growing up with a father who watched awful Republican "news" and thought all minorities were criminals had made her careful to guard against any hint of racism in her own thoughts.

Brian Bingle was looking at her, she realized, waiting for her to continue.

"Um, yes, Brian? Will you please turn off the lights? Thank you, Brian!"

She had worked on the presentation for hours, timing each slide to give her improvement goals time to sink in.

But now, in class, it felt too slow. Two students had put their heads down as soon as the presentation started, and now, several other students had started whispering. Yesenia was staring away from the Smart Board, and Kaytee followed her gaze to the clock. It was getting late. They'd have to skip the norm- and expectation-setting activity for today. If only the slides would move faster . . .

But the slides did not move faster.

Instead, the bell rang, and the last of Kaytee's improvement goals flashed on the screen unnoticed as students stuffed papers into their backpacks, pushed back their chairs, and shoved noisily toward the door.

"Don't forget to turn in your exit tickets!" yelled Kaytee.

THE
CURRICULUM STANDARD
OF THE DAY
ACHIEVEMENT INITIATIVE

NICK WALLABEE WAS not at the emergency weekend principals' meeting—at least not physically. Instead, his giant face presided over the room from a large screen connected to a computer at the Malibu Innovation Festival, where famous innovators solved the problems of the world in highly publicized meetings.

The festival had caused such a surge of innovative energy in Nick Wallabee that he'd called this emergency meeting to announce the Curriculum Standard of the Day Achievement Initiative, which had caused Dr. Barrios to drive home early from a visit to his in-laws, which had in turn caused a long bout of silent treatment from Mrs. Barrios.

At least he wasn't alone.

All the Believers Zone principals sat with him in the windowless room full of motivational posters, trying their best to look happy. The implied message had been lost on none of them: Some of the people in this room would end the year "resigning" to "spend more time with their families."

That was what people always said, wasn't it, when they had to pretend they weren't being fired? On top of everything else, you had to pretend you wanted to spend more time listening to your son and his wife argue about their home renovations, or watching your daughter's kids play video games at the table in restaurants.

An anxiety Dr. Barrios had been suppressing crept back into his chest. None of the other principals were sitting next to him. They'd offered conciliatory smiles from across the room, but it was clear they were keeping their distance from the colleague whose armpit had been front-page news. Could he blame them? The image surfaced from the depths of his memory even now, spraying him with shame. He'd become the visual representation of the mess Wallabee promised to clean up in the district. For the first time in his career, Dr. Barrios was first in line to be the principal who wanted to *spend more time with the family*.

Why was it, anyway, that no one could just say *fired*? His own father had been *let go* (as if he'd been trying to escape) after nearly thirty years as the manager of a discount auto-parts store. No one wanted to hire a manager who was five years from retirement age, and the elder Barrios had roamed the house for months, fixing light bulbs, demanding that relatives bring their cars over so he could investigate squeaks and rattles. Eventually, he took the only job that would have him: bagging groceries at Fiesta Supermarket, shrinking as he took orders from a store manager who still had acne.

Dr. Barrios took another sip of cafeteria-grade coffee and checked his image at the bottom of the screen, trying to figure out how to best make eye contact with Nick Wallabee's giant face.

The face looked off into the middle distance, eyes narrowed with intensity, as if Wallabee was posing for a picture on an innovation-conference poster. Then it turned back toward the screen. "All teachers are to have the Curriculum Standard of the Day written on their boards. If they don't, I'll expect their Believer Scores to reflect this."

A waiter crossed behind Wallabee, holding a tray of something that looked delicious. Dr. Barrios had not eaten breakfast.

"Any questions?" asked Wallabee's face.

No, sir, thought Dr. Barrios. He was letting other people ask the questions from now on. Ever since the day of the press conference, he'd become clear about one main thing: Miguel Barrios, EdD, did not want to spend more time with his family. No, sir. No, thank you. He wanted to keep his job. If Wallabee wanted some new thing written on the board, it would be written on the board.

One of the other principals raised a hand. "When will we receive a list of the standards to be covered?"

"Soon." Behind Wallabee, a group of vaguely famous faces began chatting.

"Will we be getting any new materials or books?"

"This is not about bells and whistles," said Wallabee, steadily raising his voice until the faces behind him turned in his direction. "This is about leadership! *This is about making sure our* children *have teachers who* believe *in them!*"

Wallabee turned to the faces behind him. "Sorry, fellas," he said. "Nothing makes me more emotional than talking about the kids."

Then he turned back to the screen again. "I have to go. I'm about to be on a panel. But you'll receive an e-mail with the first standards to be covered. Is everyone clear?"

The principals sat in uneasy silence.

Finally, someone ventured the question they were all thinking. "When exactly do we start this initiative?"

"Tomorrow," said Nick Wallabee's face, and the screen went black.

ELEMENTS OF POETRY

"**W**HAT'S A MOSQUE?"

"A mosque is . . . a religious center for Muslims." Lena scanned her students' expressions, then added, "It's like a church. But for Muslim people."

"Muslims believe in God?"

Lena adjusted the headband that held her curls away from her face. She considered the many paths the discussion might take from here and the difficulty of navigating back from any of them to her original lesson plan.

Two years ago, in her interview with Dr. Barrios and Mrs. Rawlins, she had said she'd love to work with low-level readers—had, in fact, produced quite a monologue on how important it was for teachers to get away from the *deficit model* of education, which focused on what students didn't know, and instead focus on *bringing the community into the school*, connecting course material with the rich tapestry of students' interests and life experiences. This monologue had inspired vigorous head nodding from Mrs. Rawlins during the interview and had probably gotten her the job.

Also, they really needed someone to work with low-level readers.

What Lena hadn't anticipated, however, was the vast amount of explaining she'd have to do when she introduced . . . almost anything. Today, for example, she was showing a video of a Palestinian American poet speaking about the backlash against Muslims after 9/11. But when students didn't know what a mosque was, it was hard to discuss poetry about anti-Islamic hate crimes. Harder still was any discussion of comparative religion or the differences between mono- and polytheism. It went without saying she couldn't talk about atheism—Texas was no place to question whether there was really some bearded white man in the sky who cared whether you were still a virgin. Often, it was best to supply just enough background to keep the class moving forward.

"The Jewish, Muslim, and Christian religions all believe in one God," said Lena. Then she pressed Play.

A burst of static from the PA speaker drowned out the first line of the poem. "Good morning, students and teachers. Thank you for an interruption. On today we will begin implementing the Curriculum Standard of the Day Achievement Initiative."

Lena sighed as she paused the video. *Not* on *today*, she mentally corrected, *just* today. Her finger hovered over the Play button as if this would make up for lost time.

"Teachers, please check your e-mail and then write today's Curriculum Standard of the Day on the board in its entirety."

Lena opened her e-mail. If she found the standard quickly, she could probably finish writing it before the announcement ended. Mrs. Rawlins, the more grammatically questionable of the school's two assistant principals, was never happier than when speaking over the PA.

But the first thing Lena saw was not the Curriculum Standard of the Day. It was an announcement from her favorite poetry club: Nex Level was back in town.

The moment wrapped its arms around her, warming her with hope.

For it was Nex Level whose words had reawakened her soul over the summer, at the rally against police brutality. The ferocious rhythm of his poetry had merged with her own thoughts, igniting the blaze of inspiration within her. And he'd be performing next Friday.

The PA clicked off, and Lena restarted the poem. She always shared this poem in the days before September 11, as the country—and Texas in particular—geared up for an intense bout of American pride. This eloquent Muslim woman, born and raised in Brooklyn, her brother in the navy, was an example of the lesson Lena most hoped to teach: There was power in poetry. The right words, arranged in the right order, were like the combination to a lock, opening doors long sealed shut by stereotypes and typecasting.

Lena Wright knew plenty about stereotypes and typecasting. As a teenager at a performing-arts magnet school, she'd been eternally cast as the finger-snappin', neck-rollin', streetwise black friend who was fond of the phrase *you go, girl*. (Occasionally, she played the Puerto Rican friend—equally sassy, but with a different accent.) Even at parties, expectant white people surrounded her, clapping off beat and waiting for her to break it down on the dance floor, or making solicitous eye contact as they chanted along to decades-old rap lyrics. *Go, Lena, it's your birthday! This is how we do it! I got ninety-nine problems, but a bitch ain't one!*

In college, she had avoided theater classes altogether; it was time to write her own lines for a change. She channeled her performance skills into spoken-word poetry, joined activist groups on campus, blasted her professors with essays on the racist imagery in Shakespeare's works.

And then she'd graduated and moved to Texas.

It was a choice she had trouble explaining. *Why not New York?* asked her classmates. *Why a former slave state?* wondered her parents. Why leave a city like Philadelphia for a giant, hot expanse of paved-over farmland with no real public transportation? Which was to say, *Why the South?*

But the South was the point exactly. Moving south held the promise of going back to something older, something *real*, a solid point of connection from which her branch of ancestors had long ago departed. All she knew was that she'd teach in a community like this one, guiding students in meaningful discussions, leaving them with a sense of pride in their heritage.

Which was why, her first year, as she watched a cluster of black girls sit out picture day because they hadn't had their hair done, she'd felt a surge of responsibility. If she could only find the right words, in the right order, she could reach them and make them understand. *We don't need other people's hair to be beautiful. We don't need other people's poetry to be brilliant. Everything we need is already inside us.* It was that night that she'd shaved her head, a poem forming in her mind to the rhythmic buzz of the clippers.

The next day, she had performed it for the class. *I'm strong and brown like a tree/ Gonna stand tall and true/ Cut off the leaves*—Lena pointed toward her newly shiny scalp—*Wave my branches/ And let my roots show through.*

The room had exploded in applause, and Lena concealed her delight by shuffling some papers on her desk.

Miss Wright?

She'd looked up, following the voice to a dark face framed by a shiny, improbably light brown head of hair. *Yes, Tyesha?*

Tyesha used one acrylic nail to push a silky strand from her face. She seemed confused. *You all black, Miss Wright?*

Of course. Why?

Oh. We thought you was mixed.

THE SCIENTIFIC METHOD

"**I HAVE A** story for you. But you have to figure out the ending." Seven years earlier, when Hernan first started teaching biology, he would have launched right into the directions for the class's first experiment. These days, he started with a riddle.

"There's this crow—one of those big, black birds you sometimes see on telephone wires." He shouldn't have had to explain what a crow was, but he'd seen even the simplest concepts derail students' understanding.

"The crow hasn't eaten in a long time. He's about to die from hunger. All of a sudden, he sees a worm floating in a pitcher of water, and he knows his last chance to survive is to eat this worm." Here, Hernan lifted a graduated cylinder from his demonstration table. A plastic worm floated on top of a few inches of water.

"The crow tries to put his beak into the top of the pitcher, but he can't get his head in far enough without getting stuck." Hernan pinched his fingers together to form an imaginary beak, pushing them halfway into the mouth of the pitcher. "There's only a little water left in the pitcher, so the worm isn't high enough for him to reach it, but he knows that if he gives up, he's going to die of hunger. Then, finally, he figures out—"

A burst of static from the PA speaker stopped him.

"Thank you for an interruption." Mrs. Rawlins's voice crackled. "Please stand for the Pledge of Allegiance and the Texas Pledge."

There was a notable difference between the speed at which students oozed upright for the pledges and the velocity with which they sprang from their seats at the end of class. Watching students stand up in this context reminded Hernan of *The Road to Homo Sapiens*, an illustration of the stages of evolution long ago banned from Texas textbooks. Mrs. Rawlins was already saying, ". . . one nation, under God," when the last student erected himself into *Oreopithecus* posture.

"Come on, Lamont," urged Hernan. "You're not ninety years old."

"Teachers, please be reminded to write today's Curriculum Standard of the Day on the board in its entirety."

Hernan walked around the room, placing upright plastic tubes on each lab table. These last-minute announcements always dragged on the momentum of the class.

A girl squinted into her plastic tube. "The hell? Is that a dead worm?"

Instead of answering, Hernan grabbed a Ziploc bag of tweezers from his demonstration table and handed it to her. "Pass these out for me, Nilda. One on each table." Then he quickly checked his e-mail, clicking the embedded link and scrolling to the biology standard: *Students will use the scientific method during laboratory investigations and experiments.*

Lamont, who seemed to slide a few inches in his chair every few minutes, had slouched to a 45-degree angle.

"Lamont, you see that stack of papers on the front table? Will you grab those and give one to each person? Great. Thanks."

Hernan wrote *Scientific Method* on the board as Lamont passed out the instructions for the experiment.

MATERIALS

Water-filled cylinder or tube
Floating worm
Tweezers
Directions

1. The tweezers represent the beak of the crow. You must hold them in one hand and cannot alter them in any way.
2. You can use any materials you find in the room, but you must

only use the tweezers to handle them. (Remember: Crows have no hands!)

3. The tube must remain upright and on the table at all times.
4. You cannot add water to the tube.
5. Solve the problem by removing the worm from the tube using only the tweezers.

"The first group that figures out how to remove the worm from the tube gets extra credit." Another strange phenomenon Hernan had observed: Even students who didn't do their regular assignments would work for extra credit.

"And I'll give y'all a hint." Under *Scientific Method*, he wrote: *Step one: Make observations.* "This means look around carefully. Notice things. Pick things up and feel them. Use all five senses."

As always, students spent the beginning of their observation time arguing among lab partners and jiggling the tubes to see if the worm was real. Eventually, however, they settled into trying to solve the puzzle. Hernan walked around the room, observing. Aside from his plants, the room had the attributes found in most high school science labs: rows of rectangular lab tables; shelves of tools for mixing, measuring, and filtering; two sinks, one of which worked. Scattered among these lay bolts, screws, and other small metal objects Hernan had placed around the room the day before.

He wrote the next step on the board. *Step two: Propose a hypothesis.*

"Okay, everyone, hopefully you've had some time to make observations. Now it's time to form a hypothesis—that's an educated guess about the answer to the experiment."

He wrote the last four steps on the board:

Step three: Design a controlled experiment to test the hypothesis.
Step four: Do the experiment.
Step five: Reject or fail to reject the hypothesis.
Step six: Draw conclusions. Then, if you need to, go back to step one.

He knew there would be much work to do before students fully understood the steps. The schools that fed into Brae Hill Valley considered it a matter of survival to focus on each year's tested subjects, and only a few grades took science tests.

"We'll discuss all this later," said Hernan, gesturing toward the board. "For now, just work on forming a hypothesis."

Eventually, a student would notice the bits of metal hidden around the room and figure out that if they dropped these in the water, the worm would float to the top of the tube. In the meantime, Hernan circled the room, offering occasional pointers. His mind wandered to Lena: The year's first happy hour was on Friday, and he hadn't heard from her yet. Maybe she'd forgotten. Maybe Lena was just being polite when she asked for his number. Or maybe he should have taken her number instead. Then again, would he have even called? He wasn't one to make things awkward with a coworker.

"Mr. Hernandez." In the doorway stood Hernan's least favorite assistant principal, Mr. Scamphers. He was giving Hernan the look one might give a child who had indeed put someone's eye out in a game he'd warned them would only be fun until someone got hurt. "You are out of compliance with the Curriculum Standard of the Day Achievement Initiative."

"We're working on the scientific method," said Hernan, pointing to the board. "Isn't that the standard?"

"The standard is to be written on the board *in its entirety*, Mr. Hernandez, as per this morning's announcement."

"Sorry." But then, since Hernan wasn't actually sorry, he added, "It's just that we were already in the middle of the lesson when that announcement came on."

"Well, I'll certainly make a note of that." Scamphers scribbled on his clipboard.

Before Hernan could wonder why this was worth noting, a burst of activity erupted from a lab table near the window. Someone had made a correct hypothesis. Now students were all hunting for bits of metal to pick up and drop into the water, just as crows did in the wild.

High school science experiments were like this. Everything that determined the outcome was already in the room, working as it always did, as predictable as the laws of gravity or volume displacement. They were only new if you hadn't noticed them before.

It was Nilda who first called, "We got it!" She held her worm up like a trophy.

"Nice," said Hernan. "Congratulations to the whole group on using the *scientific method* to find a solution!" He couldn't resist looking at Mr. Scamphers as he emphasized the words.

But Mr. Scamphers offered no sign that he had understood. He marched out the door, his clipboard cradled stiffly in one arm.

Hernan turned to the student who had vindicated him. "Nilda, why don't you tell us what your hypothesis was?"

Nilda shrugged. "I saw everyone putting these metal thingies in the water, so I tried to get more of them than everyone else."

Hernan sighed. "You were supposed to form a hypothesis first."

"Yeah, but Mr. Hernandez, sometimes you just gotta go for it."

Sometimes you just gotta go for it was not the takeaway of the lesson, but the bell rang before Hernan could answer, and the students filtered out of the room. It was early in the year, he reminded himself. There was still time. He watered the plants along his windowsill before the next wave of students arrived, feeling a vibration he at first assumed was coming from the air conditioner. Then he realized it was his phone, announcing a text message from inside his pocket.

This Friday. Papacito's?

A smile crept onto Hernan's face as he realized the area code was from Philadelphia.

See you there, he typed back.

PRIMARY AND SECONDARY SOURCES

"**I'M CONCERNED ABOUT** a couple of my students."
Kaytee avoided saying their names: Yesenia Molina and
Jonathan Rodriguez. She didn't want to set off one of
Mrs. Towner's parents-who-don't-speak-English rants.

"I know." Mrs. Towner nodded sympathetically. "These kids are bad."

"No, no, they're actually really smart kids! But it's like they're so
used to being failed by the system that they're sabotaging their education by talking in class."

Mrs. Towner looked confused.

"I called home to try to invest their families, but I could only reach
one parent."

"Single mom?"

"No. Well, I mean, I don't know. The mom said she would talk to her
son, but the next day nothing changed. And the girl—"

"No surprise there. Most of the parents who support education
moved their kids to the suburbs years ago. Or they go private. Like my
husband and me—we both went here, but we busted our butts to send
our kids to Catholic school."

Mrs. Towner, Kaytee's assigned mentor teacher, was always quick to
share that she'd attended the school as a student. She was even quicker
to add, *It sure wasn't like* this *when* I *went here.* From what Kaytee could
gather, the school district had desegregated after Mrs. Towner's senior
year. She'd returned from teaching college to find a diversifying mass of

teenagers who—according to her—got worse every year. Conversations with Patty Towner were like archeological digs in which each layer of sediment revealed a new, well-preserved stereotype. These were exactly the type of conversations TeachCorps had warned them about.

"Listen, hon, I'm going to share something with you that someone once told me. A couple years ago, I went to a professional development session, and they gave us each one of these." Mrs. Towner opened her desk drawer and pulled out an oversized Q-tip. "You know what the letters in Q-tip stand for?'"

Kaytee shook her head.

"Quit Taking It Personally!"

"Oh."

"I know, isn't that great? Whenever this job is getting to me, I just open my desk drawer and look at this and repeat that to myself: Quit taking it personally."

Kaytee had a sudden, strong desire to be back in her own classroom.

"But you know what? I think you need this more than I do now." Mrs. Towner handed the Q-tip to Kaytee as if passing an Olympic torch.

"Wow. Thanks so much. Really. I appreciate it." Kaytee was backing out of the room. There was nothing she wanted less than to stand near Mrs. Towner's open door holding a two-year-old Q-tip. "But I should go now. I have a ton of work to do."

"No problem, hon. Have a great weekend. And remember—Q.T.I.P!"

Kaytee hurried back toward her classroom, so focused on holding the Q-tip away from her body that she didn't see Lena Wright until they nearly collided.

"Girl. Why are you running back *into* the building on a Friday afternoon?" Her eyes traveled to Kaytee's hand. "And why are you holding a giant Q-tip?"

Kaytee glanced over her shoulder. She didn't want to offend her mentor teacher, but it felt urgent to let Lena know she wasn't doing this by choice. "It's supposed to stand for 'quit taking it personally,'" she whispered. "I'm trying to find a place to throw it out."

"You don't need a Q-tip," said Lena, not whispering at all. "You need a drink. It's payday Friday. We're all going to Papacito's."

Maybelline Galang huffed past them without saying hello and reentered her classroom. Kaytee watched, weighing her options. On the one hand, she had work to do. She'd fallen behind on grading exit tickets, which TeachCorps had warned them would make it hard to maintain high expectations. On the other hand, this was the first time Lena Wright—or any of her colleagues—had ever invited her to happy hour.

"Okay. I'll meet you there."

Before she left, she ducked back into her classroom to stuff the exit tickets into her TeachCorps tote bag. The Q-tip she dropped in the garbage.

"I mean, I get not wanting to pay taxes," Lena was saying when Kaytee arrived. "I just don't get all this focus on what's going on inside other people's butts."

"Because it's a sin for a man to lay down with another man," answered Breyonna. "It's written in the Bible."

Hernan Hernandez, who sat facing Kaytee at one end of the table, gave her a smile that suggested Lena and Breyonna just might be crazy. At the other end of the table were Candace and Regina, who taught at nearby schools and whom Kaytee gathered were from Breyonna's sorority.

Lena was smiling directly at Breyonna now, her eyes telegraphing a conversational knockout punch. "Have you actually *read* the Bible?"

"I grew up in the church choir."

"Because you know the Bible says it's okay to have slaves, right?" Lena leaned forward. "There's even, like, directions for how to treat your slaves. And, meanwhile, there's only one line in the whole Bible that can even be *interpreted* to say that being gay is a sin."

"Well, it should be obvious."

Kaytee wondered if Breyonna regretted inviting Lena and Hernan—and, by extension, Kaytee—to fill the empty seats at her table.

But Lena either didn't notice or didn't care. "I just don't get how it's possible for black people to agree with Republicans. On anything."

Kaytee wasn't sure if it was okay, as the only white teacher at the table, to laugh at this remark. She settled for a small *hmm* that could be taken as a laugh if appropriate.

Regina and Candace laughed. But it was okay if they did it.

"I'm not a Republican," said Breyonna. "I just think being gay is nasty."

The food arrived, and hands reached in toward wings and nachos. Kaytee took a celery stick from the wing plate. It crunched loudly when she bit into it, intensifying her self-consciousness. She wondered if she was the only one at the table on a diet.

Lena turned at the sound of the crunch, her face lighting up as if she'd just thought of something. "Hey! Remember that presenter a couple years ago who gave us Q-tips?"

"Oh, yeah," said Hernan. "She was like, *Keep this big, dusty Q-tip in your desk and stare at it when you're having a bad day*." He was addressing the table, though he seemed mostly focused on Lena's reaction.

"Yup, that's the one. Anyway, guess who I saw outside Patty Towner's room holding a giant Q-tip?"

Kaytee blushed. "I was on my way to throw it out."

"You threw out the Q-tip?!" Hernan opened his eyes wide. "You were supposed to keep that in a safe place!"

Kaytee looked at him, surprised. "You kept yours?"

"Nah. Just kidding. I used it to clean my ears."

Lena laughed, and Hernan's fake shock melted into a smile. "It gave me a warm, fuzzy feeling when I used it, though."

"Mrs. Towner gave it to me. And she gave me this whole speech about how I'm not supposed to take it personally if my kids don't succeed." Kaytee hoped her tone communicated enough incredulity. She didn't want anyone here to think she was like Mrs. Towner. She was the *opposite* of Mrs. Towner. "Actually, I was trying to get advice about some students who have been sabotaging their success by talking in class. I wanted—"

"I know," said Candace. "These kids are bad."

"For real," said Breyonna. "And y'all know I went to the Hill—but we sure didn't act like these kids."

"No, no." Kaytee tried to clarify. "They're actually really smart kids!

But it's like they're so used to being failed by the system that they're . . ." She trailed off as Candace and Breyonna began to look bored.

"We gotta help this girl out," said Lena, "before she gets kidnapped by the Q-tip people. Give her some *real* advice about Brae Hill Valley."

"Don't put your lunch in the teachers'-lounge fridge," offered Breyonna.

"For real." Lena turned to Kaytee to explain further. "They always tell us we can't have those little fridges in our rooms, but everyone does. People *steal* at this school."

"I used to take a bite out of my sandwich before I put it in the lounge fridge," said Hernan. "Then one day someone stole it anyway. That's when I got my own fridge."

Lena laughed. Hernan straightened in his seat.

"And try to get honors classes." This, like nearly everything Regina said, sounded like a complaint. "They actually do their work, so you get your TCUP score bonus."

Kaytee looked at Breyonna, who taught the honors classes in the history department, but Breyonna was digging in her purse.

"Wait," said Lena. "I thought the scores depended on whether we believed in students enough."

"Yeah," said Hernan, "and we get to take ownership of that this year. It's super exciting."

"A real paradigm shift," agreed Lena.

"Based on *real* research and statistics."

"You're so crazy, Hernan!" Candace interjected.

"Not just crazy," said Lena. "Crazy *and* you owe me a drink. Remember the bet we made?"

"I remember," Hernan admitted, then signaled to the waitress. "Next one's on me."

"What we need," said Regina, as if sensing the threat of incoming cheerfulness, "is a neck-tattoo statistic."

They all turned toward her.

"They want to send us data like, *This many black students passed a test in some other teacher's class, and this many are passing in your class.* And that's not even the point. I mean, I'm black. Breyonna and Candace are black. We can pass a test."

"Yeah, exactly," added Lena. "I can pass a test."

"How 'bout you tell me how many thirteen-year-olds *with neck tattoos* are passing a test in another teacher's class. Then compare my neck-tattoo kids with their neck-tattoo kids. *Then* tell me what kind of teacher I am."

Kaytee made another *hmmm* sound that could have been a laugh, though she hoped it was clear she was *not* laughing at thirteen-year-olds with neck tattoos, who were trapped in a cycle of generational poverty that was certainly not funny.

"Actually," said Lena, "I've got some kids with neck tattoos who are even smarter than the other kids in the class. They're just a different kind of smart."

"You should see our students this year," said Breyonna. She launched into a story about a group of girls she called *Pookie and them*, which led Regina to follow up with a comment about *Quay'Vante and them*, which Kaytee gathered were fictional names, chosen because they sounded like the type of names that represented generational poverty among African Americans.

This time, Kaytee refused to laugh. She reached back to feel her TeachCorps tote bag, which hung from the back of her chair with the stack of exit tickets inside. If she graded some of them at the table, right here at happy hour, maybe it would serve as an example to these other teachers, who had nothing to say about the kids except that they were *bad*. Her thoughts flickered quickly to her blog.

Breyonna looked at her phone. "I got to go soon, y'all. Roland and I are going to dinner with some other people from the marketing department at his bank. I mean, don't get me wrong—wings are good and all, but I'd rather have some crab legs and filet mignon, y'all know what I'm saying?"

"Forget the TCUP bonus," said Candace. "I gotta get me a rich fiancé."

"Well, you chose the wrong career," said Regina. "Ain't no men in teaching."

"Hey!" Hernan placed both hands over his heart as if he were deeply offended.

"You know what I mean, Hernan. Okay: There are a *few* men in the teaching profession. But Hernan is the only good one."

"Better," said Hernan. "Much better."

Candace smiled at him.

"That reminds me," said Lena, "if you all are into the spoken word scene, there's this poet, Nex Level, who's gonna be performing at Club Seven next Friday."

"Sorry, Roland and I are taking a weekend cruise." Breyonna signed her credit-card slip and headed out.

"Anyone else?" asked Lena, looking toward Regina and Candace.

Kaytee took advantage of the distraction and slipped the exit tickets from her bag.

"Ain't no men at poetry clubs," said Regina. "Those things are always ninety percent women."

"I'll go," said Hernan.

A chorus of *Oohh, Hernan*s rose from Regina and Candace.

"Cool," said Lena. "Um . . . I'll give you the details at school?"

It was now or never. Kaytee took a deep breath, then pushed her plate aside, placing the exit tickets on the table. She felt eyes on her as she began writing, but she did not allow herself to look up. She had just finished grading the third ticket when she felt a kick under the table.

"Girl, what are you doing?" whispered Lena.

"Just grading some papers." Kaytee tried to sound nonchalant, as if such student-focused multitasking was a natural extension of happy-hour fun. "I need to get some feedback to my students soon so they—"

"Put them away!" Lena hissed. "You're killing everyone's buzz."

THE MYSTERY HISTORY TEACHER

www.teachcorps.blogs.com/mystery-history-teacher

"QUIT TAKING IT PERSONALLY"?

I was told today, in a whole bunch of different ways, that I should "quit taking my students' failure so personally." There's an attitude toward our marginalized students of color that seems to come from every other teacher at my school. I won't go into detail.

But then she deleted the last sentence, because perhaps she *would* go into detail. She was still hungry after eating only celery sticks at happy hour, and she'd stopped grading papers after Lena kicked her under the table. This meant the exit tickets still loomed over her weekend.

But it was more than that. She'd expected the teachers at happy hour, of all people, to care as much about low-income students' success as she did. Instead, they'd sounded just as bad as Patty Towner. Kaytee wondered, suddenly, if she was the only teacher at her school who *took it personally*.

And then she began typing.

She changed what she had to in order to keep the story anonymous but left the main ideas intact: how, even at a table full of her colleagues, she'd felt like the only advocate for her students. How she'd had to remind *her own mentor teacher* that the kids were not hopeless. How the teacher next door, maybe the worst offender of all, taught lessons about democracy but ran her classroom like a dictatorship. By the time Kaytee reached the last paragraph, she'd nearly forgotten how hungry she was.

Today I tried to lead by example and show my colleagues that when it comes to breaking down barriers for students, there's no such thing as time off—even if that means grading papers during happy hour. Maybe I'm the only one, but I'll say it: My students' futures matter to me. And I am *not* going to quit taking them personally.

COMMENTS

Yellow Brick Road University Teachers! Get an online masters degree at www.yellowbrickuniversityonline.com.

NaughtyTeacherDetentionXXX Have you been a bad boy? Cum see me after class! Check out my naughty detention pics and so much more. www.naughtyteacherseemeafterclass69.com

CLICK HERE TO WRITE AN ADDITIONAL COMMENT ON THIS POST

MAKING HEALTHY CHOICES

"**O'NEAL RIGBY! WHAT** are those girls doing up there in the stands?"

"Yelling my n—" O'Neal began, then stopped, his smile disappearing. This was the wrong answer.

"Yelling. Your. Name." Coach Ray spoke slowly, using what he'd heard players call his *calm-before-the-storm* voice. "Why? Because they like football so much?"

O'Neal Rigby stared at his cleats. He knew what was coming. "No, Coach."

"Do girls like football, *O'Neal?*" Coach Ray used Rigby's first name on purpose—*Rigby* was what crowds screamed when things were going well.

And things were not going well.

"No, Coach."

O'Neal Rigby was the star of the Killer Armadillos. Usually, he was everything a coach could ask for. But he lost focus when girls were around, clowning and doing these stupid little dances when he caught the ball and then, almost immediately afterwards, making some idiot mistake. With the first game of the season coming up, the Killer Armadillos had no time for mistakes. Plus, after what had happened last year, the whole keeping-your-dick-in-your-pants thing could not be reinforced too much.

"What *do* girls like, *O'Neal?*" He was leaning in now, staring right into the face mask of Rigby's helmet.

"Attention. Coach."

"And . . . ?" All of the other players were gathered around now, listening. Every one of them knew the rest of the sentence, and fuck if O'Neal Rigby was going to get back on the field without finishing it.

"Football equals attention."

Coach Ray could have kept going if he wanted to. If he really wanted to drive the point home, this was when he'd ask the player whether he was a boy who liked football or a girl who liked attention, in which case he might want to go ask Ms. Watson if she had a cheerleading uniform in his size.

But he saved those moments for when he really needed them.

Right now, that didn't seem to be the case. O'Neal Rigby, despite being three inches taller than his coach, looked as sorry as a child. Which was part of the whole thing: In a way that a kid who'd just turned eighteen could never understand, he still *was* a child. But a child who was six foot five, over 250 lbs, and already getting attention from the local media could easily be convinced that he was an adult. As a result, the moment a top player was about to cross into the bright end zone of opportunity was also the moment he was most likely to pull some knuckleheaded fucking fumble that cost him a free ride to college and sometimes even got him a criminal record on top of that, not to mention getting the school's name in the paper and leaving the coach hanging on to his job by a thread. *Fucking Gerard Brown.*

But Gerard Brown was not the topic right now.

The topic was Booker T. Washington High School, who the Armadillos would be playing in their first game, and who were known for coming into the season ready. No way Booker T. was going to lose because of some girl.

Coach Ray addressed the whole group now. "The first game sets the tone for the year. So why don't y'all tell me right now—how's this season supposed to end?"

"Championship!"

"And how's this season *gonna* end?"

"Championship!!!"

"You think you're just gonna show up on the day of the fucking game and decide you want to win?"

"No, Coach!"

"Remember, your game face is not just for the game. And it's not just for your face. Everything y'all do between now and that first game is gonna decide whether we win. So get those inner game faces on, and go play. *Let's go!*"

That inner game face. That was what he always came back to. That was what you needed to do football right. On the field, you didn't think about last year, or the heat, or the fact your truck needed fixing, or that God, who had to know men communicated anything worth knowing through sports, had seen fit to send you two daughters whom you now had to support with almost half of each paycheck. Keeping an inner game face meant blocking out any thoughts that didn't fit your current objective.

Here was the current objective: to get ready for the first game of the season. And to remind this year's star team member that he was more team member than star.

And so Coach Ray was thinking of nothing else as he caught O'Neal Rigby by the arm, just before they went back out onto the field, and said, "Learn from other people's mistakes, son, or your mistakes are gonna be the ones people learn from."

Like mine, he didn't think. Didn't think about it at all.

FUNCTIONAL ORGANIZATION OF DATA

THREE-RING BINDERS WERE the highest level of the organizational hierarchy. They were not like flimsy manila folders, which one could fill with leftover work sheets, then stash in some accordion folder inside a file drawer. They were not like pocket folders, which one could stuff with meeting notes and forget in a pile. Binders required full attention. One had to neatly label each divider before anything could go into them at all.

And so, with this year's data binder in front of her, Maybelline couldn't possibly have time to notice the whistles and yells on the football field outside her window. These were not important. What was important were the pre-test results, which Maybelline had already printed. She would have her data binder finished a full week before the official due date, probably before any other teacher in the school.

Out in the hallway beyond her door, she heard sounds of teachers leaving for the day. These were the same teachers, Maybelline was sure, who would have to rush to finish their binders by the deadline. Most of her colleagues fell behind on paperwork. They forgot to print out data. They waited too long to grade papers. Then, before they knew it, they were accepting stacks of makeup work from students—the ultimate sign of a weak organizational system. Maybelline Galang never accepted makeup work.

She sliced open a fresh box of plastic sheet protectors. What better way to show that one had not waited until the last minute than to encase each data printout in its own glossy sheet protector? The time would come to provide documentation. And when it did, Maybelline would be ready.

It would be a different story for some of her colleagues. Lena Wright, for example, probably kept her data in some overflowing manila folder belching its contents onto a shelf. One look at Lena's paperwork would be enough to show any observer she was more concerned with organizing happy hours than organizing data.

Maybelline slipped the final, completed form into its sheet protector with what should have been a victorious swish. So why did something about it feel empty?

Maybe it was because, even with the deadline only a week away, Dr. Barrios hadn't sent out the goal-setting cover sheet until this morning. This suggested that, once again this year, he wouldn't be coming around to check the binders, which meant, *once again*, he would not know who'd finished on time. Maybe he didn't even care if everyone procrastinated on their data binders, just as they did on everything else.

Everything except football. *That* they took seriously.

The racket from the field seemed to be directly below her window now, the pounding of players' cleats trampling her own sense of accomplishment. Suddenly, she was consumed with the need to show Dr. Barrios that, even though he'd sent out the cover sheet *way* too late, she had finished early.

She headed to the office to sign out for the day, taking the binder with her.

The principal greeted her with a wide smile. "Ms. Galang! You're here pretty late!" He always said this when she stopped by his office after school hours.

"I'm always here until this time. Sometimes even later." That was another thing that bothered her: How could he not notice which teachers stayed late? If she were running a school, she'd keep an eye on the staff parking lot, noting the order in which teachers went home. "Actually, I just finished my data binder, even though we didn't receive the goal-setting sheet until this morning, and I thought you might want to see . . ." She opened the binder, its sheet protectors glowing like treasure under the office lights.

"That looks great, Ms. Galang!" Dr. Barrios's hand inched toward his desk phone. "Listen, I have a call scheduled right now, but Mr. Scamphers handles most of the evaluation stuff. I'm sure he can help you."

"I don't need help," clarified Maybelline. "It's finished already."

"Okay, great. Take it over to Scamphers. He's a genius at this stuff!"

Dr. Barrios put the receiver to his ear, squinting at a paper on his desk as if it required careful attention.

Maybelline's frustration grew. She didn't need Mr. Scamphers to be *a genius at this stuff.* She had finished *early.*

Even as she thought this, however, she fulfilled the request.

Mr. Scamphers looked up at her from his desk, his moustache hiding too much of his mouth to reveal a readable facial expression.

"I just stopped by because I finished my data binder and . . ." She trailed off, unsure what to say. Mr. Scamphers had always seemed so dismissive.

"Great! You're the first one." His tone was more enthusiastic than she'd expected.

"Actually, I had most of this done a week ago, but—"

Scamphers lowered his voice. "But our *principal* didn't send out the last form until this morning, right?"

Something in Maybelline's heart clicked into alignment. "Exactly."

Mr. Scamphers gestured toward the wall separating the two offices, his voice still low. "I reminded him. I told him, *The DTSGSF is to be completed and submitted no more than thirty days into the school year.* But what can I say? The main office here doesn't exactly do things the way I would."

"Well, some of the teachers around here don't do things the way I would." She stepped into the office and placed the binder on his desk. She felt brave, all of a sudden. "Then again, it must be hard to make a good data binder if you haven't looked at the data."

"Interesting." Mr. Scamphers's thick moustache lifted on one side in what was now almost definitely a smile. "*Someone* in the administration should look into that."

"Yes," said Maybelline, "I think someone in the administration should."

She gathered the binder in her arms and hurried back to her classroom on light feet, barely even noticing the flyers announcing the first football game of the season.

Moments like this called for proper documentation.

By the time she finished typing and left, it was later than she'd planned. She knew Allyson and Rosemary would be waiting, giving her that look they both got when she explained how busy she was at work. The farther she drove, and the more she pictured the look, the more she thought maybe this wasn't the best day to bring up the clothes.

Allyson had stopped complaining about the outfits she was allowed to wear to school. But Maybelline also noticed, on many afternoons, a conspicuous lack of the smudges and pen marks and lunch stains that signaled a day in fifth grade. She suspected Allyson was changing into Gabriella's clothes.

And yet the timing always seemed wrong to bring up such a messy subject, especially on a day when she'd been *the first teacher in the whole school to finish organizing her data binder*. Better still, Mr. Scamphers had all but promised he would check everyone else's work.

The binder sat, radiant, on the passenger seat of Maybelline's car. It seemed almost to be smiling at her. *You*, it seemed to be saying, *have done everything right.* She didn't move it to the back seat until she pulled up in front of Rosemary's house, where Allyson slipped wordlessly into the car in her unwrinkled school clothes.

NATURAL SELECTION

THE LENA WHO climbed into Hernan's Jeep on Friday evening did not look like the Lena who taught down the hall from him at Brae Hill Valley High School. Her lips were the color of shiny pomegranate seeds. Her eyelids shimmered. She smelled like an island to which Hernan would gladly have bought a one-way ticket.

But all he said was, "Nice dress."

It wasn't even really a dress, but rather a continuous piece of fabric that wrapped around her, staying in place due to some undiscovered law of physics. Tiny seashells hung from the bottom, clicking against each other as she settled into the passenger seat. "Thanks. You look good, too."

Hernan wore jeans and a green polo shirt. He'd been to Club Seven once. It was tucked into one of the sketchier side streets near downtown, and if he remembered correctly, it didn't have much of a formal dress code. Now, with Lena sparkling at his side, he wondered if he should have dressed up more.

"So," said Lena, "I guess this is where we start talking about school and then keep talking about it for the whole night?"

"Yeah, well, that is the default setting."

But they didn't. Their conversation flowed as easily as the freeway's nighttime traffic, not even pausing until Hernan pulled onto the exit ramp.

"Wait," said Lena, as he turned down a side street to park, "you know where Club Seven is?"

"Yeah, my sister's college friends threw this Latin-music party there." Then, realizing this might make him sound like the type of twenty-nine-year-old who spent his time at college parties, he added, "It was a while ago. You?"

"Yeah. I'm kind of a regular on poetry night."

Hernan turned off the car and walked around to open Lena's door. They crossed the street together, close enough to renew his hope that this might be a date.

It soon became clear that Lena was more than a regular. The bouncer knew her by name and waved the two of them past the cashbox. They got drinks and found a table next to the stage, where a woman in tiny shorts was reading into the microphone from behind a paper.

"I'm ready to find a man who respects me for me," she said, shifting nervously from one exposed leg to the other, "who sees *all* I can be/ If you can see me as more than just the skin I'm in/ I can see past your past sins/ and at last we'll build something that's build for last-*in'*." Then she hurried off the stage as the crowd clapped politely.

The emcee reappeared, his skinny build and giant Afro giving him the appearance of a walking microphone. "One more time for our new poet. She a poetic virgin, y'all. Show her some love!"

The applause blended into an old school hip-hop song that reminded Hernan of his college days in Austin. By the time he turned to share this with Lena, however, the emcee with the microphone hair had appeared at their table.

"This is Deejay Jay Jay," said Lena, rising from her chair to hug him, "from Radio Four-Twenty."

The deejay handed Lena a clipboard, then turned to greet Hernan. "You a poet, too, or just here to watch your girl perform?"

"Just watching."

"Well . . . enjoy." Deejay Jay Jay waited for Lena to hand back the clipboard, then vanished into the backstage darkness.

"I usually try to do a poem when I come here," Lena explained. Her eyes perused the room as if she were expecting someone.

Hernan, too, surveyed the club. Except for a dim glow near the bar, most of the illumination came from the spotlights focused on the stage, red on one side, blue on the other. The colors highlighted the contours of poets' faces as they performed. There was a poem about smoking weed that got a lot of applause, poems by women in various stages of heartbreak, a lone white guy doing a poem about being the lone white guy doing a poem. Also, Hernan had been right about the dress code: Most of the guys in the club were wearing jeans. The women were dressed up, though, and Hernan watched two skinny women wobble toward the bar, tugging at their dresses. Nearby, a group of bigger women talked and laughed loudly at a table, as if to say, *This club was built around us.*

And then there was Lena, who projected a mix of assurance and insecurity that made her hard to categorize.

The music paused, and Deejay Jay Jay came back onstage. "One more time for our favorite white guy! Okay, okay—our only white guy."

"I think I'm up next," Lena whispered. "Wish me luck!"

"Next up, we have the teacher y'all *wish* you had when you were in high school, here to drop some inspiration. Let's give it up for Miiisss Leenaaa Wriiight!"

"Good luck," called Hernan as Lena hurried into the darkness.

A moment later, she stepped out onto the side of the stage, beaming at the cheers of the crowd.

"Okay, y'all. This poem is called 'What You Really Need to Know.'"

"Yeah!" came a yell from the back of the room.

"Lesson one: Never hide." The blue spotlight caught the angle of her cheekbones.

"Lesson two: Show your pride." The red light highlighted her eyelids and full, shiny lips. "Because *your* fate is *not* for the world to decide."

From the stage, she exuded a confidence Hernan had never noticed in person. She slowed, sometimes, to let certain lines sink in, then suddenly sped up, rhyming within rhymes in a display of verbal acrobatics that would have left most speakers breathless.

"You say/ you want extra credit/ well, I don't give that/ you go *get* it." The crowd fell under Lena's spell, listening, watching, listening-and-watching, listeningandwatching until the senses became inseparable, and Hernan felt himself pulled along with them. He was one of those rare scientists who knew magic when he saw it.

Then, at the end of a fast-paced drum roll of a stanza, Lena stopped, looked around the room, and raised one eyebrow dramatically. "And that's—" She held the microphone out to the audience.

"What you really *need to know!*" The crowd finished the poem for her.

"Thank you," Lena whispered. Then she left the stage to a roar.

A moment later, she emerged from the stairwell, accepting compliments with the smile of a celebrity as she made her way back to Hernan.

"One more time for Miss Wright!" said Deejay Jay Jay. "I bet there are a lot of guys out there hoping to be Miss Wright's Mr. Right, if you know what I mean."

Hernan knew.

Lena slid back into her chair and let out a breath, giving him a conspiratorial look.

"Nice job," said Hernan.

"Thanks," she mouthed.

The speaker near their table drowned out any further chance at conversation.

"Next up, we got a man who's been missing from the scene for a minute. He's been letting the whole country know how we do it down here, but now he's back to show he ain't forgot about us. I guess you could say he's here to take us to the . . . Nex . . . Level!"

The room burst with the biggest applause of the night as a tall man with dreadlocks stepped between the red and blue lights. He withdrew the microphone, then raised the stand with one hand and slowly placed it behind him, flexing his muscles—it seemed to Hernan—a bit more than necessary.

"Tonight"—Nex Level smiled—"I got something for the ladies."

The cheering sounded noticeably more female now. The guys in the audience were busy arranging themselves into confident, heterosexual poses.

"Or maybe I should say"—the poet licked his lips—"my queens."

Hernan crossed his arms and leaned back in his chair.

"I gotta be careful with the words I choose, 'cause the words we use/ contain the power of suggestion. That's why when I rhyme/ I say it's high time we question . . ."

This was no longer the intro to the poem, Hernan realized. It was the poem itself. Nex Level's language had picked up speed and lifted into the air without warning. It seemed dishonest somehow.

"The mechanism by which/ we learn to call a woman a bitch/ when what we mean is"—Nex Level paused, then slowed his cadence—"fellow soldier."

From somewhere in the dark, a woman's voice called, "Rewiiiinnn-nddd!"

Nex repeated the lines. "I said it's high time we question/ the mechanism by which/ we learn to call a woman a bitch/ when what we mean is . . . *fellow soldier*."

Hernan, apparently, had missed the *mechanism by which* this lesson was learned. He did not call women bitches.

"Strong sistas holdin' the whole world on their shoulders/ hustlin' home from two jobs/ to throw down in the kitchen/ overcoming overwhelming odds under unfit conditions . . ."

Shouts and claps and finger snaps crackled behind Hernan's head as he watched the stage. He didn't really follow the poetry scene, but he'd still heard of Nex Level. Over the summer, a video of the poet's performance from a rally against police brutality had dominated Facebook for days. Even Hernan's sister Lety was a fan. What he noticed now, watching from up close, was the way Nex Level locked eyes with various women in the audience who were "through with hopin' and wishin'/ sick of single-handedly handling life's mission . . ."

The poem seemed to be nearing its end. Hernan snuck a look at Lena.

"Understandably/ asking for a man who understands you."

Lena's eyes were fixed on the stage.

"Ladies, I know life got you stressed/ but true beauty manifests . . . in how you *handle* what life hands you." It was on this last line, which set off a chorus of shrieks and applause, that Nex Level aimed his gaze directly at Lena. Then he smiled.

From the corner of his eye, Hernan saw Lena smiling back.

Moments later, Nex Level descended from the stairs behind the stage, his eyes reconnecting with Lena's as he emerged from the darkness. He offered an innocent grin, shrugging as if to say he didn't know what the fuss was all about. Hernan waited for him to pass, but he lingered near their table as the applause died down.

"Nice poem," said Lena.

"You, too. So you're a teacher, huh?"

"Yeah." Lena giggled. "This is my friend Hernan. He works with me."

Hernan's hopes for the night plummeted. One didn't need to know much about human courtship rituals to know *friend* was code for *ruled out as a potential mate.*

"Oh, yeah? Where y'all teach at?" The question was directed at both of them but clearly meant for Lena.

"Brae Hill Valley High School," she answered.

"No shit. You work at the Hill? Them roughnecks don't give you a hard time?"

"Nah, I'm from Philly. We got worse schools up there." She didn't seem to mind that she did not sound like an English teacher.

"Well, I wish I had a teacher like you when I was in school."

Hernan hoped Lena recognized Nex's lame-ass pickup line for what it was.

But she gave no sign of this. "I saw you at that rally over the summer. Love your stuff."

"You mean you never saw me rhyme before? Don't tell me this is the only poetry spot you go to."

Lena nodded.

"Well, we gotta get you to another club one of these days—all that talent you got. How about I give you my number?"

"Nah," said Lena, though her voice held a flirtatious modesty. "I don't take men's numbers."

Hernan's heart soared. She'd asked for *his* number at the back-to-school meeting.

"If you want to talk to me, you'll call me."

Hernan's heart sank. She'd asked for *his* number at the back-to-school meeting.

"Oh, I see. So you the old-fashioned type. Well, Missss Lena"—Nex swept out an arm and bowed in an exaggerated display of gallantry—"any chance I could get *your* number?"

Hernan rose from the table. "I'm gonna get another drink."

"Hey, I got a hookup on drinks here," offered Nex Level. "When you go up there, just tell them you with me."

"That's okay," said Hernan. "I'm good." Seven dollars was a more-than-reasonable price for an excuse to leave the table. The plastic cup of Jose Cuervo was a bonus. Hernan squeezed the wilted sliver of lime into the tequila, then tossed it into the trash along with the straw. He sipped slowly, keeping his eyes on the stage, until he glanced over and saw Lena sitting alone again.

"Sorry about that," she said as he slid back into his seat. "I've been wanting to see if he would come do some poetry for the kids."

"Okay. Well . . ." The statement didn't seem to call for an actual response so much as a beat of response-like noise.

"Most of his poetry isn't like that," she added.

Hernan looked at his watch to avoid looking at Lena. She didn't really owe him anything, he reasoned. She'd been planning to come here anyway. And she'd invited everyone at happy hour. It was he who had jumped at the possibility, and then later offered to pick her up. He was the idiot who thought they might be on a date. At least he hadn't done anything to give himself away.

"You look like you're ready to go," said Lena.

"Yeah. It's getting late."

They cheerfully avoided the subject of Nex Level the whole way home.

"So, you think we won our first game?" asked Hernan.

"Oh, wow," said Lena, "that was tonight, wasn't it? To be honest, I don't really pay that much attention to football."

"Uh-oh. Don't tell the rest of Texas."

Lena drew out her laughter as far as it would stretch. Then she asked, "Did you have fun?"

"Yeah. Good club." He tried to sound like he meant it. "You're very talented."

He turned up the radio to drown out the silence that followed.

CHARACTERIZATION

"**THINK BACK TO** the first day of school, when you met your teachers. How did you figure out what kind of teachers they were going to be?"

"Their attitude."

"Okay," said Lena, "their attitude. But how did you know what kind of attitude they were going to have? What did they do?"

"Like, if they yell at you the first day and say you can't come in the class without a notebook. Like how Ms. Grady—"

"Okay, Rico, but we're not mentioning names."

"Sorry, Miss. If *a teacher* yells at you the first day and says you can't be in class without a notebook and asks if you thought you were coming to the circus."

A few other students laughed.

"So, one of the ways you can figure out what type of person you're dealing with is by paying attention to what they say." Lena wrote on the marker board as she spoke.

Five Methods of Characterization

1. Character's words.

"Yes," agreed Rico. "That's exactly what I meant."

Rico Jones, a short, expressive kid with a tattoo on the side of his neck, was the student Lena had first thought of when the topic of neck tattoos came up at happy hour. He seemed capable of original observations on any subject. During class discussions, he sparkled. Reading, however, was a different story. When called upon to read aloud, Rico was like a car with a weak battery, starting and stopping, losing momentum with each try, finally resigning himself to bump slowly along the page in a clatter of mispronounced words. Lena knew if she didn't point out his errors, he'd never learn to fix them. Yet the thought of correcting teenagers' reading in public filled her with humiliation on their behalf. In her hesitance, she often let errors slide.

"What else do authors do to help you get to know a character?"

Rico raised his hand again.

"Someone I haven't heard from yet." Lena looked around the room. "Their actions?"

"Good. Their actions. Good." Lena wrote, *2. Character's actions.*

The clock was ticking toward the bell. She hoped her students would come up with the remaining items on the list without too much prodding. The Curriculum Standard of the Day, posted online even later than usual today, had caught Lena in the middle of an entirely unrelated lesson. Now, she was trying to cover the required material as an add-on during the last fifteen minutes of class.

"How about in the first few seconds? What forms your very first impression?"

"Their attitude?"

Before Lena could point out that someone had said that already, another voice chimed in. "Their clothes?"

"Good." Lena wrote, *3. Physical description.* "And not just their clothes, but the way they look, the expressions on their faces. Anything physical that the author thinks is important enough to describe." She knew she was filling in information students hadn't actually supplied, but she didn't have time to do the whole *guide-on-the-side-not-sage-on-the-stage* thing that professional development trainers were always talking about.

"Raise your hand if you've ever known about a teacher before you even stepped into a classroom."

A few hands went up.

"Okay. So number four is: *What other characters say about the character.*

And there's one more thing—something the author might know, but no one else does."

Near the back of the room, someone unzipped a backpack.

Quickly, Lena wrote, *5. Character's thoughts.*

"Okay. Just copy this list into your notes. And at the end, write this." She talked loudly as she scrawled on the board in giant letters. "*A plot is the development of character over time.* Then you can pack up, and we'll talk about this again during our fiction unit. Just remember: No character? No story. Perfect character? No story. Character who never changes? No story."

The bell rang. Students folded the day's work sheets and shoved them into their pockets. One girl removed her sweatshirt, the better to display her cleavage and non-uniform shirt in the hallway. Another left the classroom and began making out with her boyfriend almost immediately. On a normal day, any of these actions would have annoyed Lena, but today nothing could put her in a bad mood.

She had a date tonight.

There was something about Nex Level's features that made Lena never want to look away: the intensity of his eyes as they focused on the road, the hint of a scar above his eyebrow. It made him look unafraid, as if, in some other life, he might have been an African warrior. Lena wondered if everyone noticed this about him, or if it was something only she saw.

"Whatchu looking at, boo?"

"Nothing." She hoped the lightness in her voice kept him from thinking she'd been staring. "Just trying to figure out where you're taking me."

He stopped at a red light and turned to look at her fully. "I was gonna bring you by this poetry spot I go to on Wednesdays. Let you show off your talent a little bit."

"Sounds good." The words felt overly eager coming out, as if they held traces of how many times she'd rehearsed her newest poem, hoping for exactly this.

"Only problem is, this place ain't downtown, like Club Seven—

actually, it's kinda hood. I don't want to take you anywhere you feel uncomfortable."

"Don't worry about me. I work at the Hill, remember?" She dropped the nickname Nex Level had used for Brae Hill Valley when they'd met, hoping to spark his memory.

"Oh, right. Yeah, you'll be aright."

They were on the freeway now. Slow, thumping music pulsed through the speakers. Lena tried to think of something that might be worth talking about over the music but instead settled on looking out the window until Nex pulled off at an exit she'd never taken before. It was a ramp she'd always assumed led to an industrial road, and there were, indeed, darkened factories visible in every direction. Yet up close, she could see there were also houses. They were in a neighborhood—one so economically and physically ravaged that she tried to conceal her alarm.

Never had she imagined the city held such a place.

The poor neighborhoods in Philly were cramped blocks of row houses that pulsed with life. Young men swaggered on corners, and in summer, families drank together on front steps while bedtimeless children swirled around their feet. The area where she worked and lived also held the marks of a bad neighborhood, with its check-cashing stores, curbside car repairs, and stray dogs.

But the streets rolling past Lena's window now were so desolate they might have been backcountry roads. Empty, litter-strewn lots stretched into the distance, dotted with only a few sagging houses and boarded-up remnants of stores. On one dark sidewalk, a woman wearing a shower cap pushed a stroller, turning occasionally to yell at a toddler who trailed behind her. On another, a pair of teenage boys walked slowly, as if there was no destination they could ever imagine being in a hurry to reach. Lena averted her gaze as they looked in the direction of the car. Nothing stirred but the sounds from cars headed the other way, the rumble of their music merging briefly with the beats inside Nex's car as if by the hand of some cosmic deejay.

"Don't worry." Nex's voice pushed its way between her thoughts. "We're not getting out here."

"Me? I'm not worried." Lena realized her hand was resting near the door's lock button. She moved the hand, now unsure where to put it, settling it finally on her knee. "I was just thinking this poetry spot must not be too crowded."

Nex released a deep laugh that dissolved her hesitations.

She wanted to make him laugh again.

They turned onto what seemed like the main street in the area, finally arriving at a strip mall whose parking lot, considering the emptiness that surrounded it, was remarkably packed. Most of the stores were closed at this hour, but a hive of activity surrounded an open door in the corner. The line to get in stretched past the darkened windows of the other businesses. Cars idled in the lot, waiting for spots to open.

"Okay," joked Lena, "I take back what I said about it not being too crowded."

Nex laughed again. His eyes shined.

Lena wondered what he might have looked like as a child.

There was only one remaining spot at the end of the lot, blocked off by two orange traffic cones. Nex jumped out to move the cones, then pulled into the spot.

"You sure you can park here?"

"*Reserved* parking." He winked at her as he turned off the motor. "My friends own this poetry spot. I told them I can't be waiting around trying to park a car—not when there's this girl I'm trying to impress."

Lena knew game when she heard it. Hell, she had game herself. Yet in spite of this, she pictured Nex telling his friends who owned the club, *There's this girl.* She let herself out of the car and followed him to the open door. A fat bouncer leaned on a stool in front of it. He locked hands with Nex, their grips drawing each other closer until their chests crashed and receded.

It was only then that the bouncer looked at Lena, standing a few feet behind Nex. "Ten thirty. Ten dollars for everyone." Gold glinted from his bottom teeth.

"Nah, this our new poet right here. She a teacher."

The bouncer's eyes assessed her with approval, then turned friendly. "A teacher, huh? Wish they had teachers like you when I was in school."

"Heh." She was never quite sure how to answer that remark.

"Where you teach at?"

Lena waited for Nex to jump in and say *the Hill*. Finally, she answered, "Brae Hill Valley High School."

"Oh, shit. That's where I went."

The statement warmed her like an embrace. "Yeah?"

"I heard y'all won your first game last week against Booker T."

"Yeah . . . We won!" Lena vaguely remembered students talking about the victory but hoped she wouldn't have to offer any details in front of Nex Level. She was relieved to feel him moving toward the door.

"So, whatchu teach?"

But Lena pretended not to hear. Answering the question felt less important than making an entrance at Nex's side.

"Oh, it's like that, huh?" The bouncer's voice followed her as she stepped into the dark club.

It was true. This wasn't like Club Seven.

It wasn't a club at all, really, but rather an empty storefront space lit by strings of seasonless Christmas lights. The inside was larger than Lena would have guessed, and she found herself following Nex as he slipped through the mass of packed bodies. Everyone was black, she noted—there were no token white poets here. And most were women, many of whom seemed eager to greet Nex Level as he made his way toward the "bar"—really just a folding table in a back corner where someone was mixing drinks from a cooler. Lena reached for Nex as she tried to keep up. He gave her hand a quick squeeze and then let it fall.

When they reached the folding table, she pressed in next to him, standing on her toes to whisper her drink order in his ear. None of the women in the crowd looked at her directly, but she felt the beams of their envy pointing her way, and she gripped her cup in one hand as they pushed their way toward the stage, reaching for his fingers with the other.

Again, he squeezed her hand and then released it.

"You're not a big hand holder, huh?" she asked, when they'd finally found a spot with a good view. She hoped she sounded casual.

"Yeah. Not into that public affection stuff. Sorry."

"No, it's cool. I'm really not, either."

"See? Now, that's what I like about you—I can take you anywhere." He put a hand on her lower back and let it rest there.

The poets onstage became a blur. She was conscious of nothing but his warmth and her own cautious pressure as she leaned into him without turning in his direction.

He could take her anywhere.

It wasn't until they were back in Nex's car that Lena, exhilarated by the night and high from her success onstage, worked up the nerve to ask the question. "Hey, I was hoping you could come to my class one of these days—do some poetry for the kids."

"Come on, now. I bet they get plenty of inspiration from you."

"Definitely. I just think they would really like some of your police-violence stuff. Like the one you did . . . at . . . the . . ." And then she stopped, because she knew then that he would lean in and kiss her. It was inevitable at this point. She had smoothed scented oil onto her wrists and neck and collarbone, and she was giving him a look that had never failed her. It was a look that suggested some shared secret. It had worked on every man she had ever drawn in to her.

Now, sitting in Nex Level's car, several drinks in each of their systems, his smooth, dark face leaning toward hers, it felt if all her years of writing poetry, all the time spent perfecting this very look, had come to this moment.

She knew better than to think this would lead to love. She wasn't even sure she believed in love. But he'd said he could take her anywhere. And Nex's version of *anywhere* was exactly where she wanted to go.

The kiss was long, soft, and surprisingly gentle. As they parted, she noticed for the first time the tattoo on Nex Level's neck. It peeked out above the top of his shirt like a shared secret.

Knowledge, it said.

Suddenly, there was nothing she would not have done to get him to come to her classroom—and nothing she would not have done to hide how badly she wanted him to come.

"So . . . ?" She hoped she wouldn't have to elaborate.

He looked into her eyes and smiled. "So . . . what do I get out of the deal? You gonna cook me dinner or something?"

THE
RESEARCH-BASED BEST
PRACTICES THAT WORK™
ACHIEVEMENT INITIATIVE

DAREN GRANT, OF TransformationalChangeAdvocacy-ConsultingPartners, was still talking. "But then I realized that to really scale up and make that macro impact for low-income students, I'd have to step out of the classroom and apply the leadership skills I'd learned as a teacher."

Dr. Barrios nodded, his gaze drifting to the hiker's backpack that sat next to the consultant's chair. A metal water bottle dangled from the side, as if Daren planned to hike somewhere in his suit directly after this meeting. It was strange to see an African American kid—or young man, as the case might be—carrying hiking gear. Dr. Barrios had always associated hiking with white people. This was probably wrong of him.

To be fair, he was trying to like Daren Grant. This had taken less effort earlier in the meeting, when the younger man described how his high school teachers, due their stereotypes and low expectations, had only encouraged him to apply to state colleges.

He'd seemed so earnest that Dr. Barrios almost chimed in with his own related stories. Counselors had often tracked him into automotive arts classes despite his high grades. He'd even spent a year in a class for non-English speakers during elementary school, though it was his Spanish that was barely passable. Both of his parents had been born in Brownsville, Texas.

But it had quickly become clear that Daren Grant's story was not an invitation to share. Rather, it was the personal-hardship segment of a tightly engineered narrative that continued with Daren Grant's acceptance into (and graduation with accolades from) Cornell, which, sure, it wasn't Harvard, but it was solid Ivy League, right up there with Princeton or Yale—even better than those schools by some measurements, according to Daren Grant.

They were now in the Daren-Grant's-résumé segment of the narrative, which included two years of "leading from the classroom" before moving to TransformationalChangeAdvocacyConsultingPartners. TransformationalChangers, as Dr. Barrios thought of them, always seemed to have taught for exactly two years. Then they moved on to work at places whose names were capitalized words stuck together. They seemed both impossibly young and impossibly self-assured, their Adam's apples bouncing excitedly above their shirt collars as they talked.

"We have abundant data on best practices that work in the startup sector"—bounce—"and in transformational schools like the Destiny charter network"—bounce— "which we're using to innovate and catalyze disruptive change."

"Absolutely." *Disruptive change*, wrote Dr. Barrios on a notepad. *Abundant data.* He had spent enough time around consultants to know it helped to respond with the same terminology they used. It reassured them that, in the jungle of jargon-filled edu-calls, he was a member of a symbiotic species.

"We like to start with the question, *What could be true if . . . ?*"— bounce—"Then we use that thought experiment to craft a vision for the school."

What could be true if . . . ? wrote Dr. Barrios.

"For example, one of the concepts we're working on is, What could be true if younger teacher-leaders could have the respect and authority that comes with seniority, but without having to work at a school for a long time?"

Dr. Barrios checked the time on his computer screen. It wasn't as late as it felt, but it wasn't early. Morning e-mails were already stacking in his inbox.

"Our research has shown that the best teacher-leaders are followers of the best practices we've isolated in our program."

Best leaders are followers, wrote Dr. Barrios. Something seemed off about the statement, but he didn't want to say anything that might prompt an explanation, especially not now: Daren Grant was reaching into his backpack to retrieve a glossy folder. If handled correctly, the handing over of promotional materials signaled the end of a consultant meeting.

Grant slid the folder across the desk: *Research-Based Best Practices That Work*™. Underneath the words, a diverse group of young leader-followers stood in various inspiring poses.

Dr. Barrios leafed through the papers inside. Then he reviewed his notes, trying to string together the arrangement of words most likely to make Daren Grant go away.

"Thank you so much, Mr. Grant." He smiled. "It's great to hear you're taking such a research-based, macro approach toward transformational, disruptive change. And, naturally, we love innovations based on abundant data."

Daren Grant made no move to get up.

"I look forward to sharing these best practices with our teacher-leaders."

Still no motion.

"I'll certainly get in touch as needed." Dr. Barrios offered a conciliatory gesture as he reached for the receiver of his desk phone. "Thanks for stopping by."

A subtle amusement crept into the younger man's expression, as if it were this moment, rather than the promotional folder, that the meeting had been building toward. "Maybe I didn't make this clear, Dr. Barrios. Superintendent Wallabee has already brought us on board to partner with the Believers Zone."

"Ah." Dr. Barrios recalibrated. "Well, welcome aboard!"

"He directed us to start with your school."

"Oh." The cabin pressure had changed. Dr. Barrios, waiting for a cue, dropped his eyes to the folder. Now it seemed as if the young leader-followers were staring at him, all with the same smug expression as Daren Grant.

"I'll be visiting classes starting tomorrow, so if you can just make sure all teachers have the Research-Based Best Practice That Works of the day written on their boards, that would be awesome."

Dr. Barrios missed the education consulting companies of the past. They sold textbooks and gave benign presentations, but they had little interest in walking around an enormous high school building and visiting actual classrooms. Not so with the ChangeAdvocates: They'd show up the next day, iPads and refillable water bottles in hand. Barrios looked again at the backpack, which now seemed to symbolize the inexhaustible energy and freedom of youth. Daren Grant would never have to publicly say he wanted to spend more time with his family. Daren Grant didn't have a family. He probably didn't even have a girlfriend.

"Good morning, Killer Armadillos." Mrs. Rawlins's voice came on the PA. "Teachers, please remember to write the Curriculum Standard of the Day on your board in its entirety."

Dr. Barrios gestured toward the speaker. "Should the teachers still write the Curriculum Standard of the Day, or . . .?"

"Absolutely." Grant unscrewed the metal water bottle, leaving its top dangling from the backpack, and leaned back for a long, Adam's-apple-activating sip. Apparently, AdvocatingForTransformationalChange required one to stay hydrated. "Our program is in addition to any existing initiatives. But this is the priority, so let's make sure they write this one on top."

"I just mention it because some of the classrooms have limited board space."

"Well, an innovative problem-solving approach to that might be to have them write in smaller letters!"

Dr. Barrios replayed the words in his head, searching for a hint of sarcasm, but Daren Grant seemed almost robotically earnest.

"Remember, we're your partners in this." Grant twisted the bottle back into its cap. He spoke in the tone of someone who had won and could now afford to be gracious. "Just think of me as the angel on your shoulder—but with research-based best practices that work!"

ALL STUDENTS ON TASK, ALL THE TIME™

"**IF YOU WERE** trying to create a sustainable environment in a lunar colony, what would you need?"

Kids called out answers. Hernan repeated them as he filled up the board.

"Water."

"Water."

"Shelter."

"Shelter."

"Food."

"Food."

"McDonald's."

"That's food."

And so it went: *Heat. Electricity. PlayStation. iPhone. Come on, let's be serious. Soap. Shampoo. Oxygen.*

"Definitely oxygen," confirmed Hernan. "And, just a hint—plants provide oxygen, so if you calculate how much oxygen you need and get enough plants in there to produce it, you won't have to worry about pumping in air."

"Is that why you have so many plants in here—so we don't run out of oxygen?"

Laughter.

The kid did have a point, though: Hernan had filled every available space in the lab with plants from the various terrestrial biomes of

Texas. The hobby reconciled him to the long days spent indoors. The plants, who didn't realize they should have been in prairies, or marshes, or sand plains, did what they could to survive. Some hoarded sunlight, flattening their giant leaves against the windows and blocking the security grates from view. Others learned to survive on tiny scraps of sun, thriving despite the odds against them. Some died. Hernan planted new seeds in the soil they left behind.

He finished giving the directions for the lunar colony activity and the class began working. They were just settling into a state of homeostasis when an unknown student entered. It was never a promising sign when a new student entered on a Wednesday in mid-October. Less promising still, he did not address Hernan but instead headed toward a seat at the far end of the room.

Hernan positioned himself in the student's path. "Good morning."

The newcomer repeated the greeting with weary irritation, as if he were the teacher and Hernan had walked into *his* classroom unannounced.

"You're a new student?"

"Mmm-hmm."

"And your name?"

"Angel."

"Great. Sit in that chair next to my desk, and I'll be right with you."

Hernan stopped to check on a few other students before returning to his desk to review the transfer papers, which confirmed his original hypothesis: Angel had been sent by Destiny.

Destiny was short for Demographics Don't Determine Destiny, a nearby charter school and the source of much grumbling among Brae Hill Valley faculty. The most common gripe was that Destiny dumped its worst students into Brae Hill Valley to improve its own test scores, though this wasn't an entirely fair complaint. After all, district schools also unloaded such students when they could. This was possible because students often lied about their addresses when enrolling for school, a practice that was not allowed but that schools overlooked in the case of high achievers or top athletes. It was when students started fights or failed classes that schools started investigating. Happy was the administrator who discovered that a troublemaker's "home address" actually belonged to a cousin, or a family friend, or the Irazu Dollar Discount & Pet Store. This allowed the school to gleefully disenroll problematic kids, shoveling them off to their actual neighborhood schools in time for testing season. Brae Hill Valley received its share of these midyear transfers. It also used this same game of hot potato to hand off students to other district schools. All of which was to say the animosity toward Destiny wasn't really about the transfer students.

It was about the admissions process.

To attend the Demographics Don't Determine Destiny charter network, families had to sign a strict discipline agreement: Students would dress in uniform every day. They would redo unsatisfactory homework. They would angle their bodies in the prescribed eager-to-learn posture in their seats, visually tracking teachers' movements like seagulls eyeing a sandwich. These requirements alone deterred the authority challenging, the energy draining, the test-score-lowering, and the special-education-requiring.

But there was more. In a move that was either ingenious or infuriating, depending on where one stood, families had to sign these agreements—and complete the rest of the complicated admissions process—*before* the first day of school. This meant that while Destiny could "counsel out" problematic students at any time, district schools could never, under any circumstances, send midyear transfers to Destiny. Hernan tried not to let such baggage influence his reaction to new students, however. They all deserved a fresh start.

He pointed Angel toward what he hoped would be a welcoming lab group.

As he walked toward his newly assigned seat, Angel retrieved a handful of orange chips from a bag he was holding and shoveled them into his mouth.

"Angel," said Hernan, "I don't allow food in this class. Please put those away."

Angel shoved the bag in his pocket at an unconvincing angle. Within minutes of arriving at his lab table, he'd taken it back out and placed it on the chair next to him, fully displaying the name of the product and its dubious health claims. Due to concerns about childhood obesity, the school was no longer allowed to stock regular Reetos products in the vending machines. They were, however, allowed to sell (BAKED!) Reetos, which contained all the same chemicals at nine fewer calories per bag.

Hernan made another round of the classroom, silently picking up the bag of chips as he passed Angel.

Angel looked up. "Hey, man, those are mine."

"No eating in my classroom."

"I wasn't even eating them. I just had nowhere else to put them."

"You're holding two in your hand right now."

Angel sulked in silence for a while. Then he looked up, his expression taking on a puppy-dog quality. "Can I please get them back if I participate?"

"If you want to, you can come get them at the end of the day. It will give us a chance to talk."

Angel drew in a deep breath and let it out slowly, as if to show this was the very limit of patience that could be expected of him. It was unlikely that he would come back for the chips. Nothing dissuaded teenagers like a mandatory heart-to-heart conversation with a concerned adult.

Hernan was about to check on the next lab group when the classroom door opened again, revealing another visitor, this one slightly too old to be a new student. He wore a suit and carried a backpack, and he informed Hernan that he was observing classes at the school.

"Student teacher?" Hernan guessed.

"Oh, no, ha-ha. I'm from TransformationalChangeAdvocacyConsultingPartners. We're just making sure everyone's following today's Research-Based Best Practice That Works."

Hernan was glad he'd remembered to write the newest thing-to-write-on-the-board of the day. In its entirety.

The visitor walked to the back corner of the room and took a seat behind Angel, who Hernan hoped would hold it together as the class finished the activity. He restrained himself from looking nervously toward the corner. But there was no sign of a commotion, and when the bell rang, both newcomers slipped out along with the rest of the class.

Alone in the room, Hernan turned to his plants. He'd planted this year's hopeful crop of bluebonnets less than a month ago. Their sprouts were just beginning to inch upward, leaves spreading to gather sun-light. Not that this was a guarantee of anything: Bluebonnets were the state flower and could be found in front of every hotel and government building in Texas, but they were really only adapted to the sandy soil in the eastern part of the state. To grow anywhere else, they required well-timed watering and optimal seed-soil contact. Even then, some of the seeds took years to germinate. Some never sprouted at all. But that didn't mean they weren't worth planting.

As Hernan bent to water the base of the closest plant, something caught his eye. It had an irregular shape and was a fluorescent orange color Hernan was pretty sure didn't exist in nature. He bent closer, tilting the pot for further inspection, until finally he identified the substance: a wet glob of partially chewed (BAKED!) Reetos.

COMPLETE ANSWERS USE
COMPLETE SENTENCES™

THE PARENT CONTACT number in Yesenia's records did not work. Or, more accurately, it *did* work but led to Yesenia's own cell-phone voice mail, which was a full minute of Yesenia's voice saying, "Hello? Hello? I can't hear you. Talk louder!" followed by laughter, followed by Yesenia's voice saying, "Nah, I'm just fucking with y'all. Leave a message."

This left no one with whom Kaytee could discuss the tremendous potential that might be unleashed if Yesenia ever returned to class. What Kaytee never discussed, even with herself, was that she sometimes felt relieved when the morning bell rang and Yesenia's seat remained empty. She'd caught herself thinking that Yesenia, when she did show up, used much of her potential to make Jonathan Rodriguez yell.

Not that Jonathan needed much provoking: Even without Yesenia around, he communicated in animated student sign language with anyone who would participate, then started whispering, then sometimes forgot he was whispering and burst into full-volume conversation. But above all, he interrupted. Off-topic commentary flew out of him like sparks from a live wire. Kaytee's reprimands led to arguments, which took up even more class time. She had tried everything she could think of but still spent each day bracing for the inevitable moment when Jonathan would break whatever hold she'd gained on the class's attention.

This week, with some trepidation, she'd moved his seat to the front corner of the room, separated from the rest of the class by Brian

Bingle. She hoped it was a good decision. Brian, with his tattooed forearm and clenched jaw, had turned out not to be a behavior problem after all. On the contrary, he came in each day, directed his intimidating gaze at the board, turned in his completed work at the end of class, and pushed in his chair before leaving. The angry look from the beginning of the year had settled into seriousness, intensifying back to anger only when other students disrupted a lesson. Now, as Jonathan waved his arms to catch the eye of a kid in the middle of the room, something menacing flashed in Brian's expression.

"Okay!" Kaytee forced herself to sound cheerful. "Let's go back to discussing our bell-ringer activity. If you could make one change to improve this school, what would it be?"

Brian raised his hand. Kaytee was about to call on him when Milagros Almaguer, who was usually silent, said, "The food."

"Good job, Milagros! But remember: The Research-Based Best Practice of the Day is that you have to answer in a complete sentence, using language from the question."

Milagros looked dejected.

"That's just a reminder to everyone." Kaytee gave Milagros what she hoped was an apologetic look. The Best Practices of the Day were supposed to make students more ready for college, and Kaytee definitely wanted her students to be ready for college. Also, she'd heard a consultant was coming around to check on them. "So, for example, if I ask what change you could make to improve the school, your answer might start with, *One change I would make to improve this school would be . . .*"

Milagros stared down at her notebook.

"Do you want to try again, Milagros?"

Milagros shook her head.

"But the food *is* nasty here," interjected Jonathan. "I found a fingernail in my burger the other day."

Kaytee decided to ignore him. "Milagros, we'll come back to you, okay? Who else wants to share their answer? If you could make one change to make this school better, what would it be?"

"Actually, I think it might have been a whole finger."

There was some laughter at this, and Kaytee drew in her breath to respond, bracing for an argument.

But then Brian said, "Enough." He spoke softly, but there was a warning note in his voice.

Jonathan, without directly acknowledging Brian, settled quietly back into his seat. Kaytee felt herself relax.

Brian raised his hand.

"Yes, Brian?"

"One change that would make the school better would be to stop letting people skip in the cafeteria line."

Kaytee gave him her best *there-are-no-wrong-answers-in-here* smile, though she'd been hoping for an answer that was . . . bigger. She wanted students to address the systemic racism and low teacher expectations that were holding them back. Not the food. Not the lunch line.

"The thing is that no one stops people from skipping, so no one can get lunch unless they skip the line," said Brian. "And if nobody says anything about that, then how anybody supposed to respect the other rules?"

Other students nodded.

Kaytee tried again to conceal her disappointment. "That's an excellent start, Brian, and good job using complete sentences in your answer! But let's try to think of something that would really improve *educational equity*, and maybe even society as a whole, in a really fundamental—"

"I always cut in line," Jonathan said. "How I'm gonna get lunch otherwise?"

Kaytee was considering how to handle the interruption when Brian whipped his head around. "Shut the fuck up, Jonathan. Ain't nobody trying to hear your mouth all the time."

Katyee's intestines contracted. Brian had told Jonathan to be quiet earlier, but he hadn't cursed, hadn't sounded so angry or ready to fight. She knew now that she'd made the wrong decision. She should never have moved Jonathan next to Brian, and now it was too late. Whatever happened next would be her fault.

Outside the door, she could hear the rumble of adult voices. She recognized one of them as belonging to Mr. Scamphers, which meant the other voice was probably the consultant. They were coming into her classroom now, of all moments.

Kaytee held her breath.

The door opened.

She forced herself to smile as the consultant walked into the room, holding an iPad. Mr. Scamphers followed him, clipboard in hand. They were both taking notes. She squeezed the marker in her hand, bracing for an explosion.

But there was no explosion.

Instead, something wonderful happened.

Jonathan Rodriguez shut up.

THE MYSTERY HISTORY TEACHER

www.teachcorps.blogs.com/mystery-history-teacher

FROM THE CLASSROOM TO THE WORLD

Today, we worked our way toward a meaningful discussion about what students would do to improve their school. (During an observation, no less!) At first, they focused on surface-level details, like the food and the lunch line, but eventually I was able to guide them to think about more big-picture solutions, like having a truly representative student council or a way for students to share feedback about their teachers. I've always believed my students can grow up to change the world. It's good to see that, finally, they are starting to believe this about themselves.

COMMENTS

DanceGurl11 I just wanted to say you're blog is very inspirational. It reminds me of my favorite movie, *Show Me You Care and I'll Show You My Homework*. More teachers should be like you, instead of giving up on there students. Maybe you should write a book or a movie about you're experience so you can inspire more teachers to be great like you!!

NumberOneTeacher I, like you, am one of the few outstanding educators who believe all children can succeed. I recently sat down with a child in my class who reads below grade level and said, "You are so smart! Why are you reading below grade level?" He told me I was the first teacher who ever told him he was smart! Can you imagine? There truly should be more teachers like us in this world.

44 MORE COMMENTS ON THIS POST

Even before she'd installed the spam-blocking program, Kaytee had never gotten more than ten comments on her blog before. But now, as she finished writing about the day's events from her couch, she looked at her previous post and found there were almost fifty.

Why? she wondered.

She typed the name of her blog into Google, shocked at how many references turned up. Apparently, the post she'd written after happy hour had caught the attention of the woman whose memoir about her four years of teaching had inspired the movie *Show Me You Care and I'll Show You My Homework*. Now an international motivational speaker, she had linked to Kaytee's post from her own blog, and the comments had been rolling in ever since. They made Kaytee feel as if she were floating. The movie had been one of her biggest inspirations to join TeachCorps. Only later had she noticed that the teacher in the movie had only one class.

But now, as she read the growing thread that compared her to the movie's star, Kaytee thought she understood even that. After all, if she were making a movie, she'd want it to be about her first period. There was Brian, who looked tough but was really just misunderstood. Then there was Jonathan, whose behavior was improving, at least most days. And Milagros, hopefully, would overcome her embarrassment and participate again. Then again, Milagros was so quiet she would probably be more of an extra than a main character. Maybe Kaytee would even track down Yesenia, who was perhaps pregnant and working some menial job, waiting for a teacher to talk her into giving school another try.

Yes, the movie would definitely have to be about first period. It certainly couldn't be about her perpetually bored third period. No one wanted to watch a movie of kids falling asleep on their arms. The problems in her other classes, too, were mostly things like careless spelling and half-done homework that wouldn't transfer well to the big screen.

And then there was seventh period, the class that filled Kaytee with increasing dread as the end of each day approached. The students in seventh period weren't as loud as the ones in first period, but they were so negative, so mean. Just the thought of them propelled Kaytee into the kitchen. She opened another cheesecake-flavored yogurt that, even in her most optimistic mood, she had to admit didn't taste like cheesecake at all.

THE LOVE OF LEARNING
(LOL) FACTOR™

"**I JUST WANTED TO** know what this consultant is supposed to be looking for, exactly." Maybelline had rushed to Mr. Scamphers's office as soon as the bell rang.

"The *consultant*." Mr. Scamphers's moustache lifted into a sneer.

"He barely even looked at my data binder."

"Mr. Barrios has me showing that kid around like some type of tour guide."

"And then he made me do this cheer with the class, like, when I said, *the equation*, they had to say, *must balance*. We had to practice it until they were all saying it at the same time." She hoped she wouldn't have to demonstrate. It had been humiliating enough the first time around.

But Mr. Scamphers was looking off in another direction. "He probably thinks he's going to be a principal before I am."

"Sorry, what's that?"

Mr. Scamphers turned back to her. "You know what we have in common, Ms. Galang?"

Maybelline primed herself for another compliment, perhaps on her organizational skills, or how quickly she got things done. She really was quite organized and quick at getting things done.

But Mr. Scamphers was on a new subject. "You and me, we're the wrong color to make it in a school system like this. I mean, you're Chinese—"

"I'm Filipina."

"Well, you know what I mean. You have the ethnic last name, at least. But a white guy like me? Forget it."

This conversation was less encouraging than Maybelline had expected.

"My whole career, they say, *Jump*, and I say, *How high?* They want multiculturalism? I say, *Olé!* They want to make Mr. Barrios the principal? I say, *Fine. I'll wait.*"

Maybelline noticed, for the first time, that Mr. Scamphers never said *Doctor* Barrios. It was always *Mister*. Or just plain *Barrios*.

"Well, I'm done waiting. Next time I get the chance, *I'm* going to start acting like the principal."

"It seems like a good principal would check everyone's data binders." She was relieved to find a way back into the conversation. "And write up anyone who hasn't—"

"I'll tell you one thing," said Mr. Scamphers, though he seemed to be talking mainly to himself now. "I am not about to answer to some *kid*. With a *backpack*."

"Yes. I noticed the backpack, too."

The assistant principal looked at her, blinking, as if he'd forgotten she was there.

The hallway back to her classroom was plastered with homecoming-game flyers. They flapped into Maybelline's field of vision like fans of an opposing team. The conversation with Mr. Scamphers was supposed to have been reassuring. Instead, it had turned into . . . something else, with that vaguely disturbing reference to her last name, and then the talk about the consultant's backpack. Why the backpack bothered Mr. Scamphers so much was unclear.

She only knew why it bothered her.

Even twelve years earlier, during her first year of teaching, Maybelline had been more organized than the other teachers. She calculated, corrected, and left each night with a clean desk. When she controlled the details, everything worked just as it was supposed to.

It was when the kids entered the room that chaos took over. They were so messy and unruly. They talked loudly and talked back and didn't follow directions and didn't care.

All except a few.

Andres Medina had been one of those students, that first year, who plugged away, never quite getting it. He was one of only a few students who accepted Maybelline's offer of help during lunch, showing up so consistently she suspected he had no one to eat with in the cafeteria. Under her direction, his skills began to improve, bit by bit. And Maybelline was pleased. She was eager to prove to her students—and to her new bosses—that hard work and attention to detail paid off.

Unfortunately for Andres, he had also developed some teacher's-pet tendencies. During class, he raised his hand to answer every question. When Maybelline dropped something, he jumped out of his seat to hand it to her, and when his classmates threw balls of paper at the wastebasket, it was Andres who scooped up the shots they missed. He stayed afterward, too, picking up textbooks his classmates had dropped on the floor or left open on desks.

"You don't have to do that," Maybelline said, but she was too overwhelmed to turn down help with any real conviction.

The other students in Andres's class were terrible. One of them, Sandro Velez, had the power to silence other students with his eyes. Sandro wore bandannas around his wrist or hanging from his back pocket, and once, when Maybelline called on him to solve an easy algebra problem, he answered, "T don't equal shit." Then he looked around to see if anyone had a problem with this. No one seemed to.

Sandro and his friends talked through Maybelline's lessons as if they were sitting in front of a muted television. Other groups of students saw this and started their own conversations, until Maybelline was straining her voice every day, feeling as though she was speaking underwater. Only Andres continued to answer her questions—this even as Sandro and his friends made girls laugh with muttered insults or threw pencil erasers at Andres when he bent to open his tattered backpack.

The two boys were the same size, somewhere in the medium-to-husky range, and both were Latino. But the similarities stopped there. Sandro was muscular in the way that men who'd been in prison were muscular. He had all the signs of experience with the juvenile justice system: the homemade tattoos, the determination to get around rules, the admiration of trouble-loving girls. Andres, on the other hand, was droopy and lumpy. His arms flopped at his sides, and he smelled vaguely of mildewed clothing. One got the feeling he rarely had home-cooked meals but instead fed himself from a shelf of junk food in an empty house. He had probably always clung to his teachers for reassurance.

After a while, to Maybelline's great relief, Sandro began skipping class. The absences were occasional at first, then stretched for days at a time. Finally, he seemed to disappear altogether, leaving the class to build up a shaky dynamic in his absence. Andres continued to wave his hand in the air for questions, but the insults relented. There were even moments of order and tranquility during which Maybelline felt like she was actually teaching algebra.

It was a particularly quiet day in mid-October when Sandro showed up again. Most students had textbooks on their desks, and Maybelline was explaining the quadratic formula when she saw Sandro open the door. He stood, surveying the class in silence. Maybelline kept talking as if, by not acknowledging his presence, she might keep it from becoming real.

This is how it happened that Andres, who was looking at his work, didn't see Sandro slip into the chair next to him.

The silence didn't last long. As soon as he'd arranged himself in the chair, Sandro turned to a friend and began whispering urgently.

Maybelline raised her voice to be heard over his, almost by reflex.

Sandro gave Maybelline what he probably thought was a charming grin. "Don't worry, Miss, I'm gonna leave right now. Just gotta talk to my homeboy over here about some, uh, math problems."

Andres, with the increased confidence that he had built up during Sandro's absence, turned to his right with a sharp, "*Ssshhh!*"

His eyes met Sandro's as he turned.

At this point in the story, Maybelline's memory always switched to the type of grainy picture found on old VHS videotapes.

Sandro stared at Andres without blinking for what seemed like several minutes.

Andres looked down at his textbook.

A voice somewhere in the room said, *Oooh, he told you to shut up!* There was laughter.

He was like, Shhhhhhhhhhhhhh! The voice called out again.

Students turned to one another with a chorus of exaggerated shushing sounds, the day's lesson abandoned.

Stretching his legs out in front of him, Sandro leaned back in his chair, arms behind his head, turning an amused face toward Maybelline. "You know what? I changed my mind. I'm gonna stay."

Andres's eyes remained locked on the book in front of him.

Maybelline forced her mouth to continue describing the quadratic formula. A voice somewhere in the room said, *Miss, you said that already,* but she could not attach the words to a face nor a body. She had a feeling that she was about to see a crushing triumph of evil over good. Could she get Andres out of the room? Could she get another adult into the room? There was an emergency call button next to the door, but to press it was to admit that she didn't believe Andres could defend himself.

There was also a wastebasket next to the door. Maybelline grabbed a paper from her desk and brought it to the wastebasket, leaning her arm against the button in a move that felt more conspicuous than she'd hoped.

Mrs. Rawlins's irritated voice came through the intercom. "Fight?"

Maybelline froze. She'd assumed that pressing the button would prompt a security guard to quietly rush to her aid, although later, looking back, this would seem silly.

"Helloooo? Do you have an emergency? Is there a fight?"

"Uh, no. Sorry, I pressed the button by accident." Maybelline hoped Mrs. Rawlins could read the desperation in her voice. She was already starting to notice looks passing among some of her more drama-hungry students. For reasons she had never understood, kids liked watching each other get hurt.

"Well, be more careful, please. We're short-staffed on security. We can't have them running all over the place." There was a click as the intercom shut off.

Around Maybelline, the class was already making its ready-to-go sounds. The time students spent packing up had expanded since the start of the year, so that now, even before students shoved through the door and scattered into the hallway at the end of each class, there were several minutes of binders snapping and loud talking and laughter and students standing up and moving around the classroom, and it was during this confusion that Sandro sprang to his feet, yanking Andres sideways from his chair by his backpack.

Awww, shiiiiitttt! yelled a girl's voice. *They gonna fight!*

Andres struggled awkwardly to disentangle himself from the backpack.

Students crowded around to get a better look. Two of Sandro's friends closed in, ready to jump on Andres in the unlikely event it became necessary.

"Am I being too loud for yo bitch ass now?" Sandro yelled into Andres's ear.

Andres managed to pull one arm out of his backpack strap. "Sorry, man, I didn't—"

He never had a chance to finish. Sandro had a lock in his other hand, and he crashed it into Andres's eye with a sickening crunch.

Andres fell immediately to the floor.

The crowd pressed inward in its excitement. Maybelline lunged for the emergency button, pressing it over and over, but this time she got no answer at all. Bodies pressed in at the doorway as voices in the hall yelled, *Fight! In that new math teacher's class!*

Maybelline propelled herself into the center of the crowd on a wave of adrenaline.

"Stop!" she begged, grabbing at Sandro's shirt.

Andres was in a ball on the floor, curled up and covering his face as Sandro kicked him in the back.

Suddenly the crowd near the door thinned, and a deep voice roared, "GET. THE FUCK. UP. OFF HIM." A thick pink arm reached through the mass of bodies, grabbing Sandro in a chokehold.

Coach Ray.

He dragged Sandro into the hallway, where two security guards were just beginning to push their way through the crowd.

Maybelline turned back to Andres, who lay curled up on the floor, clutching his eye with a bloody hand. The rest of the class filed out, avoiding the red-faced football coach.

One skinny kid, imitating a character in a then-popular movie, leaned over Andres's crumpled frame and squealed, "You got knocked the *fuck* out!"

Handing Sandro off to the security guards, Coach Ray addressed Maybelline's next class of students, who were leaning into the doorway to see who was hurt. "Go across the hall to my room and sit down. Now. Oh, and shut up."

"I got them," he said to Maybelline. "Go check on the kid."

Andres had struggled to a sitting position by the time Maybelline closed the door. "I'm okay, Miss," he said, and then lay back down. There was urine on his jeans.

Maybelline called an ambulance from her classroom phone.

"I'm sorry," she whispered, as two paramedics carried Andres away on a stretcher. She couldn't tell if he heard her. The area around his eye seemed more than just swollen. Something about it seemed rearranged, misshapen.

School was over by the time the ambulance left, and Maybelline crossed the hallway to Coach Ray's room. The walls were bare except for a few football posters and some health-class textbooks stacked against an empty bulletin board. Chalk writing on the board announced that the day's lesson was *Health and Fitness*.

"Thanks for everything," said Maybelline. She tried to step back into the hallway before her tears spilled.

"That's all right, Ms. Galang. You ain't the first teacher at this school to have a fight in your class. Or the last." He offered her a Chick-fil-A napkin from his desk drawer.

Maybelline pressed the napkin to her eyes. She was surprised the coach knew her name. They had never interacted before.

"Ask anyone in this place. We got some crazy kids here, and security ain't worth a thing. But if anything happens, just remember, you got me across the hall."

When Maybelline returned to her classroom, Andres's backpack was still lying on the floor. She put it in her classroom closet, as if keeping it safe might in some way transfer to its owner.

Andres never returned to Brae Hill Valley High School. He never transferred to another school, either, as far as Maybelline knew. The contact numbers she got from the office led to disconnected lines. After three months of showing up at lunch and staying after class, Andres Medina had disappeared as tracelessly as a soap bubble.

Coach Ray, on the other hand, appeared often. In the weeks following the fight, he made a habit of stopping by the classroom. He warned students that he'd handle any complaints from Ms. Galang personally. There were football players in most of her classes, and Coach Ray marched them to her desk, advising them that if they wanted to see him happy in practice, Ms. Galang had better be happy at the end of the day. Then, one day, he asked her to dinner.

The whole thing would have been a short fling, a few months of uncommunicative dating based more on gratitude than anything resembling love—if not for the mishap that led to Maybelline's pregnancy, and eventually to Allyson.

Never, in the years that followed, would Maybelline turn her back to her students. Never would she misplace a paper, or fall behind and have to accept makeup work. She would leave no room for error or chaos. Even her classroom closet was flawless, filled with neat stacks of workbooks and labeled boxes. All except for the farthest corner, on the lowest shelf, where Andres Medina's backpack sat in a disorderly lump.

FORTIFY BACKGROUND KNOWLEDGE™

MY PLAN IS TO *be a vetinarian and one day have my own vetinary clinick.*

Lena sighed. Papers in which students shared their career plans were always the worst. They wanted to be veterinarians, CSI technicians, psychologists, and a host of other advanced-degree-requiring professions they'd seen on TV, all of which, in displays of tragic situational irony, were likely to be misspelled. Layers of fatigue settled upon her each time she corrected a concoction of letters such as *nowindays* or *oftenly*, or fixed punctuation that seemed almost randomly sprinkled across the page. Yet there was always one paper that made her finally decide to pack up for the day, her comment-making capacity depleted. This paper felt like it might be the insurmountable one.

Except she *couldn't* leave. Report-card day loomed, and the ever-present piles on her desk now threatened to engulf her. If she didn't finish at least one stack of essays today, there was no way she'd have her grades done on time. She clicked open her grading pen, positioning it over the paper.

My plan is to be a vetinarian . . .

To make matters worse, it was one of those earnest three-page efforts that called for some encouragement to balance out her corrections.

. . . my own vetinary clinick.

And she wasn't just supposed to correct the spelling errors, either.

She was supposed to write something meaningful on this paper, something that could conceivably begin to bridge the chasm between its author and a person who might, one day, *actually own a veterinary clinic*. Then she was supposed to do the same thing for the next paper, and the next, and the one after that, despite her waning concentration. And despite the weather; Texas's oppressive summer heat had finally faded, giving way to the type of breezy mid-October day that made her colleagues tell lame jokes about whether she'd brought the cold down with her from Philly. Fresh air drifted through the open window, hinting at the exciting possibilities that lay outside. It was one more reminder that grading these assignments threatened to cut into Lena's own more pressing assignment for the night: cooking dinner for Nex Level.

My plan is to be a . . .

VetERinarian, she wrote, circling the first misspelled word.

"Hey, Ms. Wright." It was Daren Grant, the consultant, sipping from his water bottle and preparing to pee the clear pee of the righteous.

"Hey." Lena hoped her tone communicated just how little enthusiasm Daren Grant's presence inspired. He had visited her classroom for the first time that morning. Afterwards, he'd sent a follow-up e-mail that ended with the phrase, *Make it a great day!*

"Just dropping off a quick work sheet to help you fortify background knowledge for students." Daren Grant had the informal tone of someone who nonetheless was about to issue a formal directive. "If you could just have them write down the background information they're missing—and of course provide meaningful feedback, ha-ha—then it will be really easy for me to confirm that you're fortifying background knowledge." He held up his iPad to show her what looked like a digital checklist.

"You want me to ask students to write everything they *don't* know? On one page?" Also, more importantly, was Daren Grant asking her to grade a whole extra stack of work sheets, right before report-card day, so he could check one box on a checklist?

"Our strategy is to have teachers use what students don't know as a starting point, and then perform actions that will make students know those things."

"Isn't that . . ."—Lena was confused—"pretty much the *definition* of teaching?"

"Exactly! Love that attitude. Just go ahead and make copies of this when you get a chance." With that, he handed her the paper and breezed into the hallway.

The last of Lena's grading motivation whooshed out like air from an untied balloon. She promised herself she'd grade at home if she had time, and it was with this thought that she stuffed the whole pile of papers into her bag, hoisted them onto her shoulder, flung them into her car, drove them home, lugged them up to her second-floor apartment, and dropped them just inside the front door, where she promptly forgot about them.

It was time to *throw down in the kitchen*. Ever since Nex had said he might come to her classroom if she cooked him dinner, that line from his poem had been repeating itself in her head. *Strong sistas* knew how to *throw down in the kitchen*.

It made her glad that she'd fortified some of her own lagging background knowledge when she'd first moved to Texas. Cooking, she knew, was something she should have learned as a child, from the type of tough-yet-loving grandmother featured in gospel genre movies. She should have spent Sundays in a kitchen full of aunties and cousins, amid arguments that ended in tearful embraces as everyone realized blood was thicker than water. There were supposed to be children running around and cornbread in the oven, and everyone was supposed to have a good singing voice.

Actually, Lena did have a good singing voice. She'd played several roles in musicals at the performing-arts high school. It was all the rest of it she had missed out on during her siblingless, cousinless, petless childhood. The Wrights did not gather in the kitchen on Sunday mornings. They sat in silence, reading the *New York Times*.

The thought that her cooking skills might one day reveal these deficiencies had prompted Lena, shortly after moving to Texas, to buy a book of home-style Southern recipes and practice them on her own. The fried chicken was a lost cause—she could never get the inside fully cooked before the outside burned—but she'd mastered the meatloaf and found a baked mac'n cheese that was hard to mess up.

These, combined with store-bought cornbread, had become the one full meal she could make with confidence.

The smell of the food filled her apartment as she showered, shaved, touched up her toenail polish, dusted on some inconspicuous makeup. Then she cleaned, flinging loose shoes and unfolded laundry into the closet, lighting a candle, and rubbing at the marks her ironing board had left on the carpet. Finally, to her relief and delight, she removed the dishes from the oven, each of them at just the right moment. They sat golden-edged on top of her stove, giving the whole place a sense of home. She had just dabbed scented oil behind her ears and was brushing her teeth in her newly clean bathroom mirror when she heard a knock at the door.

She opened it, greeting Nex Level with a long, slow kiss. He told her the food smelled good. She told him he smelled good. He put the gym bag he was carrying on the floor, next to her bag of ungraded papers. Lena set their plates on the coffee table and opened two beers, taking a long sip of hers and trying not to watch as Nex took his first bite.

Finally, he turned to her. "Hey, beautiful lady . . ."

"Mmm-hmmm?"

"You got any hot sauce?"

And thankfully, she did.

"CAN WE STAY in here during the pep rally?" The pleading voice belonged to Jermaine Hadler, who spent most class periods casting longing glances toward "Professor" LaQuandrea Jackson. A hoodie sagged over his bony shoulders like a vampire's cape.

"Sure," said Hernan. He always stayed in his room during pep rallies, offering refuge to the shy and the crowd averse.

"Fuck yeah!" said Jermaine, though he seemed to realize even as he said it that the words didn't roll off his tongue right. Students who learned coolness as a second language never quite lost their accents.

Hernan knew that real nerds didn't dress up for Nerd Day Thursday. They ignored it, just as they ignored Pajama Day Monday, Halloween Costume Tuesday, and all the other school-spirit dress-up days that led to the homecoming pep rally. The rally itself usually fell on School Color Friday, which was okay for nerds because it allowed anyone in a red shirt to blend into the crowd unnoticed. This year, however, there had been a scheduling glitch. The pep rally had been pushed up to Thursday and would thus be filled with screaming nonnerds dressed in taped-up glasses and high-waisted shorts—a scene from which actual nerds would stick out disastrously.

The athletes and cheerleaders and band members had all left class earlier in the day, excused through a succession of hall passes and administrative e-mails. Unserious students also took advantage of the chaos. They ducked into bathrooms to cause various types of mischief, or snuck down the street to hang out at Taco Loco, or skipped school completely, filtering through the proverbial cracks of the proverbial system and into the proverbial streets.

In the end, the kids left in the lab were girls like LaQuandrea, with her ever-present book and unironic glasses, who got stuck nodding along while groups of boys talked about computer games. Or they were boys like Jermaine, who got stuck listening to groups of girls talk about menstruation. Most of them would not attend tomorrow's homecoming game. Instead, they'd spend the day wishing football itself, along with all the other winner-take-all alpha-dog showdowns of high school, would cease to exist.

The class had just finished a unit on dinosaurs. Hernan always saved this topic for homecoming week. No one appreciated the *Tyrannosaurus rex*, that huge, awkward predator already extinct for millions of years, like sophomores with bad skin and difficulty making eye contact. Something about homecoming week called for a reminder that even the largest of us were small, that the continents were once a big, continuous land mass and might be again, and that, in the time scale of evolution, humans were no more significant than a grain of sand.

Outside, drums signaled the beginning of the pep rally. The students in the room drifted toward the noise like a siren song. They pushed aside leaves and branches to peer through the windows as the field filled with shouting, shoving teenagers. The dance-team girls wiggled their pleated skirts, their flawless makeup accentuated by matching nerd goggles. Coach Ray yelled the names of the game's starting line as, one by one, jocks came crashing through banners made from bulletin-board paper.

"Jeffeerrrrsssooooonnn Jeeeaaaaaannnn!"

The crowd roared as "Haitian Sensation" Jefferson Jean tore through the paper, his muscles bulging through plaid shorts and high socks.

"OOOOO'Neeeeeeaaaalllll Riggggggbbbbbbbyyyyyyyy!!!!!" The name brought the loudest roar of the day. Rigby stood on stage, basking in celebrity, pulling his nerd suspenders off one shoulder like a Chippendales dancer preparing for a strip tease.

Hernan's closed classroom windows were powerless against the shrieks and whistles.

"Why do people act like animals?" asked LaQuandrea, squinting through the tendrils of a snailseed vine. One strip of hair had managed to escape her ponytail. It stuck straight up in the air like a messy antenna.

"Because we *are* animals," said Hernan.

"Hey," said a voice from the doorway. "Could I stay in here?"

It was Angel, out of uniform as always but not dressed as a nerd. Hernan tried to conceal his surprise. Angel seemed an obvious pick to skip school on a day like today.

"You can, if you're sure you don't want to go to the pep rally."

"Nah. I just get in trouble at those things." Angel found a spot in a back corner of the room, put his headphones on, and laid his head on a lab table.

Outside, Coach Ray shouted that the Mountain Lake Native Americans were going *down*. Two thousand voices roared their agreement. Inside, under the shade of the foliage in the windows, the students fell into their own natural states. They played fantasy card games, drew pictures, or talked in the hushed tones of those whose conversations were mocked when overheard. Hernan took the opportunity to tend to the plants in his window. Some of them had climbed all the way to the ceiling. Others had withered. Hernan bent to remove a clump of brown leaves from one of the pots.

"Mister. Her. Nandez."

Hernan turned toward the voice.

Mr. Scamphers was in the doorway, clutching his clipboard in a pose that signaled moderate threat. "You do realize there is a pep rally going on outside?"

As if to underscore how hard it would be to miss this fact, drumbeats thundered through the window.

Hernan said, "Yeah. But I usually stay up here with students who . . ." He gestured toward the kids in the room. He didn't want to say the words *shy* or *awkward* aloud.

If Mr. Scamphers picked up the nonverbal cue, he hid it well. "Who are supposed to be at the pep rally, you mean?"

Hernan tried a different approach. He pointed to the board, where he'd written the Research-Based Best Practice of the Day. In its entirety.

"But *Every Minute Counts*, right? Like today's e-mail said, forty-five seconds per day adds up to six extra days of instruction per year!"

He smiled, inviting Mr. Scamphers to join him in appreciating the joke. The assistant principal was, after all, wearing thick black nerd glasses that combined with his moustache to look like a Groucho Marx mask.

But there was no indication that Mr. Scamphers found the situation, or Hernan's words, or possibly anything else in the world, funny. Instead, he gestured toward Angel, sleeping under his headphones in the corner. "Is this what you call making every minute count?"

"But there's a pep rally going on."

"Ah, so you *have* noticed there's a pep rally. I guess we're back to why these students are not at it."

"I do this every year. Doctor Barrios has never said anything about it."

"You're saying you make a habit of ignoring administrative directives?"

"No, it's just . . ." Hernan wasn't sure what else to say. He had always assumed the administrators knew he let students sit out the pep rally in his room—or at least that they wouldn't care.

"Excuse me, sir?" The voice was coming from the corner.

Everyone in the room turned to look.

Angel had picked his head up and was now addressing Mr. Scamphers in a polite, deferential tone that Hernan would not have guessed was within his range. "We're in here because Mr. Hernandez doesn't just teach. He inspires!"

Mr. Scamphers's eyes narrowed. "Is that right?"

"Yes. Absolutely. Mr. Hernandez is one of those special teachers who knows that a hundred years from now, it won't matter what kind of car you drove or what kind of clothes you wore. All that will matter is whether you've made a difference in a student's life. And Mr. Hernandez sure has made a difference in mine." Angel turned to Hernan. Tears seem to be welling in his eyes. "Thank you, Mr. Hernandez."

Hernan watched him, speechless.

Even Mr. Scamphers seemed stunned, though he quickly recovered. "I will talk to you later, Mr. Hernandez. For now, I am making a note of this situation." He wrote furiously on his clipboard and then stomped back into the hallway.

"Angel," said Hernan, "I don't know what to say. Thank you!"

"No problem," said Angel. "I read it on a mug. Anyways, I hate that motherfucker." With that, he placed his head back on the desk and slept until the bell set the whole school free.

"And you know what they say," said Regina. "Men are like cars. You got your old cars with good engines. Then you got cars that look shiny but keep breaking down on you . . ."

The usual happy-hour crew was at Pappadeaux Cajun Seafood, next to the giant lobster tank near the entrance. Hernan had told them the story from the pep rally, and Lena had laughed so hard she'd snorted, softening the awkwardness he'd felt around her since their not-date at the poetry club. Now, however, the conversation seemed to be drifting back to a topic the women had been discussing at some earlier point.

"Well, what can I say?" Breyonna smiled. "I like luxury cars."

"Sounds like a passionate affair," said Lena, checking her phone for what seemed like the twentieth time since Hernan had arrived.

"Hey," said Breyonna, "it don't matter how fine a man is if he's driving his mama's car, putting in five dollars of gas, talking about *I filled up the tank*."

"We talking about your brother again?" said Candace.

A brief look of anger or hurt seemed to blink across Breyonna's face. But then she turned to the table, smiled sweetly, and said, "Candace is more of a bus-pass girl."

"You know what I heard the best kind of car is?" said Hernan. "A Jeep. Not brand new, but clean. And fully paid off."

They all laughed.

"A Jeep is a good car," said Candace.

"I'd go with a car that has a good engine," said Regina, "if there were any cars with good engines out there. Which there are not."

"Girl, your problem is you always test-drive cars too soon," said Breyonna. "Then they're not for sale anymore. Just saying."

"That is *not* always what happens," said Regina.

Lena jumped in. "Maybe she's not *trying* to buy a car. Maybe she's just looking for a really good rental."

There was a cascade of laughter from the rest of the table. Even Kaytee laughed.

"Yeah!" Regina rebounded, eyeing Breyonna. "*Just saying.*"

Hernan stared into the lobster tank.

Breyonna stretched out her ring hand conspicuously. "Look—y'all can give it up on credit if you want to. *I'm* just saying, ain't nothing you can do in a bedroom that can make a man love you."

Lena seemed to be considering this as she glanced down at her phone again. Then she looked up with the smile of someone keeping a delicious secret. "Who said anything about love?"

Hernan turned his attention back to the lobsters in the tank. Their claws were clamped shut with thick rubber bands, but they climbed on top of one another anyway, programmed by nature to struggle toward the top of the pile. It never occurred to them that they'd all be on someone's plate by the weekend.

TIMELY, SPECIFIC FEEDBACK™

COACH RAY COULD barely hear the marching band over his own fury. He shoved open the locker-room door, banging it into the wall. His players already knew better than to stand directly behind the door. They waited farther inside the locker room, leaning against lockers, sitting on benches in exhaustion. Even though it was only halftime. Even though the Native Americans were ahead by twelve points.

Their idleness made a vein throb in Coach Ray's forehead. "What the fuck is this? Why do I see players on a *losing team* lounging around like fucking mermaids?"

The players who were sitting stood up. Those who were standing straightened.

Ray pushed through the crowd. When he got to the corner of the locker room, he turned, took a long breath. Started slowly. "Boys, how is this year supposed to end?"

"Championship!"

"And how's this year gonna end?"

"Championship!!!" They were trying to sound excited. But trying was not enough. That was the whole point.

"Well, you tell me something: How in the *fuck* you think we're gonna make it to the championship when you give up on the game after the first touchdown? Native Americans score on the first drive? You come back. *You* score. You don't give up and start playing like a bunch of pussies."

"Coach?" It was O'Neal Rigby, who should have known better right now.

Coach Ray wheeled on him. It was Rigby who'd pissed away the team's early momentum, clowning for some girls on the sidelines after his first touchdown. "Oh, *you* want to talk? *You*. Didn't I hear you before the game talking about *They can't block me. I'm the man?*"

"Sorry, Coach, I was kidding. But, Coach——"

"Were you *the man* when you dropped the next fucking pass?"

"But Coach——"

"Coach?" Jefferson Jean, who'd arrived only a year earlier from Haiti, was the second biggest star on the team. He was only a junior. Yet recruiters were already talking about free rides to colleges where the professors, like his high school teachers, would continually mix up his first and last names.

Something was off, though. Jefferson Jean almost never spoke unless his coach spoke to him first. Looking around the locker room, it seemed to Coach Ray that some of the other players, too, were trying to communicate something. Coach Ray followed their eyes, the slight movements of their heads, until he saw a stranger, only slightly older than the players, nearly hidden behind the two tallest linemen. He was holding an iPad and carrying a backpack.

Coach Ray compressed a surging wave of rage. "May I help you, young man? Do you need some help finding the visitors' locker room?"

The players turned to see the younger man's reaction. Sometimes assistant coaches from other teams tried to spy on sideline conversations, but sneaking into the locker room was pushing it. That took serious—

"No, ha-ha." The visitor stepped from behind the players. "I'm actually working with TransformationalChangeAdvocacyConsultingPartners to help create a climate at your school where all students are prepared to succeed academically. So I just wanted to get a sense of how the football team operates. I'm Daren Grant, by the way."

He held out his non-iPad hand.

The way Daren Grant said *succeed academically* had revealed a glimpse of how the scene looked to him: a giant, red-faced white man with a Hill Country accent yelling at a group composed mainly of black teenagers. The consultant was black, too, but something about him suggested a delicate, bicycle-helmet-wearing childhood far away from contact sports and sharp objects and hurt feelings. All this made Coach Ray move forward until he was slightly farther into the visitor's personal space than polite conversation would dictate. "Well, maybe you can sense the climate in some other part of the school. We've had a successful season so far."

Just hearing himself say this added to his anger. He never reminded his team of their previous victories during a game. There was no past tense in football.

"I definitely understand that, but Superintendent Wallabee told me I had unlimited access to all parts of the school, and he suggested I check in . . ."

"Let me get this straight." Coach Ray employed the slow cadence he sometimes used when smacking down players' excuses, pausing after each word as if holding it to the light to examine its ridiculousness. "Nick. Wallabee. Told. You. To. Come. Into. My. Locker. Room. During. A. Homecoming. Game."

"Uh, well, actually, he said we were welcome any time? And I'm sure you know that today's research-based best practice is timely, specific feedback? So it just seemed like a good time to observe how y— how the football team uses that?"

Coach Ray stared, unblinking. He was somewhat gratified that the consultant had slipped into a speech pattern in which everything sounded like a question.

"I just thought that as a coach, you might—" Grant stopped as if he'd just thought of something. A sly look of reclaimed confidence crept onto his face. "Also, this team had some issues last year that weren't quite resolved? So Nick Wallabee was concerned about that." He gestured as if to say, *I don't think you want to discuss this right now.*

It was true. Coach Ray did not want to discuss this right now.

"Okay, well, enjoy the view." He imagined kicking Daren Grant through the locker-room doors, field-goal style. But instead, he turned to his players. They still had a game to win, which meant he still had a talk to give before halftime ended.

"Your families are out there in the stands, and we got the Native Americans in our house. *Our house.* You gonna let these mother—these *other people*"—he struggled to keep his speech curse word–free— "come into *your* house and beat you in front of your families because you're playing like little, scared—" Here he paused, mentally scrolling through the words he would normally use, dismissing most of them before finally settling on, "cheerleaders?" Which got the point across well enough.

"No, Coach!" said the team in unison.

But that wasn't enough, because now Coach Ray was thinking about Gerard Brown and this never-ending shit storm that flared up whenever the fuck it wanted to, like right now, when he had some pussy with an iPad and a backpack standing in his locker room with that *too-many-of-our-young-men-can-pass-a-football-but-not-a-test* smirk on his face. During a homecoming game.

Coach Ray knew he was supposed to have reported the Gerard Brown incident as soon as he'd heard about it. He hadn't. It wasn't like it was the first time a football player had gotten a girl pregnant. But then, when the player happened to be nineteen and the girl turned out to be fourteen, it suddenly didn't matter that the girl dressed the way she did, and hung out next to the locker-room door, and did football players' homework and a whole lot more, if the rumors were true. It was the player who lost his scholarships and became a registered sex offender. And yeah, the girl got called some names and had to change schools because people were threatening her, and Coach Ray could admit that the whole thing was a shit show for everyone involved. Still, he didn't feel bad for pretending he knew nothing when the cops and news crews showed up. Whatever happened back in March had, in Coach Ray's mind, existed in a gray area where the answers were different for men who did the world's dangerous jobs—men who, unlike Daren Grant, would understand that coaches did not throw their players to the dogs.

Ray stepped closer to Rigby, until his mouth was just inches from the player's nose. "You want to play Division One, right? And I'm talking to all these recruiters for you. What do you want me to tell them? *He can't play when girls are around?*"

"No, Coach." Rigby was saying the right things, but there was limpness to the exchange. Maybe it was that Rigby knew he was too good a player to take out of the game. Coach Ray wasn't one of those coaches who would sacrifice a win just to teach a player a lesson. But, no, it wasn't that. It was as if Rigby, or maybe the whole team, saw Coach Ray trying to talk like some . . . *lady* to avoid offending this newcomer.

Coach Ray tried to lock back in, looking hard at each player before he spoke. He'd learned from his own coaches that silence, when used properly, could intimidate better than yelling.

But there was no silence. Instead, there was the voice of Daren Grant, who on top of everything else was one of those high-efficiency talkers who felt the need to fill every pause. Apparently, he'd taken the moment not as a tactic but as a sign that the coach had run out of things to say and had decided to come to his aid. "The important thing is to do your best out there, guys! And remember, there's more to life than football."

Someone was gonna have to teach this kid something. Nobody talked to a team that belonged to another coach. In the *locker* room. During a *homecoming* game. When the team was down by *twelve* points.

Coach Ray imagined using Daren Grant to demonstrate the type of banned tackling technique that would have been flagged as a personal foul during a game. Then, just as quickly, he rechanneled his anger. *Inner game face.* In high school he'd learned that the best way to get the ball into the end zone was to push forward, blocking out all thought, until he heard nothing but the wind around his helmet—until it seemed as if he were moving full speed while everyone around him followed in slow motion. The kid wanted to see how the team worked? Well, let him see why the Killer Armadillos were an undefeated team. Let him type anything he wanted into that fucking tablet.

Coach Ray turned his attention to his players, ignoring Daren Grant's comment as if it were a nonissue that had non-happened. "You better get ready to knock the *shit* out of them, or we ain't done here." He leaned his full weight on the word *shit*. Nobody was coming into his locker room and making him afraid to talk. "This is not mother*fucking* camp. This is not motherfucking cheerleading practice. If I see you going easy out there, I am personally whooping your asses, you hear me?"

"Yes, Coach!" Ray's infusion of anger had pumped the team back up.

The yes, Coach snapped Coach Ray fully back into himself. He'd found some of these boys in middle school, had gotten them addresses, still drove some of them home after practice. He'd spent hours in the kitchen of Jefferson Jean's unair-conditioned apartment, convincing his mother that even after the concussion, football could be Jefferson's ticket to where she wanted him to go. And he knew how many former players' hopes rested on O'Neal Rigby's shoulder pads. These boys knew that there was no almost in football. There was no Just do your best. Football was a yes-or-no game, and the men who played it right weren't afraid of pain. They were afraid of losing.

"I dare y'all to come to me talking about you did your best," said Coach Ray. He wanted Daren Grant to understand how far he stood outside the bond between player and coach. "Now go out there and play like you want this. We're not gonna do our best. We're gonna pound these motherfuckers!"

With that, the players swarmed like hornets onto the lit field. When the first drive after halftime ended in an Armadillos touchdown, and when the kicker nailed the extra point that followed, Rigby didn't even acknowledge the girls on the sidelines. The whole team remained as steadfast as Jefferson Jean. One wave of young men after another crashed into the opposing players with all their might.

It was the Native Americans who were relaxing now. One of their star defensive players even had the audacity to blow a kiss to a girl in the bleachers, palming the lower half of his face mask and then extending his arm, spreading his fingers as if flinging his team's chance of victory into the wind.

Or at least that might as well have been it, because right after that, a Natives receiver dropped a perfectly good pass on third down, and from there it became anybody's game. Bodies leaned forward from the lit stands. Coach Ray yelled from the sidelines, the rush of blood in his ears drowning out his own voice.

Finally, with less than a minute left on the scoreboard, Jefferson raised his mighty throwing arm and sent the ball sailing. Rigby jumped, catching it right between two defenders. The crowd exploded as Rigby crossed into the end zone with the ball under his arm, then got even louder as he made a dramatic show of placing it gently on the ground, pretending to pack dirt around it as if planting a football tree.

But Rigby wasn't done. He raised his arms to the sky, turning slowly to face each section of the stands. The cheering grew. There were still a few seconds left on the scoreboard, but not enough for the Natives to do anything that mattered. Rigby reveled in the moment until Jean and the rest of the team reached him, crashing into one another with happiness so intense it looked almost like rage. The excitement flared upwards into the stands. Homecoming was the one game the whole school came out for, and now swarms of people jumped and shrieked and hugged and ran onto the field in celebration.

A burst of nostalgia mixed with Coach Ray's pride. This was another thing that nonplayers like Daren Grant could never understand: Wasn't nothin' better than being a star football player, on a winning team, in a town that loves football.

By the time the players had showered and changed out of their uniforms, most of the fans were gone. Dr. Barrios and a whole lineup of teachers had stopped by with congratulations, but then they, too, had drifted away. The players who lived nearby walked home with friends or family members. And Daren Grant hadn't showed his face again since halftime, though Coach Ray sure did hope he'd seen the show.

In the end, the glowing field was empty. Only Jean, Rigby, and two other players remained. These were the players whose families lived too far, or worked too much, or missed games for other reasons that never got discussed. But for the moment, the boys were bursting with triumph. They joked, bragged, and cheerfully insulted one another as they climbed into Coach Ray's truck for the long ride home.

THE
NUMBERS

"**C**SOTD AND . . . ?" Dr. Barrios reached into his memory, grasping for clues to what the letters might stand for. He sometimes suspected Mr. Scamphers, who was nearly bouncing in his chair on the other side of the big desk, made up acronyms as he went along.

"RBBPTWOTD. Research-Based Best Practice That Works of the Day. I'm creating forms for teachers to chart each student's progress on the CSOTDs and track which RBBPTWOTDs they're using."

Okay. So CSOTD stood for Curriculum Standard of the Day, and Mr. Scamphers was creating a chart. All was as expected.

In the other chair, Mrs. Rawlins withdrew a small bottle of lotion from her purse. "*My* question," she said, squeezing a dot of lotion into her palm, "is why none of the teachers ask these low-performing kids *why* they're failing. When a student comes into my office, I say, *How you doing in your classes, son? How is everything at home?* That's all the best practices *I* need."

Mr. Scamphers, who was as tightly wound as the spring on a mouse-trap, was eager to clamp down on any initiative that scrambled close enough. Mrs. Rawlins, on the other hand, had the relaxed demeanor of someone just waiting for the world to catch up with her simple, commonsense solutions. Now, having shortened Mr. Scamphers's acronym to a phrase of her own choosing, she massaged the lotion slowly into her hands as if they were sore from the effort of keeping things so simple and commonsense.

The two assistant principals resented one another, annoyed Dr. Barrios, and were blights upon the teachers of the school. Yet he needed them more than ever right now. The fearsome Office for Oversight of Binders and Evidence of Implementation was sending their people for a midyear audit.

Or maybe *people* was not the right term. OBEI auditors showed little interest in human-style interaction. It was not clear whether this was an actual requirement or a byproduct of the personality needed for the job, whose level of tedium no ordinary mortal could bear. OBEI officers tunneled through paperwork like worker ants, poring over professional development sign-in sheets, attendance rosters, and test-material storage records, unearthing tiny crumbs of data that might signal the trail to a violation. Dr. Barrios could not imagine what would ever make someone willingly take such a job.

Except for one thing: OBEI officers had power.

They reported directly to the school board and, in extreme cases, the press. This made them more terrifying than the superintendent himself. Dr. Barrios didn't know of anything he'd done wrong, but the thought of such scrutiny made him feel like he must be guilty of something.

His chest tightened as he read the assistant principals the list. "They'll be looking at attendance, parental involvement, teacher participation in professional development, discipline—although discipline should still look good."

Mrs. Rawlins nodded confidently. "It's just like I always say: Children don't *care* what you *know* until they *know* that you *care*!"

Dr. Barrios tried to keep from massaging his temples. Everyone knew the real reason discipline numbers looked good: Mrs. Rawlins was the assistant principal in charge of discipline, and she rarely enforced any actual consequences. This not only kept suspension numbers low, it also meant few teachers bothered to fill out referral forms in the first place—and these were the two ways the district calculated discipline numbers. It was, of course, these same two tendencies that caused actual student behavior at the school to skid downhill, but this was no time to make changes to the one set of numbers that felt assured.

Mr. Scamphers, not one to be out-complimented, was sliding steadily forward in his seat. "We also have the PHCDMADC meeting next month. I'll document anyone whose data binder doesn't reflect a sense of urgency regarding the pre-test scores."

"That will be great, Mr. Scamphers." Later, Dr. Barrios would try to figure out what PHCDMADC stood for. But for now, how to bring this up delicately? He had made no move whatsoever to assign Believer Scores to teachers. "We are running a little behind on the Believer Scores, if one of you wanted to . . ."

Mrs. Rawlins leaned backward, suddenly quite busy squeezing another dot of lotion into her palms.

Mr. Scamphers, on the other hand, was almost hovering in front of his chair.

"I'll do it," he said.

PARENTAL INVOLVEMENT

ANY OTHER YEAR, Maybelline wouldn't have pushed the subject of Allyson's birthday party. The birthday fell in the weeks before the state football playoffs, and Coach Ray had once explained the life of a football coach like this: "If you're having dinner with your family on Thanksgiving, it means you lost."

Of course, the Killer Armadillos rarely lost. How could they? Coach Ray recruited the best players from middle schools all around the city. Then he helped them lie about their addresses so they could play on his team. He even picked some of the players up in the mornings and drove them to school, just so they could help him win football games.

The only reason Maybelline had mentioned all of this in front of Allyson was to show that the Killer Armadillos' homecoming victory wasn't really about good coaching: It was just about getting around the rules. But Allyson had reached a different conclusion. Ever since the conversation, she'd been wondering aloud what would happen if she couldn't go to Grumbly Elementary anymore. She'd have to go to school closer to home, she reasoned, and this would be on her father's way to Brae Hill Valley. Maybe he'd pick her up, too.

It wasn't an empty threat. Allyson's grades had dropped, and low grades triggered the type of address-checking schools did as testing season closed in. Maybelline was now on the receiving end of the *your-child-has-not-done-his-or-her-homework* calls she so flawlessly documented in her own parent-contact binder.

As the day crept slowly toward lunch, she checked her e-mail again. Coach Ray still hadn't answered her message.

Instead, there was an e-mail from Mr. Scamphers, addressed not to the whole faculty but directly to her.

Well, the OBEI people checked all the administrative binders today and left very happy. I'm sure you can guess who spent yet another day covering for our "wonderful" principal.

Maybelline swallowed hard. A few days earlier, Mr. Scamphers had stopped by her classroom to talk about the Office for Oversight of Binders and Evidence of Implementation, which searched for signs of ethical violations, testing irregularities, and neglected administrative tasks. Never had she imagined such a place existed. Ever since, she'd been picturing the auditors who might visit her room and flip through her binders, marveling at the way every column balanced, assigning her a perfect score. Just the thought of it had given her the courage to e-mail Coach Ray.

But now, as she read Mr. Scamphers's description of the visit, all she could pull from it was a single devastating fact: The OBEI auditors had already *left*. Everything they cared about was in the principal's office.

Her earlier confidence drained away. There would be no auditors to notice her exceptional effort. Maybelline Galang was just a regular teacher, working in this regular classroom, right down the hallway from the source of her biggest miscalculation.

When the lunch bell rang, Maybelline closed her eyes, mentally preparing herself for the walk across the hallway. *Did you read my e-mail?* That was the way she planned to start. She took pride in not having asked Coach Ray for much over the years. Hopefully, she wouldn't have to ask him out loud to come to the birthday party.

"Miss?"

Maybelline's eyes snapped open as she realized she wasn't alone.

Jennifer Reyes, from fourth period, had stayed behind after the bell. "Is it okay if I check my grade?"

Maybelline opened the grade book on her computer. "You have a C."

Jennifer did not turn to leave.

"No makeup work," Maybelline reminded her.

"Miss—I think I'm pregnant. I mean, I am." Then Jennifer sat at an empty desk, put her head in her hands, and began to sob.

Maybelline took out a box of tissues. This would take a while. It had always been clear that some students knew she and Coach Ray had a child together. Maybelline could not be sure whether this information was passed down through successive years of students or whether Mrs. Friedman-Katz or Mrs. Reynolds-Washington spread it anew each fall. All Maybelline knew was that nothing she did as a teacher should have suggested she wanted to hear about students' personal problems. Most days, she directed them to open their books, silently follow the directions on the board, and maintain this pose for as much of each class as possible. And yet, every year, girls who "thought" they "might" be pregnant ended up crying next to her desk. It was as if they expected her to provide some equation into which they might plug the variables of their lives and answer the one question they couldn't ask aloud. The whole idea was ridiculous. What would such an equation even look like?

On one side:

1. You have a boy who is telling you he wants this baby and that this will work out. Or maybe you have a boy who is telling you he doesn't want this baby, but you are sure he'll change his mind.

2. Your sister or your best friend or your cousin had a baby last year, and look at all the attention she's getting.

3. You believe a baby at any stage of development is a tiny little life. You have always imagined abortion clinics as dark, dirty places in which expressionless men hack at your insides and leave you with a lifetime of guilt.

4. Others have warned you that a baby will change everything. But when they do, a small voice inside you whispers that you have always wanted everything to change.

But then, on the other side:

1. Your child will need food, and time, and health insurance, and so many other things you don't know if you can provide.

2. Your mother will be angry. Worse than that, she will be ashamed. And even when the anger and the shame are through, you will watch her come home older and older in her thick white nurse's shoes. She says she wears them because they are comfortable but still rubs her feet as she watches TV in the apartment you share. It is only slightly bigger than the one you grew up in. Meanwhile, your sister's family lives in a big house with high ceilings and wedding pictures in frames.

3. Your sister had an abortion when she was in high school. You are the only one who knows this.

There was not an equation in the world that could answer this question. There were simply too many variables, each of which raised further questions. For example, did the baby's father even look up when you told him the news? Or did he just keep staring at a football game on TV and then ask, as if he'd had this conversation before, *So, what are you going to do?* And where will he be when your daughter is ten years old, with a birthday during football season?

Maybe at your classroom door, while you wait for a pregnant teenager to finish crying on the desk in front of you.

"Sorry," Coach Ray called in from the doorway. "I can see you're busy." He gestured toward Jennifer, who had picked up her head at the sound of his voice and was wiping her eyes on her sleeve. No one wanted to cry in front of a football coach.

"No, I'm not busy. I mean, I am, but . . ." Maybelline hesitated, unable to discuss the topic in front of Jennifer. "Did you read my e-mail?"

"I did, but you know football. Take an hour off during championship season, you give the other guys an hour to get ahead of you." Coach Ray glanced at Jennifer, switching to the voice adults used when they thought they were obscuring their meaning from nearby children. "So, unfortunately, I can't make it to the birthday party."

He pulled a hundred-dollar bill out of his wallet and handed it to Maybelline. "I was going to buy her a present, but I figured at this age she probably wants to go shopping herself." He offered an apologetic smile. Then he left.

As the door closed behind him, Jennifer's eyes filled with tears again.

Maybelline pushed her own frustration aside. "Sorry, Jennifer."

"That's okay, Miss. I think I figured out what I'm going to do."

"Are you sure?"

Jennifer nodded.

"Okay. Sorry I couldn't be more helpful."

"Don't worry, Miss. You were."

MEMBERSHIP

HERNAN HATED WHEN kids left garbage on the ground for the custodians to pick up. It wasn't because he was Mexican, okay?

Well, maybe it was because he was Mexican. Every summer since eighth grade, he had worked for his father's landscaping company, grooming flowers around golf courses and fancy hotels.

Meaning he'd picked up his share of other people's garbage.

One morning in particular had lodged in his memory. It had been late May, graduation season. Hernandez Landscaping had gotten a job with a hotel near a private university. The job itself was a standard one: Pull weeds. Mow the lawn. Edge the bushes into neat rectangles. When they arrived, however, they found the courtyard littered with beer cans and plastic cups. They'd spent several unpaid hours that day bent over in the Texas sun, picking up the celebratory trash of college graduates.

I don't care how much school a person has, Hernan's father said. *A person with* education *knows to pick up his own garbage.*

"He rubbed his back as he said it. Like this." Hernan stooped as if in pain, rubbing his own back to demonstrate for his students. "Then my friend realized that of course his father's back hurt: He was decades older than the kids who threw the garbage on the ground in the first place. He'd been doing this job since before they were born."

When he told personal stories in class, he always pretended they'd happened to a friend. It seemed wrong to burden students with his memories. Every year, however, there came a moment that brought this story spilling out. It was usually a day like today, when he'd opened his classroom door to find the hallway littered with what seemed like a whole vending machine's worth of plastic bags.

The kids sat quietly until LaQuandrea Jackson broke the silence. "Mr. Hernandez, stop playing. You know your 'friend' is really you." She shaped her fingers into quotation marks as she said the word *friend*.

Hernan forced out a small laugh, trying to take focus away from the observation. This was the first time a student had figured this out. But then he stopped. "Yeah, LaQuandrea. It was me."

"So why don't you just say it's you, then?"

"I don't know," said Hernan. "I just don't."

A boy behind her chimed in. "He doesn't want us to know he had to pick up garbage, stupid."

"No, that's not it," Hernan said. It was strange how he spent so much time frustrated that students were not listening to him, only to get nervous when it seemed they might be listening too hard. "There's no shame in a job where you have to clean."

LaQuandrea swung around in her chair to address the boy. "I'm not stupid. Your mom is. And he probably didn't tell us because that's not the point. He just wants us to stop leaving our trash."

"I think it's time to get back to learning about DNA," said Hernan.

Hernan's father had moved to the city to do landscaping work from a town in Mexico where everyone moved to Texas to do landscaping work. Most of them had variations of the same plan: They'd save money, offer their children slices of American opportunity. Then maybe they'd retire back home one day, newly rich in a town that would always be poor. This was the idea, at least. There were enough grandfathers still stooping painfully in the sun to show this wasn't how it always worked out.

To this churn of immigrant dreams, Hernan's father had brought one tiny adaptive edge. As a teenager, he'd worked in La Huasteca National Park. There he had learned enough about plants to make them grow where no one else could. He passed this knowledge along to Hernan, who began experimenting with selective breeding, helping his father grow hardier plants and, over time, a bigger business. By the time Hernan's younger sister, Leticia, was old enough for high school, the family owned a plant nursery with a greenhouse and a home in a working-class suburb.

Lety would go on to study communications at a local university. Their older sister, Mayra, who'd become a citizen long after the prospect of college had passed, worked in a salon. Both sisters hated gardening.

Hernan, on the other hand, had spent his high school years assuming he'd take over the company. Hernandez Landscaping and Plant Nursery had become a business some men would have been proud to pass on to their sons.

When he mentioned this, however, his father gave him a look that ended the subject. "I don't work in people's backyards so my son can work in a backyard. I work so you can study. You want to work with plants? Study plants."

Hence the biology degree, and the science-teacher gig, and the students building DNA strands from beads and wire as the day advanced toward lunchtime. When the bell rang, Hernan grabbed his container of leftovers from the small fridge behind his desk. He left the usual crew of quiet misfits behind in the room and walked as fast as he could, hoping to beat the microwave line.

The teachers' lounge of Brae Hill Valley High School wasn't big enough for much actual lounging. It held one small table, a fridge no one used, and a machine that sold the same selection of (BAKED!) Reetos and (WHOLE GRAIN!) Fudgelicious products as the student vending machines. The biggest draw was the microwave. When Hernan arrived, Lena was already there, heating up her food. She offered him a *sorry-you-have-to-wait* smile that only increased the irritation he'd felt toward her since happy hour. He turned his attention toward the other people in the room. Coach Ray and Kaytee stood along the wall, holding their own lunches and watching the microwave eagerly.

Mr. Weber, who sat at the table, was the most promising source of distraction. He stirred clumps of Wake Rite instant coffee into a mug and frowned from under baggy eyebrows as Hernan greeted him. "Hernandez, you still don't want to be a union member with everything that's going on?"

"Trust me, you'd be the first to know."

Mr. Weber never got tired of warning Hernan that if he didn't join the teachers' union, his students would drink the chemicals in the science lab, or he'd be accused of rape, or Texas would lower teaching salaries to three dollars a day—and he'd be on his own. "Okay, well, I just hope you don't get tired of teaching test-taking skills every single day."

"I don't teach test-taking," said Hernan.

The microwave beeped, and Lena withdrew her lunch. "Never?" she asked, disbelieving.

"Never," confirmed Hernan. "I teach actual science."

"Well, I'm sure you can fake it when you have to." Her voice held a note of concerned reprimand, as if she was some type of expert on the topic of faking things and had noticed a shortfall on his part.

Then again, he thought with renewed irritation, maybe she was. He remembered the way her voice—even her grammar—had changed when she'd talked to Nex Level in the club. "I don't have a reason to be fake," he said, with more edge than he'd meant to.

Lena looked at him for a moment in silence, her eyes a question mark.

He held her gaze.

"I don't know about y'all," said Coach Ray, "but I *got* to be in the union. If a kid gets hurt on the field, I'm the first one they're gonna look at. Plus, they saved my ass on that Gerard Brown thing." He withdrew his lunch from the microwave and left the lounge.

Lena followed him out.

Mr. Weber, sensing he might now command more of Hernan's attention, returned to his theme. "I'm just looking out for you, Hernandez. Being in the union's like having car insurance: You hope you don't need it, but you get it just in case. It's different for the people who are just gonna leave after a couple years." He nodded toward Kaytee. Mr. Weber made no secret of his feelings about TeachCorps recruits.

"I told you already, I'm not going anywhere." Kaytee pulled open her frozen box of Low-Cal Cuisine with more force than necessary. "I just feel like we should focus on working for kids, not on contract rules that only benefit adults."

"Hey," said Hernan, addressing Mr. Weber before he could answer. "I heard your favorite movie's coming out over Christmas break."

"You mean *How the Teachers' Union Stole Christmas*?" Weber glared. "Don't tell me you're going to see it."

"Nah. Looks boring."

"It's called *How the* Status Quo *Stole Christmas*," said Kaytee, "and I *am* going to see it. Because as a *teacher*, I care about why our education system is *broken*."

The microwave beeped, and Hernan moved toward it, but Kaytee's lunch was one of those things you had to stir and put back in. The way it was looking, he'd be lucky to make it back to his room and scarf down his food before the bell rang.

Mr. Weber ignored Kaytee. "Just wait, man. You're going to wish you'd joined."

"Look," said Hernan, "I'm not into politics. But you have to admit, there are some teachers who shouldn't be in the classroom, and y'all do make it hard to fire them."

"Exactly!" Kaytee retrieved her lunch, started to leave the lounge, and then turned back toward the vending machine.

"If you're talking about Comodio, they could fire him at any time. They just have to make sure they go through all the steps."

Finally, Hernan put his lunch in the microwave. "Well, I'll start worrying after that happens. As long as Comodio's around, I'll assume I'm safe."

He was about to hit the Start button when Maybelline Galang rushed into the lounge. She was holding a stack of papers in one hand and a still-frozen lunch in the other, an insulated bag dangling from her arm. She looked at the clock, sighed, and started to back out of the door.

Something about the expression on her face, however, made Hernan say, "Hey, go ahead."

Maybelline looked shocked. "Are you sure?"

"Yeah." He took his lunch out of the microwave and held her stack of papers so she could put hers in.

"Wow. Thanks." Maybelline set the microwave for four and a half minutes.

Mr. Weber looked at the clock. "I guess you're eating lunch cold."

"Sorry," Maybelline mumbled to Hernan.

"Don't worry about it. I can eat my lunch cold. You can't eat yours frozen."

"Oh, yeah," said Mr. Weber. "That's another thing: Kids can come to our classes at any time and act however they want. But try getting back to your room even one minute after the lunch bell as a teacher."

"Well, on that note . . ." Hernan left the lounge, lukewarm leftovers in hand.

When he reached the end of the hallway, the floor outside his door was spotless.

ATTENDANCE

"**S**TOP TAPPING YOUR pen." All morning, Lena had paced the room like a panther in a cage, infuriated by behavior that should have been merely irritating. She'd woken up several times during the night, alternating between excitement about Nex Level's visit and worry that he wouldn't come. Before bed, she'd checked in with a casual text, reminding him that her students were excited. Her *students*, she'd been careful to say. Not her. In the morning, she'd sent him an e-mail with directions to the school. But Nex hadn't answered either message, and now Lena checked her phone with increasing frequency.

There was a knock at the door. She lunged for it, but it was only a student, who handed her a pass that said he'd been taking a makeup test. Then he looked around the room, confused. "Miss? I thought you said we were having a guest speaker."

"We are. I think. Just have a seat for now."

Nex Level is not coming.

She let the full sentence play in her head, forcing herself to feel its finality before a small, hopeful whisper from her subconscious added, *Well, probably not, but . . .*

But nothing. It was time to accept the situation: She had no lesson plan and a class full of increasingly restless teenagers. There was already some hopeful rumbling about having a free day. "Okay, um, for now, we're going to talk about symbolism in *Of Mice and Men*. Take out your study guides from yesterday."

"*Yesterday*, Miss?"

The class giggled.

"I mean—not yesterday. The study guides from *the class before the pre-test*, okay? Is that better?" Lena offered a smile to show she was joking at her own expense. This wasn't her students' fault. They'd just finished two days of pre-tests followed by two days of pre-test review. She'd promised them a guest speaker at the end of it. Now, instead, she had them digging in their backpacks for long-forgotten work sheets, trying to regain momentum on a novel the week before Thanksgiving. The least she could do was be pleasant.

A hand went up. "Yes, Luis?"

"Miss, the date is wrong on the board."

Lena breathed deeply. She could handle aggression, attitude, and attention-deficit disorder. Whining, though, she could not take. And Luis Alfonso was a whiner. Worse still, he was a whiner who luxuriated in correcting his teachers.

"Okay, Luis. Go ahead and change that while everyone gets their study guides out."

"Miss, did you know your 'quote of the day' has been up for three days?"

"Luis. Your study guide."

Luis shuffled through a folder until he found the page of questions. Then he beamed at Lena as if he expected her to scratch him between the ears.

Lena focused on the other side of the room to avoid looking at Luis. "Rico, where's *your* study guide?"

"I didn't get one. I wasn't here that day."

"Were you going to say something about that or were you just going to sit there?"

Before she could further pursue this topic, the classroom phone rang. Lena tried to restrain her hope that it might be the secretary from the main office, voice brimming with female approval, calling to tell her a handsome visitor was on the way down the hall.

"Okay, Rico." Lena crossed her fingers as she picked up the phone.

"Just grab a copy of the packet off my desk. Right there . . . Good morning, Ms. Wright's room."

It was not the main office. It was the school's reading coach, rounding up students for makeup pre-tests.

"You know we just missed four class periods in a row for these things, right?"

"I know. Trust me. But Scamphers keeps coming in here, and OBEI is already on us because attendance was so low on the test days."

Lena sighed. "Okay. Who do you need?"

"Can you send Kendrick Bridges, Rico Jones, and . . . I'm not sure how to pronounce this one—Last name Brooks."

"Rico, Kendrick, Djedouschla, you need to see the reading coach to make up your pre-test, so just put your papers in your binder—in your *binder*, Rico. Don't just stuff it into your backpack."

The three test-takers stepped into the hallway, where Rico immediately shoved his study guide into his backpack.

"Okay, where were we? Your work sheets. Okay . . . There's a lot of hand-related imagery in this novel. What do hands symbolize?" She always felt a little like she was forcing things when she asked these types of questions. What were the chances the author was really sitting there going, *Hey, let's add some hand symbolism in here so English teachers have something to put on a work sheet!*

"Miiiissssss?!" Luis Alfonso waved frantically, cutting off her mental reception.

"*What*, Luis?"

"For the homework, did you want us to write the questions? Or is it okay if we just number them?"

Lena inhaled deeply, the air pressing against her lungs. Suddenly, she wanted badly to hurt someone's feelings, and now there was Luis, with that *look* on his face. Something inside her reared up like a cobra, ready to strike.

But no—she caught herself. This wasn't about Luis. This was about . . . This was about . . . Her thoughts stuck there, like a scratched CD, unable to get to the end of the sentence. She looked at her phone, itching to push its button and rest her eyes on its glowing screen. A loud buzz interrupted her thoughts. The phone? No—not the phone.

Too loud . . . Then someone shouted, "Fire drill!" and gleeful chatter spread through the room. Students stuffed papers into backpacks and shoved chairs back from desks, cheerfully speculating whether they'd all be burned alive.

Outside her door, other teachers were already ushering their classes toward the emergency exit. Lena and her students followed. She rarely ventured this far down the hallway—the main office and the teachers' lounge were both in the other direction. But she knew Hernan's door was the last one before the exit, and as she drew closer, she saw it was propped slightly open. Was he inside? She strained toward it, separating herself from the flood of students who poured through the exit, reaching for the door handle as if for a lifeboat.

She slipped into the room, taking what felt like the day's first complete lungful of oxygen. There was something fresh about the air. As she looked around, she saw why.

There were plants everywhere.

Vines climbed all the way to the ceiling, and leaves stretched out against the windows, shading the room in a cool green. On the opposite wall, a purple light cast its glow over a row of sprouts. It was like being in an indoor garden—an indoor forest.

"Wow." It came out as a whisper. She'd never seen a classroom that looked like this.

Hernan was at his desk. He'd looked up from grading papers and was watching her take in the room.

"This is amazing! I never knew you did all this."

"What can I say? I'm good at making things grow."

Lena wanted to say more. She wanted to ask if she could stay here forever, in this tiny oasis. But all she said was, "You're not going out for the fire drill?"

"During my planning period? Nah. There would have to be a real fire. Even then, it's just a maybe."

Mrs. Rawlins's voice came on the PA. "Thank you all for an interruption. Teachers and students, we have technicians here working on the fire alarms. This is *not* a fire drill. Please return to your classrooms."

Groans came from the hallway as the current of teenagers reversed its course.

"Uh-oh," said Hernan, "you better get back before you waste valuable learning time."

"No, no, no, no." Lena felt despair pool in her veins. "Please . . ."

"Wow. You *really* don't feel like teaching."

"No, it's not that." And then, even though she hadn't meant to say anything, the story tumbled out. There was supposed to be a guest speaker. And it was Nex Level. And he had not showed up. And she was so, so stupid. She sensed from the look on Hernan's face that she did not need to explain further.

On the other side of the door, students ambled slowly back into the school, prodded by teachers and security guards, in no hurry to return to the day.

Hernan looked at her for a long moment.

She looked back at him.

The noise in the hallway was receding.

Finally, he stood and walked toward her. "Come on. I'll walk you back to class."

She felt his hand on her shoulder, and somehow this allowed her to move her feet in the direction of the door. Slowly. Reluctantly.

By the time they stepped out of the room, most of the students had already reentered their classrooms. The hallway was almost empty again, except for a lone dreadlocked figure heading toward them from the direction of the main office.

"Sorry I'm late," said Nex Level.

SUSPENSIONS

THE MYSTERY HISTORY TEACHER

www.teachcorps.blogs.com/mystery-history-teacher
Our New Historical Scholar Groups

Today we're discussing the origins of World War II and the Cold War. I'm planning to introduce the facts as quickly as possible so we can get into the process of historical inquiry and discuss how various forces led to the war. For this activity, I've also created new collaborative groups. Every student will work with classmates they haven't worked with before. I want them to see that if they work together, they can overcome anything.

COMMENTS

Back2Basix Teach more facts! For too long, we've been teaching so-called "thinking skills." Now our kids don't have any foundational knowledge. No wonder we're falling behind Finland on international tests.

OpenUREyes101 @Back2Basix WRONG!!! Our students are overloaded with facts! In Finland, students learn thinking skills. In the United States, it's all about facts, all the time.

That's why our kids don't know how to think, and it looks like you don't, either. #stupid

Soon2BDrJ @OpenUREyes101 @Back2Basix As a doctoral candidate who has researched cocreative processes, it is clear to me that both of your conjectures re: facts vs. thinking skills are based on limited pedagogical knowledge, as well as the assumption of a false dichotomy between evidentiary information and evaluation proficiency. #Stupid.

YouWongIRight Everyone just get ready to learn Mandarin Chinese, because that's what your grandkids are going to have to learn in order to get jobs.

125 MORE COMMENTS ON THIS POST

"Please read your info cards aloud. If anyone knows what any of these factors had to do with World War Two or the Cold War, please raise your hand. Who wants to start?"

A long moment passed. Then Michelle Thomas let out a hiss of air and lowered her head to the desk.

Welcome to seventh period, thought Kaytee. Her last class of the day wasn't rowdy like first period, but the students emitted rays of toxic negativity that crisscrossed the room like lasers. The strongest of these emanated from Michelle Thomas, who directed most of her mean-girl energy toward Diamonique, whose name suggested sparkling confidence but who was in fact a thick-limbed, sullen girl whom Michelle and several of her friends enjoyed needling with low-volume insults. No one in seventh period ever spoke loudly. When they did participate, after much sighing and eyerolling, they did so in barely audible voices, not so much derailing lessons as waterlogging them with hostile disinterest.

The dread of seventh period settled upon Kaytee during lunch each day, undermining her efforts to grade papers and compelling her toward the teachers'-lounge vending machine.

"Michelle, why don't you start? The card is on your desk."

Michelle sucked her teeth and mumble-read a fact about Dwight Eisenhower. Other students followed, murmuring their facts about Japanese Americans, the Holocaust, the invasion of Normandy, and the decision to drop the atomic bomb.

Kaytee pushed on. "Okay! Now we're going to get into our new historic scholar groups, so please listen for your name. First group: Edgar, Evelyn, Michelle, and Diamonique."

"I don't want to work with that bald-headed bitch," said Michelle, barely loud enough to be heard.

"Yo mama a bald-headed bitch," said Diamonique, in an equally quiet voice.

"No side conversation about your historic scholar groups, please."

Kaytee ignored the low-volume commentary that followed. She'd planned to get the kids into their groups first. Then she would give them the pep talk she'd prepared, about how modern workplaces required people to work together even if they didn't think they liked each other. "Next group: Iliana, Krystal, Djedouschla, and Lamont."

"Roach," said Iliana, looking at the floor.

"No commentary, please, just get together with your historic scholar groups."

"No, a *roach*," repeated Krystal, following Iliana's gaze.

"Roach," affirmed another voice.

"*Roach!*"

It took Kaytee a moment to realize her students were not insulting one another but referencing an actual cockroach, a muscular, Texas-sized beast of an insect larger than a man's big toe. The creature ambled from the center of the room toward the door. It had a lopsided swagger that made it seem confident but was most likely caused by a human hair wrapped around one of its legs, behind which dragged a fluffy tumbleweed of dust and other debris including a bright orange (BAKED!) Reetos crumb, which rested at the top of the dust clump as if riding in a carriage.

There was a chorus of scraping sounds as students dragged their desks away from the roach, leaving a crater of empty space in the center of the room. The roach continued to strain toward the door. Its slow, deliberate progress distorted the sense of time, which made it difficult to assess the speed of the events that followed.

The first of these events was that Kaytee turned to grab a can of Raid, which was wedged next to her data binder on the shelves behind her desk.

Concurrently, Michelle Thomas muttered, "Look what crawled out of Diamonique's backpack."

"It crawled out of your mom's pussy, bitch," Diamonique muttered back.

Kaytee, in the brief interval during which her hand curled around the can of Raid and her forefinger craned toward the nozzle, rethought her decision to put the girls in the same historic scholar group. The scraping of desks continued behind her, widening the empty circle toward which Kaytee now turned, can of Raid in hand, ready to aim a stream of poisonous liquid toward the roach but already sensing a more serious commotion in the center of the room, which, as she continued to turn, registered as Michelle and Diamonique locked in what looked like a slowly swaying wrestlers' hold. Diamonique clutched the top of Michelle's shirt, punching the girl's face with her free hand. Michelle's acrylic fingernails looped through Diamonique's braids, loosening them from the scalp while the nails of the other hand clawed at Diamonique's eyes.

The rest of the class formed a circle just wide enough to accommodate the fight, jostling one another for the best view.

Kaytee, already in midturn, pointed the can of Raid toward the center of the action, ready to spray. But then her central nervous system kicked in, freezing her finger before she pressed the nozzle and instead activating her feet, which propelled her toward Michelle and Diamonique as she shrieked, "Oh my God! Stop!"

She had already pushed her way to the inside of the circle when she realized she was still gripping the can of Raid.

"Stop it!" she screamed again, and dropped the can, which rolled toward the feet of the onlookers.

Droplets of blood dotted the floor. A detached braid had fallen into one of them, painting a red streak across the linoleum.

"Oh my God, stop it!" Kaytee leaned in from behind Diamonique, trying to dislodge Michelle's hand from the larger girl's hair, but it was locked in tight. Diamonique was still punching Michelle in the nose with short, noiseless punches that spattered more blood onto the floor. Kaytee gave up on Michelle's hand and leaned in farther, trying to grab Diamonique's wrist. At the same instant, Diamonique drew her arm back for another noiseless nose punch, her elbow connecting with the area under Kaytee's eye so forcefully that Kaytee stumbled backward, stunned by pain.

"Ow! Oh my God!" Kaytee clutched her eye as she fell to the floor.

The girls stopped fighting in surprise.

"Oh, shit," said Michelle. In spite of her bloody nose, she seemed somewhat inspired by this new twist in the story.

Diamonique seemed physically unhurt beyond a few scratches and the missing braid, but angry tears filled her eyes as she turned and ran into the hallway.

Kaytee grabbed the edge of a desk and pulled herself up just in time to see Ms. Grady appear in the doorway, glaring at Michelle.

"Michelle Thomas." She did not sound as if she was raising her voice, yet the words, accompanied by the look in her eyes and the scar down her cheek, held a force that seemed impossible to disobey. "Get some toilet tissue from the bathroom right now. Then sit your behind in my classroom and do not move."

"Yes, ma'am," said Michelle quietly. She hurried from the room, one hand under her nose.

"Everyone else, put these desks back and sit in your seats. You, young man"—Ms. Grady pointed at a bystander—"go find security. And you, call a custodian and tell him we have blood on the floor."

The students she'd addressed scuttled into the hallway. The others stared at the floor.

"Are you okay, Ms. Mahoney?"

Kaytee nodded, trying to look like she was okay.

Ms. Grady turned back to the students. "You all know better than to act like this in school. I will be back, and I want to see everything in this classroom looking exactly the way it did when you walked in here. Do you understand me?"

"Yes, ma'am."

With that, Ms. Grady disappeared. Kaytee surveyed the room with fresh shame as she imagined how it must have looked to her neighbor. Desks were shoved to the walls, pointing in every direction. Droplets of blood decorated the empty space in the center of the room. The can of Raid had rolled through the blood and then been kicked by students, leaving a crosshatch of red arcs across the floor. Kaytee watched in a daze as a custodian arrived to mop up the blood and her students moved the desks back into rows, their faces solemn.

As they worked, the roach strolled into the hallway unharmed, dragging the hair, dust, and (BAKED!) Reetos crumb behind it.

An hour later, when the last bell had finally rung, Kaytee made her way to Mrs. Rawlins's office. Michelle Thomas's mother was already there.

"This is Ms. Maloney," said Mrs. Rawlins, "Michelle's teacher."

"Ms. *Mahoney*," Kaytee said by way of both introduction and correction. She held out her hand, not knowing exactly how this was supposed to go.

The woman uncrossed her arms for a limp handshake.

"Ms. *Mahoney*," repeated Mrs. Rawlins. "I must have gotten you confused with one of the other first-year teachers."

"This is my second year."

"I'm sorry, sweetie, you look very young. Doesn't she look young?"

"Yes," said Michelle's mother, eyeing Kaytee. "She sure does."

Diamonique's mother arrived next, holding a baby in one arm and pressing a phone to her ear with the other as she approached the office door. "Mmm-hmm. Mmm-hmmm. That's right. And I told her if I have to go up to that school one more time, it's gonna be some—" She looked up and saw the other three women watching. "Anyway, I gotta go."

"You must be Diamonique's mother," said Mrs. Rawlins.

"Yes." The woman tucked the phone into her bra and surveyed the scene warily.

"Baaaaa," said the baby, reaching for the phone in his mother's tattooed cleavage.

"And you!" Mrs. Rawlins plucked the baby from its mother's arms. "You look just like my grandbaby!"

Diamonique's mother's wariness seemed to soften as Mrs. Rawlins performed the regulation toe squeezes and baby noises. It occurred to Kaytee that it was hard for an administrator to seem tough while rocking a baby in her arms.

Mrs. Rawlins looked up from jiggling the baby as the girls walked in, accompanied by a security guard. "Well, if it isn't two of my little troublemakers!"

Little *troublemakers?* wondered Kaytee. Diamonique towered over both Kaytee and Mrs. Rawlins. Michelle was smaller but was by no means *little*.

"Hello, Mrs. Rawlins," said Michelle, whose nose was no longer bleeding.

Mrs. Rawlins wiggled the baby's pinkie toe between her thumb and forefinger. "Now, what's this I hear about you two fighting?"

"Sorry, Mrs. Rawlins," said Michelle, blinking at the assistant principal with waiflike innocence. "We were playing around."

Playing around? thought Kaytee.

But it was Michelle's mother who spoke next, mostly addressing Mrs. Rawlins. "Like I was saying, I think the teacher might be overreacting here."

Mrs. Rawlins, still stroking the baby's foot, turned to Kaytee to explain. "Ms. Thomas was concerned that—since you're so new to this community—you might not be familiar with some of the communication styles of the children here."

Kaytee's eye throbbed. The area between her cheekbone and eyebrow had been puffy and red when she'd examined it. Now it felt like it was darkening to a bruise.

"I don't think this was an issue of communication styles. There was blood all over my floor."

"I have to say that just doesn't sound like my daughter," said Michelle's mother.

She sounded so convincing that Kaytee wondered if the universe might contain a completely alternate version of Michelle Thomas, one who never sucked her teeth or rolled her eyes or called anyone a bald-headed bitch.

The baby was attempting to stick Mrs. Rawlins's finger in its mouth.

"Yes!" said Mrs. Rawlins. "You are a *cutie!*"

"She really likes you!" said Diamonique's mother. She smiled, revealing a missing tooth that made her look more tired than tough, yet still just as eager as Michelle's mother to change the tone of the conversation.

"I was *there*," said Kaytee. "I got hit in the eye."

"But that was an accident, is my understanding of this situation," said Michelle's mother. She emphasized the articulation of each word in a way that seemed reserved for talking to white people, or possibly for talking to white people in the presence of other black people who would recognize it as a voice for talking to white people. Kaytee experienced a flicker of concern over whether the previous thought might be a form of pathologizing underserved families as *other*—that thought, plus also her suspicion that Diamonique's mother might have a repertoire of weary looks for speaking to authority figures and was maybe employing some of those here.

But a much bigger concern soon eclipsed both of these.

Mrs. Rawlins, now offering her index finger to the baby's itty-bitty hand, did not look like someone who was about to lay down the law. "Well, this does seem to have been more of a misunderstanding than a real fight."

"This was *not* a misunderstanding!" Kaytee's voice sounded younger and more shrill than she meant it to.

"Of course, the girls owe their teacher an apology."

"I'm sorry my actions caused Ms. Mahoney to fall," said Michelle.

"I'm sorry, too," said Diamonique, looking at the floor.

"All right, then, I want you two to shake hands."

The girls shook hands in a way that seemed almost congratulatory. Kaytee looked around the room in disbelief.

"Many of our beginning teachers struggle with classroom management when they first come here," Mrs. Rawlins explained to the mothers, as if she were apologizing. Then she directed a mentorly smile toward Kaytee. "In my experience, a lesson that keeps students interested can stop problems even before they start!"

"That is true." Michelle's mother nodded as if she, too, had experience planning interesting lessons that stopped problems before they started.

"For real," agreed Michelle, who had discarded the angelic smile. "Her lessons be boring sometimes."

Kaytee's heartbeat thumped in the bruise around her eye. Her jaw clamped itself shut, as if afraid of what might come out if she opened it. Then Mrs. Rawlins deposited the baby back into its mother's arms and both girls back into Kaytee's class, effective the Monday after Thanksgiving.

FACULTY ENGAGEMENT

THE PRE-HOLIDAY CROSS-DEPARTMENTAL Midyear-Assessment Data Chat (PHCDMADC for short) was conducted in the school's media center, formerly known as the library and currently the home of Creepy Mechanical Santa. This was a life-sized, motion-sensitive, dancing Santa Claus that Mrs. Reynolds-Washington had donated from her own collection of Christmas decorations. He greeted visitors by running jerkily in place and saying, "Ho ho ho! I hope you've been good this year!"

The years in the school's supply room had been rough on Santa. He'd developed some programming glitches, one of which caused him to stop midsentence, give one jerky kick, and yell, "Ho!" Other times, he would jog cheerfully, red-cheeked and smiling, for several minutes on end.

When Hernan arrived for the PHCDMADC, Creepy Mechanical Santa was in the middle of some serious cardio. The media specialist was cutting out a laminated sign that said, *Students, please stay three feet away from Santa at all times.*

"Has he been doing that all day?" Hernan asked her.

"On and off. At lunch we had a whole line of kids doing the Santa Dance like it was the Electric Slide. They got it down pretty good, but this thing is driving me crazy."

Hernan offered a sympathetic smile. On the other side of the large room, he could see teachers gathered for the meeting. The tables farthest from Mr. Scamphers had all been filled. There were a few empty seats in the front, where Maybelline Galang was watching Mr. Scamphers expectantly. And there was one seat in the middle, next to Lena.

"If you'll hurry up and take a seat, Mr. Hernandez," said Mr. Scamphers, "we're trying to get started here."

"Sorry." Hernan sat next to Lena.

"I think Santa just called me a ho," Lena whispered.

Hernan nodded. "He can be very judgmental."

Mr. Scamphers gave them a look that was meant to project authority, yet failed so spectacularly that Hernan had to force himself to think of something unfunny. He grabbed a meeting agenda from the table and squinted at it. Behind him, Creepy Mechanical Santa started jogging again. The whole group turned to see Mrs. Towner entering the room.

"Ho ho ho! Ho hoooooooooooo . . ." The sound slowed to a groan as Creepy Mechanical Santa froze with one hand extended toward Mrs. Towner.

Hernan couldn't help whispering, "You think Santa knows something about Mrs. Towner that we don't?"

Lena let out a small snort of laughter. Then she pressed the back of her hand against her lips and stared into the distance as if she, too, was trying to think of something unfunny.

"Sorry I'm late," said Mrs. Towner, taking a seat in the front and pulling out her data binder. Tiny bells adorned her shirt. They jingled as she turned around and loudly whispered, "Did y'all get my holiday e-mail?"

Lena wrote on her meeting agenda and slid it toward Hernan: *Hey, I thought that e-mail was just for me!*

"Me, too," Hernan whispered, nodding sadly.

Mrs. Towner was one of many teachers who liked to visit electronic holiday love upon her colleagues. Each December, the inboxes of Brae Hill Valley ranneth over with a cornucopia of kittens dressed as reindeer, Bible verses in large, colorful fonts, and reminders that Jesus was the reason for the season. Mrs. Towner's e-mails, especially, trended toward sentiments too personal for a group e-mail format: *May God watch over you and your lovely family. I feel blessed to have you in my life. Even if I don't say it every day, I love you.*

"As I was *saying*," said Mr. Scamphers, "data from the midyear assessments show that our students are weak on the compare-and-contrast standard. We'll be giving students a review packet to complete over winter break."

"Wait," whispered Lena, "weren't all the compare-and-contrast questions at the end of the test? Because a lot of students didn't finish."

"Well, it's nothing twenty pages of work sheets can't fix."

Mr. Scamphers turned again toward the source of the whispering. "Mr. Hernandez, I don't see your data binder."

"Sorry," said Hernan. "It's in my classroom."

Mr. Scamphers turned away with an icy look. "Well, I am happy to see that *most* of you brought your data binders."

"Oooh, you in trouble," Lena murmured, in the voice teachers used to imitate students. "Didn't you get today's all-caps e-mail about bringing our data binders?"

Hernan shook his head. "Science-fair stuff keeps filling up my inbox."

The citywide science-fair coordinator sent several updates a day to participating teachers, many of whom hit Reply All whenever they had questions. Then other participants hit Reply All to ask the original respondents to stop hitting Reply All, which drew angry responses from other people who hit Reply All to say they had planned to stay out of this, but this was getting ridiculous, and would everyone *please stop hitting Reply All?!* These e-mails, combined with holiday greetings from colleagues and multiple forwards of posts from some supposedly inspiring history teacher's blog, had filled all of Hernan's available inbox space. This prompted automatic e-mails each hour from the system administrator, reminding him that his inbox was full. As a result, Hernan had been pruning his inbox after every class, sometimes deleting things he normally would have read. Apparently, this included Mr. Scamphers's binder reminders.

"As an example to those of you who need it"—Mr. Scamphers glared at Hernan—"we'll be looking at Ms. Galang's data binder during this meeting."

At this cue, Maybelline sprang into action, standing up and raising her binder so they could all see its plastic-encased pages. Then she passed it to Mr. Scamphers like a sacred scroll.

"For real?" Lena let out a long breath and studied something on the opposite side of the room.

As Mr. Scamphers cradled the open binder in his arms, something in his moustache caught Hernan's eye. On closer inspection, the object turned out to be a large booger, which dangled ominously over the plastic sheet protectors.

"I did a few extra things, too." Maybelline was addressing them slowly, as if they might need time to take notes. "I subdivided the names by standard. Then I color-coded the students' names based on how they did on each specific standard."

"This is beautiful, Ms. Galang, just beautiful," said Mr. Scamphers. Then, turning to the unwashed horde of teachers who were not Maybelline Galang, he added, "This is an example of the sense of urgency I'd like to see from all of you regarding these binders."

Maybelline confirmed this with a grave nod. Mr. Scamphers, perhaps because of his own sense of urgency regarding the matter, had begun breathing heavily. This caused the moustache booger to flutter, its rhythm lining up perfectly with that of Creepy Mechanical Santa, who, for reasons known only to him, had resumed jogging.

Hernan looked around to see if anyone else had noticed the booger, but most of his colleagues were now thumbing through their own inferior data binders. Breyonna was looking at a bridal magazine in her lap. Kaytee was examining her eye in a makeup mirror. Lena, who was still trying hard not to look at Maybelline, was staring in rapt concentration at Creepy Mechanical Santa.

As a result, only Hernan saw the moment when the booger finally sprang loose from Mr. Scamphers's moustache and landed on one of the sheet-protected, color-coded pages of Maybelline's exemplary data binder. It would remain there, Hernan imagined, like a pressed flower, until another meeting prompted Maybelline to display it once again.

Which was why, by the time Mr. Scamphers replaced the binder on the table and looked up, Hernan was hurrying out the door of the media center, both hands over his mouth, laughing so hard tears streamed from his eyes.

"I hope you've been good this year," called Creepy Mechanical Santa behind him.

THE
CROSS-DISCIPLINARY
COMPARE-AND-CONTRAST
HOLIDAY REVIEW PACKET

THE LAST REVIEW packets had been tucked into book bags, the last bell had rung, and the school had emptied out for winter break. Dr. Barrios should have felt relieved.

Instead, he paced the newly empty hallways, filled with apprehension.

He and his wife had gone to the theater last night. There had been a local preview of *How the Status Quo Stole Christmas*, "the story of one man's heroic efforts to beat the odds and save a city's schools."

The trailers had been on TV for weeks. In them, Nick Wallabee knelt next to the desks of an enthralled Mexican girl and delighted African American boy while a caption flashed across the bottom of the screen: *The status quo says Consuelo and Jamal don't deserve an education. Who will stand up and say they do?*

Cut to: Nick Wallabee striding through school hallways, Nick Wallabee speaking passionately into a microphone, Nick Wallabee standing outside the school administration building, the sun bathing him in a prophetic glow. Even in the trailers, the scene was uncomfortably familiar. And so maybe Dr. Barrios should have known exactly what he'd see in that movie theater. Maybe he even did.

But that didn't mean he was prepared.

Sneaking looks at the audience around him, Dr. Barrios saw the expressions of the thousands who would soon be watching the movie throughout the country. Maybe millions. There were projections that the documentary's success would rival some of the biggest hits in the inspiring-teacher genre, maybe even reaching the level of *Show Me You Care and I'll Show You My Homework*.

Mr. Weber swore this was only because of the marketing budget provided by Global Schoolhouse Productions, but it wasn't just that. Even Dr. Barrios had to admit the movie had a way of grabbing one by the emotional jugular vein and holding on tight. There was the scene, for example, in which Jamal helped his grandmother rise from her wheelchair, and then later the montage of Consuelo feeding and caring for a stray puppy, all to the soundtrack of a children's choir singing "Wind Beneath My Wings." By the end, when Nick Wallabee showed up at an elementary school to pass out books, the whole audience was sniffing back tears.

But the most famous moment of the film, the moment that would get picked up by TV shows and referenced endlessly, was when Nick Wallabee, standing in front of the school administration building, delivered his iconic lines to the principal of a failing school.

I'm expecting school leaders to stand up for student achievement, not just sit in the stands defending the status quo.

Dr. Barrios felt his wife's smooth palm covering his hand in the darkness.

We've got too many students who can win on the football field but not in college and the workforce.

The audience knew what was coming and leaned toward the screen to receive it.

I ask you, Dr. Barrios: Are you a leader who will do whatever it takes to win for children? With that, Nick Wallabee strode away in his lean, tailored suit. Only the principal remained on-screen, heavy and uncomfortable and covering his face, his armpit gushing as if the very idea of believing in children activated his sweat glands.

The visual metaphor was unmistakable: Transformational change vs. the status quo.

David vs. Goliath.

Compare and contrast.

SATURDAY, DECEMBER 24

KAYTEE'S MOTHER WAS calling from the kitchen, but Kaytee stood where she was, glaring at her father. "See? That's what I mean. Why does it matter what *color* they are?"

"Hey, I can't help it if they were black." Her father reclined in his chair, hands up as if to show the situation was out of his control. "If it was a group of white kids skipping in line, cursing, and throwing popcorn, I would have said *white kids*."

"*Would* you have?"

Silence.

"I mean it. Do you really think you would mention their race if they were white?"

"Well"—Roy Mahoney's eyelids drooped as if expressing something so obvious it didn't take much energy—"it so happens they *weren't*."

It had seemed like a good idea, at the time, to suggest that her parents see *How the Status Quo Stole Christmas*; some of her father's favorite rants were about *worthless unionized bureaucrats in the public sector*, which meant the film promised a small patch of common ground for table talk at Christmas Eve dinner. Maybe it would even help her parents understand why she was so passionate about educational inequity—or at least why she couldn't stand Mr. Weber. How could Kaytee have known, when she made the recommendation, that they would end up at a theater with a group of black teenagers who happened to be behaving badly and that this would loom larger in Robin and Roy Mahoney's memories than anything about the actual film?

Then again, this proved her point exactly. "See what I mean? Imagine living in a country where every time you do anything wrong, your race is mentioned. You can't just be a *kid* at a movie theater making noise or skipping in line. You have to be the *black* kid. And rather than make any effort to understand your world view, those in the majority just write off your whole *culture* as—"

"Kaytee! I said come help me carry this pie."

Kaytee gave an exasperated sigh as she headed into the kitchen. Her mother handed her a freshly baked apple pie, along with a hard stare that said all she wanted was to have a nice holiday dinner with Kaytee, Kaytee's brother, Cuyler, and Aunt Susan and avoid another scene like the one at Thanksgiving, and was that too much to ask?

"Sorry," Kaytee muttered. "I'm trying."

"Try harder."

Fine. She would try. Kaytee returned to the dining room and placed the pie on the table, smiling sweetly at everyone except her father. "Pie, anyone?"

But Roy, who had not been in the kitchen to receive his wife's warning look, wasn't done. "How about this: Maybe after a long week of rolling up my sleeves and breaking my back at work, I want to spend my hard-earned money on a movie and enjoy it. Maybe that's *my* right. Or are people like me not allowed to have rights anymore?"

People like me, as her father used the term, were white men with white-collar jobs who used manual-labor imagery to demonstrate their work ethic. Roy Mahoney wasn't afraid to *get his hands dirty* or use *a little elbow grease* at the regional distribution-management job he'd earned *with his own sweat*. That was how he *kept a roof over their heads* in this meticulously exclusive suburb and how he *put food on the table*, the biggest threat to his ability to do so being the swarthy swarm of diverse "others" baying at the windows about their "rights."

Kaytee was trying. She really was. But she couldn't help herself. "Are you assuming *they* didn't pay for their tickets with hard-earned money? Or is everyone automatically on welfare if they're not a distribution manager for some *meat* company?" Then again, the meat-company thing was probably the wrong way to go. She already knew how that conversation went, and she wasn't even a vegetarian anymore.

"Right—the meat company that paid for your college, so you could go work at a school where the kids punch the teachers in the eye."

"Roy, please," said Kaytee's mother, who had materialized at the door of the kitchen. "We said after Thanksgiving that we weren't going to bring up the eye again."

But of course he would bring up the eye. Roy Mahoney could never understand it was like on the *front lines* in the fight for educational equity. Kaytee had an urge to press the spot where her bruise had been, just to see if she could still feel the pain. Over Thanksgiving, when the bruise was still fresh and she'd had to explain it to her family, it had been a symbol of Mrs. Rawlins's unfairness, but now it seemed like a *battle scar*. A *medal of honor*. From the *trenches*.

"Dinner was great, Mom!" The moral high ground had shifted to not ruining the holiday for her mother, and Kaytee was determined to occupy it, even under fire.

But she hadn't counted on Aunt Susan joining in. "Kay, I just want to say I think what you're doing is great. It's like my charity work in church: Even though you know a lot of these kids are hopeless, you're still out there doing your best."

"Thanks, Aunt Susan, but teaching isn't charity work."

"Yeah." Cuyler jumped in. "They pay her like three whole dollars an hour."

"Mmm, good pie!" Kaytee refused to let her brother get to her today.

"Anyway," Kaytee's mother added, "it's not like this is forever. She went to one of the best colleges in the country, for heaven's sake." She placed a placating hand on her husband's arm. "The law-school recruitment letters are still coming in. These two years with TeachCorps are more like . . . a stepping stone."

Kaytee knew her mother was only trying to help. She knew she was about to make a scene. And yet she could not stop herself.

"No!" She pushed her chair back and stood to face her parents. "Teaching is not a stepping stone! And, no, Aunt Susan, these kids are not *hopeless*."

"And, Cuyler, you want to know what I make?" She held her brother's gaze for a thick moment. "*I* make a *difference*."

This was a line from a poem Mrs. Towner had e-mailed her, but hearing herself say it aloud, to her brother of all people, filled her with such a sense of power that she whipped back to face her mother and father again. "For your information, I *am* going to teach forever. You can throw out the law-school letters."

With that, she stormed out of the dining room and down the hall to the dark office that had once been her bedroom. She hadn't finished her pie, but she didn't care. A sense of purpose that had been knocked out of her during the fight had finally returned.

From the dining room, she could hear her mother's concerned voice, too muffled for Kaytee to make out the words.

Then her father's angry roar: "Sometimes you just want to go to a goddamned quiet movie theater!"

Kaytee logged in to her blog for the first time in weeks. She wasn't going anywhere. As she wrote, she absentmindedly pressed the area under her eye.

SUNDAY, DECEMBER 25

HUNTSVILLE, TEXAS, WAS home to forty thousand people and nine prisons. A fifth of its residents were directly employed by the Texas Department of Criminal Justice. Others guided tours at the prison museum, or sold barbecue, or manned the gas stations where families stocked up on snacks after visiting incarcerated relatives. Anyone else who worked worked at Walmart.

The Ray family had always lived in housing provided at reduced cost to prison guards. They moved from time to time, but the houses looked the same and always ended up smelling the same: like a combination of Kentucky Fried Chicken, cigarettes lit from the kitchen stove, and several cats that came and went as they pleased. These had been the smells of Coach Ray's childhood. Not that anyone here called him Coach Ray. Inside the Huntsville town limits, he became Samson Ray Jr., former corrections officer. Son of Samson Ray Sr., current corrections officer. Brother of Dale Ray, corrections officer currently on administrative leave. SJ for short.

Samson Jr. knew better than to expect a greeting from Dale, who kept his eyes fixed on the TV as if no one had entered the room.

His father acknowledged him with a curt, "Hey."

"Brought y'all some shirts." Samson Jr. handed them the stack of Killer Armadillos gear he'd brought from his apartment.

"I ain't wearing this bullshit," said Dale.

"They're for the kids."

"My kids got their own shirts from their own school." Dale tossed the shirts on the couch in a lump, though Samson Jr. expected the kids would end up wearing them anyway. In Dale's house, the need for clean laundry eventually overrode matters of principle.

When Samson Jr. and Dale had been in high school, the counselors gave talks each year about the warning signs of *hypervigilance*. That was the official term for how people acted when their job included a real risk of being doused by urine, or bitten by someone who might have hepatitis C, or attacked by a prisoner who'd been taken off psych meds to save the prison some cash.

Their father had been a mean drunk, though he'd mellowed out some as he'd gotten older. For Dale, it was a good day if he was only drunk. On top of this, Dale's mental alarm system was always scanning for signs that Samson Jr., coaching in the *Negro league* in the city, thought he was better'n everyone back home. Which, truth be told, Samson Jr. did. The one thing football had surely done for him was keep him from becoming Dale.

It had taken a long time to do anything else.

Like many of his teammates who'd busted out of their hometowns on athletic scholarships, Samson Jr. had taken the easiest classes in the easiest major, keeping his grades just high enough to play. He was sure he'd go pro at the end of it all. Instead, he'd found himself back in Huntsville, degree hanging limp in his hand, working a prison-guard job he could have gotten right out of high school. It was the future no Huntsville kid ever dreamed of but most of them ended up with.

And so he gave himself back to Huntsville, piece by piece. He began making late-night visits to a girl named Cici, who'd had a crush on him before he left and saw his return as an act of romantic fate. The fact that Samson Jr. never called her his girlfriend, that he never took her anywhere, that the Ray family had a long tradition of men who resented women for roping them into relationships in the first place: These were details that could be overlooked in the name of destiny. Cici seemed sure they were falling in love and would one day build a happy family surrounded by prison walls.

"Women will be your downfall," Samson Sr. warned, three beers into any given night. "Soon's one of them says she wants to get married, you best run the other way. Otherwise she'll get pregnant and get you stuck with her."

Sure enough, after a year of fielding late-night phone calls and visits, Cici announced she was pregnant.

"Told ya," said Samson Sr.

It had never been the physical violence of prison guarding that bothered Samson Jr. Confrontation kept him from getting bored. Restraining inmates didn't feel much different from the challenges of football. If anything, it was an outlet for the frustration of being back home.

It was the stark racial divide of the corrections system that got to him. Samson Jr.'s college years had been a brotherhood of sweat and sacrifice that included many black teammates. Guys from Detroit and North Memphis and the South Side of Chicago all brought the same heart, the same willingness to block for him when necessary. And he recognized in them, on some wordless level, the same tight knot of fears he'd taught himself to crush down and outrun. After four years away, he no longer felt at home in the world of meaty white guards whose incomes flowed from the prison's existence and the mostly black and brown convicts who would lose their years behind its walls.

He never was much of a father to baby Britney, and after a while, Cici gave up on him and married *a real adult*, a guy who'd gone to their high school and now worked for the prison system as an elevator inspector. It was then that Samson Ray Jr. moved away, heading two hours away to become Coach Ray of the Killer Armadillos.

He hadn't made it to the NFL. But at least he'd escaped from prison.

Cici, Britney, and Jim the elevator inspector lived in a real house, financed through a program that helped responsible prison employees *achieve the American dream of home ownership*. The real house had a real Christmas tree in one corner, plus Christmas tree–scented candles in most of the other corners, combining to create a Christmas aroma so thick it felt like an assault.

Britney was playing video games with her cousin on the living room carpet. She didn't look up until Cici said, "Put that thing on pause and go say hello to—"The sentence finished with a hand wave. She had long ago stopped encouraging Britney to call Samson Jr. anything fatherly.

Britney sighed as she pushed herself off the floor. Her nails were long and painted a color he hadn't known nail polish came in. Several bracelets jingled as she greeted him with a stiff-elbowed hug. He was struck by the changes in her. The adults in Huntsville looked the same every year. If anything, they were a little fatter and more tired around the eyes. Britney, on the other hand, seemed new each time he saw her. She was old enough to be one of his students now, with a near-completeness that made him wish he knew what the hell to say to her. Maybe the words existed that could make up for these years of being a stranger, a gesture of her mother's hand. But he did not know them.

"You got tall," he said.

"Yeah. That happens."

"Well, I didn't know what you wanted for Christmas, but I figured girls your age like to shop for themselves, anyway."

Samson waited for confirmation of this statement, but Britney just stared at him from under thin dashes of eyebrows.

He opened his wallet and handed her a hundred-dollar bill. "Just your size, right?"

"Great. Thanks." Britney tucked the bill into the pocket of her jeans, which showed off several inches of her skinny teenager's back as she lowered herself onto the floor and restarted the game.

Jim the elevator inspector came into the living room.

"Hey. You want a beer or something?" It was clear this was not really an offer. Rather, it was the type of thing expected of upright men who owned their homes and kept their yards clean.

"Nah, thanks. Just came by to say merry Christmas to everyone."

"All right, well, you have a good one, now."

"Look, Dad," called Britney from the floor. "I'm winning the game!"

"Nice job," began Samson Jr., but he quickly fell silent.

She was talking to Jim.

"Nice job," said Jim, reaching down to squeeze Britney's shoulder.

The three adults stood for a moment, surrounded by the Christmas tree's light and the video game's cheerful music.

"So," said Cici, "I'll walk you out?"

On the front porch, she pulled out a cigarette. "Anything going on with you?"

"Just football."

Cici laughed. "I guess that's still your whole life, huh?" She seemed hopeful that the answer would be yes.

"Yeah, you know me." The truth was, things weren't really going all that well. The Armadillos hadn't made it to the championship after all, and now there was this new movie out about how kids played too much football and were failing their classes, which made Daren Grant feel even more comfortable sitting through practices and typing his secret notes.

But Samson Jr. wasn't about to discuss these things with Cici. "How's everything here?"

"Great," said Cici. "Britney's doing great."

"Yeah. Looks like you're doing a great job with her."

"A lot of it is Jim," said Cici. "He's really been a . . . you know, a figure for her."

"Right. Seems like it." Samson Jr.'s hand crept toward his pocket.

"There is something I wanted to talk to you about, though." Cici took a long drag on her cigarette and squinted into the distance.

"Anything you need." He pulled out the stack of bills he'd brought for just this moment. Every family had a holiday tradition, and this was theirs. Cici would gently poke at his shittiness as a father, making sure to add that child-support checks didn't nearly cover the cost of raising a kid, and after a while he would give her an extra few hundred bucks. That always shut her up and cleared him until the next year.

But this time, Cici waved the money away. "I'm not asking for money, SJ."

"Okay." He kept the bills in his hand, just in case.

"Seriously, we don't need it. Jim just got a promotion."

"Nice. So he's what now, an elevator inspector *inspector*?"

There was a time Cici would have laughed at this, or anything Samson Jr. said, no matter how stupid. But that time had long passed.

"Look, SJ, I don't hate you anymore. I'm not even mad at you. But Jim and I have been talking for a while now, about . . . I mean, he really has raised Britney. We might as well make it official."

"What's that supposed to mean?"

"Adoption paperwork's all done. We just need you to sign."

Here, again, he was supposed to say something, and probably should have, and probably wanted to, but instead his inner game face turned on, blocking out any reaction. "Well, okay. If that's what y'all want to do."

"And you don't need to stop by on Christmas anymore."

"Oh. Okay."

"Not that anyone will notice much of a difference."

The money was still in his hand. Unsure what to do with it, he held it out to Cici.

She pushed it away in disgust. "I guess maybe if Britney were someone you could teach to run with a helmet on, you'd care more, right?"

"I should probably go. Got a long drive home."

He drove fast. The suffocating mixture of smells from the two Huntsville homes lingered on his clothes, following him back to his apartment like a restless spirit.

Whenever the Killer Armadillos lost a game, Coach Ray could not even look at televised football. But as he sat on his couch and flipped through the channels, he hungered for the background noise of commentators, the scoreboard that made it clear who was winning, who was losing, and by how much.

He'd had to cancel his ESPN subscription to get his truck fixed. Such was the life of a high-school football coach paying double child support. But never had its absence weighed upon him so heavily. He would have been fine watching any sport, really. Boxing highlights would have done the trick. Baseball. Even golf.

But nothing was on but a bunch of stupid family Christmas movies. Damned basic cable.

MONDAY, DECEMBER 26

"HAPPY DAY AFTER** Jesus's Birthday!" said Lena's father.

"Happy Day After Jesus's Birthday," Lena and her mother echoed, their wine glasses clinking in the half-empty restaurant.

This was the closest thing the Wrights had to a holiday tradition. On December 26, when most of the country was home eating leftovers, it was easy to get in to the type of restaurant where it was, as her mother liked to say, *just impossible to get a reservation.* Flying on Christmas Day was also less of a hassle, and so ever since Lena had started college, she'd joined the planes full of Asians, Muslims, and Orthodox Jews who flew on Christian holidays. This year, she'd taken the last flight out.

So you're going to Philly, huh? I guess I can't bring you over for the holidays, then. Nex had said this three weeks earlier as they'd lain together, their heads on the same pillow, staring up at a poster she'd taped to her ceiling. It was the first night he'd ever shared a poem he was working on.

Racially charged rhetoric results in mass incarceration / Prisons locking up our prophets with a profit motivation . . .

Lena remembered only pieces of the poem. It was the night itself she'd relived in detail, until lines of poetry had become linked in her memory with lines from the conversation that surrounded it. This verbal remix played in her head even now, as she stared at the menu in a formerly abandoned music club, reborn during gentrification as a soul food–inspired bistro.

Lately, she'd begun imagining Nex's reaction to her daily activities. It almost felt as if he were hovering over her shoulder, a hologram. This was fine, even motivating, when she was in front of a class. But here, holding a menu that for real contained the phrases *nouveau neck bone* and *drizzle of chitlin reduction*, she cringed. Breyonna had it wrong: The trendiest, most expensive restaurants did not serve filet mignon. They served artisanal versions of the food poor people ate.

"So," Lena's mother was saying when Lena tuned back in to the conversation, "I guess the other teachers at your school must resent you for working so hard."

"What? No—why would they?" But it was too late. They were on this again.

Her parents had seen *How the Status Quo Stole Christmas* the day it came out. They took it for granted that she was one of the good teachers Nick Wallabee claimed he would put in every classroom. With Nex hovering over her shoulder, this detail became as frivolous and humiliating as the restaurant itself. Only the most progressive, educated parents assumed their children were solving the problems of the world.

Raised to represent the real with dreams unrealized / raw grip on reality rarely recognized / boxed into shadow boxes before we ever commit a crime / told, This is where your road ends unless you learn to dunk or rhyme. Lena had read a book about private prisons and had almost mentioned it at that moment. But then she didn't. She'd long imagined a scene like this one, the two of them sharing poetry in the dark. It felt important to tread lightly.

Again, her mother's voice: "Well, considering the quality of teaching they've been getting away with, they're probably worried about any challenge to the status quo."

"The teachers at my school are fine," said Lena. "I've never met anyone like the teachers described in that movie." This wasn't entirely true. Mr. Comodio was pretty bad. But there were more than a hundred other teachers at her school who were fine, plus the inaccuracies in the movie would have taken all night to explain, and moreover, she was desperate to get off the subject before the waitress, who seemed always within inches of their table, arrived with their food.

"Here we have the braised neck bone and grits with fatback essence, and the slow-roasted pig foot garnished with one flash-fried collard green leaf."The waitress placed tiny plates in front of Lena's parents.

"And the catfish for you, ma'am." She had a respectable Afro and a calculated subservience in her voice, and was pretty enough that Lena imagined Nex's hologram watching her with approval. "Don't worry. It's not spicy."

So you're going to Philly, huh? I guess I can't bring you over for the holidays, then. It was the day after this that Lena had bought her plane tickets, choosing the last flight out on Christmas. But when she mentioned her late flight time, Nex had not repeated the invitation.

This morning, she'd sent a quick *hope-your-holiday-was-good* message, carefully crafted not to sound like she was demanding a response. Now she wondered if she should have just waited to hear from him. Or maybe she had sent her own text too early in the morning, and Nex, after a long night of partying with his family, was still recovering. Or *had* he texted her? Maybe she just hadn't heard her phone inside her purse. Her father considered it a crime of restaurant etiquette to check a cell phone at the table.

She excused herself to the bathroom, phone cupped in her hand.

No new messages.

"I definitely agree with what that superintendent says about football, though," her father was saying when she returned to the table. They were still on the documentary. "These students are risking concussions for a negligible chance to make it in professional sports, and in the long run, no one ever makes it in football. You should see the statistics."

"I always say football is for boys whose mothers don't love them!" said Lena's mother, laughing. She did, in fact, always say this when the topic of football came up.

"It's really a sport that exploits kids whose parents don't have high-paying jobs and can't afford to—"

The waitress was heading toward the table again.

"Can we talk about something else?" begged Lena.

"How's everybody doing here?" said the waitress.

"Just talking about football," said Mr. Wright, with a wink at his wife.

"Oh, yeah?"The waitress brightened, this time in a way that seemed genuine. "My son is a wide receiver at his high school. I told him, *Boy, you better get some scholarship money off of that, because college is expensive.*"

"*She* teaches high school!" said Lena's mother, pointing to Lena.

"Really." The waitress's smile seemed to cool back into potential-tip-inspired enthusiasm. "Where do you teach?"

"It's in Texas," said Lena, relieved that she did not teach in Philadelphia—in addition to the city's having a notoriously broke school system, this would have left her at risk of actually meeting one of her students' parents under these circumstances.

"In the inner city!" added her mother.

Lena tried to mentally compress Nex Level's hologram, as if forcing a genie back into a lamp. She could not let the reality of this moment touch the memory of their last night together. Near the end of the night, she'd finally made some comments on the poem. She'd been conscious of his eyes on her as she spoke, and wondered if he sensed, as she did, the possibility of their combined energy on stage.

You're smart, you know that? And you got a beautiful smile.

Thanks . . . I try.

Did you have braces?

"Texas"—the waitress's voice pulled her back to the restaurant table—"didn't they just make a movie about the schools down there?"

The look Lena gave her parents said, *Please don't.*

Finally, they finished dinner and stepped out onto the snowy sidewalk.

A driver picked them up at the corner and wished them a merry Christmas, though his name and accent suggested he might not celebrate Christmas, either.

Lena checked her phone again, more out of habit than hopefulness. But this time, a new message glowed at the top of the screen. Her heart jumped. She must have been in such a rush to get out of the restaurant that she hadn't felt the vibration.

Hope ur having a great time in philly. love ya.

Love? He'd said *love!*

He probably didn't mean it exactly like that, of course. And she had no intention of saying it back. Or, if she did, she'd say something borderline, like *You, too.*

Anyway, there was time to think about it. After hours of waiting on her end, it was Nex's turn to wait for an answer. She put the phone back in her purse.

But still, he'd said *love*!

The inside of the car was toasty as the Wright family glided through the evening snow. They were far from the restaurant now, and Lena felt something wash over her that felt almost like holiday spirit. *Love.*

"Thanks for dinner," she said to her parents, "and happy Day After Jesus's Birthday!"

She caught the driver's eye as he looked at her in the rearview mirror.

JESUS HAD BEEN conspicuously absent from the Hernandez household during Christmas. Hernan's older sister, Mayra, had made repeated phone calls, leaving drunker and angrier messages each time. *Your son is here waiting for you*, she'd yelled into the phone, *in case you care!* There had been no response.

But on New Year's Eve, Jesus returned. With a giant blue bottle of tequila in each hand, he slid open the door from the backyard, letting in a draft of *cumbia*, loud voices, and air bursting with the smells of grilled chicken and meat.

"What up, Jaime Escalante!" Jesus thought it was hilarious to compare Hernan to the balding, middle-aged math teacher from the movie *Stand and Deliver*.

"What up, Speedy Gonzalez." Jesus had once been pulled over for speeding on the way home from traffic court, where he'd been handling another speeding ticket.

As Hernan's nephew ran in from the living room to greet his father, Hernan went to the kitchen, where Mayra was washing dishes. "Speedy Gonzalez is here. Did you know he was coming?"

"Yeah," said Mayra.

"Okay, then."

Mayra's wet hand grabbed his sleeve as he turned to leave the room.

"Listen," she whispered, "don't say anything about Christmas, okay?

It was a misunderstanding. We squashed it already, and Jayden's really excited to see him."

"Hey," Hernan held up his hands like a player avoiding an out-of-bounds ball. "That's your business."

"Speaking of business, did Papi tell you about the bluebonnet thing?"

"No. What?"

"Ask him. You know I don't know nothing about plants."

The two siblings fell silent as Jesus entered the kitchen. He put the tequila bottles on the kitchen table and waited for Mayra to turn around, but she had started scouring dishes with great concentration. Chito, the Hernandezes' pit-bull-mixed-with-some-smaller-dog, came into the kitchen and pressed his face into the side of Hernan's leg.

"Damn, Hernan," Jesus said. "Y'all still got that Chihuahua-wannabe pit bull?"

"You know it," said Hernan, scratching behind Chito's ear.

"Surprised they even let you in the dog park with that thing."

"Surprised they let you come back over the border with that much cologne on."

Mayra let out a laugh without turning from the sink.

"I see someone's in a good mood." Jesus turned his attention to Mayra and wrapped his arms around her from behind. Then he kissed the side of her head and spun her so she could see the two bottles on the table. "I brought a little something back from Mexico for you, *mi amor*."

Mayra leaned into his embrace noncommittally. Hernan sensed that she wanted privacy and started to leave again, but Lety was already on her way into the kitchen, accompanied by her blond skater-dude boyfriend, Geoffrey.

"Whassssuuuuuuuppp!" said Geoffrey.

"Hey, Gee-off," said Hernan.

"Hey, Gee-off," said Mayra.

"What up, Jerk-off?" said Jesus.

"What up, homes?!" Geoff reached out to Jesus for a proactive bro hug, which Jesus headed off with a fist bump.

There were a number of things Hernan and Mayra found irritating about Geoff, the first being that he verbally pronounced both the E and the O in his name. Even more annoying was his habit of flitting around Jesus like a fruit fly near a ripe banana.

"Bro! I've been meaning to talk to you about . . . that thing." Geoff thought he was very secretive about the fact that he bought weed from Jesus.

Mayra scrubbed aggressively at a pan in the sink.

"Okay, but later," said Jesus. "I'm with my lady right now."

"Yeah, man. Yeah. Sure. No hurry. But later, right?"

"He just said that, Geee-off," said Mayra.

"Cool." Geoff looked around the kitchen. "Hey, who brought the tequila?"

"I did." Jesus was warming to the distraction. "Straight from Meh-hee-co."

"Hell, yeah! Is there a worm in it?" Geoff adjusted his man headband excitedly.

"Tequila doesn't always have a worm in it, Geeee-off," said Mayra.

"Sometimes it does." Lety's voice tightened with baby-sister defensiveness.

Geoff was too focused on the tequila bottles and Jesus's attention to be fazed. "So, we getting started on some shots or what?"

"Why not? It's New Year's Eve, right?" Jesus unwrapped his arms from Mayra.

Lety got out glasses and cut a lime from a bowl on the table. Jesus poured portions of clear liquid into the glasses.

"*Saludos!*" said Geoff as he held out his glass to Jesus.

Mayra raised an eyebrow at him.

"Hey, remember my friend Maritza?" Lety asked Hernan, changing the subject. "From when we used to throw parties at Club Seven? I saw her the other day, and she asked about you."

"The one with all the Hello Kitty stuff?" asked Hernan.

Mayra nodded. "And the Precious Moments collection."

"Who cares?" said Lety. "She's pretty. And I think she likes Hernan."

"If she's cute, who cares?" said Jesus. "That's your problem, Jaime Escalante. You're too picky."

Geeee-off laughed a bit too enthusiastically.

Mayra shot Jesus a chilly look.

"Just trying to help," said Jesus. "We got to get Jaime Escalante here a girlfriend."

Geoff cackled as he grabbed a tortilla chip. "For real, homey!" A piece of the chip fell on the floor as he bit into it, and Chito scrambled over to retrieve it.

Geoff squinted at the dog. Then he turned to Hernan with a flash of inspiration in his eyes. "Bro! For real, though, you know what you should do? Get a skateboard and have your dog pull you down the street on your skateboard. Any chick will fuck you if she meets you while your dog is pulling you on a skateboard." Geoff glanced over to gauge Jesus's reaction.

"Don't curse in my parents' house, Geeeee-off," said Mayra. "I already told you that before."

"Sorry. Tequila's kind of kicking in. This is some good shhh . . . sttuff."

"And how do you know that, anyway?" asked Lety. "About the skateboard?"

"My friend told me," said Geoff. There was a careful architecture to the word *friend*, leaving just enough room for the possibility of air quotes.

Hernan took his tequila to go, making his way through the rest of the party. Even with an uncle in Iraq and two cousins in Afghanistan, the Hernandezes had an overflowing New Year's Eve crowd. Texas's winter weather was the payoff for its sweaty summers, and the temperature was perfect. Music played. Meat sizzled. Eyes and teeth sparkled under the lights that lit the yard.

Hernan found his father in a folding chair against the fence, laughing at a joke someone had just told. His face turned weary when Hernan asked about the bluebonnets. For Hernandez Landscaping and Plant Nursery, the first few months of each year bustled with orders for the flowers, which bloomed in March and reached their full, blue-violet glory near the end of April. Lately, though, rust-colored dots had begun appearing on the saplings, growing into larger circles until they hollowed out the leaves and shriveled the stems. When crews rushed out to replace the flowers, the new ones soon developed the same tiny spots. It wasn't just the Hernandezes, either. The infection was spreading fast, threatening to make the year a brutal one for Texas gardeners.

Hernan promised he would try to help, though he wished he'd learned about the problem earlier in the holiday break. With more time, he could have buried himself among the rows of plants, sampling leaves and studying them under the microscope he kept in the nursery office. But school started in two days.

As it was, there was barely enough time to get his lesson plans in order, and he'd promised to help his nephew with the compare-and-contrast packet his third-grade teacher had given him. Apparently, the compare-and-contrast questions had been at the end of *all* the TCUP pre-tests. The resulting data dictated that every kid in the district needed to practice the skill of comparing and contrasting, which in reality just meant circling the keywords listed in the packet.

A paragraph that compared was likely to contain the terms *alike, all, also, both, have in common, share, similar, the same as*.

A paragraph that contrasted would say *contrary, even though, however, opposite, on the other hand, unlike, yet*.

Anyone who found enough of these terms, the test-prep logic went, would know what kind of paragraph they were reading. They'd figure out the rest from there.

On the last night of a break, teachers often reported similar dreams. Common themes included showing up to school in pajamas or bathrobes, waking up late, or completely forgetting how to get to the school, taking a string of wrong turns in unfamiliar terrain.

Another shared nightmare involved schedule changes. In these, teachers learned they'd be teaching classes of several hundred students in enormous, irregularly-shaped rooms, or on open fields where even the loudest of voices would be lost in the wind. In time, they would all settle back into their familiar routines. Their shared dread would recede as they realized they had not, in fact, forgotten how to teach over vacation. Still, on that last night they would all sleep fitfully, checking their clocks in panic and twisting their sheets into ropes. Most would wake the next morning in similar states of crankiness, powering through the day on coffee and adrenaline.

Hernan, on the other hand, experienced exactly the opposite. Unlike his colleagues, he slept soundly and woke the next morning remembering no dreams at all.

WHATEVER
IT TAKES
TO WIN!

THE LARGE CHAIR in which Dr. Barrios sat probably looked comfortable on camera. Next to him, on a decorative end table, rested a pitcher of water and an empty glass. They mocked his thirst, daring him to pour himself a drink. Not a chance. He could already imagine the headline: "Failing Administrator Drinks as Students Thirst for Knowledge." Underneath would be a photo of him holding a glass of water, leaning back in this too-soft chair, on this too-bright stage, in front of these too-excited audience members selected by the Education Sensation TV producers.

Already, he had submitted to a coating of heavy, chalklike powder in the makeup room. Now he sat next to the other two panelists on the stage, a teacher's-union representative and one actual teacher, avoiding eye contact with the camera.

Host Melinda Morningside was still reading from the teleprompter, her head straight, her torso angled slightly forward. "If you're just joining us, this is Education Sensation TV, and we want to hear *your* voice. Please tweet to us using the hashtag EdSensationTV. Again, we have a tweet here from someone who saw the documentary and says the status quo is unacceptable! And here next to me is a teacher here who agrees with that completely."

It was not, in fact, clear what the teacher thought of the tweet. Melinda had cut her off as soon as she'd begun speaking. "Actually, that's not exactly—"

"But now we want to hear what *you* have to say!" If Melinda Morningside noticed the interruption, she hid it well. "We've equipped each seat with a computerized voting clicker, generously provided by Global Schoolhouse Teachnology! Thanks to Global Schoolhouse Teachnology, everyone in our audience can vote on the question on this screen: How important *is* our children's success?"

The audience fumbled with the gadgets next to their seats. A crowd-participation reporter put down his microphone to help those with their hands raised. The teacher was crossing her arms, clearly frustrated, but Dr. Barrios did not feel sorry for her. He hoped his own time in the spotlight would be equally short. *Please*, he thought, *let Melinda Morningside cut me off.* No follow-up questions. No chances to make the crowd angry.

The whole setup reminded him of the megachurch TV programs his mother had watched when he was in high school, after she got sick. Sinners, nonbelievers, and people with all manner of afflictions would climb to the stage, where the famous preacher would release the Holy Spirit into their bodies. The force was always so strong they fell backward, into the arms of strong men who stood waiting to catch them. It had seemed like a lot of pressure. What would happen to the one person whom the Holy Spirit did not knock off his feet? Did he just have to stand there, unsaved, in front of all those hopeful people? But they always fell. The crowds always broke into euphoric applause. His mother always smiled weakly at the TV, nodding as she smoothed the blanket over her knees.

Several more Education Sensation staff members were now in the audience helping with the voting clickers. A man with headphones held up three fingers, counting down silently as Melinda swiveled back to the camera.

"While we're waiting for our audience to weigh in on this important question, let's hear from our next panelist"—her smile disappeared and she shook her head slowly, narrowing her eyes—"a representative from the teachers' union."

A round of boos came from the audience.

Unshaken, the union rep smiled and leaned her own torso toward the camera.

Melinda Morningside's face, meanwhile, had become a photogenic mask of disgust. "It looks like everyone here is wondering why your union is willing to rob children of their futures just to defend the status quo."

"Melinda, I'm glad you asked, because if there is one thing our union definitely cares about, it's kids! That why it's more important than ever to say no to one-size-fits-all, cookie-cutter solutions and save public education." She shoveled in the last phrase before anyone cut her off. Then she smiled, back straight, like an Olympic gymnast who'd just finished a perfect routine.

Dr. Barrios marveled at her composure.

Melinda Morningside had turned so far away from the union rep she had to speak into a different camera. "So, I guess the real question is, do we care more about the rights of adults or the rights of our students to get an education? We know what this union representative thinks"— here, she paused and made the most ladylike version of a gagging noise Dr. Barrios had ever heard—"but I think it's time to hear from *you*, our studio audience. Thanks to Global Schoolhouse Teachnology, your survey votes have been counted. Let's see here." She looked up at a screen above Dr. Barrios's head. "It looks like ninety-eight percent of you said our children's success is either important or *very* important! Wow, this is an audience that cares about kids! Please, everyone, give yourselves a hand for caring about kids so much!"

They did.

Dr. Barrios snuck a look at the teleprompter, which said, *Pause for Level 5 applause.* Even the audience's reaction was part of the script.

And just like that, Dr. Barrios understood why the union rep looked so calm. She already knew how this worked. She'd said her lines, and now her part was over. His could be over, too, just like that.

But what, exactly, was his part? Why had Nick Wallabee's secretary been so adamant that Dr. Barrios participate? He mentally traced the arc of the show, trying to figure out how the script might end. They'd clapped benignly for the teacher, then ignored her. They'd booed the union representative. What did that mean for Mr. Status Quo himself? Were they saving the worst for last?

"And now," Melinda Morningside continued, "if you care about kids as much as I think you do, you'll *really* love our next guest. He's the star of a recent documentary, and you may remember he had some tough words for one failing principal."

The lights went down. Dr. Barrios braced himself as the clip began playing on the screen above his head. The familiar words cascaded over him in suffocating waves.

Too many students who can win on the football field but not in college and the workforce . . . Dr. Barrios: Are you *a leader who will do whatever it takes to win for children?*

Then Melinda Morningside's voice, which seemed to come from every direction at once: "Well, it so happens the man behind those words is here with us today. Please welcome *Superintendent* Nick Wallabee!"

Pulsing strobe lights eviscerated the darkness. Music pounded. Nick Wallabee strode onto the stage to wild applause.

He did not sit down.

Instead, Melinda stood up, joining him at the front of the stage like a dance partner. "Superintendent Wallabee, we all know you mean business. But we want to hear you tell us yourself: How much *are* you willing to do for our children?"

"Well, Melinda, I'm glad you mentioned business, because here in this school district, we're in the *business* of educating children."

Melinda Morningside was nodding vigorously.

"And just like any great business, we do"—Wallabee paused until everyone in the wide room was leaning toward him—"whatever it takes to win!"

The crowd cheered like a concert audience hearing the live version of their favorite song.

A knot began forming somewhere in Dr. Barrios's chest.

"And the main thing any successful business owner can tell you is that when they have competition, it forces them to make their businesses stronger."

The audience sizzled with the promise of schools that ran like successful businesses.

"That's why we're opening up our school system to that same businesslike competition. In fact, we're telling businesses, *If you think you can educate our students better than our district schools, come on in and do it.* And if our district schools want to keep their students, well, they'll have to do . . . *whatever it takes to win!*"

Here, Wallabee paused for Level 7 audience applause.

"And today, I'm excited to announce that Global Schoolhouse School Choice Solutions has responded to that challenge! They'll be opening several schools, and every one of them will be equipped with top-of-the-line answering clicker technology!"

Melinda Morningside, who'd mostly been supporting Nick Wallabee with dramatic facial expressions, lifted up the Teachnology clicker with a wink.

The formless unease growing within Dr. Barrios's chest began to take shape. The schools Wallabee was describing were for-profit charter schools. They weren't just *comparable* to businesses—they *were* businesses. They took in the same per-pupil funding as public schools, paying the district a nominal fee to "oversee" them. The lack of regulations applying to charter schools allowed them to cut costs and keep the difference. Dr. Barrios had heard stories of schools that bought supplies from companies owned by the same parent corporation, or rented space from themselves, sometimes closing in the middle of the year if they didn't turn a profit. Maybe he shouldn't have been so surprised, though. Making money, after all, was the way businesses won.

But Wallabee wasn't done. "They're also offering a virtual–charter school option so our greatest teachers—those who really believe in children—can reach beyond the walls of their classrooms and believe in thousands of children at once!"

The room exploded.

Dr. Barrios snuck a look at the union representative. He wondered if she got as furious about virtual charter schools as Mr. Weber, who could go on for hours. Compared to a real school, with a lunchroom, and air conditioning, and teachers, it cost almost nothing to educate students online—and for-profit companies knew it. Some had entire sales teams working on commission to get families to choose the virtual option. *Closing the deal*, they called it.

The union representative was now notably less composed. She was talking angrily into her microphone, but it appeared to have been turned off, as were the lights on her side of the stage. The only light was on Nick Wallabee and Melinda Morningside.

Which meant Dr. Barrios, too, was in the dark. This realization allowed him to take what felt like his first full breath in hours.

"To help spread the word about our new school-choice options," continued Wallabee, "we're going to have all our teachers write one Winning Strategy on the board each day. They'll also wear T-shirts that remind students that just like any successful business or winning sports team, our schools will do—"

From the back of the audience, someone yelled, "Whatever it takes to win!"

"It so happens we have a few of those T-shirts right here," said Melinda Morningside. "Let's get that gentleman back there a T-shirt!"

A crew member rolled a T-shirt cannon onto one edge of the stage.

"And how about the rest of you? What are we willing to do for our children?!"

"Whatever! It takes! To win! Whatever! It takes! To win!" This group was *not* going home without free T-shirts.

It turned into a chant so loud that at first Melinda Morningside had to yell to be heard. "I love the energy in here! But"—her voice dropped to a normal speaking tone, and the crowd quieted to listen again— "there is one person we haven't heard from yet, and it's a testament to Superintendant Wallabee's leadership that this man is here with us today."

A spotlight turned on, shining right into Dr. Barrios's eyes, bearing down on him like a train in a tunnel. His makeup felt heavy and itchy, but he dared not raise an arm to touch his face. Whatever Melinda Morningside asked next, there would be no answer that could satisfy this crowd. He was only seconds away from another floundering humiliation, broadcast live to the city, to the world, to his family.

"Let's hear now from the principal we saw in that video, Miguel Barrios!"

Dr. Barrios smiled weakly, bracing himself for a chorus of boos.

But instead, the crowd grew silent.

And now Melinda Morningside was turning toward him with a flawless expression of interest. "Doctor Barrios, you got a big warning earlier this year, but Nick Wallabee has told us he's worked hard to make sure your school is all about business. So we all want to know one thing: What are you willing to do for our children *now*?"

Still no boos, no angry faces. On the contrary, the crowd was staring at him with an intensity so familiar that he understood all at once, like a flash of the Holy Spirit.

The look in everyone's eyes was not anger: It was hope. For the first time in months, Dr. Miguel Barrios, EdD, was not here to be booed, or yelled at, or put on notice. He was here to bear witness, to testify to the mercy and greatness of a force more powerful than himself. He was here to be saved. All he had to do was say his part.

A surge of gratitude overtook him, so strong that his arms felt weightless, rising toward the ceiling of their own accord. He pulled as much air into his dry throat as he could and yelled, "Whatever . . . ! It takes . . . ! To Win!"

The end of the sentence was lost in the rapturous applause of the crowd.

TRAINING

THE TEACHCORPS WORKSHOP facilitator put a finger to her lips as they entered the silent room. She was thin, blond, and perfectly formed except for her mouth, which seemed a few gradations too high on her chin. She handed Kaytee a marker, then pointed toward several large squares of paper stuck to the walls.

What does a well-managed class LOOK like? said one.

What does a well-managed class SOUND like? said another.

The room was a model of silent participation. The only noise was the occasional squeaks of markers as workshop members added phrases like *on task* and *organized* to the growing list.

Achievement-oriented thoughts and actions, wrote Kaytee.

Her blog post that morning had been short, but within an hour it had already attracted 195 comments. She'd had to pry herself from the computer to make it to the training session on time. Now, positivity coursed through her veins. She visualized herself in her own classroom, finger to her lips, guiding students through a silent task during which no one bumped into anyone else, or purposely broke the silence with loud questions, or threw paper, or let out long sighs or defiant cheek-sucking noises—

She caught herself. She was thinking of Michelle Thomas again.

Diamonique had become more cooperative since the fight and sometimes looked at Kaytee with what seemed like remorse. But Michelle—

No, Kaytee thought. She would not do this. She rerouted her concentration back to the TeachCorps training space, which was clean and quiet, with modern office furniture and large, sun-filled windows.

Still silent, the facilitator motioned for everyone to sit. Then she began taking attendance. "Kaytee?"

Kaytee and another girl raised their hands at the same time.

"Sorry. There are two of you!" The facilitator's eyes stayed open as she smiled. The white parts of them were outstandingly white. "Katie with an I-E."

Kaytee lowered her hand.

"Jordan?" called the facilitator. Kaytee looked toward the one guy in the workshop, but Jordan turned out to be one of the five girls. Her hair was in pigtails. She was wearing the type of funky, ultrastylish pants that could only be worn by girls thin and funky enough to also wear pigtails.

They were all thin. Even the guy had the wiry build of someone who biked everywhere, with long, sinewy arms jutting from his plaid shirt. The girl sitting next to Jordan was so skinny that her elbows reminded Kaytee of a praying mantis. They all sipped water relentlessly, not even glancing at the bowls of candy in the center of each table. Kaytee, too, tried to ignore the candy. Despite the weight-tracking chart in front of her scale, she had managed to gain another three pounds since the start of the school year.

"Aman . . . thay?"

The one black girl in the room, also thin, raised her hand. "It's Amantha, though. Like *Samantha* but with no S."

"Sorry." The facilitator smiled her open-eyed smile again. "Aman-*thuh*? Am I pronouncing that right?"

"Yes."

A few of the workshop participants reached into their bags and retrieved papers they'd brought to grade during any downtime. Kaytee immediately felt guilty for not bringing any student work.

"Okay!" The facilitator's voice was a model of calm and cheer. "I just want to start by saying that I am a *facilitator*, not a boss or expert. I am just here to *facilitate* as we all learn from one another. So, just to clarify the norms and expectations before we begin, our most important norm is that we commit to unpacking our assumptions so we can co-investigate our subject matter from a stance of respect. Also, please keep your phones on silent."

They fumbled with their phones, then looked back at the facilitator, who now held up a decorated shoebox. "I'd like to start by having everyone in here physically unpack their preconceptions and assumptions and put them in this assumption box. I'll model by going first." She mimed the opening of a large, invisible package in front of her, lifting out what looked to be about six to seven pounds of preconceptions and assumptions and laying them gently in the box. Then she passed the box to Jordan, who poured out the contents of a slightly smaller invisible package before passing the box to the praying mantis–elbowed girl, whose invisible burden managed to be even smaller.

When the last tiny parcel of assumptions had been safely unloaded, the group began to applaud, but the facilitator stopped them with a raised hand.

"One last norm I'd like to introduce in here is that instead of clapping, we *raise the roof*!" She demonstrated by jerking her palms into the air with an emphatic *Woo-hoo!* "Now you try it."

"Woo-hoo!" Most of the group pressed their palms against an imaginary roof beam just above their heads.

"Amantha—am I pronouncing that right?"

"Yes."

"I didn't see and hear you raising the roof."

Amantha-am-I-pronouncing-that-right raised her palms and said, "Woo-hoo."

"That was great! Now, you all may notice that I just demonstrated one of the TeachCorps classroom-management principles, which is that when a student is not participating, you need to remind them they are part of the group and you expect them to participate. That's part of setting high expectations for everyone. Now, let's all raise the roof again for one hundred percent participation in this activity!"

Kaytee woo-hooed along with the rest of the group. She tried to imagine asking her own students to raise the roof. All she could picture, however, was a lethargic chorus of eye-rolls and lackluster, one-handed roof raises, punctuated by a long sigh from Michelle.

Focus, Kaytee reminded herself, as the facilitator moved to the next agenda item, on schedule to the minute.

It was all so well planned. Unlike the materials from district-led workshops, the TeachCorps folder had no missing or misstapled pages, no obvious spelling mistakes in the handouts, nothing to distract Kaytee as she took notes, growing more optimistic as she wrote. This was what she had been missing, this sense of being part of a movement full of people so . . . *right* that they needed their own set of protocols, their own words, almost their own language, to express how right they were. The sense of shared rightness comforted her, carrying her along like a gentle stream.

It was almost time for lunch when the facilitator closed her notebook, reminding them again that she was just the facilitator, not the boss or the expert.

"We are all here to be thought partners for one another," she reassured the group. "So I'd like to invite you to share out specific classroom challenges you'd like to deep-dive into with the help of the thought partners in this room."

Kaytee drew in a breath.

The thought partners in the room sipped water, flipped through their stacks of student work, said nothing.

"My class is actually going very well," volunteered Jordan.

"Mine too," said Katie-with-an-I-E. "I pretty much already do all of the stuff we've discussed." She closed the folder in front of her gently, as if to illustrate how little she needed the information inside.

An edge had crept into the air. The thought partners eyed one another like gladiators entering an arena.

"I'm having a problem," Kaytee heard herself say. "I mean, a *challenge*."

She felt the eyes in the room snap toward her.

"Before Thanksgiving break, there was this incident—two girls got into a fight in my class." Even as she spoke, she was aware of condensing the story, careful not to give the wrong impression to her thought partners. She continued. "One of them has gotten better, but the other one has more of an attitude than ever."

But that wasn't the whole story, either. There were more details she had to share if she really wanted a deep-diving co-investigation, and she forced herself to keep talking, to elaborate when necessary. She was surprised by how unburdened she felt. For the first time, she understood how much she'd needed to share this experience with people who might understand—who might even be able to help. The story was a heavy load she'd been carrying for a long time.

"First of all," said the facilitator, "let's raise the roof to honor Kaytee's willingness to speak her truth in the sharing space we've created!"

"Woo-hoo!" The group pushed its palms toward the ceiling.

"Now, let's open the floor up for some clarifying questions."

Jordan spoke first. "I noticed that you use the word *attitude*, which is a highly subjective word? When you say that the girl has an attitude, are you sure that you're not just interpreting her actions based on your assumptions about her home culture?"

Kaytee's sense of relief skidded to a halt. Asking if someone was making assumptions about a student's home culture was the TeachCorps-endorsed language for questioning whether the person might be racist.

"I don't think so—I mean, she's always putting her head down while I'm talking, and every time I ask the class to do something, she—" Kaytee caught herself before she did an impression of Michelle's eye-rolling, cheek-sucking sigh. That would have definitely made her seem like a teacher who was making assumptions about a student's home culture. Several thought partners, including Amantha-am-I-pronouncing-that-right, seemed to be watching her in anticipation of just such an impression. "I, uh, think it's fair to say she's being deliberately uncooperative."

Katie-with-an-I-E jumped in. "I'd just like to piggyback on Jordan's question and ask, what were you teaching when the fight started? I've noticed that, since I make sure my class material is relevant to students' lives, they're much less likely to get off task."

"Actually—" Kaytee tried not to sound defensive. Suggesting a teacher's lessons were not relevant was another way of saying the teacher might be the type of person who made assumptions about students' home cultures.

"One thing I always make sure my students know," said the guy in the plaid shirt, "is that even though they're Latino and African American, I don't expect any less from them academically."

"Remember, clarifying questions only!" The facilitator's tone reaffirmed that she was just facilitating, not posing as an expert.

"Sorry," said the guy. "I mean, I'm wondering if you've been explicit about your high expectations for your students? Like I have? Also, my students respect me?"

The thought partners in the room nodded.

Kaytee had the feeling she was losing a contest. A teacher who did not articulate high expectations would be the same type of teacher who did not plan relevant lessons because she was making assumptions about students' home cultures. She looked longingly at the candy bowl in the middle of her table.

"As a person of color myself," said Amantha-am-I-pronouncing-that-right, "I've found that sharing my firsthand experience with educational inequities has helped me invest students in my high expectations of them."

The contest ended abruptly. The non–person of color thought partners in the room shared a shudder of collective defeat.

"Okay, Kaytee!" said the facilitator. "It's your turn again. Do you have anything you'd like to add?"

Did she? Yes, she did! With a surge of gratitude, she realized she hadn't told them about the roach. "Actually, I forgot to mention: This all started because there was a roach in my classroom. I had this great lesson planned, but then this giant cockroach walked in." She demonstrated its size with her hands. Everyone had to agree that this could disrupt even the culturally relevant classroom of a non-assumption-making teacher.

But the interest of the thought partners had drifted to their own culturally relevant teaching practice.

"We made up a multiplication rap," offered the praying mantis–elbowed girl.

"We do 'fiesta fuego firecracker cheers' when someone gets an answer right," said a brunette girl next to Katie-with-an-I-E. She pronounced the Spanish words with a flourish that confirmed she was probably Latina and thus also a person of color who could share first-hand accounts of educational inequities.

"Oooo-kaaaay!" The facilitator sounded nervous, as if she'd just realized the group might really think she was only there to facilitate, not to be the boss or expert. "It looks like we're moving onto the suggestion part of our co-investigation, so I'd like to share out a story that might be helpful. Last year, when I was still teaching, a bee flew into the classroom, and the kids started to get off task. I knew we were wasting learning time, and my students could not afford to waste one minute that could be used to prepare them for college. So . . . I killed the bee and ate it!"

The room grew silent.

"I wanted to send the message that we do not let anything get in the way of student achievement," explained the facilitator. Her high mouth tightened into a smile.

Finally, Jordan said, "I think that deserves a roof raise!"

"Woo-hoo!"

"I'm sorry." Kaytee was confused. "Are you saying I should have. . . ?" She trailed off, gagging at the thought of the roach's spiky legs against her tongue.

"Obviously, she isn't saying you should have eaten the roach," said Amantha-am-I-pronouncing-that-right. "It's a metaphor."

"Right," said Jordan. "For not making assumptions about students' home cultures."

"And making sure your lessons are culturally relevant," added Katie-with-an-I-E.

"And setting high expectations," added the guy in the plaid shirt.

"That's right!" said the facilitator, offering another open-eyed smile. "But most of all, it's about making sure you don't let *anything* get in the way of your students' success. Right, everyone?"

"Wooooo-hoooooo!"

"In fact, before we break for lunch, I wanted to share out one more piece of inspiration. This is a passage from my absolute favorite blogger on the TeachCorps blog site: the Mystery History Teacher!"

Kaytee swallowed hard.

"Oh!" exclaimed Jordan. "I love that blog. I sooo relate to it."

"*I was told today, in a whole bunch of different ways, that I should 'quit taking my students' failure so personally.'*"

Kaytee looked to see if anyone was looking at her. No one was. They were all just smiling, nodding with familiarity as they listened to her anonymous words. She tried not to listen, but chips of meaning broke off and lodged themselves in her ears. *Today I tried to lead by example . . . No, no, no*, thought Kaytee. *My students learn democracy by practicing democracy . . . Please, make it stop*, she pleaded internally. *Way too many classrooms in my school that are dictatorships . . .* Ms. Grady! She'd written that about Ms. Grady!

The images cascaded through Kaytee's thoughts: Ms. Grady's harsh words on the first day of school. The fierce scar. The face at her door on the day of the fight.

The can of Raid rolling across the bloody floor.

Kaytee's heart pounded in her ears, blocking out the rest of the passage until a final volley of woo-hoos told her the facilitator had finished.

The thought partners were gathering their things for lunch now. The praying mantis–elbowed girl performed her multiplication rap for the brunette who was probably Latina. Jordan and Amantha-am-I-pronouncing-that-right announced they were skipping lunch, then began grading papers with an efficiency that seemed almost hostile.

Kaytee reached out and grabbed a piece of candy from the bowl.

SELECTION

AFTER ALL THE lectures from teachers, the hand waving of politicians, the cautionary movies, and other warnings about how no one ever makes it in football, an interesting thing sometimes happens.

Every now and then, someone makes it in football.

More specifically: Janoris Swan, former star of the Brae Hill Valley Killer Armadillos, was now a highly paid NFL running back, all the more famous for playing on the team in his hometown. On the first Wednesday of each February, at his former coach's request, Janoris came back to the school for National Athletic Signing Day. There, he shared the story of how he had made it—not just into college but all the way to the NFL and, this year, all the way to the Super Bowl. And this year's Super Bowl, just days away, would be played *here*, in the exact city where all those gloomy folks had once warned him no one ever made it in football. This was the story ESPN used in their profiles of Janoris and the story Coach Ray had expected when he'd handed his former player the microphone.

But Janoris was going off script.

"I didn't do much work in high school," he told the gathering of students and families. "In college, neither. Matter of fact, tell you the truth, I barely went to class. But I'll tell y'all one thing: College women *do* love football players."

Coach Ray's head snapped toward Janoris. *What the fuck?* Didn't the

NFL have media trainers who taught players not to say dumb shit in front of a microphone? Plus, Janoris had to know that if another player messed up, the whole football program was in danger—which meant he should have known better than to say something like this in front of O'Neal Rigby. Rigby had miraculously kept his grades up and made it through his final season without getting in trouble. But senioritis for athletes only got worse after signing day.

Coach Ray waited for the look to land, or for Janoris's own common sense to kick in and get him back on topic. But maybe Janoris had forgotten. Or maybe he didn't care. Maybe, as his muscles and celebrity and bank account grew, his high school coach shrank in the rearview mirror.

"In fact," Janoris continued, "my whole time in college, I don't think I ever—" *Slept alone* was the next phrase. Janoris had told Coach Ray this story about a million times, and it was clear he was going to finish it if nobody stopped him. To make matters worse, Daren Grant was in the gym. He'd arrived just before the ceremony to hand Coach Ray his mandatory *Whatever It Takes to Win!* T-shirt and was still hanging around, taking notes, pretending he wasn't getting a contact high from being around a real NFL player.

Coach Ray lunged toward Janoris and grabbed the microphone. "Ha-ha! What a joker!" He clapped Janoris's wide shoulder in a way that was meant to look friendly but still serve as a warning. "Janoris, why don't you say something *inspiring* and *educational* to our young players and their families today?"

"Sorry, Coach. I just get nervous and start talking." It wasn't clear if Janoris meant this, but he switched tracks. "Okay, y'all. Being serious now: One thing Coach Ray used to tell us is that your game face is not just for the game, and it's not just for your face. We can't just show up and *look* like we want to win."

That inner game face. You can't just look like you want to win. As Janoris said these lines, it wasn't just the words that sounded familiar. Coach Ray recognized the Huntsville cadence that rolled through the words when he said them to players, year after year, on busses and in locker rooms. Janoris Swan, famous NFL player, could still recite the pep talk as clearly as if he'd listened to it this week. And maybe he had. Maybe players saved Coach Ray's words in their memories to be pulled out as needed, just as he had saved the words of his own coaches.

"We can't just decide we want to win when we get *off the bus*," Janoris continued. "We gotta want to win when we *wake up*. We gotta want to win while we're *brushing our teeth*. We gotta want it while we're—"

"Watch it, son."

"Sorry, Coach. I'm just trying to say it's your *inner* game face that counts. And even now, no matter what I'm trying to do, even off the field, I think about putting on that inner game face. So keep that inner game face, y'all. No matter what you doing."

The families in the gym whooped and hollered. Coach Ray understood their excitement. Few things inspired him as much as seeing kids sign those scholarship papers. These were the few, the tough, the hardworking and uninjured, the lucky starfish plucked from the beach by an invisible hand and tossed back into the sea.

Now, one by one, the players came up and took the microphone. Each made a short speech or told jokes they'd practiced for the occasion. Then, in a moment of drama, they reached inside the lectern to pull out the hats representing their chosen schools. They placed the hats on their heads and signed the letters of intent that would unlock their athletic scholarships. Cheerleaders waved pom-poms. Mothers and grandmothers burst into tears. Everyone posed for pictures.

O'Neal Rigby went last. Aside from Janoris Swan, Rigby was the star of the event. "Nothing matters but that inner game face," said Rigby, echoing Janoris. Then, with his family standing behind him, he reached into the lectern, pulled out the hat of a Division I school, and placed it on his head. The crowd in the gym screamed, previewing the years of screaming fans that might line the stands of Rigby's future.

Just don't make any mistakes, nagged a voice in the back of Coach Ray's mind, but he used his own inner game face to squash it into silence.

"I want to just say one more thing." Janoris Swan had at some point made his way behind the lectern again. "It's about my coach."

The room quieted as all eyes swooped toward his massive frame.

"Coach Ray, if it wasn't for you, I wouldn't be where I am today. That's why I wanted to make sure you could be in the stands for my biggest game yet." He reached into his pocket and held up a small rectangle of glossy cardboard.

Coach Ray stared in disbelief. Even from across the room, he knew what a Super Bowl ticket looked like.

"Coach, you were like a father to me." Janoris's voice wavered. He took a deep breath before continuing. "I thought this would be a good way to say thank you."

Then he stepped from behind the lectern, crossed the gym, and pressed the cold, crisp rectangle into Coach Ray's hand. It felt electric, as if the camera flashes were sparks coming directly from the ticket itself.

"Janoris?" It was Daren Grant. He had crept up behind them and was now ruining the moment, in true Daren Grant style. "Do you think you could also remind everyone that doing whatever it takes to win doesn't just mean—"

"'Scuse me, chief." Janoris cut him off. "I'm trying to talk to my coach."

Coach Ray wanted to laugh. Well, more accurately, he wanted to yell into Daren Grant's face, *That's right—I'm Coach Ray, bitch! I in-vented doing what it takes to win!* But instead, both he and Janoris Swan acted as if Grant was invisible. That was nice, too.

"Sorry I could only get one of these," said Janoris, "but if you want tickets to games during the regular season, I could get you a few. All you got to do is let me know."

Just when the moment seemed like it could not get any better, Janoris stepped away, and Coach Ray read the ticket in his hand.

Mid-deck. Front row. Fifty-yard line.

Suddenly, like so many of the family members in the gym that day, Coach Ray found himself wiping away tears.

PLANNING

"**So, you know** who Janoris Swan is, right?" Lena stood, dressed in nothing but Nex's white tank top from the night before, ironing her *Whatever It Takes to Win!* T-shirt.

Nex stepped out of her bathroom, a towel around his waist. Flecks of water clung to his abdominal muscles. He looked at her as if unsure whether she was joking. "Everybody know who Janoris Swan is."

"Yeah . . . no, of course." Lena wished she hadn't started with the question. *Of course* everybody knew who Janoris Swan was. And everyone in *Texas*, obviously, knew the *Texan* who played for the most famous team in *Texas*. Which was about to be in the *Super Bowl*. But she had to get through this part of the conversation so she could get to the part she'd been practicing. "I was just gonna tell you a story about him. He went to the Hill—the school where I work? And our football coach was his coach in high school."

"For real?" Now Nex sounded impressed. He unwrapped the towel, draping it around his neck as he stepped into his boxer shorts.

"Yeah, so on Wednesday, he came to our school and gave the coach a front-row ticket to the Super Bowl." Or was *front row* only for basketball? Lena became self-conscious again.

"Shit." Nex pulled on his pants. "I need to coach me some high school football."

"Yeah, I know, right?" Lena waited for him to say more. The conversation, in her mental rehearsals, had a natural progression: She would tell Nex about Janoris Swan giving the ticket to Coach Ray, which would lead to the topic of the Super Bowl and Super Bowl parties, which would remind Nex to invite her to his cousin's party. He'd mentioned the party in passing a few weeks earlier, and she'd been determined to recoup the opportunity she'd missed over the holidays.

But none of these transitions occurred. Instead, Nex silently retrieved a fresh pair of socks from his bag. The night before, they'd wasted no time removing their clothes as soon as he'd walked in. Now, they seemed locked in the reverse scenario, and she realized with sinking dismay that he was halfway dressed—halfway gone. She'd have to move the conversation forward herself.

"So, yeah, I was thinking I wanted to watch the game—the Super Bowl—somewhere good. Since a player from the Hill is going to be in it, you know?"

"Well, I don't think you gotta worry." Nex pumped some of Lena's body lotion into his hands, smoothing it over the muscles of his chest and arms. "They playing it everywhere."

"I was just thinking more of a party type thing, you know? I don't really want to watch the game at a bar."

"Hey, you know where my shoes went?"

She gave herself a mental shove. "How about you? Where you gonna watch it?"

"Probably over by my cousin's house."

"Yeah?"

"Yeah." Nex tugged his shirt over his head. The sleeves bulged around his powerful shoulders.

Breyonna's happy-hour admonishment came back to Lena like an echo. *Look—y'all can give it up on credit if you want to . . .*

But that was ridiculous. She'd never expected anything from Nex. And, really, it wasn't like she had given him anything. They were both just having fun. If anything, it was Nex who'd sounded disappointed that she couldn't come to his family's house for the holidays. It was he who'd texted *love ya*. It was he who had said, on their first date—

"I thought you said you could take me anywhere." Regret washed over her immediately. She hadn't planned to speak the thought aloud.

Now she wished she could go back in time and revise her words, edit them until they were perfect, memorize them like a poem.

Nex gave her a long look that was difficult to interpret. Was he surprised she still remembered what he'd said? Or worse—did he not remember saying it?

Suddenly, she had to ask. "Is this whole thing . . ." She gestured back and forth between them. She couldn't bring herself to say *relationship*, but she couldn't say the term *giving it up*, either. "Is this like I'm opening some . . . line of credit for you that you're never going to pay back?"

Nex's eyes narrowed. "You saying you think I got bad credit?"

"No, no. I didn't mean it like that." It was all coming out wrong. Now she sounded like she'd bought into the stereotype that black men had bad credit, and she hadn't been trying to say that at all.

"Have I ever asked you for money?" He looked angrier than she'd ever seen him. "Have I ever asked you for *anything*?"

"No—I just wanted . . ." She stopped, unsure how to fill in the blank. But Nex had already found his shoes and put them on.

"Never mind," said Lena. "I have to get ready for work."

"Cool." He stepped out into the sunrise, closing the door behind him.

The copy machine had been broken all week. Even now, it was only *working* in the loosest sense of the term. Every fifteen copies or so, it shook, then sputtered to a halt and displayed an error message, leaving the teacher whose documents were inside to open and slam a series of plastic doors while apologizing to the colleagues waiting in line.

"It starts in middle school." Mrs. Friedman-Katz reached into the copier and pulled a crumpled paper from its depths. The machine started again with a promising whir. "We have kids here who had no business passing eighth grade in the first place."

Lena mentally calculated her wait time. Mrs. Friedman-Katz was, as always, accompanied by Mrs. Reynolds-Washington. Behind them was Daren Grant, holding a thin folder marked *Confidential*. He was the only one among them not wearing the mandatory *Whatever It Takes to Win!* T-shirt. His shirt and tie served as further reminders that he,

Daren Grant, was there to make sure students were learning and was not just some *teacher*.

"It really starts in elementary school," insisted Maybelline, who stood behind Daren Grant holding a huge stack of packets. "I'm responsible for teaching so many skills that the kids should have learned in the lower grades."

Lena's planning period was rapidly becoming a write-off.

"I'd say it starts with giving teachers some authority," said Mrs. Reynolds-Washington. "When I was in school, they could whoop us. Now we can't even have fridges in our classrooms."

"Actually, it starts with high teacher expectations." Daren Grant placed the first of his confidential papers on the glass. Apparently, they were not too confidential to copy on the *one* machine teachers needed to use during their planning periods. "We have abundant data on that."

"I have a fridge in my classroom," said Lena. She refused to let Daren Grant dominate both the copier and the conversation.

A few of the teachers laughed. Many of them kept fridges in discreet corners of their rooms.

"All the real problems, though? They start in the home," said Mrs. Friedman-Katz. "If parents paid more attention, we wouldn't have all these kids killing each other out there, all these babies having babies . . ." She trailed off in a way that indicated that she could easily go on. It would never be said, if a student committed some unspeakable act, that Mrs. Friedman-Katz had not seen it coming.

"Babies having babies," echoed Mrs. Reynolds-Washington, shaking her head.

Lena sighed at the thought. Of all the stupid decisions teenagers made, having a baby seemed the most shortsighted, the most long term, the most easily preventable. Every time she saw a pregnant girl walking the halls of the school, she felt the urge to scream, *Why are you not getting an abortion* right now?! Sometimes she wondered if she was the only person in Texas who felt this way.

Breyonna, who'd just arrived, chimed in. "What kids are really missing these days is a foundation in the church. I grew up in the church, and we all learned some respect."

"I know that's right," said Mrs. Reynolds-Washington.

"I'm going to need to see some data on that," said Lena. "Abundant data, if possible."

Hernan probably would have thought this was funny, but nobody in the copier line seemed to notice the sarcasm except Maybelline, who glared as if data were a member of her family whom Lena had just insulted.

"Well," said Mrs. Friedman-Katz, "a background in any religion, really."

Lena began gathering her things. The bell was so close to ringing that even if the machine started working perfectly she would never be able to finish her copies.

"For black folks, though, it starts in the church," said Mrs. Reynolds-Washington. "That's one of the things we all have in common—well, church and football."

If Lena had been in a more confident mood, she would have pointed out that there were plenty of black people who observed other religions or even no religion at all. But in her current state of mind, she doubted all of her own perceptions. The words *church and football* had thrust the morning's conversation back into her consciousness.

You think I got bad credit? Again, she wondered why oh whyohwhyohwhy she'd said the word *credit*.

She knew only one thing in the world, which was that this conversation could not conclude with the words *church and football*.

"It starts," she said, "with birth control."

A small weight lifted from her as everyone laughed.

Well, everyone except Maybelline. But she never laughed at anything.

KEEPING SCORE

"**B**YE, **MOM. HAVE** fun *not* watching the Super Bowl," called Allyson as she and her grandmother left for Rosemary's party.

The door slammed behind them, and Maybelline peered out the window to the scraggly lawn of the apartment complex. Among the beat-up cars of her neighbors' party guests, Rosemary's SUV gleamed like a trophy. The back of the truck faced Maybelline's window, parked at just the right angle to show off a new sticker adorning its bumper: *My Child Is an Honor Student at Grumbly Elementary School!*

Allyson had received no such sticker.

Spanish yells bounced in from the hallway. Loud, unintelligible conversation pressed through the wall from the Pakistanis. From the sound of things, they'd invited at least twenty guests to watch the game on their illicit satellite dish. It seemed as if everyone in the city, no matter where they came from or what language they spoke, had united to watch this silly American game.

Even Allyson loved football now. In fact, her love for the game seemed to correlate inversely with her mother's distaste for it. She'd even begun talking about becoming a cheerleader, though Maybelline had told her this was out of the question.

But there was no time to think about that, or Rosemary's party, or even the Super Bowl itself, where, according to the usual sources of gossip, Coach Ray would be sitting in the stadium, right on the fifty-yard line. None of this was Maybelline's concern. She had work to do.

Right at this very moment, for example, she was finalizing a spreadsheet of all the failing students whose parents she had contacted, with additional notes in cases where the contact information hadn't worked. There were ways, she knew, of getting the test scores of certain students removed from a teacher's evaluation. She only needed documentation that they had not done their work, or had not come to class, in spite of her best efforts. The key was to prove that she had done her part. The rules changed every year, and few teachers kept up with the paperwork involved. But Maybelline always did. This year, she'd started finalizing her spreadsheets as soon as she'd seen Daren Grant at the copy machine with his confidential folder. She was sure there was something in there about her—perhaps a complaint that she didn't do math-related cheers with her students.

And then Lena Wright had said that thing about birth control.

And everyone had laughed.

Even now, Maybelline seethed as she remembered it. Even Daren Grant had laughed. Had he even heard all the other things Lena said? That she didn't pay attention to data? That she had a fridge in her room, which was *clearly* against school policy? But the consultant had barely seemed to notice. Lena's disregard for rules would, just like Rosemary's, go forever unpunished.

Another roar vibrated the plaster of the living room wall. A wooden cross, one of the few mementos Maybelline's mother had carried on her journey from the Philippines, inched over with each cheer until it hung from its nail at a crooked angle. It felt as if the whole city was intruding on the apartment, images forcing their way onto Maybelline's mental computer screen: Coach Ray cheering from the front row of the gleaming stadium. Her mother and daughter celebrating on Rosemary's clean leather couch. Lena Wright, at some party full of glamorous, childless people, all of them laughing at jokes about birth control.

Then again, with all the work she had to do, Maybelline didn't have time to think about this. She turned her attention to the district website, searching for this year's documentation requirements.

But the new rules were not there.

Even though it was already February, whoever was in charge had not bothered to post the updated version. Without the new rules, she could do nothing with the neat rows of the Excel spreadsheet in front of her. There was no way to protect her test score data from students who had not done their part.

The thought made the entire universe feel like an unbalanced equation.

There had to be someone who could make this right, someone who understood that there were rules, and there were rewards for following these rules and consequences for breaking them. Before she knew what she was doing, she opened her school e-mail account, attached her spreadsheets to a new message, and sent it to Roger Scamphers.

More cheering came through the wall, louder this time—the type of cheering one might hear for a team that had pulled ahead. It made her feel ridiculous for sending the e-mail. Why hadn't she waited? Why hadn't it occurred to her that Mr. Scamphers would be watching the game, just like everyone else in the city, in the state, in the country? Watching the Super Bowl, Maybelline realized, was the exact inverse of being lonely.

She did not pursue this thought. There were other things that needed to be done, important things that were best done today. She clicked through files on her computer screen, looking for the next item that needed her attention.

A pinging sound interrupted her. Mr. Scamphers had written back!

This is great work, Ms. Galang. You can count on me to handle this. And I hope, in the future, I'll be able to count on you, too. Especially since it looks like I may be up for a promotion to principal after all. All I can say for now is that someone very important knows I'm in charge of the Believer Scores at our school and is counting on me to make sure they line up with test scores. I could use help from someone with your attention to detail.

Something lit up inside Maybelline as she printed and filed the e-mail. She worded her answer carefully. He had not asked her to mention specific colleagues—at least not yet. But she wanted him to know she was more than willing to help.

> *Well, there are definitely some teachers who don't believe our school's data means anything. If you're looking for a place to start, you might look at people who ignore other school rules, like the one about not having refrigerators in the classroom.*

The noise next door sounded distant now. Another message appeared.

> *Thank you, Ms. Galang, I believe I know exactly who you're talking about. Keep up the good work. I have a feeling that both your test scores and your Believer Score will be fantastic this year.*

By the light of the computer screen, Maybelline smiled. Mr. Scamphers already had his eye on Lena Wright. Had he heard whatever it was Lena had been whispering about Maybelline's binder during the PHCDMADC meeting? Whatever it was, it had made Hernan Hernandez run out of the room laughing. Lena thought she was so funny. Well, she'd see what was funny when the Believer Scores came out. A serenity settled upon Maybelline—the sense of having righted a great imbalance.

But it didn't last long. The apartments on both sides erupted in cheers again, and this time the noise spread all the way down the hallway, out of the apartment complex, and down to the street outside her window, where cars honked and music blasted and shrieks filled the air as the whole city exploded in the uproarious, disorderly joy of fans whose team had won the Super Bowl.

Maybelline tried to ignore the noise. There was other work she'd planned to do today, and it now seemed more urgent than ever. She worked without turning her face from the screen, blocking out any sense of time until she heard keys rattling in the door and the voice of her mother, who was excitedly rehashing the game with a neighbor from El Salvador.

Then Allyson ran into the apartment, breathless, as if she'd run up the stairs. "I saw my dad on TV!"

"Oh. Is that right?" Maybelline turned from the computer slowly, trying so hard to communicate her disinterest that it took her a moment to register Allyson's outfit. Not even an *outfit*: a glittery cheerleading uniform. Not even a uniform: Really, it was no more than a white swimsuit and a strip of sequins barely pretending to be a skirt.

Now Maybelline turned fully toward her daughter. "What are you wearing?"

"Gabriella gave it to me. It's just like the ones they wear at the game!"

Maybelline looked up and saw Rosemary, who could have easily stayed in the car but had silently followed Allyson into the house.

"*You* gave this to her?"

Rosemary shrugged. "Gabriella had two."

"I don't want her wearing that."

"Well, then, maybe you should have picked her and Mom up yourself."

This was how Rosemary operated. One could never be sure when she was plotting a punishment for some unnamed offense. Even when it came, there was only a hint—though there *was* always a hint—that her vengeance was anything but an innocent blunder.

Maybelline turned away, deliberately ignoring her sister's words. "Allyson, you cannot wear that. Go take it off."

"Why?" whined Allyson.

"It's not appropriate for a girl your age." She did not add that it was also not appropriate for Allyson's body type. Allyson's prepubescent nipples pressed against the shiny fabric, her belly button clearly visible in the center of a wobbly stomach. The skirt cut off just below her underwear, revealing stocky, eleven-year-old legs.

"The girls just wanted to show some team spirit," said Rosemary.

"This is between Allyson and me." Maybelline did not even turn her head as she said it.

But Allyson had already sensed the crack in her mother's defense. "Yeah, we just wanted to show some team spirit."

"I said take it off."

"Why is this the only place in the world where fun is just, like, *not allowed?*" Allyson stormed off in a shiny, pudgy fit, looking less like a professional cheerleader than anything Maybelline could imagine.

Maybelline turned back to her sister. "Please do not get into arguments between my daughter and me." The *please* was not meant to be polite. It was meant to show that even at a time like this, Maybelline had not lost control of her manners.

"Well, since it looks like I'm helping to *raise* your daughter . . ."

Their mother hovered nearby, pretending not to listen. She always did this when tensions between the twins heated up, turning every argument into every other argument they'd ever had, all of which Maybelline should have won over the years. She had done everything she was supposed to, and yet some invisible force always pulled Rosemary ahead. Now it was Rosemary who had an honor-roll sticker on the back of her truck, and Rosemary spending her husband's money and hosting parties in her spacious home.

"Yes, Rosemary, so I've heard." Maybelline snuck a look at her mother, who was now straightening the cross on the wall with exaggerated concentration. "Sorry some of us have to work for a living."

"Oh, I see what this is about. Well, excuse me for waiting until I was married to have a kid."

This was something Rosemary had never said—should not have said. Not when Maybelline, for all these years, had kept her sister's biggest secret.

It begins with birth control.

Maybelline felt something familiar rise up within her. An equation had become imbalanced, and she needed to correct it. "I know you did. I was the one who drove you home from the clinic in high school, remember?"

She'd meant it as a hint, in coded language that she thought only Rosemary would understand, but immediately she could see she'd been wrong. Their mother turned, staring at Rosemary with hurt eyes. Rosemary's mouth hung open. The noise of the street had dimmed to only the occasional defiant car horn. Somewhere, a door slammed.

Inside Maybelline's chest stirred a troubled sense that she'd done something irreversible, that instead of righting an imbalance, she'd pushed much too far in the opposite direction. But the feeling that made Maybelline's heart pound wasn't fear. It wasn't regret.

It was the uproarious joy of someone whose team had won.

DEFENSIVE STRATEGY

"**IF BIRDS CAN'T** talk, how do they even know which bugs are poisonous?"

It wasn't a bad question, but Hernan still snuck a look at the clock as he answered. He was eager to leave school. He needed to examine the bluebonnets in his father's greenhouse before they all caught the fungus. It *was* a fungus—he'd been able to confirm that much, and now he just hoped there would be some way to keep it from spreading. Every day, however, there was something that kept Hernan at school too late to do any experimentation. The science fair, with all its accompanying headaches, had barely finished when his department head had volun-told him to do TCUP tutoring. Meanwhile, in gardens all over the state, tiny brown spots were appearing on the leaves of bluebonnets, growing larger until they consumed the plants.

The sight of Mr. Scamphers at the door snapped Hernan back into the moment. The door had been locked. He was sure of it. Yet the assistant principal had entered without so much as a warning jingle from his keys.

"I see you're busy." Mr. Scamphers's voice was unusually pleasant. "I just need you to sign this."

Hernan signed distractedly.

"Oh, and I'll be e-mailing you to schedule a support dialogue," Mr. Scamphers said, and left briskly.

"Uh-oh," said a student. Even teenagers sensed that a *support dialogue* was not as positive as the phrase might suggest.

"Don't worry about it," said Hernan. He tried to follow his own advice but instead found he suddenly had a strong interest in reading the paper he had just signed.

Lack of professionalism, the paper said, *inbox full, causing e-mails to bounce back*. This had been during science fair and the holiday season.

Classroom-management issues documented by outside observer: student eating chips in class and spitting in plants near window.

Hernan remembered Angel joining the class for the first time, Daren Grant sitting behind him. Then, later the fluorescent glob of (BAKED!) Reetos in the flowerpot.

The third and final offense had been handwritten that very day. *Violation of school regulations: fridge in classroom*. Hernan almost laughed. Didn't every teacher ignore that rule?

So much for leaving right after the bell.

The assistant principal did not seem surprised to see Hernan at his office door at the end of the day. "Yes, Mr. Hernandez, how can I help you?"

"I was wondering if we could discuss the paperwork from today."

"We can. But you already signed it."

"I just want to explain that on the day the outside observer came in, I had a new student who had only been in the class for fifteen minutes. The problem described on this paper was with him."

"Well, Mr. Hernandez, I have no control over what an outside observer wrote about your class, but I can assure you that you are responsible for all of your students." It was clear the assistant principal was enjoying this.

"Okay, but also, when my inbox was full, during the holiday season, that was because of science fair–related e-mails. Every time they—" The look on Mr. Scamphers's face told him the discussion was useless, maybe even counterproductive.

"Okay, well, I tried." Hernan turned to leave. Clearly, there was no point in bringing up the fridge.

"Mr. Hernandez, one more thing: I noticed you have an excessive number of plants in your room. Those are a violation of the fire code. You'll need to take those home by the end of the week."

"But I've had those for years," said Hernan.

"As we've discussed, Mr. Hernandez, just because you've gotten away with something in the past doesn't mean it's allowed. I'll be putting this directive in an e-mail, so you'll want to make sure your inbox has space to receive incoming mail."

This time, Hernan did not bother to answer. He went back to his classroom and gathered as many plants as he could carry. His apartment was too small to hold them all, but every summer, he moved them to his father's greenhouse during the last week of school. Now, he supposed, this would be their permanent home.

It was still light when he parked his Jeep on the grass outside the greenhouse and carried the first pot of bluebonnets inside. He'd find the rows of flowers that hadn't caught the fungus yet and place the ones from his classroom among them. Eventually, they'd go out as part of some larger order, living out their lives anonymously in the hedges of a hotel or government building.

But when he turned the corner to the bluebonnet section, he found himself frozen, staring as far down the rows of blue flowers as his eyes could see. The leaves of every one of them were dotted with tiny brown circles.

CRUNCH TIME

THE FACULTY MEETING was almost over. Almost. Over. Except it wasn't, because of the three hands still waving predictably in the air. Two of these hands, shiny-nailed and adorned with multiple rings, belonged to Mrs. Reynolds-Washington and Mrs. Friedman-Katz. The other belonged to Don Comodio.

Dr. Barrios weighed his options.

Finally, concealing his dread, he said, "Yes, Mrs. Reynolds-Washington?"

"It sounded like you were trying to tell us to teach nothing but test-taking skills from now until the TCUP. *Is* that what you're telling us?"

"I don't think that's exactly what I said." Dr. Barrios stirred an amiable laugh into the statement, though of course that was exactly what he had meant. It was one of those things principals didn't say in so many words, like the fact that seniors were not supposed to receive failing grades. But the topic of the meeting was crunch time, which was the portion of the year when teachers were expected to *emphasize test-taking skills*, which was a euphemism for teaching almost nothing else.

Mrs. Reynolds-Washington and Mrs. Friedman-Katz were still staring at him, heads tilted to the left, waiting for his explanation.

"Just, please, write the test-taking skill of the day on the board," said Dr. Barrios, reciting from the most recent Nick Wallabee memo.

"Is this in addition to the Curriculum Standard of the Day?" said Mrs. Friedman-Katz. She and Mrs. Reynolds-Washington tilted their heads to the right.

"Yes. Those, too."

"*And* the Research-Based Best Practices?" said Mrs. Reynolds-Washington. Both women folded their arms.

"*And* the Winning Strategies? And the shirts?"

"Yes." *Sorry*, he wished he could add, *about everything*.

There was a series of tired sighs in the auditorium as teachers absorbed the news.

"Doctor Barrios! Over here!" Don Comodio's hand was still in the air, waving wildly.

Ignoring Mr. Comodio was still an option. It was late. Teachers were already checking their cell phones, folding their meeting agendas, zipping and unzipping their bags. These were the adult equivalents of students snapping binders shut before the bell.

Dr. Barrios was as eager to leave as any of them. It would be another late night in a week that—in addition to the usual impositions on a principal's time and blood pressure—included another tense budget meeting. On the other hand, crunch time was no time to seem undemocratic.

Dr. Barrios sighed. "Yes, Mr. Comodio?"

"What's the policy on black pants that are faded so they look gray?"

"Uh, black pants that look gray?" The question didn't even make enough sense to dismiss quickly. It had to be clarified, *then* dismissed.

"Well, the uniform policy calls for black pants, but one of my students has black pants that are faded so they look gray. My question is, are they still part of the uniform?"

"Yes, Mr. Comodio. Faded black pants are still part of the uniform." Dr. Barrios breathed in with the intention of dismissing the meeting.

"We all need to remember some of our students can't afford new uniforms every year," volunteered Mrs. Friedman-Katz. "I could give you several examples right now."

Most of the teachers were now in Olympic-runner starting position, ready to race toward the door. Mr. Weber, from his intensely visible spot in the first row, was looking at his watch, ready to evoke Statute

III, Item 4 of the teachers'-union contract: *Thou shalt not keep instructional staff detained in meetings past the time of 3:40 p.m.*

"We can discuss this some other—" began Dr. Barrios.

Mrs. Reynolds-Washington broke in. "Anyway, half the kids don't even obey the uniform policy in the first place."

There were murmurs of *That's true* and *Sure don't.* A few brave teachers crept toward the back doors. They gave their best body language signals for *Picking up the kids, can't stay, so sorry, but I heard the important part, right?* The coaches rose as one from their seats in the back row. Players were on the courts and fields. Heaven forbid there was some injury out there when the coaches were in a meeting.

"I couldn't agree more, Mrs. Reynolds-Washington," said Mr. Comodio. He turned to address the crowd. "It's only one step ahead of bringing guns to school."

The parents on staff were on their phones now, apologizing in hushed voices to babysitters and mothers-in-law and elementary-school office personnel.

"Some of these kids already bring guns to school," Mrs. Friedman-Katz offered, shaking her head to let the record show she disapproved of this behavior.

Mr. Comodio nodded solemnly. "And iguanas."

This conversation was not going to end organically.

Dr. Barrios leaned into the microphone again. "Mr. Comodio, we can talk about individual concerns another time. Meeting's over, everyone. See you tomorrow."

There was a burst of enthusiasm as teachers gathered in the aisles, catching up with friends from faraway classrooms before they headed out to prepare for night-school classes, feed kids, walk dogs, grade papers in front of the TV, or do whatever teachers did when they no longer had to be in the Brae Hill Valley High School auditorium.

The crowd and noise receded until Dr. Barrios stood alone at the lectern, staring out at the rows of empty chairs. What he hadn't shared during the meeting was that crunch time wasn't the biggest news. It wasn't even the biggest crunch. Money was draining fast from the school system, much of it into the hands of Global Schoolhouse School Choice Solutions. Their for-profit and virtual academies were *closing the deal* with more and more families, promising shortcuts to a diploma and even offering incentives, like free computers. Other groups, too, had been claiming their pieces of the school-funding pie. Families who had always sent their kids to private schools were now getting voucher money to help with tuition, and public-school money was draining into ever more questionable alternatives. Some were not public. Others barely seemed like school: There were religious academies that didn't allow gay kids, charter schools located inside private golf clubs, glorified homeschool setups whose students didn't even take the TCUP test.

Next year, class sizes would balloon more than they already had. Even then, there might not be a big enough budget to keep all the teachers on staff. Principals were supposed to begin assembling paperwork to fire teachers who might receive low Believer Scores. There had been hints that older teachers, with their higher pay, were especially valuable targets.

Dr. Barrios had not started any such paperwork.

But the clearest starting point was Mr. Comodio. When the subject of bad teachers came up, teachers who should be fired immediately, it was impossible to keep from picturing Mr. Comodio's face. In addition to making stupid comments in meetings, he wore ill-fitting, unprofessional clothes and wrote lesson plans only sporadically. His digital grade book remained empty for the first seven weeks of each quarter, at which point it inexplicably filled up with Bs for every student. He had told at least one class of students that Christopher Columbus was the first US president. Amazingly, Don Comodio seemed to have no idea what a tissue sample of instructional failure he was. There had always been people who turned out to be bad at teaching, but most of them had the decency to quit. They filed out as part of the larger exodus of teachers who'd just had it with some aspect of the job. Not Don Comodio. He stuck around, contributing his opinions as if he were some type of valuable team member, validating anyone who complained that teachers' unions made it too hard to fire low performers.

But the true reason there was no paperwork on Don Comodio had nothing to do with the union. It was that Dr. Barrios could not stand the thought of firing anyone, least of all a man in his late sixties who would wander the earth competing for jobs with people in their twenties. Plus, in this one rare case, Dr. Barrios knew a secret that the Reynolds-Washington–Friedman-Katz rumor mill had missed: Don Comodio had cancer.

Which was why, when Mr. Scamphers had offered to take charge of the paperwork for teachers who would be "nonencouraged to continue employment with the district," Dr. Barrios had gladly accepted.

IDENTIFY AUTHOR'S PURPOSE

SO, FINE. NEX Level hated her. (Did he?) Or he was avoiding her. (Was he?) Or maybe she'd just hurt his pride. She still cringed when she thought of her comment about opening a line of credit. In any case, it was over—Nex hadn't been in touch since their argument, and she refused to contact him, though there still were times she couldn't help hoping, when she pulled out her phone between classes, that she might find he'd sent her a message. He probably wasn't going to, though. Which was fine.

What she really missed was poetry. Since their first date, she had not gone to a single poetry venue on her own. She hadn't even written anything new. It was as if poetry itself was Nex Level's domain, and she dared not enter unless he held open the door. This was the part of the situation that seemed most unfair. (Wasn't it?)

The slowness of after-school tutorials invited such mental digressions.

In front of her, in a circle of desks, sat five low-level readers in various states of disrepair. Other teachers talked about how rewarding it was to work with students individually, but Lena preferred even her rowdiest class to this slow hour at the end of the day, trying to extract the author's purpose from a passage about Helen Keller. As the group stammered through the story, the effort not to feel depressed exhausted her.

Two paragraphs into the story, after every student had pronounced the word *vaguely* wrong, after Lena had explained what *to and fro* meant, clarified that a *honeysuckle* was a type of flower, and decided to completely ignore the word *languor*, she paused to ask a simple recall question. No one could answer it.

She tried again. "Okay: How did Anne Sullivan teach Helen Keller what a doll was?" There was a forced excitement in her voice that she hated but was powerless to stop.

"She gave her the doll and traced the letters onto her hand." Chantel, a massive girl with patches of dry, itchy-looking skin on her hands and wrists, was always the one who provided the merciful answer in the end. She was eager to please and had a sense of focus in spite of her low reading level. In a world that was even half fair, Chantel would have been the type of gifted teenager able to lose herself in books, a late bloomer whose future shined in from beyond the rusty gates of high school and who understood that any book could be a self-help book if you read it right. Instead, here she was, stumbling syllable by syllable along with the others.

"Very good! So how do you think she showed Helen what a cup was?"

"A picture?" ventured a girl named Amarylis who was almost definitely pregnant.

"Remember," said Lena, "she's blind."

"Oh."

"Okay! Let's start reading again!" Where was this cheerful voice coming from?

The group mumbled through another paragraph, incomprehensible, uncomprehending. Lena marveled at Anne Sullivan's patience. How many times must she have traced those letters on Helen Keller's hand before the meaning sank in? Nothing brought Lena into more direct contact with her own disillusionment than tutoring low-level readers. She had entered teaching expecting students who, with the right question or book recommendation, would demonstrate some untapped well of deep, original thinking. Instead, she'd found that teenagers who had never read a full book were unlikely to share original thoughts. They were much more likely to parrot clichés from social-media celebrities or believe made-up news, or say things like *It doesn't really matter whether you vote*—or require bribes to come to tutoring sessions, where they stuttered through passages about Helen Keller.

Lena cheerfully summarized the paragraph they had just finished. Then she asked the students to close their eyes and trace the word *doll* into their own hands. "If you were Helen Keller, would you feel happy at learning a new word?"

"Yes," said Chantel.

"If I was blind and deaf, I'd just kill myself," said Rico.

Rico's attendance was even more sporadic in tutorials than it was in class, yet when he showed up, Lena found his presence refreshing. His neck tattoo, which was supposed to make him look tough, contrasted with his Kermit the Frog–like build. He also bit his nails even shorter than Lena bit her own. But it was his sarcasm that made Lena suspect he felt the same way she did, sitting in this circle, reading these passages full of subliminal positive messages. Must every story be a life-affirming testament to the strength of the human spirit? Was it even responsible to insist that every ugly duckling would become a swan, that every little engine could make it over the hill, that all the puzzle pieces needed for a happy ending were already in the box and one only needed the grit to fit them together?

Lena summoned her theatrical skills to keep the excitement in her eyes. "Have any of you ever learned something that makes everything start to fit together, like a puzzle, and it makes you want to say, *aha?*"

More silence. Amarylis tapped her foot, thumping her knee anxiously against the leg of the desk until she caught Lena looking at her.

Lena tried to keep her own foot from tapping. "Can you imagine the way Helen Keller felt when she finally understood what water was?!"

"Yes," said Chantel.

They finished the passage, moving on to the first question in the author's-purpose practice packet. *What is the most likely reason the author wrote this passage? To persuade? To entertain? To inform?* Amarylis was wiggling her foot again, pulling at a string on the threadbare knee of her jeans.

Lena suppressed a sigh. Even if the students in front of her did pass the TCUP, by some Anne Sullivan–caliber miracle, they would never be the type of readers who thumbed through a newspaper or perused the racks of a bookstore or stayed up all night to finish a novel. Watching one of her favorite activities become an instrument of torture made Lena's soul feel . . . threadbare.

Lately, she'd found herself wishing the whole scene were simply someone else's problem. She imagined being far away, becoming a person who nodded sympathetically to complaints that somebody should do something to fix this whole education thing—the way people did with prostate cancer, or genocide in South Sudan.

Finally, the tutoring session ended.

"Great job today, everyone!" Lena lied.

Threadbare soul. The phrase popped into Lena's head again—more insistent this time. She jotted it on a corner of the practice packet with its pages of relentless questions about the *author's purpose.*

The truth was, she wasn't even sure there *was* such a thing as an "author's purpose." There was more than one reason for writing anything, and some of the best authors never revealed their purpose at all. But she would never have tried to explain this. Not with Level 1 readers. Not during crunch time.

When she got home, she took the marked-up packet from her bag and stared at it. *Threadbare soul.* She imagined Rico biting at his tiny slivers of fingernails, Amarylis tapping her foot, picking at that hole in her jeans.

Pulling at the strings of my threadbare soul. She turned on some background music and sank into a chair, pen in hand. What rhymed with *soul*? *Trying to meet this artificial goal? Taking its toll?* No. These sounded forced. *Forget about rhyming,* thought Lena. What was this concept she was trying to capture? She bit her thumbnail, a habit that was especially pronounced in times of worry or heartache, but also when ideas were coming to her.

A lyric from one of the hip-hop chart-toppers she'd suffered through during long-ago parties floated into her head: *I got ninety-nine problems, but a bitch ain't one.* Her students had so many problems. *Ninety-nine problems, ninety-nine problems . . .* The line kept repeating itself to her like an itch asking to be scratched—like the uneven edge of a fingernail, begging to be bitten into a straight line.

Students with ninety-nine problems apiece. Yes, that worked. Now, what rhymed with *apiece? Harassed by police?* No, that topic really was Nex Level's territory. Truth be told, her personal experience being harassed by police was limited.

Ninety-nine problems apiece.

Problems like what? It occurred to her that she didn't know that much about her students' problems outside of school. Was she supposed to? Teachers in movies knew everything about their students, and that mystery-history-teacher blogging lady seemed like she did, but Lena didn't know how any teacher could handle it—the problems of adults combined with the reading skills of children, multiplied by so many students. She thought of Chantel shifting uncomfortably in her chair, Rico checking his watch then looking at the clock as if asking for a second opinion, as if the tutoring session would never . . . *cease? Problems that never cease?* No. That felt thesaurusy, and, anyway, it wasn't quite the point. So what *was* the point? What was this message she was trying to dredge from the dark sea of her subconscious, tugging it up word by word? *At least. Increase. Decrease.* None of these words had a grip on the core of the thing. It was about the way the air tightened around her in the room, the way she felt trapped, like an insect in amber, as she listened to sixteen-year-olds stumble over syllables and pronounce letters that were supposed to stay silent, the sounds of frustrated teenagers tapping pens and *tapping their feet, shifting and creaking the seats, struggling students with ninety-nine problems apiece . . .*

And there it was: the right line, the right rhythm, the blast of concentrated truth that artists chased with each brushstroke and singers searched for in the notes of a song. This was the writing experience Lena had always wanted to share with her students. Could she? In that moment, it didn't matter. A portal had opened, and everything Lena knew about teaching, everything she knew about life, was hers to pin down perfectly on the page, never to be forgotten, never to escape, never to step casually out of her door into the morning sun. If there was another purpose to being an author, Lena certainly couldn't think of it right now. The sounds of the poem rose up around her. They drowned out the melody of the music, a plane in the sky, the whole tangled concept of author's purpose, the unringing phone at her side.

INCREASE COMFORT WITH LEARNING TECHNOLOGY

THE MYSTERY HISTORY TEACHER

www.teachcorps.blogs.com/mystery-history-teacher

TECHNOLOGY, EQUALITY, AND SO MUCH MORE

Not to brag—well, maybe a little. Today's lesson not only fulfills all the new district requirements, it also introduces a culturally relevant project that relates to my students' unique home cultures. It even increases comfort with learning technology—our crunch time strategy of the day! First, we're going to watch some online clips of marches from the Civil Rights movement and uprisings by oppressed people around the world. Afterwards, we'll have a class discussion about what all of these protests have in common. Then we start a project in which students research the Civil Rights leader of their choice and discuss how this person's techniques might apply to a current civil rights issue, like transformational change in our public schools. In your face, educational inequity!

COMMENTS

BackToTheClassics Please. Students are already comfortable enough with technology. At this point, a motivated student could get an entire college education through a smartphone.

Or they could watch porn and play video games. Guess which one most of them would do.

TechTeacher1 If students like video games, why not experiment with game-based learning and #gamification? It's up to us to become #techsavvyteachers and keep course content up-to-date and fun! Technology is the #futureofeducation, so get with the obgyn!

TechTeacher1 Oops. I meant get with the *program*, not *obgyn*. #stupidautocorrect

---

212 MORE COMMENTS ON THIS POST

"Ooh, Ms. Mahoney's trying to show us something inappropriate!"

"Ms. Mahoney in trouble!"

The students were growing restless. Kaytee, meanwhile, was trying not to panic.

Last night, previewing protest videos on her laptop, she'd forgotten that the district's Internet filters erred on the conservative side. The filter blocked not only profanity but language that might in any context apply to violence or pornography. Science websites mentioning horny toads or camel humps were out of luck, along with valid educational uses of the words *hit*, *bang*, *blow*, and *spread*.

If Kaytee had remembered this, she would not have chosen a video entitled "The Long, Hard Struggle for Black Equality in Action." But she had, and now, instead of playing the video, the Smart Board displayed an ominous red X and a warning about potentially inappropriate content. She tried the Cesar Chavez clip, "Fighting for Improved Farm Hand Job Conditions." Blocked. Even the seemingly clean-titled piece about international protests was blocked, which confused Kaytee until she realized the narrator's first name was Dick.

Her shoulders slumped as the day's lesson plan slipped from her grasp.

"Just go to YouTube, Miss!" suggested Jonathan Rodriguez.

Kaytee shook her head, so dejected she said nothing to Jonathan about talking without raising his hand. "We can't get YouTube on the school computers."

Jonathan laughed. "Everyone knows how to get around that filter."

Apparently, this was true, because the class began to bubble with purpose, calling out tips for getting around the content filters until Brian Bingle said, "Y'all don't need to all shout at her at the same time. Just let Jonathan do it."

Perhaps it was a testament to Brian's leadership skills that Kaytee did not protest. Or perhaps a whole day with no lesson plan was scarier than getting in trouble for tampering with the Internet filters. In any case, she stood to the side as Jonathan fiddled with the computer. Within thirty seconds the YouTube icon filled the Smart Board, and when the video started and Dr. Martin Luther King Jr. began speaking, every face in the room turned to watch.

The day only got better from there: Almost everyone participated in the discussion, and when Kaytee introduced the research project, there was barely a grumble. Three more classes passed, each of them engaged, as if riding the current of energy from the class before. This was the feeling of becoming a great teacher. This was what her racist father and mercenary brother and even her well-meaning aunt and mother would never understand. This was the reason Kaytee Mahoney had never stopped believing.

For the first time in a long time, she felt full after finishing her lunch. She sat at her desk, satisfied, with no desire to visit the vending machine at all. Instead, she passed the time by reading the comments on her blog. There were 244—another record. The Smart Board was still connected, so her words and the reactions they inspired lit up the whole wall, larger than life. TeachLikeABawzz said, *Hope you don't mind if I steal your lesson plans, LOL*. Kaytee didn't mind. Iluvtchingrm422 described a personal anthropology project in which students looked up their high schools on YouTube to see videos shared by their contemporaries.

A personal anthropology project! Kaytee loved the idea—loved her readers. She clicked the YouTube screen, searching for anthropology-quality videos from Brae Hill Valley High School. There were a couple of pep-rally cheers, some footage of O'Neal Rigby at Signing Day, a few clips from football games. There was the now-ubiquitous clip of Nick Wallabee and Dr. Barrios from *How the Status Quo Stole Christmas*, plus some segments of the follow-up show on Education Sensation TV. Unfortunately, that was about it. Kaytee's excitement drooped as she imagined watching 180 hastily created collections of these videos. She was about to switch back over to her blog comments when something caught her eye.

"Bray Hill Vally Teacher Gets Knocked Down in Fight." The misspelling of the school's name must have kept it out of the top search results, because it had far more views than any of the videos above it.

A metallic taste filled Kaytee's mouth as she clicked on the title.

The action, recorded on some student's cell phone, had the same shaky, handheld quality of the street-protest videos she'd shown earlier in the day. This time, though, it was Michelle and Diamonique whose life-sized images filled the Smart Board, hands vise-gripped into one another's hair as students around them shouted encouragement.

Then Kaytee saw herself on-screen, pushing through the crowd, aiming toward the action with a can of Raid, yelling, "Stop it! Oh my God, stop it!"

There was a clatter as the can hit the floor, and the camera turned briefly to follow it, zooming in on its label as shoes kicked it out of the way. The shot wobbled back up to show Kaytee, desperate and clumsy, reaching in from behind Diamonique, then falling backward, shrieking, "Ow! Oh my God!" The video ended on a freeze-frame of Kaytee, sprawled on the floor, one hand cupping the area below her eye.

She knew she shouldn't read the comments.

Then, once she started reading, she knew she should stop.

But it was as if she'd fallen into quicksand. The words pulled her in, swallowing her, until there was nothing but the opinions of these strangers, laughing behind their screen names about how *absolutely fucking hilarious* it was to watch her get hurt. Also under discussion were the girls and their fighting skills, with a whole side debate about whether these bitches really could even fight anyway (mostly no to that, surprisingly), whether any bitches could even fight (yes to this, with a link that promised a close-up of a girl's tooth getting knocked out), the body types of every visible female in the video and whether or not they might be worth fucking, and whether it was possible to get arrested for putting up a fight video on YouTube.

And then, just when it all seemed as if it couldn't get any worse, **LastMannStanding** noticed the can of Raid.

TEACHER GOT SOME ROACH SPRAY. CAN YOU BLAME HER?
This was followed by a subcomment from **BuildTheWall45:** *Hey, she figured out the new way to clean up our inner cities.*

Mighty Righty: *Thought that was what police target practice was for.*
It kept going. Chains of subcomments formed under one another like the tunnels in an ant farm, growing more hateful the deeper Kaytee read.

ScrubBrush10: *My only question, is why even try to teach them first? Just give every innercity teacher a can of raid at the beginning of the year*

DeploreThis: *Wed save a lot of money on welfare.*
Tom: *YOU STACK EM UP. I'LL GET THE BULLDOZER.*

NoMoreTaxes: *Next thing you know the elites will be trying to get raid out of the storesFilling innercity classrooms with roaches at taxpayers expense.*

ScrubBrush10: *Thats what there filled with now. And illegals.*
Tom: *Better idea . . . round up these animals that have taken over our iner cities and mass transport them to muslum countries so we can make room for the Islamic Ailiens that demand refuge.*

There were pictures, too: Michelle and Diamonique's heads Photoshopped onto the bodies of cockroaches. Images of the students superimposed onto a picture of a gas chamber. Then a still shot of Kaytee, holding the can of Raid straight in front of her, facing a crowd of Nazis who appeared to be saluting in return. She felt dizzy. The world seemed to be swirling around her, a tornado of hate heading straight in her direction.

As she stared at the Nazi photo, however, she realized something even worse.

She was not the hate's target. She was its mascot.

The bell rang, dousing her in the icy reality of the moment. She was in school, lunch was over, and the hall was filling with noisy teenagers heading for her door. She clicked frantically at the corner of the screen, shutting the YouTube window only seconds before the first students entered the room.

But not before she noticed one last line at the bottom of the screen.

9,682 more comments on this video.

PROCESS OF ELIMINATION

UNION MEETINGS GENERALLY reinforced Hernan's decision not to become a union member. The meeting currently in progress in Mr. Weber's dusty auto shop was no exception.

The problem was not, as suggested by Nick Wallabee's documentary, that the union was made up of bad teachers trying to protect their jobs. There were plenty of good teachers in the union. The problem was that the union, being the irrevocably democratic institution that it was, held meetings in which everyone really *was* treated equally and everyone's opinion really *did* count. Thus, attending a union meeting was like watching a choir performance in which the most off-key singers stood closest to the microphone—and performed a series of solo numbers.

As if to illustrate this very phenomenon, Don Comodio jumped to his feet as soon as Mr. Weber called the meeting to order, demanding to address the injustice of the *Whatever It Takes to Win!* T-shirts.

"Mr. Comodio, if you can just wait, we're going to——"

But Mr. Comodio had already worked himself into a state of uncontainable indignation. "I told Dr. Barrios I dripped some red Popsicle on my shirt and asked if I could get a free replacement, and Barrios is telling me no, because this is the second time it's happened."

Mr. Weber pressed his lips together and raised his substantial eyebrows.

Another teacher chimed in furiously. "You got the first replacement for free? They made me *buy* a replacement. And my shirt was damaged on school property!"

Indeed, T-shirt issues seemed to be the main reason for the day's high turnout. Everyone had gotten one shirt for free, but the requirement to wear the shirts every day meant either daily laundry or paying out of pocket for additional shirts. Even Hernan had to admit it was an inconvenience.

"I have an update about the shirts." Mr. Weber raised a hand for silence. "We found a clause in the contract that says the district cannot dictate staff uniform on any day except every other Monday. So you only have to wear the shirts on the first and third Monday of each month."

Cheers of liberation rose from the crowd.

Mr. Weber sped through the other updates. Then, before anyone could mention the T-shirts again, he said, "Okay, everyone, you know how this works: If you don't have anything specific to discuss, you can go."

Most of the attendees headed toward the door. Others collected in the corners of the room, forming small whirlpools of disenchantment, or gathered near Mr. Weber in the hopes of overhearing gossip.

Don Comodio barreled toward Mr. Weber, filling in the details of his story as he crossed the room. "So I told Barrios, *Fine. Just watch. I'm going to wear the shirt with a Popsicle stain every day and see how you like it.*"

"Hernandez!" Mr. Weber crossed the room toward Hernan with an enthusiasm he had not shown earlier. "Didn't you say you wanted to talk about something?"

Hernan waited for Lena to pass on her way out.

"Hey, Hernan," she said. "I didn't know you were a union member now."

"I'm not."

"He's not," confirmed Mr. Weber.

Breyonna followed Lena out the door, the two of them discussing some poetry event Lena had invited Breyonna to. Hernan forced himself not to listen.

"Okay, Hernandez, what's up?"

"Mr. Scamphers had a support dialogue with me."

Maybelline, who was standing nearby, began flipping through some papers in a folder she was carrying.

Hernan lowered his voice. "He wrote me up for having a fridge in my classroom. And he said I don't take data seriously."

Maybelline looked up again and stared at Hernan for a couple of seconds like she wanted to say something. Then she gathered her things and hurried out of the room.

"See?" said Mr. Weber, when the two of them were alone in the room. "This type of shit is why I told you to sign up in the first place."

"I know." Hernan had been expecting this. "It's probably too late now, right?"

"I hate to say it, Hernandez, but you're on your own. If disciplinary action is already started, it's like trying to get insurance after you already crashed your car."

"Yeah. I kinda figured. Thanks, anyway." Hernan turned to leave.

That probably would have been the end of the conversation, but Don Comodio came thrashing back into the room again, quite possibly to share more thoughts on the Popsicle-stained T-shirt.

"Wait," called Mr. Weber. "I'll walk you out."

They hurried down the hallway. Mr. Weber spoke quietly, looking straight ahead like an informant in a James Bond movie. "Look, Hernandez, normally I don't offer help to anyone who makes our union weaker—which is all nonmembers, like you. But I'll tell you one thing: Whatever you do, don't sign anything you don't agree with."

Hernan nodded. He didn't say that he had already signed paperwork before realizing he didn't agree with it.

"Also, whatever you do, don't talk in person, especially to a sneaky bastard like Scamphers. Send an e-mail instead. You want a written record of your side of the story."

Hernan didn't say that he had already talked to Mr. Scamphers in person and had no written record of the conversation. He'd left himself as defenseless as a glacier against climate change—or a bluebonnet against the mysterious fungus that had now killed nearly every bluebonnet plant in the city and was spreading toward the rest of the state. It was almost April. Every garden should have been aflame with the blue flowers. Instead, there were only sad patches of missing foliage, and the Hernandez greenhouse was in no position to replace them. Only the bluebonnets from Hernan's classroom had so far managed to avoid infection, springing into bloom as if they hadn't gotten the memo. But even that was probably just a matter of time.

As they reached the door to the parking lot, Mr. Weber raised his voice back to its usual volume. "I do hope you'll be joining the union next time you have the chance."

"Yeah." Hernan nodded. "For sure."

"Good luck, Hernandez," called Mr. Weber as he pushed open the door and walked outside. "I hope it works out for you."

He almost sounded as if he meant it.

SUPPORT ANSWERS WITH
SPECIFIC DETAILS

"**YOU DIDN'T TELL** me this club was ghetto as hell," said Breyonna. She maneuvered her Land Rover—her *new* Land Rover, as she kept reminding them—through the deserted streets that led to the poetry club.

Regina sat in the passenger seat, eyeing the landscape and occasionally letting out a disdainful "Whaaa?"

Lena realized she should have been clearer about where the club was located.

"This is gonna be nothing but women and broke muthafuckas," said Regina. "I wasted an outfit on this."

"There are guys," said Lena, though, as they pulled into the parking lot, she mostly saw women.

"Right," said Breyonna, "driving their mama's cars, putting in five dollars of gas, talking about *I filled up the tank*."

Candace, who had managed to sit next to Lena in the back seat without ever speaking to her directly, let out a cackly laugh. "Well, at least we get in for free."

The statement increased Lena's edginess. In her optimism about what time three sorority girls would actually be ready, she had forgotten to mention that ladies only got in free until ten thirty. The clock on Breyonna's dashboard already said 10:21. The slowness of the thumping cars in front of them now felt almost personal, as if Lena lacked some essential quality that would have forced them to move faster.

Women in tight outfits poured out of cars, hurrying to line up before the ladies' night special evaporated.

By the time they had reached the edge of the parking lot, and Breyonna had conspicuously turned on her alarm and inspected the area around her tires for broken glass, and the four of them had navigated back across the lot in their heels, it was 10:27.

The line moved slowly. At the door was the bouncer she remembered from her date with Nex Level, leaning on his stool. He'd told her he'd gone to the Hill, Lena remembered, and she smiled at him. But if he recognized her, he didn't show it. He waved in the two women just before her, greeting them like old friends. Then he looked at his watch and moved his stool so it blocked the path to the door.

"Ten thirty, everybody," he boomed to the line. "Have y'all money ready."

"I thought you said this place was free," said Candace.

Lena tried to make eye contact, but the bouncer ignored her again, waving in two guys who stepped forward with money in their hands.

The parking lot had filled almost completely now. There was only one empty spot remaining, and cars circled past it without pulling in. Lena's eyes combed the spot in spite of her efforts to redirect them, collecting the image and delivering it to some involuntary reception center in her brain.

A sliver of orange. The edge of a traffic cone.

Suddenly, getting an acknowledgment from the bouncer seemed like the most urgent thing in the world.

"Hey." Lena stood right in front of him. "Don't you remember me?"

"Ten thirty. Ten dollars." His tone suggested nothing bored him more than complaints from ladies who'd missed the ladies'-night cutoff.

She'd never been dismissed like this, especially not when she was dressed up. Now she said, with a little more attitude, "I was just tryna see if you remembered me. I work at—"

"Ten dollars, dear. If you ain't got your money ready, step to the side." He waved in another group and pulled the rope closed in front of her again.

"I'm friends with Nex Level," said Lena, hating herself even as she said it.

"Wait," said Candace, "isn't that that guy you were talking about at happy hour?"

Lena hoped Candace would fall and hurt herself.

"Everybody here friends with everybody. Ten dollars."

"Fine." She pulled out her money, ending the conversation before Candace said anything else.

As they entered the dark club, Lena headed straight to the table in the back, ordered a rum and Coke, and asked the bartender to make it strong. Then she added her name to the open-mic list. Because that was why she was here: to read her poem.

She'd drained two more drinks by the time she rejoined her companions, who had clustered in the corner to talk about the same subjects they always talked about. Lena smiled until her cheeks hurt as Breyonna described her wedding plans, which mostly consisted of a list of things she would never do at her wedding because they were tacky. Serving chicken at a wedding was tacky. Having the reception in the meeting hall of the church was tacky. And, apparently, it was tacky for the bride and groom to walk into the reception without something about a flock of butterflies and a nonrefundable deposit that Lena could barely hear but laughed at anyway, and she kept laughing while Regina complained about how there were only busted-ass men at this club, and laughed again when Candace, who hadn't spoken to Lena the whole night and might not have even been speaking to her then, said, *Hey, I thought Hernan was coming*, and laughed even harder when Breyonna said, *Girl, will you stop talking about Hernan?* Because it wasn't like Lena was here to do anything besides read her poem, but if Nex did show up, he would have to see that she was having fun. And why shouldn't she be? She had every right to be here, enjoying poetry with her friends. Anyway, she dared him to question her about why she had come out to "his" club. She had rehearsed her answers to anything he could say almost much as she had practiced the poem itself. If he called her afterwards, she'd already decided she wouldn't pick up. He would have to try more than once if he wanted to reach her after all this time. Unless he didn't try more than once. Maybe she would pick up.

Lena kept drinking as the possibilities ran through her head. She drank until the poems became a blur of topics she had heard before.

Every now and then, she looked over her shoulder, not exactly for Nex—but almost. When the emcee finally called her name, she finished the drink in her hand, passed the cup to Breyonna, and strutted to the platform. At least she thought she was strutting. She was drunker than she'd realized.

"How y'all feelin'?" she said. She waited for encouraging shouts from the crowd, but heard only a thin murmur. "We got any teachers in here tonight?"

Club Seven had always been filled with teachers who whooped and shouted in response to this question, but now, as she surveyed the crowd, she saw only Breyonna and Regina clapping. Even Candace was just standing there, checking her phone. *Bitch.*

Okay, so teachers didn't come to this place. So what? She had a good poem and she was gonna own it. "Well, I work at Brae Hill Valley High School—I mean, the Hill—and you know we got that TCUP test coming up . . ." Lena felt herself pouring words into the silence as she tried to force the crowd to open and let her in.

Eyes shifted toward cell phones. Conversations resumed. She started slowly. "Air drains from the room/ But that's not what we need . . ."

Here, she sped up. She'd rehearsed every part of the poem, along with the corresponding gestures and facial expressions and pauses, until the performance was as automatic as a part in a play. "You think it's all cool/ till you sit after school/ with sixteen-year-old students still learning to read. . ."

A few conversations stopped. They were coming back to her. When she knew her lines well, it always felt like there were two of her—one on stage performing, the other circling the room, watching the crowd react.

"Tapping their feet. . ."

The off-stage part of her saw the door open.

"Shifting and creaking the seats . . ."

She recognized the side of Nex's face as he entered, lit by a parking-lot light just outside the door. After so many weeks of existing only in her imagination, he looked somehow strange and familiar at the same time. The crowd parted to let him through—a little too wide, it seemed, until it became clear that they were letting in someone else in just behind him. A woman. Somehow, in all her mental rehearsals for this moment, Lena had skipped this possibility.

"Struggling students with ninety-nine problems apiece . . ." The part of her that was onstage switched to autopilot. The rest of her watched, as if in slow motion, as the vibrations of her voice reached Nex Level. A flicker of recognition crossed his face, turning to something that might have been worry as he looked up and met her eyes for the briefest of moments. Then he looked away, guiding the woman behind him toward the corner farthest from the stage.

The part of Lena that was performing kept moving, propelling the practiced lines into the crowd until the applause signaled that she had finished. She rushed off the stage. A few people complimented her in what seemed to be a hazy blur. She couldn't tell whether she answered them or not.

She wobbled on her heels back to the bar, away from her friends and the corner where she'd last spotted Nex Level. A guy offered to buy her a drink. He was okay-looking, though he had a cold sore that Lena had to try hard not to look at. She accepted the drink, drained it, and laughed hard as he talked. She didn't even realize she wasn't listening until he asked, "You waiting for someone?"

"Huh?" She smiled and touched his arm flirtatiously.

"You keep looking behind you. You looking for somebody?"

"No. Not at all!" said Lena, though her eyes combed the room even as she said it.

And then she caught sight of them. They'd left the corner and were mingling with the crowd. Beyond them, on the far side of the room, she saw Breyonna, Regina, and Candace looking around. It was hard to tell whether they were searching for her or diligently looking away from a guy wearing a dollar-sign medallion who was trying to start a conversation.

"I mean, yeah—I'm looking for my friends. And I just saw them. Over there." She stumbled as she turned, but the guy caught her before she fell. She looked into his eyes flirtatiously one last time.

"So, can I get your number?"

"Probably later," she said, and made her way through the crowd.

She was so drunk that it really was almost an accident when, just as she called out to Breyonna, she stepped backward and bumped right into Nex Level.

"Sorry," she said loudly, then looked back at him as if surprised.

"Don't worry about it," he said, then quickly turned away. Had he not seen her? Or, wait—had he just pretended he didn't *recognize* her?

Too drunk to be subtle now, she turned all the way toward him. "Oh, hey! Look who it is."

The woman with Nex looked at him as if expecting an introduction.

The moment pulsated around them. There had been times in Lena's life when she'd said things and regretted them later, and an equal number of times when she had regretted not saying more. Now, she was desperate for this moment not to fall into either of those categories. She needed this woman, who was giving her a look that might have been pity, to know this was how Nex treated women after months of. . . months of . . .

Months of *nothing*. The realization flashed into her eyes like a strobe light. There was nothing Nex had done, nothing he had said or promised her, that entitled her to act like she had any claim on him. It was just like Breyonna said: She'd given it up on credit.

Suddenly, Lena didn't want a confrontation.

"Now what is going on *here*?" said a voice nearby, and she turned to see Regina. Somehow, Breyonna, Candace, and Regina had appeared behind her. An understanding of the situation was just beginning to register on their faces.

Lena hoped Regina would shut up.

"Hey, isn't that the poetry dude you were talking about at happy hour?"

Lena hoped Candace would catch on fire.

"Is this somebody I should be meeting?" said the woman at Nex Level's side.

Nex leaned closed to her, lowering his voice as he answered.

It was clear that he didn't want Lena to hear what he was saying, and maybe if she hadn't been listening so hard, and maybe if the music hadn't stopped at that exact moment as the next poet took the stage, she wouldn't have heard it:

"Nah. Everyone who performs here kinda thinks they know me."

And just like that, Lena didn't want to be a poet anymore. She didn't want to do anything, ever again, that forced her to be the center of attention or search for the right words. All she wanted was to be far away from Nex Level, out of the club, back in the car, and then back in her bed, maybe forever. But she couldn't move.

"Oh. Hell. No." It was Breyonna, now. But she did not sound surprised, like Regina, or gleeful, like Candace. She sounded mad. She moved closer to Nex Level, her eyes narrowing. "Did you just act like you don't even *know* my friend, you unemployed piece of shit?"

Nex turned toward her, eyebrows raised.

"Yeah." Breyonna pushed forward even farther, poking a shiny fingernail into his chest. "I'm talking to you, *Next Generation*, or whatever your name is. I know your type, you broke-ass pretty boy."

Nex Level backed away from Breyonna with a gesture that suggested his innocence. "Look, I'm just saying your friend seems a little confused. She just don't seem like she from around here. That's all I'm saying."

Eyes were turning toward them from every direction. Lena felt like a sheep surrounded by wolves.

Breyonna looked at Nex Level like he was an insect buzzing around her plate. "Why the fuck would she want to be from around *here*? She's an educator. With an educa-*shun*. My only question is why she would ever waste her time with you."

"Let's go." Lena grabbed Breyonna's arm. She hadn't wanted Nex to know she had ever talked about him, though Candace had already ruined that. But she really didn't want this to turn into a scene about who was wasting whose time, who had an education, who belonged where.

"No." Breyonna shrugged off Lena's grip. "*Fuck* this motherfucker! This dude probably drives his mama's car to get here, putting in five dollars of gas, talking about, *I filled up the tank*."

Nex grabbed his companion by the hand, pulling her into the crowd behind him.

Breyonna looked like she wanted to follow them, but Lena grabbed her arm again, more forcefully this time. "Let's go. Please!"

"Yeah!" Breyonna yelled toward Nex's retreating figure as Lena dragged her toward the door. "That's what I thought! Now let's go get back into my *new Land Rover* and out of this Ghetto. Ass. Club."

When Lena replayed the moment, as she would often in the coming weeks, she had trouble remembering what the woman at Nex Level's side had actually looked like. There was nothing memorably pretty about her. Yet she was so conspicuously *not ugly* that Lena couldn't be sure she was not in some way beautiful. Even this, however, was not what Lena remembered most clearly. Nor was it Nex Level saying, *She just don't seem like she from around here*, though this phrase, too, was enough to shut off Lena's appetite and constrict her intestines.

What she remembered most of all was this: As Nex Level led the woman away into the darkness of the club, he'd been holding her hand.

AVOID CARELESS ERRORS

MAYBELLINE DIALED ROSEMARY'S number again. She'd called over and over for the first half hour of her planning period, but each time, the phone rang through to voice mail. This was how it worked with Rosemary: She wouldn't pick up until she'd ignored some magic number of calls.

It had been a bad decision, Maybelline knew, to spill her sister's secret on the night of the Super Bowl. She could not go quite so far as to feel sorry about it, but that didn't matter because apologizing wouldn't have worked anyway. Rosemary never admitted to being angry. The only thing to do was beg, and that only worked sometimes.

In the meantime, Rosemary had seized an opportunity to place Maybelline at her passive-aggressive mercy. The "national holiday" known as Take Our Daughters and Sons to Work Day was coming up, and Rosemary was planning to take Gabriella to the mall. That made sense: Shopping was about the closest thing Rosemary had to a real job. Except she'd invited Allyson, who was supposed to be grounded for bad grades.

Maybelline dialed again, so resigned to another round of Rosemary's voice mail greeting that she was surprised to hear a *click*, followed by an irritated, "Yes?"

"Rosemary, we need to talk about next Thursday."

"Mmm-hmm. What about it?"

"I really don't want Allyson missing school."

"Then drive her yourself." Clearly, Rosemary had been waiting to say this.

"Look, you know Allyson's school is too far out of the way for me in the mornings. If I wait for the doors to open, I'll be late."

"Well, next Thursday, school is out of the way for me."

"It's *your* neighborhood school, Rosemary. I'm the one who has to drop her at your house every morning and then get to work by seven."

"Exactly."

Maybelline tried to pull back to safe ground. Talking about work with Rosemary was dangerous territory. "And, I mean, I appreciate it. I'm just saying that when I enrolled her under your address, you knew I would need you to drive her in the mornings."

"Well, *usually* I'm pretty nice about covering for you as a parent." The mention of work had reminded Rosemary this was punishment time. "But I'm not going to be the only one who doesn't take their kid to work that day. Especially since Gabriella just made honor roll."

It was this last sentence that did it. Even as she opened her mouth, Maybelline knew she was making another mistake, but she could not stop herself. "So going to the mall counts as 'work'?"

"Yeah. You're right. It's not. So I guess you should probably take Allyson with *you* on Thursday. To your *real* job."

Maybelline was about to respond that Allyson was not coming anywhere near Brae Hill Valley High School when she developed a sense that she was not alone in the room. She turned around. Sure enough, Roger Scamphers was behind her, smiling, one hand squeezing his keys into silence.

"Listen, Rosemary, my boss just walked in. I have to call you back." She knew this sounded like a comeback. After all, one needed a job to have a boss. But there was no way to explain.

"Okay. You can try. But I'll probably be busy." Rosemary hung up.

"Good morning, Mr. Scamphers!" Maybelline tried to sound cheerfully surprised. She wondered how long he had been in the room.

"Good morning to you, Ms. Galang. I got your e-mail yesterday, but it seemed like a better idea to talk about this in person."

"Definitely," said Maybelline, relieved.

Ever since she'd sent the e-mail during the Super Bowl, she'd been waiting for a sign that Mr. Scamphers was starting a paper trail on Lena Wright. Instead, he seemed to be prying for information about Hernan Hernandez. This had nagged at her, until finally she'd sent an e-mail suggesting she might be able to help more directly.

"I am not telling anyone else this, Ms. Galang, but I trust you, and I do need someone helpful."

Maybelline nodded eagerly, waiting for him to ask exactly what she'd been hinting at in her e-mail. It would feel so good to finally say Lena's name aloud.

Mr. Scamphers lowered his voice. "Our superintendent has approached me privately to say I may be considered for a principal position next year, provided our school meets certain . . . numerical targets."

"Well, I am a numbers person."

"I had a feeling I could count on you." He moved closer. "With all this national attention, Superintendent Wallabee needs to make sure teachers' Believer Scores align closely with their students' test scores. It's a delicate situation, as you can imagine."

Maybelline nodded, though she wasn't exactly sure what she should be imagining. Then again, she'd always thought imagination was overrated.

"Especially since they've got those computer programs now. Any teacher who messed with an answer sheet would get caught in a second."

Maybelline was confused. None of this had anything to do with the misunderstanding about Hernan. Nor did it have any connection to Lena Wright's forbidden classroom fridge and disregard for data.

"Luckily, Mr. Wallabee has a close relationship with Global Schoolhouse's test-creation division. They've been kind enough to provide some preview documents ahead of the test."

"But that's—"

"I know. It's still a logistical nightmare. It's important to remember that the questions and answer choices will be in different orders on different tests, but the questions themselves are the same. The good news is that the OBEI people are in charge of test security, and I've already got them eating out of my hand. And now I'm in charge of the Believers Scores. I just need help distributing the materials to certain teachers whose discretion we trust. Teachers like you, for example."

Suddenly, Mr. Scamphers's smile didn't seem so friendly. Giving out test questions ahead of time wasn't just against the rules—it was against the law. But it was the last part, *teachers like you*, that bothered her the most.

"Mr. Scamphers"—she straightened and looked him in the eye—"I am *not* going to help anyone cheat."

Mr. Scamphers emitted a lighthearted laugh that sounded strange coming from him. "Oh, Ms. Galang! I hope *that* wasn't what you thought I meant."

"Okay. Good." Perhaps she had misunderstood.

He studied her face intently for a moment. Finally, he said, "I was only mentioning that I've taken on a lot of the responsibility for making this school run correctly."

"I understand." Maybelline felt the conversation clicking back into its groove. "Actually, that's why I e-mailed you—to make sure you knew exactly who I was talking about when I said—"

"For example," Mr. Scamphers continued, ignoring her, "I'm very good at catching students who use fake addresses to enroll here. You may have noticed that some of the failing students on that list you sent me have not returned to your class."

"Yes. Thank you," said Maybelline, though she hadn't realized what Mr. Scamphers had done with the names she'd sent him. She tried not to seem worried. Had he heard her conversation with Rosemary? Had she said enough to incriminate herself?

The long look Mr. Scamphers gave her answered both questions. "If I knew about a situation where someone was doing that at another school, it would probably make sense for me to tell the administrators there. I'm sure you can imagine."

"Yes," said Maybelline, and this time, she found she could.

"Good. So we understand each other."

She nodded. Her throat felt dry.

"Get ready, Ms. Galang. You might be calling me Principal Scamphers next year." He gathered his keys tightly in his fist and stepped into the hallway without a sound.

In the last five minutes of her planning period, Maybelline tried several more times to call Rosemary, but each time, the phone rang through to voice mail.

TESTING SEASON

DR. BARRIOS SANK into his desk chair, coffee in hand. He needed it. There was nothing like the onslaught of e-mails a principal received during testing season.

6:59 A.M.

Subject: Testing Protocol and Security Measures

URGENT: As you are all aware, testing begins next week. Administrators are reminded to follow all protocols and test-security measures. Failure to comply may result in disciplinary action.

7:01 A.M.

Subject: Sample Question of the Day Achievement Initiative

URGENT: Effective immediately, instructors at Believers Zone schools are to write one sample test question on the board each morning and discuss it with students. Please note the Sample Test Question of the Day must be erased before students are released to their testing rooms. Failure to comply may result in disciplinary action.

Subject: TCUP Assessment Pep Rally

URGENT: All Believers Zone schools are to hold a motivational pep rally in the one-week period leading up to the TCUP test. If you have not scheduled a pep rally, please begin planning one immediately.

Subject: Take Our Daughters and Sons to Work Day

URGENT: This year brings yet another increase in participation in Take Our Daughters and Sons to Work Day. Teachers and administrators are to respect students' decisions to embrace real-world work experience but also reiterate the importance of taking upcoming tests seriously. Please encourage students to look for opportunities to practice testlike questions while visiting their parents' workplaces.

METHODS OF DEVELOPMENT

WHAT WOULD AN additional paragraph at the end of this passage—

"Miss, can I go get a permission form if we're not doing anything later?" As usual, Luis's timing was so bad it seemed purposely designed to get on Lena's nerves. She'd already signed permission forms for half of her first-period students by the time Mrs. Rawlins made the announcement about the Sample Test Question of the Day initiative.

"Luis, have we ever *not done anything* in this class? Ever?"

Luis huffed back to his seat. Lena finished writing the methods-of-development question on the board. In its entirety. *What would an additional paragraph at the end of this passage likely be about?*

The PA beeped again. "Thank you for another interruption. The following teachers and their students will please report to the auditorium for a TCUP assessment pep rally: Mr. Hernandez, Ms. Mahoney, Ms. Wright . . ."

Cheering drowned out the rest of the announcement. *Pep rally! No class!*

"Miss, can I stop by the office on the way down to the pep rally?"

"I said no, Luis."

There were so many reasons to miss class at Brae Hill Valley High School: pep rallies, obviously. But also field trips. Athletic events. Personal illness, or the illness of a family memeber. Car trouble. A family member having a baby. Court dates. Headaches. Cramps. Babysitting for the baby of a family member who had a court date, or a headache, or cramps. The due date of a major project that you did not do. Fridays. Mondays. The days before or after a three-day weekend. Tuesdays on weeks when you didn't come to school Monday, which was almost like a three-day weekend. Classes where you never did anything. Classes where the teacher always made you work. The willingness of at least one adult relative to pick you up early if you said you were bored. The entire week before a major holiday. Days when you were just doing test prep. The days after the test was over, when nothing mattered any-more. Diarrhea. Constipation. The Monday after a late-night TV awards show. Classes where you hated the teacher. Classes where the teacher hated you. Rain.

But not one of these excuses was quite as delectable as the national holiday known as Take Our Daughters and Sons to Work Day. Every year, on the fourth Thursday of April, the only thing that stood between most teenagers and a whole day off from school was a form from the attendance office. Students needed only to complete this form with what appeared to be a parent's signature, then gleefully thrust it toward their teachers, who would have no choice but to excuse the student to spend the next day at work with their parents. Most parents, mean-while, assumed their teenage children were at school.

This explained the crowd blocking the hallway as Lena walked her class toward the auditorium. A long line of students waited outside the entrance of the attendance office, while others stopped immediately outside its exit, forging their parents' signatures as they pressed the forms against any available flat surface: the wall, the floor, even the backs of friends who were simultaneously forging signatures on their own forms. The entire area around the attendance office was now a noisy tableau representing the exact opposite of attendance.

Luis turned to Lena with a pleading look.

"Don't even think about it, Luis."

The only thing worse than a test-related pep rally was a last-minute test-related pep rally. The only thing worse than that was a last-minute test-related pep rally planned by Mrs. Rawlins. The auditorium, when they arrived, was rowdy even by Brae Hill Valley standards. Teachers did their best to corral their classes into adjoining blocks of seats as students streamed through the doors and threaded through the aisles, searching for their friends. Onstage, a nineteen-year-old deejay played Lena's least favorite song.

All my bros packed in my ride like a space ship . . . Pick them hands up, put 'em high like a facelift . . . Ridin' through the sky with my hand on the gear shift . . . Yeah, I got that go switch, that go switch.

Mrs. Rawlins, who was almost definitely responsible for the lack of seating arrangements, was yelling into the microphone. "Teachers, please be reminded that y'all are responsible for your students' behavior!"

Mrs. Rawlins's unshakeable belief in honoring students' interests, combined with her position next to the onstage speakers, left her unaware that she was listening to the radio-friendly version of a much less appropriate song, the lyrics of which students knew by heart and were now belting out with enthusiasm.

Niggaz all packed in my ride like a slave ship . . . Empty-head hoes getting high like a facelift . . . Ridin' on my dick 'cause they all want that good shit . . . Yeah, I got that good shit, that good shit.

Lena searched the room for partners in her misery. Maybelline Galang looked unhappy, but she did not make eye contact with Lena. Kaytee Mahoney was off to the side, pacing the aisle near her students and glaring at Mrs. Rawlins. Breyonna was there, too, but she was way up front, with a group of cheerleaders who were preparing to go onstage. Lately, Lena had felt a surge of affection and gratitude when she saw Breyonna, but the sight of cheerleaders removed any temptation to move closer.

But it wasn't just the cheerleaders that made Lena stay where she was. She was sure she'd heard Hernan's name as part of the pep-rally announcement. Or was she just imagining she'd heard it? Maybe it was some auditory mirage her mind had created because, she suddenly realized, the only thing that could possibly make the next hour bearable would be enduring it with Hernan at her side.

And then a door on the far side of the auditorium opened, and there he was, the light of the hallway streaming in behind him. He caught her eye, sharing a complicit grin as he directed his students toward the nearest empty section. Her hope deflated. She'd already wrangled her own students into a semicohesive seating arrangement, and there was no moving them now. There was nothing to do but stay right where she was, separated from Hernan by an ocean of screaming teenagers.

The pep part of the pep rally was beginning. The cheerleaders ran onstage first, performing a cheer in which they replaced the name of the opposing team with the phrase *TCUP test!* Then the football players jumped onto the stage in their uniforms, striking aggressive poses as Coach Ray bellowed into the microphone in his game-day voice, "What are we gonna do next week, y'all?"

"Beat that test!" the players yelled back.

All of this went on for as long as such things could possibly go on, after which Coach Ray handed the microphone back to Mrs. Rawlins, who looked at the clock and said, "Um . . ." in a way that suggested this had been the total extent of her planning.

Then, as if remembering that she enjoyed speaking into microphones regardless of her level of preparation, she brightened. "Students, I want to know who can tell me today's Sample Test Question of the Day!"

No one answered. The students in the audience lowered their voices, sensing that the most boisterous among them might be singled out and forced to participate. They played with their cell phones and generally avoided looking at the stage.

"Come on, now! Didn't your teachers put the question on the board this morning?"

Now it was the teachers' turn to avoid looking at the stage. Lena had barely finished writing the sample question when the pep-rally announcement interrupted her. She certainly hadn't had time to review it with her students. Looking around at her colleagues, she sensed she wasn't the only one.

"Well, all right, then." Mrs. Rawlins sounded like she was running out of peppy things to say. "Let's have our teachers come up here and give you some test-taking tips!"

The cheerleaders shook their pom-poms in approval. The deejay put the song back on, and once again the students drowned out the clean version with the original lyrics.

Got that good shit, that good shit. . . Pack it like a slave ship, a slave ship. . .

Mrs. Rawlins called up the teachers, who shuffled up the stairs to the stage with the enthusiasm of a chain gang.

For most of her life, Lena had loved performing in front of an audience. Ever since her humiliation at the poetry club, however, the thought of being on a stage had filled her with dread. Now, as she watched black and Latino students gleefully singing about *niggaz* and *slave ships*, and girls delightedly shaking their bodies to lyrics about *empty-head hoes*, her desire to be elsewhere was so heavy it weighed down her limbs.

"What's wrong?" It was Hernan's voice. He was walking up the stairs behind her.

"I hate this."

"I know. The only thing worse than a last-minute TCUP pep rally is a last-minute TCUP pep rally planned by Mrs. Rawlins."

"For real," said Lena. The relief of hearing Hernan echo her thoughts propelled her forward and onto the stage.

Got that good shit, that good shit . . . Pack it like a slave ship, a slave ship . . .

Didn't this deejay have any other songs?

"First," the music stopped again, and Mrs. Rawlins passed Lena the microphone. "Let's hear from Ms. Wright!"

The sensation of the cold metal in her hand locked Lena into the double consciousness she always experienced while performing. This time, however, the part of her that was onstage felt powerless to command the crowd's attention. The other part of her watched the room, where students were playing with their phones . . . turning around in their seats . . . laughing . . . at her?

"Make sure you get a good night's sleep," she mumbled.

She passed the microphone to Kaytee, who said something about eating breakfast and handed off the microphone to the next person as quickly as she could.

The students showed no interest. Then again, why would they? The tips were nothing new. They were repeated every year, in every class and at every test pep rally, as if circling keywords or getting enough sleep could somehow cancel out a lifetime of accumulated reading deficits. The microphone made its way down the line until it reached Mrs. Rawlins, and the teachers readied themselves to exit the stage.

But Mrs. Rawlins was looking at the clock again. "Um . . ."

Lena had a feeling something bad was about to happen.

"Okay, I have another idea for y'all. Who wants to see your teachers dance?!"

Now the students were paying attention. They shrieked, lifting their phones to capture the moment on video.

The music started again, and so did the students: *Niggaz all packed in my ride like a slave ship . . .*

This time, it seemed every face in the auditorium was roaring the lyrics, every finger pointing at the teachers on stage.

EMPTY-HEAD HOES GETTING HIGH LIKE A FACELIFT!

Lena felt her body stiffen but did her best to move to the music. Anything to move this moment forward.

RIDING ON MY DICK 'CAUSE THEY ALL WANT THAT GOOD SHIT!

YEAH, I GOT THAT GOOD SHIT, THAT GOOD SHIT . . .

Time slowed. It seemed she would never be done jerking her heavy marionette of a body as what now seemed like millions of laughing teenagers yelled at her to pack it like a slave ship. She thought bitterly about how many of her students hadn't bothered to memorize the poem she'd assigned for Black History Month. And yet they all knew the words to this ridiculous, illiterate fucking song.

When the music finally stopped, the teachers did not wait for Mrs. Rawlins to have another idea. They collectively lunged toward the stairs leading off the stage. Lena made it to the stairs first, followed closely by Kaytee, and then Hernan.

"All right!" said Mrs. Rawlins, behind them. "The pep rally is over, y'all!"

"The only thing worse than a last-minute TCUP pep rally planned by Mrs. Rawlins," said Hernan, "is a last-minute TCUP pep rally planned by Mrs. Rawlins that only takes up half the class period."

Both Lena and Kaytee froze.

"No way," said Kaytee.

"No way," echoed Lena. But when she looked at the clock, she saw Hernan was right: There would still be twenty-five minutes of class when they got back to their rooms. If it had been ten minutes, or even fifteen, she might have been able to get away with letting students "pack up" until the bell. But twenty-five minutes was legit learning time. It meant at least twenty minutes of cajoling students to work on a day when they had already celebrated the cancellation of class.

The teachers hurried down the stairs to direct their students, who were swarming into the aisles.

Behind them, Mrs. Rawlins was still on stage, doing her engage-the-youths thing. "It looks like a lot of you recorded our dance contest! Teachers, watch out! Some of you might be YouTube stars pretty soon!"

Kaytee let out a long breath. "Fuck this lady. Fuck this whole fucking place."

Lena was so surprised to hear Kaytee say something negative that for a moment she forgot to be miserable.

The moment lasted precisely until she and her students reentered the classroom. The events of the morning had adjusted the lens of some internal camera so that Lena could only focus on the most annoying possible student behaviors. And there were many.

"Stop that," Lena growled to a boy strumming the teeth of a plastic comb.

"Leave her alone," she said to another boy, who was stroking the hair of the girl in front of him. "And you—stop putting your hair on his desk."

The best option for running down the clock on first period was the Global Schoolhouse test prep workbook. Lena flipped through passages until she found one that included the Sample Test Question of the Day: *What would an additional paragraph at the end of this passage likely be about?*

The question barely even made sense to Lena. Why would there need to be another paragraph at the end of the passage? Wasn't it complete? And, if it wasn't complete, couldn't a story take almost any direction after its arbitrary endpoint? But this was not life, or literature, or even the type of material any reader would ever consume by choice. This was a test-prep practice passage. Thus, even a below-average test taker had to know the hypothetical final paragraph would contain some life-affirming testament to the strength of the human spirit. The predictability of it always made Lena want to roll her eyes. Except that she was exhausted. The pilot light inside her was flickering, as if just one small breath might extinguish it completely. In this state, she found she desperately wanted whatever moment came next to be inspiring. Life affirming, even. Perhaps even a testament to the strength of the human spirit.

It was at that moment that the door opened, and in walked Rico Jones, holding a permission form for Take Our Daughters and Sons to Work Day.

"You're late," said Lena.

"Sorry," said Rico, without looking sorry at all. "I had to get this form."

"The class is more than half over."

"The line was long." In Rico's other hand was a freshly opened bag of (BAKED!) Reetos.

He'd stopped to buy chips.

Lena felt the anger in her bloodstream building to a toxic level. "You know what? Just sit down."

"But you're gonna sign it, right?"

"Please do a little of your job, which is coming to school and learning, before you talk to me about *pretending* to spend the day at your parents' job."

Rico turned, slowly, toward an area where he might conceivably find a seat.

"Teacher tryna act like she know me," he muttered, not *to* Lena but loud enough for Lena to hear. Then, for the benefit of either himself or the closest sympathetic student, he added, "She ain't even from around here."

Looking back, the string connecting Lena to her last bit of patience had already grown thin.

But it was still Rico's last line that snapped it.

"Rico," Lena said, her voice turning treacherously pleasant, "do you *really* think you need to miss school *one week* before the *TCUP test* when you *read at a fourth-grade level*?"

Part of Lena saw the smile disappear from Rico's face, but she couldn't stop. A valve inside her had opened, releasing content packed for too long under too much pressure. Her voice grew louder and even more ominously calm as she continued. "Do you know what *that* means, Rico? That means you can't understand a book that an *eleven-year-old child* would read for *fun*. That means you will never, *ever* hold a decent job unless your reading improves dramatically, which would take a lot of work. But instead of being worried about this and working harder, you are so . . . *worried* about whether I am going to *sign a form* so that you can skip school tomorrow. Because God forbid you and your *nine-year-old reading level* go to an extra . . . *day of school*, Rico."

She'd almost said *so* fucking *worried* and *go to an extra* fucking *day of school*, but she'd caught herself in time. She'd caught herself in time, right?

The class was frozen like a movie on pause.

The part of Lena that was watching the scene caught up with the part of her that was standing in front of the class.

Stop, it said. *Stop talking.*

Her fingers felt icy. The words that had just left her mouth seemed to hover, as if inviting her to reach out and pull them from the air. In front of her, Rico seemed a bright shape surrounded by shadows, staring at her.

She became conscious of the way her body was positioned in space, as if she was watching the whole scene from outside: Lena Wright, hands on her hips, head cocked confrontationally to one side. Rico Jones, bag of chips in one hand, permission form pulled into his skinny chest. Thirty sets of wide eyes in front of her, tiny mirrors reflecting what she had become.

It was Rico who finally resumed the action, made time start moving again. "Never mind," he said. He crumpled the unsigned form into a ball. Then he turned, dropped the paper into the garbage, and continued out the door.

"Keep working in your workbooks," said Lena to the rest of the class.

And they did. No one—not even Luis—said anything until the bell rang.

There were three more class periods before lunchtime—three groups of students filing in and out at the sound of the bell. Lena told them all to work in their workbooks. She sat in her desk chair, trying to seem busy. Choosing words and saying them aloud seemed like a responsibility for which she was no longer suited. Why had she ever wanted to become a teacher? Why had she chosen a job that wedged her so tightly into the chain of cause and effect that when she made a wrong move, the dominos never stopped falling? She wanted to lie down forever, cover her face in a room full of silence.

But no, she realized. That wasn't it at all. What she really wanted was to bolt from her chair and run to the end of the hallway, straight to the plant-filled science lab of Hernan D. Hernandez.

METHODS OF DEVELOPMENT, CONTINUED

AT LUNCHTIME, HERNAN found his phone filled with text messages from Mayra. She was back with Jesus after another breakup and now wanted Hernan's opinion on a whole new round of suspicions, all of which were probably correct.

He was still reading the messages when Lety called.

"Why are guys such assholes?" she demanded.

"Well, hello to you, too. And thanks. Work is fine."

"Come on, Hernan. You know I wouldn't call you at work if it wasn't serious."

"Okay. What's up?"

"So, I was going through Geoffrey's phone while he was in the shower—"

"Nice. Very romantic."

"Hernan!"

"Okay. Sorry. What did you find on Gee-off's phone?"

"Remember that thing he said on New Year's about how any girl will sleep with you if she meets you while your dog is pulling you on a skateboard?"

"Uh-huh . . ."

"Well, he has a bunch of texts from some girl, and guess how they met."

"Oh shit. That sucks."

Lety stayed silent for a few seconds. Then she let out a sob.

"If it makes you feel better, Mayra texted me six times today about some more crazy stuff Jesus is doing."

"Again?" Lety's crying receded into low-grade sniffles. "Man, does this shit run in our family or what?"

"Hey, leave me out of this."

"Whatever, Hernan. You're just as bad as any of us."

"Meaning?"

"Meaning, like, do you even *have* a girlfriend? I told you on New Year's that my friend Maritza liked you, and you never even asked me about it. You'd rather spend all your time looking through a microscope at a leaf."

Maybe she had a point. He'd been spending all his evenings and weekends in the greenhouse, trying to figure out how to cure the bluebonnet fungus. The flowers from his classroom window were still the only healthy plants he'd seen in a month, and the mystery of this absorbed him. It would have been a fascinating puzzle if his father's business were not also on the line.

There was a knock on the door. Hernan opened it to find a student aide, who handed him a folder.

"This is from Mr. Scamphers," she said apologetically.

There were two papers inside.

Pending this year's test results, said the top paper, *you will be nonencouraged to renew your contract with the school district.*

Nonencouraged? Wait . . . he was being fired? Like this?

"Listen, Lety, I need to call you back."

The other paper in the folder was a Believer Score checklist. Mr. Scamphers had assigned him a score that fell just below what was required to renew his contract. Technically, it wasn't official until the test scores came out. But the scores would have to be near perfect to save his job, and he already knew they would be about average. He had, as usual, refused to spend the year plowing through test-prep workbooks. The science test results weren't going to save him. But obviously Mr. Scamphers knew this.

Hernan's desk chair creaked as he sank into it. Maybe this shit did run in his family. Maybe the whole Hernandez crew was programmed with some epigenetic loser switch, just waiting for the right environmental factor to trigger it. His father's plants were dying, and the business would probably die along with it. Lety, if she was anything like Mayra, would be back with Geoff in a week. And Hernan?

There was another knock on the door, and Hernan whipped it open, half expecting to find Mr. Scamphers chuckling under his moustache. Instead he saw Lena, sniffing and dabbing at her eyes with her sweater.

"Can I come in? I can't go back to my classroom right now."

Here we go again, thought Hernan. "Let me guess. The poet did something else you didn't like?"

"Yeah, but that's . . . I mean, I don't know. Maybe." A tear escaped and trickled down her cheek. "Why are guys such assholes?"

"I think your actual question is why women, given a choice of guys, chose the biggest asshole they can find."

Lena stopped crying and squinted at him. "Whoa. What's *your* problem?"

"Just what I said. If you're not getting treated right, it's because you selected a person who doesn't treat you right. And I don't have time for this right now."

The vulnerable look on Lena's face turned to surprise, then anger. "You know what? Forget it." She turned and headed back down the hall, walking slowly, as if giving Hernan a chance to call her back.

He didn't. Instead, he shut the door just in time to hear Mrs. Rawlins on the PA, wishing everyone a happy Teacher Appreciation Week. And with that, life seemed to be such a giant, poorly written joke that Hernan felt a sprout of hope spring up through his despair.

Mr. Hernandez, sometimes you just gotta go for it.

Nilda, from his first period, had said this when he was teaching the scientific method. He'd been trying to teach his students to wait, to observe, to craft a hypothesis before hurling themselves into thoughtless action. But maybe it was Nilda who was right. Maybe he had spent his whole life stuck on the observation step of the scientific method, squinting at the details while the big picture whirled by behind him. Maybe sometimes you just had to go for it.

He pulled out his phone and called Lety back.

"You know what? Go ahead and give me Maritza's number. I'll call her tonight."

SYNTHESIZING INFORMATION

BASED ON THE *information given, how does each part add to the main idea of the passage? Use details from all sources to support your answer.* This question was written on every board as Coach Ray wandered the hallway, glancing into other teachers' classrooms, in no hurry to get to his own. There were so few kids in the school on Take Our Daughters and Sons to Work Day that teachers often combined classes, the better to take turns parading through the hallways with their own children.

Only Maybelline Galang was at her desk. The few students inside her room were bent over their math books, just like any ordinary day. She never brought Allyson to the school during these days, which suited Coach Ray just fine. Still, he passed the room as stealthily as he could. Ever since Maybelline had invited him to the birthday party, he'd felt a new sense of accusation emanating from her. Or maybe it wasn't new. Maybe he'd just never noticed it before.

Finally, he reached his classroom. A cluster of the younger football players were in a corner, playing cards, talking loudly, trying to draw O'Neal Rigby into their conversation. Rigby, aware of his place in the high school hierarchy, ignored them. He lounged in one of the rolling chairs reserved for assistant coaches, arms and legs spread out like an emperor. He conversed only with Daren Grant, who leaned against a student desk in his white shirt and a tie.

Normally, Ray would have said something to Rigby about sitting in a coach's chair while an adult stood up nearby, but there was something gratifying about Grant's awkward pose, trying to look relaxed, with one butt cheek resting on a tiny desk. If Grant wanted to stand while a student took his seat, let him.

Ray sank into his own chair and leaned back luxuriously, as if to say this was the level of comfort a grown man demanded. "You okay standing like that, son?"

"Yeah, I'm fine. I don't like to spend too much time sitting down, ha-ha." There was a cheerful condescension in Grant's voice that was just begging to be body-slammed. Then he turned back to Rigby, resuming what seemed to be a one-sided conversation.

Grant had gotten sneaky since Signing Day. When he spoke to Coach Ray, he stuck to the topic of whatever game happened to be on TV the night before. Yet now there was this vibe he gave off, as if Daren Grant had decided that the best way to maximize the macro impact of Daren Grant was to humor the old redneck football coach while presenting himself as a role model of refined minority manhood.

This crusade for the souls of the players included constant, grating reminders that Daren Grant was the type of fellow who went to Cornell University. Daren Grant had a five-year plan, and a ten-year plan, and all kinds of other plans that would never rest on some rickety dream of making it to the NFL. Daren Grant was quitting his consulting gig next year to go to *b-school,* which was short for *business school.* And over the summer he was going to *take a break* and go backpacking through Europe.

"When you're done in one country," he was explaining to O'Neal Rigby, "you just get on a bus and go to the next country. And you stay in a place where you rent a bed for the night and everyone shares a bathroom, so it's really cheap."

Rigby eyed him with a mixture of suspicion and boredom. "I probably rather go somewhere I could stay in a hotel."

Coach Ray laughed. International travel was not one of the pissing contests in which high school athletes engaged. Nor did high school athletes fantasize about the kind of travel that required carrying a backpack or sharing a bathroom. The team's trip to Plano for last year's state championship had been Rigby's first stay at a hotel. Everything about the experience had thrilled him.

And yet, the moment lacked the satisfying crunch it should have had. The image of Daren Grant in Europe with his backpack and water bottle was yet another reminder that Grant lived the type of worry-free existence that would never depend on luck, or injury, or a potential knucklehead move from a teenager like O'Neal Rigby, whose post–Signing Day attitude was becoming more like Gerard Brown's every day.

Rigby should have known better. He'd been a junior when Gerard had left the school in handcuffs, his scholarship and future drying up within the week. For the type of kid who played football at Brae Hill Valley, life offered no second chances.

Rich kids could mess up and still go on to college. They could commit crimes and still go on to become CEOs. They could cheat on their taxes, or defraud sick people, or run banks into the ground, and leave others to clean up their messes. Hell, they could even become president.

Meanwhile, one screw-up could transform a kid like Gerard Brown or O'Neal Rigby from a superstar into a big guy with a criminal record who did menial jobs and made authority figures nervous.

"The thing is, when you stay at a hostel . . ."

But O'Neal had lost interest in Daren Grant's feats of exploration. He wanted to talk about his own feats of football. He eased his chair around to face Coach Ray. "Coach, did you get a chance to look at those game tapes? When I scored that last touchdown against Whatsitcalled?"

One of the younger players, Marquez, tried to nudge his way into the conversation. "Yeah, 'cause we all know O'Neal do whatever it takes to score."

"You mean, whatever it takes to *win*, ha-ha." Grant corrected Marquez in the voice adults used when they were afraid of sounding harsh.

"Shut the fuck up, Marquez." O'Neal was not afraid of sounding harsh.

"That's just what I heard," Marquez muttered, just loud enough to reclaim a bit of pride as he turned back to the card game.

Coach Ray stared at O'Neal, who waited a beat, then glanced up as if to gauge his coach's reaction. Something was not getting said.

"What is going on here?" growled Coach Ray.

Marquez studied a nutrition poster on the wall next to him.

Coach Ray kept his eyes fixed on O'Neal.

"It's nothing, Coach. Some freshman cheerleader that used to like me is acting all crazy now. She came at me. Now she trying to act all innocent."

Coach Ray felt his face redden. "Tell me you did not pull any stupid shit."

"I'm trying, coach, but these girls . . ." O'Neal raised his palms as if to show his helplessness in the situation. It was clear he was trying not to smile.

"Girls," Coach Ray hissed, "do not like football. Girls like attention. And accusing you of rape is gonna equal a *shitload* of attention."

He was so angry he forgot that this was not a subject to discuss in front of Daren Grant, who now jumped in as if someone had asked him to help. "O'Neal, this is brother to brother here: You have to look at every woman as someone who could be your sister or your mother, not as an object."

"Well, what if she act like an object?" O'Neal gave Grant a look that said he had listened nicely to the whole international-travel thing, and now it was his turn to brag. "What if she show up at my boy's house and tells us her mama think she at her cousin's for the night? That sound like somebody trying to be an object to me."

Coach Ray could not contain himself any longer. "*Boy*, were you not in this motherfucking school last year to see what happened to your teammate?"

Grant broke in again. "No need to use the word *boy*, Coach, ha-ha."

Ray whipped around to face him. "What?"

"I'm just saying—that can be taken the wrong way. Ha. Ha."

A half year's worth of rage swelled inside Ray. He heard the door to the classroom open, but ignored it, as single-minded as a player going for a touchdown. "Listen, *son*, I will call my *players* anything I want to."

He was not about to explain himself to some kid in a button-down shirt, talking to him like he was some Hill Country racist. He didn't have to tell Daren Grant he picked players up in the mornings, drove them home after late games, sat with them in the hospital after knee surgery. He was as close a thing to a father as a lot of these boys had.

"Uh, Coach?" Marquez was looking toward the door.

Coach Ray ignored him. He leveled his gaze at Daren Grant, who looked like he was trying to figure out what to do with his arms. It was time to tell this kid some things about himself that he wasn't gonna like.

"Hi, Dad!" The sound of a young girl's voice was so out of place that it took a moment for Coach Ray to realize where it had come from.

He turned and suddenly found himself staring right at Allyson, who stood in the doorway wearing a shiny white cheerleading uniform. The fabric was nearly see-through, even more revealing than the uniforms of the Killer Armadillos' cheerleaders.

Coach Ray jumped to his feet. "Hey—" It seemed he should insert some type of pet name here, *sweetie* or *dear* or *honey*, but none of these seemed like they would come out right. "Your mother let you come to school in that uniform?"

"My aunt dropped me off." Allyson entered the room smiling, as if she were sharing a secret. "My mom doesn't even know I'm here."

This last statement, however, wasn't entirely correct. Already, they could hear Maybelline Galang's urgent footsteps in the hallway, her voice growing closer as she said, "No, Rosemary, she's *not* in my classroom! I don't know where she is! I can't believe you brought her here and just dropped her off!"

Seconds later, Maybelline appeared in the doorway with the phone in her hand.

As their daughter turned to face Maybelline in the sparkly uniform, Coach Ray caught a glimpse of how the scene must have looked to her: Behind Allyson sat O'Neal Rigby, the school's most promising specimen of athletic talent. Above Rigby's right shoulder was Daren Grant, hovering like an angel in a crisp white shirt. Above Rigby's left shoulder stood Coach Ray, a vein pumping in his forehead, his face as red as his T-shirt as he met Maybelline's eyes.

SYNTHESIZING, CONTINUED

TEN MINUTES LATER, Maybelline walked her daughter through the door of her own classroom. Coach Ray's giant red windbreaker was zipped around Allyson, drooping past her knees like a dress. The students in the room looked up as if expecting an explanation.

"You need to have your work done by the time the bell rings," said Maybelline. "Remember, there is no makeup work."

The students resumed working. If they noticed her hands were shaking, they didn't show it.

She turned to Allyson. "Do you have anything from school to work on?"

Allyson shook her head.

"Okay, then draw a picture or something. I think there are markers in the closet."

Allyson, newly obedient, went to search for the markers.

Maybelline rearranged the stack of papers on her desk, as if putting them in the right order might align the universe, too. Except that she knew it wouldn't. Her attempt to help Mr. Scamphers enforce the rules had gotten Hernan fired. And Mr. Scamphers could decide at any time to tell Allyson's school she was enrolled under a fake address. Next year, if he became principal, who knew what kind of "help" he might demand from her? Maybe it was time to accept that the world would never be put in order.

The bell rang and the students filed out, placing their classwork in a neat pile on Maybelline's desk. She instinctively grabbed the first paper, ready to grade it, record it, and place it in the proper pile. But before she could do anything, Allyson's voice called to her from the depths of the closet.

"Mom? Whose backpack is this?"

IDENTIFYING WORDS AND PHRASES IN CONTEXT

KAYTEE'S STUDENTS KNEW many tricks for passing the TCUP essay test:

- Don't say *big*. Say *gigantic*, or *enormous*, or *gargantuan*.
- Don't say *walked*. Say *strutted*, or *jogged*, or *ambled*, or some other word from the power-synonym list provided by your English teacher.
- Include a semicolon somewhere; even if you're using it wrong.
- When possible, show your unique voice by using a phrase like *my uncle's brand-spankin'-new truck*.
- If you can't think of a phrase that shows your unique voice, describing anything as *brand-spankin'-new* will probably still get you some points.
- Start your essay with an attention-grabbing opener.
- *Wow!!!!!* is not an attention-grabbing opener.
- Unless you're really stuck.
- Last, but certainly not least, always do whatever you need to do to make sure you fill at least three quarters of the space provided, even if you have to end with an extra long, possibly even rambling or repetitive sentence that says the same thing more than once just to get to the next line of the paper.

This was composition boiled down to its least fuck-upable essence. Nearly every essay Kaytee had graded in the past year and a half seemed guided by these principles.

But law-school admissions essays had a whole different set of requirements. TeachCorps held workshops on how to describe teaching in law-school admissions essays, and in the past few weeks, Kaytee had started attending, copying suggested phrases such as *lead from the classroom* and *scale up my macro impact for low-income students*. These encapsulated the unique glow TeachCorps alumni presented to law schools. Law schools didn't care about semicolons; they were looking for applicants who'd vaulted life's obstacles, spat in the face of failure, and learned an important lesson along the way.

This was the real problem, because writing this essay in the first place was proof that Kaytee Mahoney was not vaulting life's obstacles. She was giving up.

Dear Admissions Committee, she pictured writing, *I want to go to law school because I will do anything in this world to get out of being a teacher.*

She let out a short, bitter laugh. There was no way to fit that one into the formula.

Above all, the workshops had advised being specific. Everyone who applied to law school knew how to use big words. They had already breezed through top-tier liberal arts colleges and could produce prose that sizzled like a hot pan touching sink water, extended metaphors that flaunted a flare for analogy. The TeachCorps bump, therefore, required *zooming in for emotional resonance*. One had to describe a particular student whom one had successfully muscled toward achievement against the odds. Only then could one explain the need to scale up one's macro impact by going to graduate school, or applying to a consulting firm, or running for office.

Kaytee logged in to her grade book and perused the names, searching for a student to zoom in on. Jonathan Rodriguez's main success was controlling his outbursts for short periods of time. Yesenia had never come back to class. And Michelle . . .

Just the thought of Michelle Thomas automatically loaded the You-Tube video inside Kaytee's brain, playing it against her will, then forcing her to relive the unendurable moment when she'd scrolled through the comments. Her bitterness returned.

I'm not sure if I've inspired any actual students, she now pictured writing, *but the video of me pointing roach spray at my class has certainly inspired thousands of white supremacist Internet trolls! How's that for scaling up my macro impact? I'm like King Midas, except instead of gold, everything I touch turns to racism!*

All she wanted now was to escape, to get far away, to become an anonymous face at a law school in a coastal northern city from which she would never have to return. And that, she reminded herself, required *zooming in for emotional resonance*.

On Brian Bingle.

Brian Bingle? Of course! Brian was one of the few students who'd accepted her offer of lunchtime help on his Civil-Rights-leader project. On the due date, his careful work was an exception to the pile of uninspiring last-minute messes she'd received.

When I think of what it means to lead from the classroom, Kaytee began typing, *the first student I think of is Brian.*

Then she stopped. The problem with Brian as an essay topic was that he had been a fairly willing participant in her teaching. More than that—his fierce expression and resolve to keep the class on track had set the tone for her whole first period. Kaytee felt her confidence peeling at the edges. *Brian* was the leader. He was the one who should be writing the admissions essay, using her as an example.

Get it together, she told herself, *unless you want to "lead from the classroom" again next year*. The application deadline was just days away.

When Brian walked into my classroom this year, his numerous tattoos caught my eye. Wait. That made her sound judgmental. Bad for law school.

When Brian walked into my classroom this year, his classmates whispered about his tattoos. But that made it sound like none of her other students had tattoos. You didn't need an amazing teacher for kids who were surprised by tattoos. Law schools were looking for amazing. She started again.

Other teachers had told me about Brian before he ever entered my history class. He'd been a character in other teachers' stories, but I believed every child deserved a chance to be the main character of his or her own story. This was the reason I chose to teach history at Brae Hill Valley High School, a school with much history of its own.

Yes. This struck the right tone. Kaytee reread the paragraph, feeling the congratulatory jolt that accompanied a job well done. She'd even left herself an opening to include the necessary demographic information, which would further prove the school needed an obstacle -hopping, equity-inducing teacher-leader like her. But the numbers could go in later. She'd finally managed to unscrew the lid, and now the essay's pressurized contents bubbled out: all those hours during lunch-time, helping Brian on his Civil-Rights-leader project while also encouraging him to study hard in his other classes and even apply to college. Leadership? Check. Determination? Check. Qualified for reasons beyond grades and scores? Check.

Except . . . there was one more thing. For the essay to really pack an admissions-worthy punch, she had to make it clear that Brian was African American. Explaining this outright would be clunky and awkward. But the name Brian was so racially neutral. He could have been any kid. And that would just not do.

Unless—she could change the name, right? The essay was supposed to be anonymous, after all. Kaytee tried to think of a traditionally African American name that would make the point. Jamal? No, that was the kid from *How the Status Quo Stole Christmas*, with the grandma in the wheelchair. She cycled through names of black Civil Rights leaders. Malcolm? Martin? No, those had become names that even white families named their children. And she couldn't use the name of a student she actually taught.

A blip of conversation surfaced in Kaytee's memory. *Pookie and them. Quay'Vante and them.*

She tried to dismiss it, but it would not leave. *Quay'Vante and them.* Quay'Vante.

Breyonna and her friends had joked about that name at happy hour, and Kaytee had refused to laugh, precisely *because* Quay'Vante was an unmistakably African American name that suggested a legacy of generational poverty, which made it completely inappropriate to joke about.

And yet, somehow, it was absolutely perfect for the essay. Kaytee used the search-and-replace tool to change *Brian* to *Quay'Vante*. Re-reading the essay, she had to admit the name change amped up her difference-making score considerably.

Her uneasiness returned. The thing was, Brian Bingle wasn't really the Quay'Vante type. He was, for all intents and purposes, a fairly accurate Brian.

Then again, it wasn't like Brian would ever see the essay. And anyway, it wasn't like all Quay'Vantes were the same, right? Really, if the law-school admissions team presumed a student named Quay'Vante was less likely to succeed than a student named Brian, weren't *they* the ones making assumptions about students' home cultures?

As she wrote, Quay'Vante's description snowballed, gathering details from multiple students, quotes in unmistakably ethnic grammar, and background information Kaytee didn't actually have access to but that seemed likely for a kid who went to an inner-city school.

The expression *inner city* felt queasily familiar. She quickly erased it, changing it to *under-resourced*, then to *high poverty*. Then, in what now seemed only a small change in the service of anonymity, she moved Brian's tattoo from his arm to his neck.

The resulting Frankenstudent was a composite character who, had he existed, would have been unlikely to come to Kaytee's classroom during lunch to work on a project. This left her no choice but to turn up the dial on her own efforts—just a bit. Just enough to draw this updated, downtrodden Brian/Quay'Vante to her classroom, sit him down, inspire him, and cause him to develop an interest in Thurgood Marshall that would *encourage Quay'Vante to envision both a history and present in which he has potential to be the main character, and to articulate this narrative so others will take notice.* Kaytee edged forward in her chair, leaning into the essay's momentum.

All she needed now was a good conclusion. But this posed another challenge: Why would anyone capable of such feats of obstacle-busting teachery leave the Quay'Vantes of the world behind? Wouldn't she want to be a teacher forever? Wouldn't she miss the rewards of working with children?

The rewards of working with children. A cynical puff of air escaped her lips. At what point in a law-school admissions essay did you say you'd been hit in the eye? At what point did you talk about being smacked down by an administrator with a stranger's baby in her arms? When did you get to mention the assumption box?

The answer was, you didn't. Not if you actually wanted to get in. Under no circumstances could Kaytee admit that law school was her escape from the very selling point that would move her to the front of the line: her experience teaching in the inner city.

The *inner city*. Why did she keep using that phrase? The queasiness returned, and then the reason for it came to her also, rushing over her with a sickening force.

Hey, she figured out the new way to clean up our inner cities . . . Just give every innercity teacher a can of raid . . . Filling innercity classrooms with roaches at taxpayers expense . . . round up these animals that have taken over our iner cities. She'd been their mascot. And now she was using their words. The comments closed in around her again, and she struggled to block them out, forcing her fingers back to the keyboard.

While I know I will miss being in direct contact with students, I also know I need a law degree to effect the widespread change that will help those with stories like Quay'Vante's achieve the goals that will lead to a happy ending.

As she wrote these final lines, she thought again of Brian's Civil-Rights-leader project. Even with her lunchtime help, the essay contained an embarrassing number of errors. It was also true that they'd talked about colleges, but even as she offered encouragement, she knew it was likely Brian would spend years completing remedial classes in a community college, or—worse—get sucked in by some for-profit enterprise that left students with few career prospects, credits that didn't transfer, and debt that made the long slog out of poverty even longer.

It had always been people like Kaytee who escaped, who wrote the law-school admissions essays, who shared their versions of history and starred in the happy endings. For all the Brians and Quay'Vantes of the world, and even (*Say it!*) the Diamoniques and Michelles, Kaytee felt a stab of guilt.

For what that was worth.

ADEQUATE
YEARLY
PROGRESS

"**W**HICH IS, OBVIOUSLY, the problem with the whole education system."

Dr. Barrios drank a sip of hospital-cafeteria coffee and tried again to find a comfortable sitting position. He'd been in the same plastic waiting-room chair for hours. At some point, he'd struck up a conversation with a woman next to him and had made the mistake of mentioning that he was a high school principal.

She'd been delivering a sustained monologue ever since. "I mean, if I ran the schools, the first thing I'd do . . ."

Dr. Barrios wasn't even trying to employ his listening face, though maybe those muscles had gotten such a workout over the past year that he looked attentive even now, as he stared at the door, waiting for news from the doctor.

There was only one more week of school. Test scores would be in soon, and then Dr. Barrios would learn whether the school had made Adequate Yearly Progress.

Adequate Yearly Progress. He turned the phrase over in his mind, shuffling it like a deck of cards. That first word was where they got you, he decided. *Yearly* and *progress* were concrete terms. But *adequate*? That was the moving target. *Adequate* was the part that got decided in an office somewhere, at the last minute, based on what would look good in the newspaper, or get someone reelected, or highlight some new defect that called for Transformational Change.

What, in any case, *was* an adequate amount of progress to make in a year? If he'd learned anything, it was that there was no happily ever after in education, no riding off into the sunset. There was only one yearly fix after another. Then, in August, the whole cycle started again. It was exhausting.

"I have a neighbor whose son is in first grade, and it's just unbelievable, the . . ."

He looked up at the woman. Her eyebrows were knitted together in disapproval. On the other side of him, the warm pressure of his wife's hand closed in on top of his, and he looked at her gratefully. The rest of the family was there, too, looking back and forth between the door and a muted television.

Dr. Barrios leaned his head against the cool wall behind him, thinking about his father. The man had worked through so many of the moments that collectively made up life. And here was Dr. Barrios, continuing the tradition. He'd been in a budget meeting during the birth of his first grandchild. He'd missed the second because of a fight that required police involvement and kept him at school past nightfall. Even now, he saw his two grandchildren so infrequently that they always seemed to be much older than the last time. Maybe, he thought, he should spend more time with them.

Could he do it? He hadn't saved as much for retirement as he would have liked to. Then again, his kids were grown. He and his wife didn't travel much. They had moderate tastes and had paid off their house years ago. Maybe they could sell the house, move into an apartment, and just hope nothing expensive happened. He considered the strange twist of fate: After all the degrees he had earned, he could spend his final years the way he'd spent his childhood, on a tight budget in a small apartment.

Was *that* adequate yearly progress?

The voice of the woman elbowed its way in between his thoughts. "What I don't understand is why more of the people who actually run the school system in this country haven't figured this out yet. I mean, come on, y'all." Then she stopped talking and stared at him, arms crossed indignantly, as if waiting for him to confirm that the best person to lead the country's school system would be a woman with neither respect for nor knowledge of nor experience interacting with public education in any way.

Dr. Barrios was trying to imagine a world where such a thing might happen when a doctor opened the door and beckoned to the whole family.

Suddenly, everything else became irrelevant.

Dr. Barrios rose from his seat and tossed his now-cold coffee in the trash. Then he turned to the woman. "Ma'am, sounds like you'd be just the person for the job."

She answered with a self-assured grunt.

Dr. Barrios reached for his wife's hand to help her from her chair. Then the two of them followed the rest of the family down the hall to meet their newest grandchild.

PHYSICAL EDUCATION

COACH RAY ALWAYS knew who was leaving at the end of the year. Teachers stopped by when they needed his players to help them move things to their cars. Anyone who needed more than a couple of extra hands wasn't coming back.

He'd heard the history teacher from the teaching corps had gotten into law school, so she'd be gone. No shocker there. The departure of Hernan Hernandez from the science department was a bigger surprise. According to Mrs. Reynolds-Washington, he'd gotten fired, and according to Mrs. Friedman-Katz, Daren Grant had something to do with it. Coach Ray had changed his mind about a lot of things over the past few weeks, but wanting to slam Daren Grant into a wall wasn't one of them.

The big news of the week, however, came when Maybelline Galang appeared at the door.

"Need players to help you with something?" asked Coach Ray.

He knew she would say no. Maybelline never asked for help with anything. It was only in the past few weeks that he had really noticed how tired she looked as she marched down the hallway with her binders and folders.

Today, however, she carried nothing but a small yellow envelope. "I just wanted to let you know I won't be at the school next year. I got a job with the OBEI department."

"No way." Then again, he could see it. "They pay better?"

Maybelline nodded. She shot a look down the empty hallway before continuing, "I needed it. I'm moving somewhere where I can put Allyson in the neighborhood school."

"Well, let me know if there's anything I can . . ." He made a gesture that suggested generalized assistance. "You need some players to carry the heavy stuff?"

"I'm fine." Her businesslike tone had returned. "I just came to give you this."

She handed him the envelope. Inside was an invitation.

"Allyson and her cousin are graduating fifth grade. We're having a small party, and since this isn't during football season . . ." The rest hung in the air between them. She was accustomed, by now, to his excuses for not showing up.

"I'll be there."

"That would be great," said Maybelline, though her tone was flat, as if to suggest maybe *great* was too strong a word. Maybe she meant something more like *okay* or *adequate*. Then she turned and walked back into her classroom, the door shutting slowly behind her.

Coach Ray folded the invitation in half and stuffed it into his back pocket. He took out his wallet to see if he had any cash on hand. How much did people give for a fifth-grade graduation, anyway?

But then he put the wallet away without opening it and took out his phone instead.

"Hey, it's me," he said to the surprised voice on the other end of the line. "I gotta ask you a favor."

SOCIAL STUDIES

THE END OF the school year at Brae Hill Valley was less of a grand finale than a slow tapering off of attendance. Even the room itself looked sparse, like the set of a TV show airing its final episodes. The shelves were empty, the walls stripped bare. The few remaining students were playing with their phones or sleeping.

Kaytee sat at her desk wearing a pair of jeans she hadn't fit into since October.

Lena appeared at her door. "Congratulations! I heard you got into law school!"

Kaytee snuck an uncomfortable look at her students. She hadn't told any of them she'd applied.

"Don't feel bad," said Lena. "You gotta do you, right? Teaching other people's children can get old."

"It's not that. I——" Kaytee caught herself before she summoned the explanation she'd used in her admissions essay. Saying it aloud in front of Lena was unthinkable.

"Hey, it's cool. I've been thinking I could use a change myself."

"*You?* No way. Don't you think you would miss teaching?"

Lena laughed. "Girl, I already miss teaching. We've been doing test stuff for months. By the way, it looks like those low-cal lunches are working. Either that, or getting into law school helps you lose weight."

There was some truth to this observation. Ever since Kaytee's acceptance letter had arrived, her craving for vending-machine food had disappeared. So had her motivation to update her blog; it now sat untouched in cyberspace, collecting unread comments. The chance to escape from Brae Hill Valley had afforded her a new lightness that extended to every part of her life.

So it had come as a surprise, even to her, when she'd realized she was going to stay. The thick envelope had arrived, and she'd opened it, waiting for excitement to kick in. She had even filled out the form that said she'd be attending. But she never sent it. The faceless racists of the Internet would not win this one.

"I'm not going to law school." She raised her voice to carry through the room. "I decided I'm not done teaching. So, if you need to find me next year, I'll be right here."

The students looked up at her. Not that there were many left: Michelle had stopped coming to school the previous week, much to Kaytee's relief. Jonathan Rodriguez and Milagros Almaguer were also part of the trickle of students who'd confirmed that they had passing grades and then stopped showing up. This morning, even Brian Bingle had stopped by to ask if he could leave early. Kaytee had given him permission, though she couldn't help feeling a bit let down.

When the final bell rang and the last class left, only one student stayed behind.

Kaytee tried to hide her surprise. "Hey, Diamonique."

"Hey, Ms. M." Diamonique hesitated. Then she said, "I just wanted to say, I hope you know I didn't mean to knock you over that one day."

Up close, it was clear that some of Diamonique's braids clung to her scalp by only a few strands of hair. Kaytee had never noticed this before, and she wondered if the braids themselves might be to blame. Perhaps years of tightly wound styles meant to make Diamonique's hair seem thicker and longer had caused just the opposite effect. This thought, that even hair could be borrowed from the future at too high an interest rate, filled Kaytee with an infinite sadness.

"Thanks for saying that, Diamonique. It means a lot."

"No problem." As she said this, Diamonique shyly pushed her hair away from her face. Her braids fell back over one shoulder, revealing a shiny patch behind her temples where there was no hair at all.

Kaytee drew in a surprised breath, immediately ashamed at her reaction.

Diamonique quickly pushed the braids forward again, concealing the bald spot. "It's okay, Miss. Stuff just be getting to me sometimes."

"What do you mean? What kind of stuff?" Kaytee made intense eye contact, hoping Diamonique would read the concern in her face and elaborate.

She hoped it would be one of those moments.

But Diamonique would say no more.

SCIENCE

I'M NOT EXACTLY religious," Maritza was saying. "I'm more like . . . spiritual."

She was, as Lety had said, cute. And she did, as Lety had promised, like Hernan. Plus, Breyonna's wedding was coming up. Hernan could not show up unemployed *and* alone.

And so he said, "Spiritual? How so?"

"Well, it's like, I'm a Libra, right? But my rising sign is Taurus. So basically, I've always felt the best energy from signs that get along with Libras *and* Tauruses."

Hernan tried to keep a positive attitude. At least there were no uncomfortable silences. Just the opposite: Maritza seemed equipped with a motion sensor that made her start talking whenever they made eye contact, churning out a stream of benign statements like *Today is a gift, and that's why they call it the present.* With so many other things on his mind, it was a relief not to have to work to keep the conversation going.

Anyway, who was he to be picky? He'd spent the day sweeping a year's worth of chip and candy wrappers from the forgotten corners of his classroom, boxing up equipment for the science teacher who would take his place—*if* the school hired another teacher. In their efforts to cut costs and compete with the new virtual charters, some schools were replacing science lab classes with semisupervised online courses.

Hernan had always told students that "natural selection" wasn't as elegant as it sounded. In reality, nature didn't select anything. The climate changed, and certain traits that had once been important for survival stopped being helpful. That was what had happened: Hernan D. Hernandez had been selected out of the school system. And now, this kindhearted, attractive woman sat across from him, talking about how it was scientifically proven that death came in threes.

The least he could do was be honest with her.

"Maritza," he said when they pulled up to her door at the end of the date, "I have to tell you something."

"Okay." She looked hopeful.

"I'm not a teacher anymore. I got fired."

For the first time all night, Maritza fell silent. Then she said, "Sorry. That sucks."

Hernan nodded.

"You know what you need to do, though? Seriously? Ask the universe for help."

He walked her to her door. They hugged goodbye. She was an excellent hugger.

"I mean it, though," she said. "Just put it all out there to the universe. I've tried it a bunch of times, and it has always worked. It's literally a proven theory."

Under other circumstances, Hernan might have felt an urge to explain that there was no such thing as a *proven theory*. Scientists could never prove theories. They could only fail to disprove them. They could only collect evidence that they were getting closer to the truth.

But Maritza didn't have to be a scientist, did she? And what did it matter if she had a Hello Kitty phone case and was now opening her door with a key on a Hello Kitty keychain? These were just details.

He got back into his car and headed toward the sky-maze of highways silhouetted against the setting sun. The entrance and exit ramps loomed larger as he approached them, as if urging him to hurry up and figure out where the hell he was going.

Ask the universe, Maritza had said. Whatever that meant.

Then again, what could it hurt?

Hernan pulled into the parking lot of a strip mall and sat there, facing the tangled ribbons of concrete, opening himself to any sign the universe might see fit to send him. Then he took a deep breath and summarized the events of the year out loud: how he'd ignored Mr. Weber's invitation to join the union, how he'd managed to become a target for Mr. Scamphers, how Angel had showed up at his door, spitting into his plants on the exact day that the consultant had come to observe the class.

Then there was the plant fungus that threatened to wipe out his father's business. Every bluebonnet in the greenhouse had now wilted and died except for the one pot Hernan had transplanted from his classroom. His flowers had survived so long it almost seemed as if they were resistant to the fungus, although that didn't make much sense. They'd spent their entire life on a classroom windowsill. That was an unlikely place to develop a resistance to anything.

The clouds didn't part. Lightning didn't strike. But somehow, saying it all out loud was comforting. Maybe a comforting presence was what he needed after all. Hernan pulled out of the parking lot and headed toward the highway. He was just about to turn onto the ramp that would take him home when he thought of something that made him whirl the steering wheel in the other direction. He pulled onto the feeder road and made a U-turn. Then he drove to the greenhouse as fast as traffic would allow.

MATH

EXCEPT FOR THOSE unlucky souls who had to teach summer school, teachers didn't have much work to do on the Friday after school let out. They turned in their grade printouts, brought their keys to the office, and floated to their cars, giddy at the thought of turning off their 5:00 a.m. alarms.

This was usually the time Maybelline prepared for the first weeks of the next school year. But today, she only added a few last papers to the binder she'd been working on, then slipped it into her purse before walking to her car. She did not stop at the office.

When she arrived at the house, Rosemary was arranging wings on a plate.

The twins eyed one another until Maybelline broke the silence. "I came to help set up for the party."

"Good thing," said Rosemary. "I'm a little behind schedule here."

Rosemary had not directly apologized for the incident with the cheerleading uniform. It was not her style to be either apologetic or direct. But she'd offered to host a joint graduation party for the cousins. And now, as she motioned toward a bag of chips that needed to be poured into a bowl, she said nothing about how unusual it was for Maybelline to show up and help. By Rosemary's standards, that was apology enough.

"So," Rosemary said finally, "you're ready for the new job?"

"I think so," said Maybelline. She was careful not to say *Of course I am*, or make her new position in the OBEI department sound too important. "It will give me a chance to spend more time with Allyson, so that's good."

"Yeah." Rosemary, too, seemed to hold herself back from saying more.

The peace between them was as intricate and fragile as a spider web. Any movement could dislodge it. Maybelline knew, therefore, that she could not tell Rosemary how well her interview had really gone. It turned out the only thing that excited OBEI officers more than a well-organized data binder was a binder full of typed conversations and printed e-mails that could get somebody in big trouble. And Maybelline had smiled and thought, *Have I got something for you.*

Allyson popped into the room, a long plastic *ConGRADulations* banner crinkling on the floor behind her. "Do you have tape?"

Maybelline was happy to see her daughter in an outfit that was appropriate for an eleven-year-old girl. She'd been less happy about having to buy the outfit at mall prices, but it was for graduation day. Plus, both mother and daughter agreed that as a soon-to-be sixth grader, starting at a middle school by their new apartment, it was time for Allyson to stop wearing Gabriella's hand-me-downs. They would work out the details later.

Rosemary spent a long time crumpling the package into the garbage. "I was thinking about looking for a part-time job. Now that Gabriella's getting older."

"Really?"

"Yeah. You think it would be hard to get a job as a school nurse?"

The doorbell rang, which saved Maybelline from having to break the news that most school nurse positions had been cut years ago. She almost felt bad for her sister, trying to get a job at a time like this with no work experience. Almost.

"Hi," said Coach Ray when Maybelline opened the door.

He'd said he would come, but she was still surprised to see him there, sweating in the sun in his red windbreaker. In his hand was the most inexpertly wrapped present she had ever seen.

"Hi," she said.

"Hi," said Allyson, who was sliding down the front hallway in her socks.

"Congratulations . . . graduate." Coach Ray handed Allyson the present, and they shared an awkward hug.

Then Allyson ripped off the wrapping so ungracefully it made Maybelline wince. Inside were a T-shirt and hat that Maybelline recognized immediately. Everyone in the city had been wearing them since the Super Bowl.

"Thanks!" Allyson put the T-shirt on over her clothes. It was just big enough for her to grow into.

"There's something else in there."

Allyson reached into the ripped paper and retrieved three cardboard booklets.

"That's three sets of season tickets," explained Coach Ray. "If you're gonna be a football fan, you better start learning about the game."

"Who's at the door?" Gabriella came sliding into the hallway, also in her socks.

"My dad. He gave me football tickets!"

"Oh my God! Can I come?"

"Maybe." Allyson looked at her father. "Who are the third tickets for?"

"You can decide who to invite to each game." He gave Maybelline an uncertain look. "I mean . . . you'll need to get your mom's permission."

Allyson turned back to her mom, ready to use one of the many methods of persuasion available to someone who was nearly eleven and a half years old.

But there was no need. Maybelline Galang had already decided, for the first time since she'd begun teaching, to accept makeup work.

LANGUAGE ARTS

AT EVERY WEDDING, no matter how objectively lovely, there is a certain percentage of people who are miserable. At Breyonna's wedding, it looked like Lena would be one of them. She was late, for one thing. After all Breyonna's joking about how black folks' weddings always started late, Lena hadn't wanted to show up too early. But now it was clear she'd overshot on the lateness thing.

By the time she entered the chapel, the bridal party was lined up at the front of the room, the preacher was giving his sermon, and the back pews, which Lena had hoped to slide quietly into, were full. Now, in addition to the discomfort of being in a church and the awkwardness of showing up alone, Lena found herself trying to walk discreetly down the aisle during someone else's wedding. White rose petals smashed under her feet as she tiptoed toward a half-empty pew near the front of the room.

There was a reason the seat was empty, she soon realized. It was along the most highly visible section of the aisle. As such, it attracted churchgoers who wanted to call attention to their worship. The woman behind Lena punctuated each of the preacher's proclamations with yells of, "Yes, Lord Jesus!" and "Mmm-hmm, that's right, dear God." Lena felt eyes turn in her direction. Whether this was because of the woman's religious ecstasy or her own lateness didn't seem to matter. Her humiliation deepened, which she probably deserved. Lately, her conscience felt so streaked and muddy that if she could have made herself believe in God, she would have taken this moment in church to ask for His forgiveness.

There was the matter of Rico Jones, for one thing. She'd apologized, and he'd said everything was cool, but it was clear he'd changed. It was nothing that would have shown up in the district's data-tracking system. Rico's attendance had always been spotty and remained so. He maintained his usual D average, and his reading scores had long ago marked him as a student unlikely to graduate. But he never raised his hand again. He never offered another offbeat observation or sarcastic remark. He spent the last month of the year staring out the window, and the few times his eyes met Lena's he did not smile. There seemed to be no way to fix things, nothing to do but watch Rico roll out of reach, like a ball gone over a fence.

Then there was the thing with Hernan. He had turned her away when she was crying, and he'd been rude about it. Yet she had a nagging sense that maybe she didn't have the right to be mad at him. She hadn't allowed this thought to fully develop.

The organ played. The choir sang. The preacher directed everyone to stretch out their arms to Jesus.

"Yes, dear Lord! Thank you, Lord!" called the voice behind Lena's head.

She fought the urge to turn around and look. Instead, she focused on a point under Jesus's ribs and extended her arms in front of her, feeling awkward and exposed. She did not belong here. Mrs. Reynolds-Washington had been right: The black community in Texas, which she'd so hoped to be part of, went to church and knew what do to when it got there. They believed Jesus was up there, listening to their joyful noise. Lena could clap along in church just like she could cheer at football games, but it would always be just a performance. Maybe she could move again, to some new place where she had never embarrassed herself. She could find another profession where she couldn't do so much damage, get things right next time. Or maybe her destiny was always to be alone, alien and alienating. Her arms, still outstretched toward Jesus, grew weary. Her wish not to be standing next to the aisle was so strong it might have been a prayer.

The fog of despair surrounded her so thoroughly that she barely heard the sound of another body shuffling into the pew next to her. Then, she felt a warm sleeve next to her arm and realized someone had arrived even later and more conspicuously than she had. When she turned, she found herself looking into the eyes of Hernan D. Hernandez.

He stretched his arms out in front of him, mirroring the body language of the people around them. "Did I miss anything?" he whispered.

"God is *so good!*" came the voice from behind them.

"A lot of that," Lena whispered, with a slight tilt of her head. As much as she wanted to stay angry at Hernan, his presence was so comforting she couldn't bring herself to put distance between them.

Finally, they were all able to drop their arms and sit, and the preacher began the business of uniting Breyonna and Roland in holy matrimony. "We put the ring on the fourth finger of the hand," he declared, his voice vibrating with conviction, "because it is the veins from *this* finger . . . that lead . . . to the heart."

"Mmm-hmm. Preach!" said the woman behind him.

"The veins in every finger lead to the heart," whispered Hernan.

Lena snuck a look at Hernan's face. There was a humor in his eyes that made her feel as though, after months of static, someone's walkie-talkie was tuned to the same frequency as hers. And he smelled great. He slid closer to her on the wooden bench, and Lena wondered if she should do the same.

But before she could move, a woman appeared at Hernan's other side. She was a beautiful Latina with long, wavy hair, making the universal *sorry-I'm-late* face as she slid into the end of the pew. Lena slid toward the stranger on her other side so Hernan could make room for the woman. Then she fixed her gaze back on Jesus's skinny ribcage.

As further proof that God, if he or she existed, was not on Lena's side, she was seated at the same table as Hernan and his beautiful date for the reception in the church's meeting hall. And not just them but also Mrs. Reynolds-Washington and Mrs. Friedman-Katz, collectors of all business of other people, plus Candace and Regina, who knew a whole lot about Lena's business.

The teachers' table.

There was always a teachers' table. Everyone, from every rung of the American socioeconomic ladder, had a cousin who was a teacher, or a friend whose wife taught, or, in Breyonna's case, a host of teacher friends and colleagues happy to spend the evening discussing topics only teachers could tolerate. One might as well put the cousin and the colleagues and the friend's wife at the same table.

Kaytee Mahoney was there, too, a welcome buffer against the rest of the group. Lena left her purse on an empty chair next to Kaytee, then escaped to the bar in the corner of the room. She'd drained her first glass of wine by the time she sat down and was considering whether it was too soon to head back for another when the emcee began introducing the bridal party. The bridesmaids and groomsmen entered the room, each dancing to different music. Then everyone cheered as the emcee introduced Mr. Roland McGee and Mrs. Breyonna Watson-McGee.

As the newlyweds strutted into the room, hundreds of white butterflies burst into the air. They fluttered in all directions, then flapped toward and coalesced against the stained-glass windows. Lena wondered if they would ever escape or if they would just flutter around, watching church events from the windowsills, until they died.

"What happens to the butterflies?" asked Hernan's date, as if reading Lena's mind. "Do they just stay in here until they die?"

"Probably," said Hernan, then gestured toward the stained glass. "Although some of them might lay eggs. There could be some caterpillars up there in a few weeks."

Breyonna's brother gave a toast as a waiter came around with plates of dry-looking chicken. Lena vaguely remembered Breyonna saying something about how chicken at weddings was tacky, and also something about never having a wedding reception in a church meeting hall, but maybe Lena was misremembering. And anyway, what did she care? She stared longingly at the bar, trying hard to seem as if she was listening to the toast. As long as she could avoid talking, she was fine. She concentrated on cutting her chicken into tiny pieces.

Then the music started, and Mrs. Reynolds-Washington started along with it. "Have you heard Maybelline Galang will be working at OBEI next year?"

Lena hadn't heard this. The thought of Maybelline Galang coming around to check data binders made a career change even more tempting.

"There really are just *so* many teachers who won't be here next year," said Mrs. Friedman-Katz. She and Mrs. Reynolds-Washington both looked at Hernan, who motioned to his date and quickly headed out to the dance floor. The voices around Lena faded into the background as she watched them dance, their twists and spins reminding her of a routine she'd learned in high school, when she'd played Anita in *West Side Story*. But Hernan's date wasn't dancing like a performer. She didn't seem like she was trying to show off for the crowd. Instead, she moved as if she and Hernan had always known one another and all she wanted was to let him guide her around the floor. *Effortless*. That was the word. Wasn't that how it felt to be around Hernan? Effortless? The thought filled Lena with an envy-tinged sadness. Lately, it seemed like every interaction in her life took more energy than she had to spare.

"Speaking of people losing their jobs"—Mrs. Reynolds-Washington's voice cut into her thoughts—"I heard our lovely bride's new husband was downsized. He's working at Fantastic Fitness now, selling gym memberships."

"I knew it!" said Candace, turning to Regina. "I saw someone who looked like him working at my gym. When I asked Bree about it, she straight up changed the subject."

Lena, now fully tuned into the conversation, felt a jolt of defensiveness on Breyonna's behalf.

"Well," said Mrs. Friedman-Katz, "I guess that explains this wedding."

"That's just what I was thinking," said Mrs. Reynolds-Washington. "For someone with Breyonna's taste, all this does seem a little—"

"I thought the sermon was really nice," Lena interrupted. Something told her that if this news were true, Breyonna would not want it discussed at her wedding. And something told her, even more strongly, that it *was* true.

Regina, who had perked up at the chance to discuss Breyonna's business, ignored Lena. "It's interesting, after all that talk about the fiancé in marketing and whatnot—"

"She's probably gonna have to trade that Land Rover back in, too." Candace really was a bitch.

"Hey, not everyone has their dream job," said Lena. Breyonna had defended her on that humiliating night at the club. The least she could do was derail this conversation.

"Right." Candace broke into an evil smile. "Not everyone gets to be a famous poet."

The message was clear: If Breyonna's situation wasn't interesting enough, Lena's business was next on the menu. Lena knew she was on weak ground. Mrs. Reynolds-Washington and Mrs. Friedman-Katz sensed incoming gossip and were straining forward in their seats. If Candace told the story of what had happened in the club now, everyone at Brae Hill Valley would hear the story by the time school resumed in August. Lena braced herself for what was coming.

But then the Electric Slide came on, and the whole room sprang into action.

"Oooooh," said Mrs. Friedman-Katz and Mrs. Reynolds-Washington at the same time. They jumped up to join the dance.

Regina, too, left the table, and Candace followed. But first she gave Lena a look that said she wasn't finished. She was only waiting for their audience to return.

One glass of wine was not enough to deal with this. Lena was about to head back to the bar when she heard laughter. Hernan and his date had returned to the table.

"I guess we're discussing your business next," said Hernan.

"Yeah," Lena sighed.

"Well, it will be a nice change for me. They've been fascinated with me ever since I got *nonencouraged to continue employment*."

"What?" The news shocked Lena out of her misery. "*You* got fired?"

Hernan nodded. "You didn't know?"

"No," said Lena. "Sorry! When did this happen?"

"Five minutes before you came to my classroom that day."

Lena's blurry understanding of their last conversation began to come into focus.

"He's gonna be okay, though," interrupted the woman at Hernan's side. The way she said it suggested she knew Hernan better than Lena ever would.

Lena tried not to hate her.

"Yeah, I'm helping my dad out with his business."

"Well . . . that's good, right?"

"Helping him out?" said Hernan's date. "I think you mean *setting him up for retirement.*"

Lena popped a final piece of chicken into her mouth and chewed it slowly.

"So," said Hernan, "how's the poet?"

She swallowed the chicken. "I wouldn't know."

"Really?"

"Yeah." She hoped her tone communicated just a bit of indignation at how Hernan had underestimated her.

"Damn, Hernan," said his date, "why can't you believe that sometimes when women say they're done with a guy, they're done?" She turned to Lena. "Guys are such assholes, right?"

Lena looked at them, surprised. Hernan's date was allowed to say this, and she wasn't?

"Oh," said Hernan, "I don't think I introduced you. Lena, this is my sister Lety."

"Nice to meet you," said Lena. A sense of possibility opened before her, but before she could process it, the Electric Slide ended, and the four women headed back to the table. Candace's smile revealed every bit of her plan for the upcoming conversation. Lena looked toward Hernan for reassurance, but his seat was empty again. He must have gotten up while she was looking at the dance floor. She was alone.

Now, she thought. Now was the time to go get another glass of wine. Find someone to dance with. Catch the eye of someone at a faraway table, start talking, and sit with them for the rest of the party. She'd always been good at finding new places to be.

Looking around the room to assess her options, she started to rise from her chair. But then she stopped. She took a breath and settled back into her seat. Gossip or no gossip, the teachers' table was where she belonged.

The four women pulled out their chairs, and Candace opened her mouth, a gleeful gleam in her eye.

Lena waited, unblinking, gathering a small fistful of tablecloth in her lap.

Then she felt a tap on her shoulder, and turned to see Hernan standing behind her.

"Wanna dance?" he asked.

She reached up to accept his outstretched hand.

TCUP SAMPLE QUESTION

WHAT WOULD AN ADDITIONAL SCENE AT THE END OF THIS STORY MOST LIKELY BE ABOUT?

A. Hernan D. Hernandez and Maybelline Galang pack the remaining items from their classrooms into one small box each before walking down the hallway for the last time. The seniors of Brae Hill Valley throw their graduation hats into the air, where they seem to hover, as if in a freeze-frame. Later, after dark, Dr. Barrios sits alone in his office. The light of a single lamp illuminates his hands as he opens the test-results envelope and looks at the scores.

B. The school's TCUP scores come under scrutiny when Maybelline Galang, a new employee of the OBEI department, investigates vice principal Roger Scamphers for illegally sharing questions before the test. In a public statement, Scamphers suggests that the tampering started *at a much higher level* and promises he is *not going down alone.* The same week, in what is believed to be an unrelated incident, Nick Wallabee resigns as superintendent. He later announces plans to open a nationwide virtual charter-school network with startup capital from Global Schoolhouse School Choice Solutions.

C. The film company behind *How the Status Quo Stole Christmas* shifts their focus to inspirational movies, preferably starring "plucky, likeable twentysomething teachers with can-do attitudes." They are currently searching for the anonymous blogger behind *The Mystery History Teacher.*

D. Millions of plant enthusiasts and landscapers rejoice at the discovery of a new compound that makes Texas bluebonnets resistant to fungus. The exact formula is proprietary information, patent registered to Hernandez and Son Plant Nursery. It is rumored, however, to involve a chemical reaction that occurs when (BAKED!) Reetos mix with a protein found in human saliva.

E. All of the above.

ACKNOWLEDGMENTS

THERE ARE SO MANY people who made this book possible. It is an honor to be able to mention them here.

Many thanks to Alia Hanna Habib, the literary agent who saw the statue hidden inside the block of marble and had the vision and patience to help me carve away the rest. To Molly Lindley Pisani, an intuitive editor who understood exactly where I was trying to go and helped me get there, paragraph by paragraph. And to Katie Herman, meticulous master of the well-placed comma and finely turned phrase. To Alan Dino Hebel and Ian Koviak for the book's great cover and to Pauline Neuwirth for its lovely interior. Also, a big thanks to everyone associated with the Miami Book Fair and Miami Writers Institute. These institutions have made Miami a city where literary dreams grow into reality.

And now, for the teachers: No character in this book was based on any real-life teacher. However, I am indebted to the hundreds of teachers who took time over the years to speak with me about their experiences, let me observe classes, or shared insights into their subject matter. Special thanks to science teacher Carlos Draschner, whose crow-themed lesson plan I used in its entirety, and Bill Harrington, whose lunar-colony activity and related comment about plants inspired aspects of Hernan's character. And to Coach Alex Terry, who showed phenomenal patience in answering my football questions.

Thanks, also, to the people who offered help and opportunities as *See Me After Class* made its way through the world. These include: Rita Rosenkranz; Michael Sprague; Arielle Eckstut; David Henry Sterry; Dave Barry; Rick Hess; Alexander Russo; Dan Brown; Larry Ferlazzo, Carolyn Guthrie, and many other generous professionals in the Miami-Dade County Public Schools; Davar Ardalan and Michel Martin of NPR's *Tell Me More*; Lori Crouch, Emily Richmond, Gregg Toppo, and the whole wonderful Education Writers Association; Ellen Moir, Jane Baker, Tracy Kremer, and Kathy Raymond with the New Teacher Center; Meg Anderson and Cory Turner of NPR-Ed; The National Board for Professional Teaching Standards; the volunteers who started the Miami chapter of the New Leaders Council; John Norton, Barnett Berry, and the rest of the folks at the Center for Teaching Quality. The doors and windows you opened offered views of the education world that would never have been visible from my classroom.

I'm tremendously grateful to the people who read drafts of this novel and provided a vital mix of feedback and encouragement: Andy Baldwin, Jennie Smith-Camejo, Nadine Gonzalez, Natalia Sylvester, Tamica Lewis, Kathy Pham, Zakia Jarrett, Nick Garnett, Ginger Seehafer, Inga Aragon, Cathy Kelly, and John and Jackie Ermer.

The work of many other writers has influenced this book and my writing in general. I am indebted to the many education journalists and memoirists who have taken time to describe what goes on in classrooms, provide context, and search out what is hidden from view. Works of nonfiction that informed parts of this book include *The Teacher Wars* by Dana Goldstein, *Hope Against Hope* by Sarah Carr, *We Own This Game* by Robert Andrew Powell, *Relentless Pursuit* by Donna Foote, *Making the Grades* by Todd Farley, *Tested* by Linda Perlstein, *The Same Thing Over and Over* by Rick Hess, *Stray Dogs, Saints and Saviors*, by Alexander Russo, *Dis-Integration* by Eugene Robinson, *The Righteous Mind* by Jonathan Haidt, *Friday Night Lights* by H.G. Bissinger, *Against Football: One Fan's Reluctant Manifesto* by Steve Almond, *Life In Prison: Eight Hours at a Time* by Robert Reilly, *The Great Expectations School* by Dan Brown, and *Teaching In Circles* by Nathan Miller. The poem that Lena plays in her classroom is a nod to "First Writing Since," by Suheir Hammad, a poem I played many times for my own students, and one that proves the power of the right words arranged in the right order. I'll stop there. But the truth is, there are so many books, both fiction and nonfiction, that have influenced my writing and continue to do so. (Mine is an English teacher's soul in the end. I always look for the symbolism. I always notice the hand imagery.) With that in mind, fellow readers are welcome to join me on Goodreads, where I catalogue every book I read in weirdly precise categories.

Finally, thanks to my family, who provided invaluable early reads, invaluable final reads, listening ears, vocal support, private pep talks, childcare, and love. Thanks to my parents, Phyllis Mandler and Gary Elden, for all the ingredients that led me to become a teacher and later a writer. *Merci beaucoup* to my mother-in-law, "Grandma Tita," who gave her time and love to help with two babies so I could work on the book. To Erica, for reading and listening to more of my words than anyone should ever have to, and Bryan, for feedback on the manuscript and interesting conversations on many of the issues I hoped to tackle in this book. Thanks to Brenda and Lucien for making holidays special and to Dony for the pictures and soundtrack that pull the whole movie together. Thanks to Stephanie, a true "lead(H)er," for sharing female business lady advice when I needed it, and to Tammie, Marty, and Wendy for encouragement and good times. Special remembrance to my two grandmothers, Sylvia Elden, a voracious reader and unfailing supporter who I always wanted to make proud, and Barbara Mandler, whose shiny red nails and outspoken negotiating skills live on in my memory. Thanks to all the Volmars, Siclaits, and Dewsburys who showed up to events, spread the word, helped with the kids, fed me fantastic food, and made life better in so many ways.

To the Z's: You are my favorite people to read books with. I hope you'll both grow up to be big readers and writers – even if it means that your minds (like your mother's) are sometimes elsewhere.

And to Claude, who always treated this book as an inevitability rather than a dream and without whom this and so many other things would never have been possible. *Muah.*

ABOUT THE AUTHOR

ROXANNA ELDEN combines eleven years of experience as a public school teacher with a decade of speaking to audiences around the country about education issues. Her first book, *See Me After Class*, is a staple in school districts and educator training programs throughout the country, and her work has been featured on *NPR* as well as in the *New York Times*, the *Washington Post*, the *Atlantic*, *Education Week*, and many other outlets. She also teaches creative writing with the Miami Book Fair. You can learn more about her work at www.roxannaelden.com.

CPSIA information can be obtained
at www.ICGtesting.com
Printed in the USA
LVHW022222311018
595313LV00003B/3/P

9 781732 098701